Also by Glenn

tHE.
DEVIL
WILL COME

Glenn Cooper graduated with a degree in archaeology from Harvard and got his medical degree from Tufts University School of Medicine. He has been the Chairman and CEO of a biotechnology company in Massachusetts and is a screenwriter and producer. He is also the bestselling author of *Library of the Dead*, its sequel *Book of Souls*, and *The Tenth Chamber*.

013711206 X

THE DEVIL WILL COME

GLENN COOPER

arrow books

Published by Arrow Books 2011

3 5 7 9 10 8 6 4 2

First published in Great Britain in 2011 by
Arrow Books
Random House, 20 Vauxhall Bridge Road,
London SW1V 2SA

www.randomhouse.co.uk

Addresses for companies within The Random House Group Limited can be
found at: www.randomhouse.co.uk/offices.htm

The Random House Group Limited Reg. No. 954009

A CIP catalogue record for this book
is available from the British Library

ISBN 9780099545736
ISBN 9780099545743 (export)

The Random House Group Limited supports The Forest Stewardship Council
(FSC®), the leading international forest certification organisation. Our books
carrying the FSC label are printed on FSC® certified paper. FSC is the only
forest certification scheme endorsed by the leading environmental organisations,
including Greenpeace. Our paper procurement policy can be found at
www.randomhouse.co.uk/environment

Typeset in Sabon by Palimpsest Book Production Limited,
Falkirk, Stirlingshire
Printed and bound by CPI Group (UK) Ltd, Croydon, CR0 4YY

The stars move still, time runs, the clock will strike,
The Devil will come, and Faustus must be damned.

from

The Tragical History of Doctor Faustus
by
Christopher Marlowe

PROLOGUE

Rome, AD 1139

He kept his curtains parted to keep an eye on the night sky but the window faced west and he needed to look east.

The Palazzo Apostolico Lateranense, as the Romans called it, was vast – surely the largest and grandest building he'd ever seen. His native tongue was Irish, which was of no use in these parts. He found conversational Latin tough going so during his visit he and his hosts limped by with English. In English this was the Lateran Palace, the residence of the Pope.

He peeled away his thin blanket and fished in the dark for his sandals. He had bedded down in his simple monk's habit, which he wore despite his right to grander attire. He was Máel Máedóc Ua Morgair – in English, Malachy, Bishop of Down, and he was here as the guest of Pope Innocent II.

It had been a long, difficult journey from Ireland, taking him through the untamed lands of Scotland, England and France. The journey had consumed the entire summer and now in late September the air

1

was already carrying a chill bite. In France he had stayed for a while with the esteemed clerical scholar Bernard of Clairvaux, a man whose intellect clearly matched his own. But he'd fooled Bernard with his faked piety and earnestness. He'd fooled them all.

Malachy's cell in the guest dormitory was a great distance from the high-ceilinged regal rooms of the Pope. He'd been in Rome for a fortnight and had only seen the old man twice: the first time for a perfunctory audience in his private chambers, the second as part of an entourage to tour the pontiff's pet project, the rebuilding of his favorite church, the ancient Santa Maria in Trastevere. Who knew how long it would be before he was summoned again to conduct his main business – petitioning Innocent to grant the pallia for the Sees (the seats of ecclesiastical authority) of Armagh and Cashel? But that was unimportant. What was vital was that he had succeeded in being in Rome on the twenty-fourth day of September in the year 1139 with midnight approaching.

Malachy crept carefully down long bare corridors, coaxing his eyes to accommodate to the darkness. He fancied himself a slithering creature of the night, gliding silently through the sleeping palace.

They have no idea who I am.

They have no idea what I am.

And to think that they swallowed me whole and allowed me to dwell within their own belly!

There was a staircase leading to the roof. Malachy had seen it before but had never taken it. He could only hope that he'd be able to make it unimpeded all the way up into the night air.

When he could climb no higher he turned an iron latch and put his shoulder against the heavy hatch until it budged and then yielded outwards. The pitch of the roof was steep enough that he had to take great care to keep his footing. To be safe he removed his sandals. The slates felt cold and smooth against the soles of his feet. He didn't dare sneak a look at the eastern sky until he'd pressed his back against the nearest chimney stack and jammed his heels against the slates.

Only then did Malachy feast his eyes on the heavens.

Over the great slumbering city of Rome the cloudless black firmament was perfect in every way. And just as he knew it would have, the lunar eclipse had already begun.

He'd spent years studying the charts.

Like the great astrologers before him, like Balbilus of ancient Rome, Malachy was a master of the heavens but he doubted whether any of his predecessors had ever had an opportunity like this. How disastrous, how catastrophic it would have been if the sky had been overcast.

He had to see the moon with his own eyes!

At the precise moment when he had to count the stars!

Complete eclipses of the moon were uncommon enough but was there ever one like tonight?

Tonight the moon was in Pisces, their sacred constellation.

And it had just completed its nineteen-year cycle, sinking once again below the sun's ecliptic to its South Node, the point of maximum adversity – the Devil's Tail, as astrologers called it.

This convergence of celestial events had perhaps never happened before and perhaps would never happen again! It was a night full of glorious portent. It was a night when a man like Malachy could make powerful prophecy.

Now all he could do was wait.

It would take almost an hour for the golden moon to slip into blackness, its orb nibbled away by an unseen giant.

When the moment came Malachy had to be ready, his mind had to be free of distraction. His bladder ached a bit so he pulled up his habit and let loose, watching in amusement as his urine streamed off the roof onto the Pope's garden. Too bad the old bastard wasn't standing there, looking up with open mouth.

The eclipse was a quarter done, then half, then three-quarters. He hardly felt the night chill. When the last of the moon's light was gone a penumbra suddenly formed, glowing thick and amber. And then Malachy saw what he'd been waiting for. There were stars shining brightly through the penumbra. Not a few, not too many.

He'd have time enough to make his count and check it once before the penumbra disappeared.

Ten.

Fifty.

Eighty.

One hundred.

One hundred twelve!

He bore down mentally and repeated the exercise.

Yes, one hundred twelve.

The eclipse began to reverse and the penumbra collapsed.

Malachy carefully scuttled back down to the hatch, descended the stairs and made his way to his room, anxious not to lose a moment.

There he lit a fat candle and dipped a quill into a pot of ink. He began to write as fast as he could. He would write all night until the dawn came. He saw it clearly, as clearly as the stars brightly imprinted on his mind's eye.

Here in the Lateran Palace, here in Rome, here in the bosom of Christendom, the home of his great enemy and the enemy of his kind, Malachy had a lucid and certain vision of what would come to pass.

There would be 112 more Popes: 112 Popes until the end of the Church. And the end of the world as they knew it.

ONE

Rome, 2000

'What does K want?' the man asked. He was seated, nervously drumming thick fingers against the wooden arms of a chair.

Although the line had gone dead, the other man still had the phone in his hand. He set it back into its cradle and waited for a city bus to pass under their open window and for its annoying rumble to fade. 'He wants us to kill her.'

'So we'll kill her. We know where she lives. We know where she works.'

'He wants us to do it tonight.'

The seated man lit a cigarette with a gold lighter. It was inscribed TO ALDO, FROM K. 'I prefer more planning.'

'Of course. So do I.'

'I didn't hear you objecting.'

'That wasn't one of his people. It was K!'

The seated man leaned forward in surprise and exhaled a plume of smoke which floated off and merged with the wafting diesel fumes. 'He called you himself?'

'Couldn't you tell by the way I was speaking?'

The seated man drew on his cigarette so deeply that the smoke penetrated the deepest reaches of his lungs. When he breathed out he said, 'Then tonight she dies.'

Elisabetta Celestino was shocked at her own tears. When was the last time she'd cried?

The answer came to her in a vinegary rush of memory.

Her mother's death. At the hospital, at the wake, at the funeral and for days afterwards until she prayed for the tears to stop and they did. Even though she was a young girl at the time, she hated the wet eyes and the streaked cheeks, the awful heaving of the chest, the lack of control over her body and she vowed to banish henceforth this kind of eruption.

But now Elisabetta felt the sting of salty tears in her eyes. She was angry at herself. There was no equivalence between these long-separated events – her mother's passing and this email she'd received from Professor De Stefano.

Still, she was determined to confront him, change his mind, turn the situation around. In the pantheon of the Università Degli Studi di Roma, De Stefano was a god and she, a lowly graduate student, was a supplicant. But since childhood she'd possessed a gritty determination, often getting her way by peppering her adversary with a fusillade of reason and then launching a few piercing missiles of intellect to win the day. Over the years many had succumbed – friends, teachers, even her genius father once or twice.

As she waited outside De Stefano's office at the Department of Archeology and Antiquity within the heartless Fascist-style Humanities Building Elisabetta composed herself. It was already dark and unseasonably cold. The boilers weren't putting out any perceptible heat and she kept her coat on her lap draped over her bare legs. The book-lined corridor of the department was empty, the volumes secure in locked glass-fronted cabinets. The overhead fluorescent lights cast a white stripe on the gray-tiled floor. There was only one open door. It led to the cramped office she shared with three other grad students but she didn't want to wait there. She wanted De Stefano to see her as soon as he rounded the corner so she sat on one of the hard benches where the students waited for their professors.

He kept her waiting. He was almost never on time. Whether it was his way of demonstrating his position on the totem pole or just scatterbrained time management, she was uncertain. He was nonetheless always appropriately apologetic and when he finally did come rushing in he spouted *mea culpas* and unlocked his office door hurriedly.

'Sit, sit,' he said. 'I was delayed. My meeting ran over, and the traffic was dreadful.'

'I understand,' Elisabetta said smoothly. 'It was good of you to come back tonight to see me.'

'Yes, of course. I know you're upset. It's difficult,

but I think there are important lessons that in the long term will only help your career.'

De Stefano hung up his overcoat and sank into his desk chair.

She had rehearsed the speech in her mind and now the stage was hers. 'But, Professor, here's what I'm having great trouble with. You supported my work from the moment I showed you the first photographs of St Callixtus. You came with me to see the subsidence damage, the fallen wall, the first-century brickwork, the symbols on the plaster. You agreed with me that they were unique to the catacombs. You agreed the astrological symbology was unprecedented. You supported my research. You supported publication. You supported further excavation. What happened?'

De Stefano rubbed his bristly crew-cut. 'Look, Elisabetta, you've always known the protocol. The catacombs are under the control of the Pontifical Commission for Sacred Archeology. I'm a member of the Commission. All publication drafts have to be cleared by them. Unfortunately, your paper was rejected and your request for funding to mount an excavation was also rejected. But here's the good news. You're broadly known now. No one criticized your scholarship. This can only work toward your benefit. All you need is patience.'

She leaned back in her chair and felt her cheeks flushing with anger. 'Why was it rejected? You haven't told me why.'

'I talked to Archbishop Luongo just this afternoon and asked him the same question. He told me the view was that the paper was too speculative and preliminary, that any public disclosure of the findings should await further study and contextual analysis.'

'Isn't that an argument for extending the gallery further to the west? I'm convinced, as you are, that the cave-in exposed an early Imperial columbarium. The symbology is singular and indicates a previously unknown sect. I can make tremendous progress with a modest grant.'

'To the Commission, it's out of the question. They won't support a trench beyond the known limits of the catacomb. They're concerned about larger issues of architectural stability. An excavation could trigger further cave-ins and have a domino effect that could lead back into the heart of St Callixtus. The decision went all the way up to Cardinal Giaccone.'

'I can do it safely! I've consulted with engineers. And besides, it's pre-Christian! It shouldn't even be the Vatican's call.'

'You're the last person to be naive about this,' De Stefano clucked. 'You know that the entire complex is under the Commission's jurisdiction.'

'But, Professor, you're on the Commission. Where was your voice?'

'Ah, but I had to recuse myself because I was an author on the paper. I had no voice.'

Elisabetta shook her head sadly. 'Then that's it? No chance of appeal?'

De Stefano's response was to splay his palms regretfully.

'This was going to be my thesis. Now what? I stopped all my other work and immersed myself in Roman astrology. I've devoted over a year to this. The answers to my questions are on the other side of one plaster wall.'

De Stefano took a deep breath and seemed to be steeling himself for something more. When it came out it shocked her. 'There's another thing I need to tell you, Elisabetta. I know you'll find this somewhat destabilizing and I do apologize, but I'm going to be leaving Sapienza, effective immediately. I've been offered a rare position at the Commission, the first non-clergy Vice-President in its history. For me, it's a dream job and, frankly, I've had it up to here with all the bull I have to endure at the university. I'll talk to Professor Rinaldi. I think he'll make a good adviser. I know he's got a full plate but I'll persuade him to take you on. You'll be fine.'

Elisabetta looked at his guilt-ridden face and decided there was nothing more to say besides a whispered, 'Jesus Christ.'

An hour later she was still at her desk, hands resting in her lap. She was staring out the black window onto the empty parking lot behind the Faculty of Letters and Philosophy, her back to the door.

They crept up in their crepe-soled shoes and came into the office unseen.

They held their breath lest she should hear air escaping from their noses.

One of them reached out.

Suddenly there was a hand on her shoulder.

Elisabetta let out a short scream.

'Hey, beautiful! Did we scare you?'

She wheeled her chair around and didn't know whether to be relieved or angry at the sight of the two uniformed policemen. 'Marco! You pig!'

He wasn't a pig, of course – he was tall and handsome, her Marco.

'Don't be mad at me. It was Zazo's idea.'

Zazo jumped up and down like a little kid, giddy at his success, his leather holster slapping against his thigh. Since she was a toddler he'd delighted in scaring his sister and making her howl. Always scheming, always a prankster, always the motormouth, his boyhood nickname, Zazo – 'Be quiet, shut up' – had stuck fast.

'Thank you, Zazo,' she said sarcastically. 'I needed that tonight.'

'It didn't go well?' Marco asked.

'Disaster,' Elisabetta muttered. 'A complete disaster.'

'You can tell me about it over dinner,' Marco said. 'You're off work?'

'*He* is,' Zazo said. 'I'm pulling overtime. I don't have a girlfriend to feed me.'

'I'd pity her if you did,' Elisabetta said.

Outside, they braced themselves against the cutting wind. Marco buttoned his civilian greatcoat, concealing his starched blue shirt and white pistol belt. When he was off duty he didn't want to look like a cop, especially on a university campus. Zazo didn't care. Their sister Micaela liked to say that he loved being in the *Polizia* so much that he probably wore his uniform to bed.

Outside, everything moved and flapped in the wind except the immense bronze statue of Minerva, virgin goddess of wisdom, who loomed over her moonlit reflecting pool.

Zazo's squad car was pulled up to the steps. 'I can give you a ride.' He got behind the wheel.

'We'll walk,' Elisabetta said. 'I want the air.'

'Suit yourself,' her brother said. 'See you at Papa's on Sunday?'

'After church,' she said.

'Say hello to God for me,' Zazo said lightly. 'I'll be in bed. *Ciao.*'

Elisabetta double-looped her scarf and headed arm in arm with Marco toward her apartment on the Via Lucca. Ordinarily at nine o'clock the university area would be bustling but the precipitously falling thermometer seemed to catch people unawares and pedestrian traffic was sparse.

Elisabetta's flat was only ten minutes away, a modest walk-up shared with an orthopedic resident who was often on duty. Marco lived with his parents. As did Zazo, who occupied his childhood room like an oversized kid. Neither of them earned enough to rent their own place, though there was always talk of sharing an apartment after their next round of promotions. Ever since Elisabetta and Marco began seeing each other, if they wanted to hang out it had to be at her place.

14

'I'm sorry you had a bad day,' he said.

'You don't know how bad.'

'Whatever it is, you'll be fine.'

She snorted at that.

'You couldn't change the decision?'

'No.'

'Want me to shoot the old goat?'

Elisabetta laughed. 'Maybe if you just wounded him slightly.'

The traffic signal wasn't with them but they sprinted across the broad Viale Regina Elena anyway. 'Where's Cristina tonight?' Marco asked when they got to the other side.

'At the hospital. She's on a twenty-four-hour shift.'

'Good. Do you want me to stay over?'

She squeezed his hand. 'Of course I do.'

'Do we need to buy anything?'

'There's enough to whip something together,' she said. 'Let's just go home.'

Ahead was the student district off the Via Ippocrate. On a warm night it would have been thronging with young people smoking at cafés and browsing the small shops but tonight it was nearly deserted.

There was a short stretch of road that sometimes gave Elisabetta pause when she walked alone late at night, a poorly lit zone flanked by a graffiti-daubed concrete wall on one side and angled parking on the other. But with Marco she was fearless. Nothing bad could happen to her while he was at her side.

There was a telephone booth ahead. A tall man was

standing inside. The tip of his cigarette glowed brightly with each drag.

Elisabetta heard footsteps coming fast from behind, then an odd, deep groan from Marco. She felt his hand slip from hers.

The tall man in the phone booth was approaching fast.

All of a sudden a heavy arm enveloped Elisabetta's upper chest from behind and when she tried to turn it slid around her neck and fixed her in place. The telephone-booth man was almost upon her. He had a knife in his hand.

A shot rang out, so loud that it interrupted the dreamlike quality of the attack.

The arm let go and Elisabetta pivoted to see Marco on the sidewalk struggling to lift his service pistol for another shot. The man who had grabbed her twisted toward Marco. She could see blood oozing from the man's shoulder onto the back of his camel-hair coat.

Wordlessly, the telephone-booth man rushed past, ignoring Elisabetta for the immediate threat. He and the wounded man fell upon Marco, their arms pounding down like pistons.

She screamed 'No!' and went for one of the flailing arms, trying to stop the killing, but the telephone-booth man threw her off, using his knife hand. She felt the blade slash her palm.

They resumed their butchery and this time Elisabetta grabbed blindly at the tall man's legs, trying to pull him away from Marco's body. Something gave, but it wasn't him – it was his trousers, which started to slide down his waist.

He rose and swatted Elisabetta violently across the face with a forearm.

She fell to the sidewalk, aware of blood – Marco's blood – spreading towards her. She saw the man whom Marco had shot squatting on his haunches, breathing hard under his stained coat.

There were shouts in the distance. Someone called out from a high-rise balcony half a block away.

The telephone-booth man approached and knelt deliberately beside Elisabetta. His stony face was blank. He raised his knife hand over his head.

There was another shout, closer by, someone yelling, 'Hey!'

The man swung round toward the call.

In the seconds before he turned back to Elisabetta and crashed his fist against her chest, just before she lost consciousness, she noticed a strange, disturbing detail.

She couldn't be sure – she would never be sure – but she thought she saw something protruding from the man's back just above his loosened trousers.

It was something that didn't belong there, something thick, fleshy and repulsive, rising out of a swarm of small black tattoos.

TWO

The Vatican, present day

Pain was his constant companion, his personal tormentor, and because it had become so intertwined with his mind and body, in a perverse way it had also become his friend.

When it gripped him hard, causing his spine to stiffen in agony, he had to stop himself from involuntarily uttering the oaths of his youth, the street language of Naples. He had a button he could push which would release a pulse of morphine into his veins but beyond occasional lapses of weakness, usually in the middle of the night when sleep seemed so dear, he avoided its use. Would Christ have availed himself of morphine to ease his suffering on the cross?

But when the worst of the present spasm receded, its passing left a pleasurable void. He was grateful for the teaching the pain imparted: that normalcy was a dear thing and a simplicity to be cherished. He wished he'd been more cognizant of this notion during his long life.

There was a gentle rap on his door and he responded in as strong a voice as he could muster.

A Silesian nun shuffled into the high-ceilinged room, her gray habit nearly brushing the floor. 'Holiness,' she said. 'How are you feeling?'

'Much the same as an hour ago,' the Pope said, attempting a smile.

Sister Emilia, a woman not much younger than the elderly pontiff, approached and began fussing with the items on his bedside table. 'You didn't drink your orange juice,' she chided. 'Would you prefer apple?'

'I'd prefer to be young and healthy.'

She shook her head and carried on with her business. 'Let me raise you a little.'

His bed had been replaced with a motorized hospital model. Sister Emilia used the controls to elevate his head and when he was safely upright she held the drinking straw to his dry lips and stared sternly until he relented and took a couple of gulps.

'Good,' she said. 'Zarilli is waiting to see you.'

'What if I don't want to see him?' The Pope knew that the old nun lacked even a rudimentary sense of humor so he let her silence last for only a few seconds and then told her that his visitor was welcome.

Dr Zarilli, the pontiff's private physician, was waiting in an anteroom outside the third-floor papal apartment with another doctor from the Gemelli Hospital. Sister Emilia ushered them into the bedroom and parted the long cream curtains over the Piazza St Pietro to let in the waning sunlight of a fine spring day.

The Pope raised his arm weakly and gave the men a small official wave. He was wearing plain white pajamas. His last therapy had left him bald so for warmth he wore a woolen cap which had been knitted by the aunt of one of his private secretaries.

'Your Holiness,' Zarilli said. 'You remember Dr Paciolla.'

'How could I forget?' the Pope replied wryly. 'His examination of my person was very thorough. Come closer, gentlemen. Can Sister Emilia get you some coffee?'

'No, no, please,' Zarilli said. 'Dr Paciolla has the results of your last scans at the clinic.'

The two men with their black suits and grim faces resembled undertakers more than doctors and the Pope made light of their appearance. 'Have you come to advise me or bury me?'

Paciolla, a tall cultured Roman accustomed to tending to rich and powerful men, didn't seem fazed by the setting of the house-call or this particular patient. 'Simply to inform Your Holiness – certainly not to bury you.'

'Well, good,' the Pope said. 'The Holy See has more important matters to attend to than calling for a Conclave. Give me the report, then. Is it white smoke or black?'

Paciolla looked at the floor for a moment, then met the Pope's steady gaze. 'The cancer has not responded to the chemotherapy. I'm afraid it's spreading.'

Cardinal Bishop Aspromonte poked his large balding head into the dining room to make sure that Cardinal

Diaz's favorite sparkling wine was on the table. It was a trifling detail for the Secretary of State and Camerlengo of the Holy Roman Church but it was entirely within character. His private secretary, Monsignor Achille, a wiry man who had long ago followed Aspromonte from Genoa to the Vatican, directed his attention to the green bottle on the sideboard.

Aspromonte mumbled his approval and disappeared for a moment, only to enter again when he heard the telephone ring. 'That's probably Diaz and Giaccone.'

Achille picked up the dining-room phone, nodded, then commanded starchily, 'Send them up.'

'Five minutes early,' Aspromonte said. 'We've trained our guests well over the years, haven't we?'

'Yes, Your Eminence, I believe we have.'

Monsignor Achille escorted Cardinals Diaz and Giaccone into the book-lined study where Aspromonte waited with his blue-veined hands clasped over his expansive belly. His private rooms were splendid, thanks to recent renovations courtesy of a wealthy Spanish family. He greeted the two men warmly, his jowls wobbling when he grasped their hands, then sent Achille scurrying for aperitifs.

The three old friends wore red-trimmed black cassocks with wide red sashes but that was the extent of their similarities. Cardinal Diaz, the venerable Dean of the College of Cardinals who had formerly held Aspromonte's job as Secretary of State, was at seventy-five the oldest but the most imposing. He towered over his colleagues. In his youth in Malaga before joining the priesthood he had been quite the boxer, a heavy-weight, and he had carried this athleticism into old age. He had large hands, a squared-off face and ample grey hair but his most remarkable feature was his posture which gave him a strong upright appearance even when he was sitting.

Cardinal Giaccone was the shortest, with a deeply lined and jowly pug face which could mysteriously change from scowl to grin with only the slightest shift of musculature. The little hair that he had left was confined to a fringe above his beefy neck. Though otherwise nondescript, if all the cardinals were to assemble on a sunny day he could always be picked out of the crowd because of his trademark oversized Prada sunglasses which made him look like a film director. He relaxed now, his worry about being late dissipated. There had been a traffic snarl-up on the way back from the Via Napoleone where, as President, he had held his monthly meeting with the staff of the Pontifical Commission for Sacred Archeology.

'The lights are burning upstairs,' Diaz said, pointing at the ceiling.

The Pope's apartment was two floors above their heads in the Vatican Palace.

'I suppose that's a good sign,' Aspromonte said. 'Maybe he has made some improvement today.'

'When did you see him last?' Giaccone asked.

'Two days ago. Tomorrow I'll visit again.'

'How did he look?' Diaz asked.

'Weak. Pale. You can see the pain on his face but

he'd never complain.' Aspromonte looked at Diaz. 'Come with me tomorrow. I don't have any formal business. I'm sure he'll want to see you.'

Diaz nodded crisply, picked up the glass of Prosecco which Achille had placed by his chair and watched the tiny bubbles rise heavenward.

The pain had been at an ebb for a good hour or more and the Pope was able to take a bowl of thin soup. He had an urge to rise and take advantage of this rare surge of energy. He rang his buzzer and Sister Emilia appeared so quickly that he asked her jokingly if she'd had an ear pressed against his door.

'Get Fathers Diep and Bustamante. Tell them I want to go downstairs to my office and my chapel. And get Giacomo to come and help me get dressed.'

'But, Holiness,' the nun demurred, 'shouldn't we ask Dr Zarilli if this is wise?'

'Leave Zarilli alone,' the Pope growled. 'Let the man have dinner with his family.'

Giacomo Barone was a layman who had been in the Pope's employ for twenty years. He was unmarried, lived in a small room in the Palace and seemed to have no interests beyond football and the pontiff. He spoke when spoken to and when the Pope was deep in thought and disinclined to chat idly they might spend half an hour in silence as they worked through ablutions and robing.

Giacomo came in with a heavy stubble on his face. He smelled of the onions that he'd been cooking.

'I want to wash and get dressed,' the Pope told him.

Giacomo bowed his head obediently and asked, 'What do you want to wear, Holiness?'

'Just house dress. Then take me downstairs.'

Giacomo had powerful arms and shoulders and moved the Pope around his chamber like a manikin, sponging and powdering, layering garments, finishing with a white cassock with fringed white fascia, a pectoral cross, pliable red slippers and a white *zuccetto* in place of the knitted cap. The act of dressing seemed to tire the pontiff but he insisted on carrying out his wishes. Giacomo lifted him into his wheelchair.

They took an elevator to the second floor where two Swiss Guards in full blue, orange and red-striped regalia stood at their traditional posts outside the Sala dei Gendarmi. They seemed shocked by the presence of the Pope. As Giacomo rolled the wheelchair past, the pontiff waved and blessed them. They made their way through empty official rooms of state to the Pope's private study with its large writing desk, his favored place to work and review papers.

The desk was really a large mahogany table, several meters in length, placed before a bookcase which contained an eclectic mix of official documents, sacred texts, biographies, histories and even a few detective novels.

His two private secretaries, one of them a Vietnamese priest, the other a Sardinian, were waiting at quiet attention with smiles on their young faces.

'I've never seen the two of you so happy to be called to work at night,' the Pope said lightly.

'It's been a great while since we've been able to serve Your Holiness,' Father Diep said in his sing-song Italian.

'Our hearts are full of joy,' Father Bustamante added with touching sincerity.

The Pope sat in his wheelchair and surveyed the piles of papers littering his once-tidy desk. He shook his head. 'Look at this,' he said. 'It's like an unattended garden. The weeds have overtaken the flower beds.'

'Essential business continues,' Diep said. 'Cardinals Aspromonte and Diaz are co-signing the day-to-day papers. Much of what we have here are copies for your review.'

'Let me use what small abilities I have tonight to tend to one or two vital ecclesiastical issues. You choose what is suitable. Then I want to pray in my chapel before I'm once again confined to bed by Sister Emilia and Dr Zarilli.'

The wine was from Aspromonte's brother who had a vineyard and regularly sent cases to the Vatican. Aspromonte was known for his liberal pouring habits and for giving away bottles as presents.

'The Sangiovese is excellent,' Diaz said, holding up the glass to the light of the chandelier. 'Compliments to your brother.'

'Well, 2006 was a marvelous year for him and really

for everyone who grows in Tuscany. I'll send you a case if you like.'

'That would be grand – thank you,' Diaz said. 'Let's pray that conditions are favorable for him this year.'

'The rains have to stop first,' Giaccone grumbled. 'Today's been mostly clear but, dear God, the last three weeks have been biblical. We should be building an ark!'

'Is it affecting your work?' Aspromonte asked.

'I just came from a meeting of the Pontifical Commission and I can tell you that the archeologists and engineers are worried about the integrity of the catacombs on the Via Antica Appia, particularly St Sebastiano and St Callixtus. The fields above them are so saturated that some trees were uprooted by wind gusts. There's fear of sinkholes or collapses.'

Diaz shook his head and put down his fork. 'If only that was all we had to worry about.'

'The Holy Father,' Aspromonte said quietly.

Diaz said soberly, 'Many are looking for us to be doing the right things, to be making preparations.'

'You mean planning for a Conclave,' Giaccone said bluntly.

Diaz nodded. 'The logistics aren't trivial. You can't just snap your fingers and assemble all the Cardinal Electors.'

'Don't you think we have to tread lightly here?' Aspromonte asked, chewing the last of a mouthful of beef. 'The Pope is alive and, God willing, he will remain so. And we must be mindful not to appear to have any personal aspirations.'

Diaz finished his glass and let Aspromonte fill it again. He looked over his shoulder to make sure they were alone. 'We're friends. We've worked shoulder to shoulder for the better part of three decades. We've taken each other's confessions. If we can't talk frankly, who can? We all know the chances are good that the next Pope is sitting at this table. And, in my opinion, I'm too old. And not Italian enough!'

Aspromonte and Giaccone looked down at their plates. 'Someone had to say it,' Diaz insisted.

'Some say it's time for an African or a South American. There are some good men who bear consideration,' Giaccone said.

Aspromonte shrugged. 'I'm told we have some excellent peach gelato for dessert.'

The Pope was alone in his private chapel. Father Diep had wheeled him in and placed him in front of his usual bronze-clad meditation chair. The ceiling glowed with stained-glass backlit panels, contemporary in style, heavy in primary colors. The floor was white Italian marble with black streaks, also a modernist pattern, but softened by a lovely old brown rug in the center. The altar was simple and elegant: a white lace-covered table holding candles and a Bible. Behind the table a golden crucified Christ floated in the concavity of a floor-to-ceiling installation of red marble.

The pontiff's hip started aching and the pain

27

intensified. He had begun to pray and didn't want to return to his sickbed just now. His infusion pump of morphine was fixed to a pole on the wheelchair but he was especially loath to medicate himself in the presence of this beautiful representation of a suffering Christ.

He fought the pain and kept the prayers flowing wordlessly for only God to hear.

Suddenly, a different pain.

It seized his throat and upper chest.

The Pope looked down with the irrational thought that someone had sneaked up and was pressing heavily on his chest.

The pressure made him contort his face and close his eyes.

But he wanted to keep them open and fought to do so.

It was as if a flaming arrow had pierced his breast, burning through layers of flesh.

He couldn't call out, couldn't take a good breath.

He struggled to keep his gaze fixed firmly on the face of the golden Christ.

Dear God. Help me in my hour of need.

Monsignor Albano entered Cardinal Aspromonte's dining room without knocking.

Aspromonte could tell from his drained face that something was amiss.

'The Pope! He's been stricken in his chapel!'

*

28

The three cardinals rushed up the stairs and hurried through the formal rooms until they entered the chapel. Fathers Diep and Bustamante had moved the Pope's slumped body from the wheelchair onto the rug and Zarilli was kneeling over his one and only patient.

'It's his heart,' Zarilli mumbled. 'There's no pulse. I fear—'

Cardinal Diaz cut him off. 'No. He's not dead! There's time to administer Extreme Unction!'

Zarilli began to protest but Giaccone cut him off and issued sharp orders to Fathers Bustamante and Diep who hurriedly fled the chapel.

Aspromonte whispered to Diaz, 'Under the circumstances, you can omit the prayers, even the Misereatur, and proceed to the Communion.'

'Yes,' Diaz said. 'Yes.'

Both Giaccone and Aspromonte helped Cardinal Diaz lower himself next to the Pope's body where he knelt and said a silent prayer.

The Pope's secretaries ran back in with a tray of communion wafers and a red leather bag. Diaz took one of the wafers and said in a clear voice, 'This is the Lamb of God who takes away the sins of the world. Happy are those who are called to His supper.'

The Pope was unable to respond, but Aspromonte whispered what he would have said, 'Lord, I am not worthy to receive you, but only say the word and I shall be healed.'

'The body of Christ,' Diaz intoned.

'Amen,' Aspromonte whispered.

29

Diaz broke off a small particle of wafer and placed it into the froth inside the Pope's mouth. 'May the Lord Jesus protect you and lead you to eternal life.'

Zarilli was on his feet now, looking mournful, 'Are you finished?' he asked Diaz. 'It's over. The Pope has passed.'

'You are wrong, doctor,' the old cardinal said icily. 'He's not dead until the Cardinal Camerlengo says he's dead. Cardinal Aspromonte, please proceed.'

Everyone dropped back while Aspromonte took the leather bag from Father Diep and extracted a small silver mallet engraved with the Pope's coat of arms.

He fell to his knees and gently tapped the Pope's forehead with the mallet, 'Get up, Domenico Savarino,' he said, using the name that the pontiff's mother had whispered to him as a child, for it was said that no man would remain asleep at the sound of his baptismal name.

The Pope remained motionless.

Another tap. 'Get up, Domenico Savarino,' Aspromonte said again.

The room was quiet.

He tapped the Pope's forehead with the mallet for the third and last time. 'Get up, Domenico Savarino.'

Aspromonte rose to his feet, crossed himself and loudly proclaimed the awful words: 'The Pope is dead.'

'The Pope is dead.'

This time the words were uttered by a man speaking into a mobile phone.

There was a pause and a deep exhalation. The man could almost hear the relief flowing from the other's chest. Damjan Krek replied, 'During Pisces. As predicted.'

'Do you want me to proceed?'

'Of course,' Krek said sharply. 'Do it tonight. Tonight is the perfect time.'

As the man walked calmly through the Piazza St Pietro, he knew that K was correct. Tonight *was* the perfect time. As word of the Pope's death spread within the Vatican, laity and clergy alike scurried to say a prayer in the Basilica, then rushed to their desks for the onslaught of work.

The man was toting a black nylon bag, the kind used to shift tactical gear. If it was heavy no one would have known. Like those of a modern Atlas his prodigious shoulders looked like they could shift any weight. He wore a dark blue business suit with a small enamel pin in his lapel, his usual attire on most days. He was not handsome but his lean angularity and midnight hair turned heads quickly enough; he had always done well with the ladies.

Instead of heading up the stairs of the Basilica he veered toward a non-public door leading to the Sistine Chapel. He picked up his pace and heard the night air whistling through his clenched teeth. He felt the SIG pistol lying tight against his heart and the Boker folding knife against his thigh. At the door, a Swiss Guard in ceremonial dress stood stiffly, bathed in floodlight. The guardsman looked the man in the eye, then glanced at his shoulder bag.

'Korporal,' the man said quickly.

The guardsman saluted crisply and stepped aside. 'Herr Oberstleutnant. Sad day.'

'Indeed it is.'

Oberstleutnant Matthias Hackel moved through the drab deserted hall, his leather-soled shoes tapping the tiles. Ahead was a locked doorway leading directly to the Sistine Chapel. He had the keys, of course, but everything on this level was covered by security cameras. While the second in command of the Swiss Guards could go virtually anywhere in Vatican City with impunity, it was better to pass through basement corridors where surveillance cameras were few.

He climbed a set of stone stairs to the first basement level and followed a corridor until he was directly under the Sistine Chapel within a rabbit warren of small and medium-sized rooms packed with uninteresting and low-value items. The Vatican had intensely secure spaces for documents, books and art treasures but the contents of these rooms were rather more prosaic: furniture, cleaning supplies, outdoor security barriers.

The room which he now entered had no cameras and was visited so infrequently that he was certain he'd be able to work without any surprise interruptions. He switched on the lights and the chamber sputtered into sickly yellow-green fluorescence. There were stacks of simple, inexpensive wooden tables, each a meter and a half long, less than a meter wide, high enough for use by a seated man. They'd been purchased in bulk in the 1950s from a Milanese factory but still seemed relatively new owing to their light use. They had been taken out of storage and carried upstairs into the Sistine Chapel only five times in nearly six decades, each on the occasion of selecting a new Pope.

They didn't look like much. But when covered in floor-length red velvet and crowned with gold-brocaded brown velvet they would take on a certain splendor, especially when laid out in precise rows underneath Michelangelo's ceiling.

The nearest table would serve a more immediate purpose. The man placed his bag on it and smiled.

THREE

Tommaso De Stefano lingered over his cigarette, seemingly fretful about his appointment. Above him, water cascaded from the fountain of entwined sculpted dolphins which had stood at the center of the Piazza Mastai since 1863. His wife had been trying to get him to stop smoking and even he wheezily acknowledged the necessity. Yet this entire Roman square was a monument to tobacco and it was, perhaps, historically appropriate to pay homage with a smoke.

Besides, he was nervous and even a bit timid. His awkwardness bore a similarity to the trepidation he felt a few years earlier when a cousin emerged from a six-year jail term for larceny. At the time he'd asked his wife helplessly, 'What do you say to a man who's life's been interrupted like this? How are you doing? Haven't seen you for a while? You're looking good?'

Behind him was the rather grand nineteenth-century Pontifical Tobacco Manufacturing factory erected by the entrepreneurial family of Pope Pius IX, now a state facility concerned with monopolies. Facing him was a more pedestrian four-story structure of red sandstone built by the same Pope in 1877 to house and educate the girls employed by his tobacco factory. It probably hadn't been an act of pure papal charity, more likely a calculated maneuver to keep a cheap workforce off the streets and free of venereal disease.

De Stefano stamped out his cigarette and crossed the square.

Though the tobacco factory was long gone the red building had endured as a school. A bevy of well-behaved teenage girls in blue and white tracksuits milled around under a sign: SCUOLA TERESA SPINELLI, MATERNA-ELEMENTARE-MEDIA.

De Stefano took a sharp breath and pushed the iron gate open. In the marble forecourt a young nun was conversing with the harried mother of a little girl who was running in circles, working off pent-up energy. The nun was black – African, judging by her accent – wearing the light blue smock of a novice. He chose not to interrupt her so he carried on through the courtyard into the cool dark reception hall. A diminutive bespectacled older nun in a black habit saw him and approached.

'Good day,' he said. 'My name is Professor De Stefano.'

'Yes, you're expected,' the nun said in a business-like manner that contrasted with the friendly way her eyes crinkled. 'I'm Sister Marilena, the Principal. I think her class is finished. Let me get her for you.'

De Stefano waited, adjusting his necktie, watching the young girls rushing past to get outside.

When she appeared, a look of fleeting disorientation crossed his face. What had it been? Eleven years? Twelve?

She was still statuesque and darkly beautiful but seeing her now in a black scapular with her hair all but obscured by a nun's veil seemed to derail him.

Her skin was milky, only a few shades darker than the high-necked white vest that she wore under her square-scooped habit, the traditional dress of her order, the Augustinian Sisters, Servants of Jesus and Mary. Though she wore no make-up, her complexion was perfect, her lips naturally moist and pink. In her university days she had dressed better than the other students and had used lovely fragrances. But even allowing for the plain garb of a nun she couldn't help but look stylishly impeccable. Her eyebrows were carefully plucked, her teeth lustrous, her nails unvarnished but manicured. And despite her billowing habit it was clear that she still cut a slim figure.

'Elisabetta,' he said.

She smiled. 'Professor.'

'It's good to see you.'

'And you. You look well.' She held out both her hands. De Stefano grasped them, then quickly let go.

'That's nice of you to say. But I think I've become an old man.'

Elisabetta shook her head vigorously at that, then asked, 'Shall we get some sun?'

The courtyard was littered with playthings for the younger children. Between two potted trees was a pair of facing stone benches. Elisabetta took one and De Stefano settled onto the other, automatically reaching into his pocket.

'I'm sorry,' she said. 'There's no smoking here – the children.'

'Of course,' De Stefano said sheepishly, withdrawing an empty hand. 'I need to quit.'

There was a longish pause, broken when Elisabetta said, 'You know, I hardly slept last night. I was nervous about seeing you.'

'Me too,' he admitted, barely hinting at how tense he still felt.

'Most of my old friends drifted away long ago. Some of them were uncomfortable. I think others thought I had become cloistered,' she said.

'You're able to see your family, then?'

'Oh yes! At least once a week. My father lives nearby.'

'Well, you look happy.'

'I *am* happy.'

'The life suits you, then.'

'I can't imagine doing anything else.'

'I'm pleased for you.'

Elisabetta studied his face. 'You look like you'd like to ask me why.'

De Stefano smiled broadly. 'You're very perceptive. Okay, why? Why did you become a nun?'

'I almost died, you know. The knife missed my heart by a centimeter. I was told that some men scared away the attackers before they could finish me off. I spent two months in hospital. I had a lot of time to think. It wasn't an epiphany. It came to me slowly but it took hold and grew, and anyway, I'd always been religious – I got that from my mother – I'd always been a believer. What I saw around me had an impact, too. All the unhappy, unfulfilled people: the doctors, the nurses, patients I met, their families. The nuns gliding through the hospital were the only ones who seemed at peace. I didn't want to go back to university life. I realized how desperately unhappy I was, how empty, especially without my Marco in my life. Once I felt the calling everything seemed so clear.'

'At the Pontifical Commission, many of my colleagues are in the clergy, of course. I've heard some of them speak about their decisions to choose a religious life. I've just never personally known someone before and after.'

'I'm the same person.'

'The same, I'm sure.' De Stefano shrugged. 'But for me a little different. Why this particular order?'

'It had to be an active community,' Elisabetta said. 'I didn't have the personality to be in a contemplative one. I love children, I like to teach. This order is dedicated to education. And I knew them. I went to school here, you know.'

'Really?'

'For eight years. Primary and middle school. Sister Marilena was one of my teachers! I was only ten when my mother died. Sister Marilena was wonderful then, she's wonderful now.'

'I'm delighted you found yourself.'

Elisabetta nodded, then looked at De Stefano steadily, 'Please tell me why you wanted to see me.'

De Stefano cracked his knuckles like a man who was about to play the piano. 'Three days ago, on Tuesday, there was a minor earthquake centered about fifty kilometers south of Rome.'

'I wasn't aware of that,' she said.

De Stefano paused for several seconds before continuing. When he spoke again there was a slight but perceptible hesitancy in his tone. 'It was hardly felt here but enough sub-surface energy reached the city to cause a small cave-in at the catacombs at St Callixtus in an area already weakened by previous subsidence and the recent heavy rains.'

Elisabetta arched her eyebrows.

'It affected the zone just to the west of the wall you studied when you were a student,' De Stefano said.

'No one ever got permission to excavate there?' she asked.

'No, the decision had been taken, and when you left, well, there was no one who pressed for a reconsideration. I certainly didn't. Archbishop Luongo was adamant at the time and he became my boss when I went to work at the Commission, so I didn't make waves.'

'But now there's been a natural excavation,' Elisabetta said.

'Messy – but quite natural, yes, you're right.'

'And?'

'That's why I'm here,' De Stefano said nervously. 'We – I – need your help.'

'*My* help?' she asked incredulously. 'As you see, I'm no longer an archeologist, Professor!'

'Yes, yes, Elisabetta, but here's the situation. We've found something that's quite remarkable – and quite sensitive. So far only a very few people know about it but there's a concern that it could get out and cause some unwanted disruption.'

'I'm sorry, I don't understand.'

'The timing with respect to the Pope's death is unfortunate. The Conclave is scheduled to begin in seven days – all the Cardinal Electors are coming to the Vatican and the eyes of the world will be on us. In the event that there might be a leak about St Callixtus, well, we'd need to have our story straight. We'd need to be able to offer some credible explanation to minimize the level of disruption which would undoubtedly occur.'

'Just what did you find?'

'I don't want to *tell* you, Elisabetta, I want to *show* you. I want you to come out there on Sunday afternoon. We'll have enough structural timbers in place by then to make it safe. Then I want you to work with me for a while at the Commission. I've got an office prepared for you.'

'Why me? You've got an entire department at your disposal. You can get any expert in the world to come at the snap of your fingers.'

'Time is critical. Today we're bringing new workmen to the site to do the heavy work. We'll have engineers

40

involved, more people on my staff. We've got areas under tarps to minimize any risk from prying eyes but despite our best efforts, people will talk. We just can't afford that, please believe me. I wish I could tell you more, but . . . The press could be informed at any time. The powers that be in the Vatican are very concerned. They are demanding that I produce a standby statement in the event of a leak but I don't know what to write. There would be an unfortunate cloud over the new Pope if this comes out, especially if we're caught fumbling for the correct words. You spent a full year doing research on the symbology outside the caved-in chamber. You've studied first-century AD Roman astrology exhaustively. You were one of my brightest students. I'm confident that you can hit the ground running. No one is in a better position to formulate an opinion quickly.'

Elisabetta stood up, vexed, her face flushed. 'That was twelve years ago, Professor! I have a different life now. It's out of the question.'

De Stefano rose in an attempt to stay level with Elisabetta but she was still almost a head taller than him. 'Archbishop Luongo is pleased that you're in the clergy. He believes you'll have the right sensitivity to the issues and he won't lose any more sleep over confidentiality. Tell me, did you retain your research notes and papers?'

'They're in my father's apartment somewhere,' she said distractedly. 'But I can't just leave my school. I can't abandon my students.'

'Arrangements are already being made,' De Stefano said, his tone suddenly more forceful, more insistent. 'This evening Monsignor Mattera at the Vatican, the gentleman in charge of all the Church's religious orders, will be calling the Mother General of your order in Malta. Your Principal, Sister Marilena, will be informed tonight. The wheels are in motion, Elisabetta. You have to help us. I'm afraid you have no choice.'

FOUR

Morning prayer in the chapel. Lesson-plan reviews. Teaching. Marking homework. Evening prayer. Communal dining in the residence. Reading and meditation. Night-time prayer. Bed.

Such was Elisabetta's rhythm, the gentle pulse of her weekdays.

Saturdays were for chapel and private prayer, shopping, chatting with sisters and novices, perhaps a football match on TV or a movie.

But Sunday was her favorite. She took Mass at the Basilica Santa Maria in Trastevere. It was here that, as a girl, she took her First Communion, here that she prayed for her sick mother, here that she saw her off with an achingly sad Funeral Mass, here that she came for confession, for solace, for joy.

It was curious, Elisabetta mused, the way her life had unfolded. As a teenager she'd been besotted with notions of adventure and travel, and archeology seemed a ticket to the exotic. But the gravitational pull of the ancient Basilica of Santa Maria proved stronger than those of Luxor or Teotihuacan. Her father, the absent-minded widower, would need her, she had decided. Zazo and Micaela, each with their own charmingly self-centered ways, were clearly not the ones to look after him properly, particularly as he grew older. So at university she set her sights closer to home and took up classical archeology.

Then Zazo introduced her to his academy pal, Marco. Good sweet Marco who wanted nothing more than to be a policeman, marry the woman of his dreams and root like a madman for A.S. Roma. He'd never leave Rome, that was for sure, so Elisabetta further narrowed her aspirations to Roman archeology and the early Christian period when the catacombs began to honey-comb the soft volcanic tuff of the city. She would stay in Rome forever. With Marco, with her family.

And then, that terrible night when Marco was ripped away from her. That night had heralded a long spell of physical healing and intense reflection after which she disassembled the person she was and reassembled the person she wanted to be.

Now Elisabetta's entire universe lay within a mere square kilometer on the western bank of the Tiber. Her school was there, her church, her father's flat on the Via Luigi Masi. They were the same few blocks that had circumscribed her childhood. The insularity was comforting, like a womb.

Mass was over. Elisabetta had taken communion from old Father Santoro, the priest who also tended to the clerical needs of her order and whose aged voice retained the timbre of a finely cast bell. She lingered under the apse vault after most parishioners had departed, soaking in the stillness. There were biblical scenes above her head set against a sea of golden tiles. The dome was fashioned by Cavallini in the twelfth century and the stories he depicted in mosaic were so intricate that she was, after all these years, still discovering images she had never noticed before. Once she had located the slender mockingbird mosaic, devilishly difficult to find, she always made a point to crane her neck and blink a silent hello to it.

In the thin light of a spring morning Elisabetta walked purposefully to her father's apartment. The people she passed fell into two camps. One group, mostly older folks, actively sought out her gaze, hoping for a smile and a blessing nod in return. The other group seemed to pretend that she didn't exist, her robes a cloak of invisibility. She preferred the latter. These walks were precious to her, private reminders of the secular life she'd left behind. She enjoyed looking in store windows, reading the movie posters, watching the easy street intimacy of young couples, remembering what it felt like to walk these streets as a 'civilian'. But nothing she saw changed her mind or chipped away at her bedrock certainties; the opposite was true. Each passage through her old domain was an affirmation. She was proud to wear her faith on her black sleeves, to openly celebrate the intense love for Christ that she carried within her heart.

When she arrived at her father's door she braced herself. He never failed to open it with a backhanded swipe, not so much out of sourness any longer but, unquestionably, out of habit.

They kissed. He was so quick with the peck that he missed Elisabetta's cheek and landed his lips on the edge of her veil. 'How was Mass?' he asked.

'It was lovely.'

'Blinded by the light?'

She followed him toward the kitchen.

Elisabetta sighed. 'Yes, exactly, Papa.'

As usual, her nose was assaulted by the heavy Cavendish pipe tobacco that fogged the air. When she was a girl she hardly noticed it, except when someone at school sniffed at her jumper and made fun. It was simply the way her world smelled. Now that she was an adult, she shuddered to think what was going on inside her father's lungs after all these decades.

Befitting a full professor, Carlo Celestino's was a spacious flat on the top floor of a clay-white apartment block on a narrow sloping street. There were three bedrooms – she'd shared one with Micaela from early childhood until Elisabetta first left for university. Zazo, the blessed son, had always rated his own room. Now their bedrooms gathered dust, locked into time warps. The door to her father's bedroom was closed. It was always shut and she had no idea what state it was in, though the rest of the apartment was at worst, only untidy. Dust and grime were the domain of the house-keeper but the woman was too scared to touch the teetering stacks of papers and books that covered most wooden surfaces of the reception rooms.

Carlo Celestino hardly fit the stereotypical image of a mathematician. He had the square shoulders, squat legs and ruddy complexion of a farmer, which made him the odd man out amongst a cadre of spindly, wan colleagues who populated the Department of Theoretical Mathematics at La Sapienza. But he'd always been different, a genetic outlier who had sprung unexpectedly from a lineage of simple dairymen, a fellow whose first boyhood memories were not of cows and pastures but of numbers whirring through his head, organizing themselves.

He'd held onto his parents' ancient farmhouse in Abruzzo and still took weekends and holidays in the rolling hills overlooking the Adriatic doing as much physical work on the hilly land as his sixty-eight-year-old body would take, letting his mind play with the theorem he'd wrestled with his entire life: the Goldbach Conjecture, a mathematical confection that his wife had claimed he loved more than her. Imagine, she'd said, with that look of exasperation that Elisabetta and Micaela would inherit, spending all your time trying to prove the assertion that every even integer greater than two can be expressed as the sum of two prime numbers! She couldn't fathom it then, and what would she have thought if she'd lived another twenty-five years? Here he was, still trying to prove the damned theorem for the sake of bragging rights which had eluded the world's mathematicians for 250 years.

Elisabetta thought her father looked tired, his thick white hair more disheveled than usual. 'How have you been feeling, Papa?'

'Me? Fine. Why?'

'No reason. Just asking. When are Micaela and Zazo coming?'

'They won't arrive before you've finished cooking, you know that.'

She laughed and donned an apron. 'Let's have a look at the joint.'

He got the lamb from the fridge and while she was unwrapping the brown paper he suddenly blurted out, 'They don't want to give me any new grad students.'

'I knew there was something,' she said, keeping her gaze on the pink meat.

'They do that when they think someone's gotten too old or too feeble.'

'I'm sure it's neither,' Elisabetta said. 'But maybe you should be glad you're not taking on new students. It's four or five years until they get their degrees. Sometimes longer.'

'The next stage will be offering me an emeritus position, then moving my office to the basement. I know how these things work, believe me.' Carlo frowned fiercely, his bushy eyebrows almost meeting above the bridge of his nose. His big fists clenched.

Elisabetta washed her hands and began sprinkling the meat with sea salt.

'What will these donkeys say when I crack Goldbach?' he sneered.

'You go and work, Papa. I'll get on with the cooking.'

By the time Zazo and Micaela arrived the kitchen window was steamed up. Zazo sniffed the air like a dog and patted Elisabetta's back. 'Keep up the good work,' he said, peering into a bubbling saucepan. 'You're almost at the finish line.'

Zazo and Elisabetta both had the graceful frames of their mother, who had been a woman with the poise and figure of a catwalk model. Zazo kept fit playing soccer after work and lifting weights in the barracks gym, and with his solid jaw and sensitive eyes he remained an eligible bachelor perpetually on the brink of commitment.

'Good to see you too,' Elisabetta said happily. 'Is Arturo here?'

'Unless he's hiding, I don't think so.' Zazo tasted the red sauce with her stirring spoon. She shooed him away and called out for Micaela.

Elisabetta heard her before seeing her. Micaela's voice grabbed people's attention like the persistent bark of a chained dog. She was complaining to her father about Arturo. 'He didn't have to swap! He knew he was invited! What a jerk!'

Micaela stomped into the kitchen. She was more like her father – shorter than her siblings, compact, with the heavier facial features of his lineage. When the children were small, people had talked about Elisabetta's and Zazo's attractive faces and Micaela's fiery attitude. Nothing had changed. 'Arturo's not coming,' she announced to her sister.

'I heard. A pity.'

'Some shit-head in the casualty ward wanted the day off and unbelievably Arturo agreed to take his shift. He's soft in the head.'

Elisabetta smiled. Pretty much the only time she heard swearing these days was from her sister. 'Maybe he's soft in the *heart*.'

'I hate him.'

'No, you don't.' The two girls finally kissed. 'I like your hair,' Elisabetta said. It was wavier than usual, similar to the style that Elisabetta herself had worn before hers was shorn.

'Thanks. It's hot in here. You must be wilting.' Compared to Elisabetta, black-clad and draped, Micaela appeared almost naked in her low-cut dancer top.

'I'm fine. Come and help.'

The dining table sat six and, when there were fewer, Flavia Celestino's chair stayed empty as if inviting her spirit back into the fold.

'How was your week?' Elisabetta asked her brother, passing the serving bowl.

'You can imagine,' Zazo said. 'We've got dozens of cardinals and their staffs arriving soon. My boss's boss is agitated, my boss is agitated and, for the sake of my men, I'm supposed to be agitated.'

'And you're not?' his father asked.

'When was the last time you saw me upset?'

They all knew the answer but no one spoke of it. It was twelve years ago. They well remembered the wild state he was in when he rushed inside the hospital to find Elisabetta half-dead in one casualty room and Marco's corpse cooling in another. They remembered how his anger had smoldered during the aftermath when at first he wasn't allowed to participate in the investigation and later when he was denied access to case files after the official inquiries stalled. He was too close to the matter, a related party, he'd been told. His lack of impartiality would jeopardize a prosecution.

What prosecution, he'd demanded? You haven't caught anyone? You don't have a single lead? The investigation's a joke.

After a year of frustration Zazo and his superiors reached the boiling point at the same time. He wanted out, they wanted him out. His natural cheerfulness had been eclipsed by sarcasm and bursts of hostility toward the upper echelons of his command structure and he'd been called on the carpet for the occasional bout of heavy-handedness during an arrest. They made him see a psychologist who found him fundamentally healthy but in need of a change of assignment to a place that didn't provide daily reminders of the outrage perpetrated against his best friend and his sister.

Zazo's commander suggested the Gendarme Corps of Vatican City, the civil police force that patrolled the Vatican, a lower-key job where the most egregious offenders he'd have to contend with were pickpockets and traffic scofflaws. Strings were pulled and it was done. He traded uniforms.

Zazo had done well at the Vatican. He regained his equanimity and rose through the ranks to the level of major. He was able to afford his own apartment. He had a car and a motorbike. There was always a pretty girl on his arm. He couldn't complain, his life was good except for those moments when Marco's ghostly bled-out corpse came to him in a flashback.

Carlo commented on the tenderness of the lamb, then grunted, 'Maybe when there's a new Pope you can get a promotion to his security detail. The new man always likes to change things around.'

Half the plain-clothes men doing close security for the Pope were from the Gendarmerie, the other half from the Swiss Guards. 'I can't work with the Swiss Guards. Most of them are pricks.'

'Swiss,' Carlo grunted disagreeably. 'You're probably right.'

After Elisabetta cleared the dinner plates, Micaela laid out the tiramisu she'd brought from a bakery. She'd been moody and uncharacteristically silent during the meal and it only took a gentle prod from Elisabetta to get her to uncork.

Micaela was in her last year of training in gastro-enterology at the St Andrea Hospital. She wanted to stay put; Arturo was on staff there, she liked her department. She'd been angling for the one open junior-faculty position. 'They're giving it to Fanchetti,' she moaned.

'Why?' her father snapped. 'You're better than him. I wouldn't let that joker put a scope up my rear.'

'He's a man, I'm a woman, end of story,' Micaela said.

'They can't be that sexist,' Elisabetta said. 'In this day and age?'

'Come on! You work for the single most sexist organization in the world!' Micaela cried out.

Elisabetta smiled. 'The hospital is secular. The Church is most decidedly not.'

The apartment buzzer rang.

'Who the hell is that?' Carlo growled. 'On a Sunday?' He lumbered toward the hall.

'Maybe it's Arturo,' Zazo said, eliciting a snort from Micaela.

Elisabetta quietly put her fork down and got up.

They heard Carlo shouting into the scratchy intercom and when he returned to the dining room he had a puzzled expression.

'There's a guy downstairs who says he's Archbishop Luongo's driver. He says he's here to pick up Elisabetta.'

'He's early,' Elisabetta said, adjusting her leather belt. 'I was going to tell you.'

'Tell us what?' Zazo asked.

'My old professor, Tommaso De Stefano, visited me. He's still with the Pontifical Commission for Sacred Archeology. He wants my help with a project. I said no but he insisted. I've got to run. I'm sorry to leave the dishes.'

'Where are you going?' Micaela asked, dumbstruck. In fact, they all stared. Elisabetta's life was so predictable

53

that this deviation from routine seemed to catch them mightily by surprise.

'The catacombs,' she said. 'St Callixtus. But please don't tell anyone.'

It seemed as though a lifetime had passed since Elisabetta had last entered these grounds. The entrance to St Callixtus was off the Appian Way which, on a late Sunday afternoon, was nearly deserted. She'd forgotten how quickly the land turned rural when one passed through the ancient southern walls of the city.

Off the main road, the avenue leading to the catacombs was lined by stands of tall cypresses, their tops glowing orange in the dwindling sunlight. Beyond was a large tract of wooded and agricultural land owned by the Church and containing an old Trappist monastery, a dormitory for the catacomb guides and the Quo Vadis? church. To the west lay the Catacombs of Domitilla. To the east, the Catacombs of San Sebastiano. The whole region was sacred.

The driver – who had remained mute during their journey – sprung out and opened the car door before Elisabetta had a chance to work the handle herself. Professor De Stefano was waiting at the public entrance, a low structure which resembled a simple Mediterranean villa.

Inside, De Stefano led her past the policeman who stood guard at the visitors' iron gate. From there they headed down a stone stairway into the bowels of the earth.

'It's a walk,' he said. 'Halfway to Domitilla. There's really no short cut.'

Elisabetta lifted her robes just enough to prevent herself from tripping. The subterranean air was dead and familiar. 'I remember the way,' she replied. She felt a disturbing blend of apprehension and excitement course through her as she remembered her previous times here and thought ahead to the imminent new revelations.

They moved briskly through the normal tourist areas. The galleries, cut by pickaxes and shovels from the soft volcanic tufo from the second through the fifth centuries AD, were somber remains of a broad sweep of history. The Romans had always buried or cremated their dead in necropolises outside the city walls for it was strictly forbidden to do so within the city limits. The wealthy built family tombs. The poor were crammed into mass graves.

Yet the early Christians stubbornly refused to mix their dead with pagan bones and most of them were too poor to afford proper tombs. A solution was found on the rural estates of sympathizers. Dig your necropolises, they were told. Burrow as extensively as you please, come and visit your dead freely, but leave our fields intact. Thus the catacombs were spawned at all compass points outside the city walls but especially to the south, off the Appian Way.

Over the centuries vast networks of subterranean galleries were tunneled to hold the remains of Popes and martyrs, commoners and the lofty. The Popes had elaborate frescoed vaults where pilgrims came to venerate them. The poor had small loculi, not much more than stone shelves cut into the rock to hold their wrapped bodies. Perhaps their names were inscribed in the stone, perhaps not. Loved ones left behind the holy symbols of their new religion, the fish, the anchor, the dove and the chi-rho cross. As time went on, the galleries were extended into multi-level mazes, miles of tunnels to accommodate hundreds of thousands of the dead faithful.

Though Christianity's early history was troubled, fortune eventually favored the new religion when, in the fourth century AD, the Emperor Constantine himself converted to it, banned the persecution of Christians and returned confiscated Church properties. Gradually, the remains of the Popes and important martyrs were removed from catacombs and buried in consecrated ground within the grounds of churches. The sack of Rome by the Goths in AD 410 put an end to the use of the catacombs for fresh burials, though for centuries pilgrims continued to visit them and Popes did their best to preserve and even embellish the important vaults.

Yet their preservation would last only so long and by the ninth century relics were transferred with increased frequency to churches within the city walls. The catacombs were doomed to a form of extinction. Their entrances became overgrown by vegetation and they were lost in time, completely forgotten until the sixteenth century when Antonio Bosio, the Christopher Columbus of subterranean Rome, rediscovered one, then another, then thirty of them, and systematically began their study.

But tomb robbers followed and over the next two centuries most marble and precious artifacts disappeared until, in 1852, the Church put all Christian catacombs under the protection of the newly created Pontifical Commission for Sacred Archeology.

Elisabetta had always felt a sense of peace inside these rough-cut narrow passageways, the color of deep sunset. How the walls and low ceilings must have come alive with a sense of motion as pilgrims passed through, clutching their flickering oil lamps! How excited they must have felt, plunging through the darkness, glimpsing the corpses in their *loculi*, the colorful inscriptions and paintings in the *cubicula* – the chambers reserved for families – until, bursting with anticipation, they reached their destination, the crypts of the Popes and of the great martyrs like St Callixtus!

Now the loculi were empty. There were no longer any bones, lamps or offerings, just bare rectangular recesses cut into the rock. Elisabetta lightly touched a remembered fragment of plaster on one of the walls. It had the fragile outline of a dove holding an olive branch. It made her sigh.

De Stefano walked quickly and confidently for a man of his age. From time to time he turned to make sure that Elisabetta was keeping up. For the first ten minutes of their journey the tunnels were those open to the public. They passed through the crypts of Cecilia and the Popes, skirted the tombs of St Gaius and

Eusebius until they came to an unlatched iron gate, its key in the lock. The Liberian Area was off the tourist path. Completed in the fourth century, it was the last sector to have been dug out, a twisting three-level network of passages.

The cave-in was at the outermost reaches of the Liberian Area. When De Stefano paused at a poorly lit intersection of two galleries and momentarily seemed at a loss, Elisabetta gently advised him to take a left.

'Your memory is excellent,' he said appreciatively.

A faint sound of metal against rubble grew louder as they approached their destination. The plastered wall which had sparked Elisabetta's interest years ago was gone, turned into dust by the collapse. Now there was a gaping opening, irregular like the mouth of a cave.

'Here we are,' De Stefano said. 'The heavy work's been done. There's good timber erected. If I didn't think it was safe I wouldn't have brought you.'

'God will protect,' Elisabetta said, peering into the harshly lit space.

Inside the chamber there were three men who were shoveling a mixture of tuff, dirt and bricks. Some kind of manual hoist system was in place to lift their buckets out of the cave-in. The men stopped working and stared at Elisabetta through the entrance.

'These are my most trusted assistants,' De Stefano said. 'Gentlemen, this is Sister Elisabetta.' The men were young. Despite the cool subterranean temperature they were soaked through with sweat. 'Gian Paolo Trapani is directly responsible for all the catacombs of the Via Antica and he's acting as foreman for the operation.'

The pleasant-looking young man who came forward had longish hair, reddened by tufo dust. He didn't seem to know if he should extend a grimy hand so he made do with, 'Hello, Sister. I heard you studied here once. It's a pity that it took a quake to make an excavation. It's such a mess now.'

Elisabetta followed De Stefano through the opening. The chamber was irregularly shaped, generally rectangular. But the margins were ill-defined because of the piles of rubble. Wooden supports, thick as railway ties, had been laid in to support the sides and the earth overhead. The space was at least fifteen meters by ten, she thought, but the cave-in made it hard to be precise. There was a shaft of light coming in from a good ten meters above. A head appeared and another fellow yelled down. 'Why are you stopping?' He was manning the block and pulleys of the bucket rig.

'Go take a break!' Trapani shouted and the head disappeared.

Elisabetta's first impression was that their work was favoring speed over science. There were no excavation grids, no signs of measurement and documentation, no camera tripods or drawing tables. The ground seemed to have been cleared in one frantic effort rather than deliberately, meter by meter. Blue tarps covered much of the floor. Only one of the walls was reasonably vertical. It was covered by a suspended tarp.

'Sorry it's so untidy,' Trapani said, looking at her

shoes and hemline, which were covered in tuff dust. 'We've been moving faster than we'd like.'

'So I see,' Elisabetta said.

She was surprised at how seamlessly she made the shift into the observational mode of an archeologist. For twelve years she'd focused on an interior space, the realm of emotion and belief, faith and prayer. But at this moment, her mind won out over her heart. She stepped gingerly through the chamber, avoiding the ubiquitous tarps, taking in details and sorting them.

'The bricks,' Elisabetta said, stooping to pick one up. 'Typical first-century Roman – long and narrow. And this.' She dropped the brick and selected a grey friable chunk the size of a small cat. '*Opus caementicium*, Roman foundation cement.' Then she picked up one of the many pieces of blackened, charred wood and thought, *There was a fire*. 'This chamber predates the earliest part of the catacombs by at least a century. It's just as I proposed. The fourth-century extension of the catacombs stopped right before it encroached on it.'

'Yes, I agree,' De Stefano said. 'The diggers of the Liberian Area catacombs were only a few swipes of the pickax away from the surprise of their lives.'

'It *is* a columbarium, isn't it?' Elisabetta said.

'Just as you suggested during your student days,' De Stefano agreed, 'it does appear to be an underground funeral chamber for pre-Christians. The aboveground monument was probably razed and likely disappeared before the catacombs were built.'

He took a clear plastic specimen bag from his pocket.

'If the first-century dating was ever going to be in doubt, this settled it. We've found several so far.'

Elisabetta took the bag. It contained a large silver coin. The bust on the obverse showed a flat-nosed man with curly hair who was wearing a laurel wreath. The inscription read 'NERO CLAVDIVS CAESAR'. She flipped the bag over. The reverse was an elaborate arch flanked by the letters S and C – *Senatus Consulto*, the Senatorial mint mark. 'The lost arch of Nero,' she said. 'AD 54.'

'Precisely,' Trapani said, visibly impressed by the nun's acumen.

'But this isn't a typical columbarium, is it?' she said, glancing at the tarps.

'Hardly.' De Stefano waved his hand at the hanging wall tarp. 'Please take it down, Gian Paolo.'

The men pulled the tarp free of its pins and gathered it up. Underneath were rows of small dome-shaped niches carved into the cement, many containing stone funerary urns. The array of niches was interrupted by one smooth panel of creamy plaster. Gian Paolo trained a floodlight on it.

The plaster was covered with a wheel of painted symbols.

Elisabetta approached it and smiled. 'The same as my wall.'

The horns of Aries, the Ram.

The twin pillars of Gemini, the Twins.

The piercing arrow of Sagittarius.

The complementary scrolls of Cancer, the Crab.

The crescent of the Moon.

The male symbol, Mars. The female symbol, Venus.

All of the zodiac. The planets. A circle of images.

De Stefano drew close, almost rubbing against Elisabetta's shoulders. 'The plaster you studied must have come from the interior wall of a smaller room. It took this cave-in to expose the main chamber.'

One symbol particularly drew her attention. She stood beneath it and raised herself on her toes for a better look.

It appeared to be a stick-figure, the trunk a vertical line, the arms C-shaped upwards as if raised, the legs C-shaped downwards. The vertical line extended above the arms to create a head or neck but it also extended below the legs.

'It's surely the symbol for Pisces, but it's traditionally portrayed on its side. Vertically, it looks more like a man, doesn't it? My original wall had the same variant. And if it's meant to be a man, what do you suppose that is?' Elisabetta asked, pointing at the segment between the legs. 'A phallus?'

The archeologists seemed embarrassed at hearing a nun utter the word and De Stefano quickly rejoindered, 'No, I don't think so.'

'What, then?' she asked.

The old professor paused a moment and told Trapani, 'All right, pull back the ground tarps.'

The men worked quickly, almost theatrically to accomplish their version of a dramatic reveal, exposing the length and breadth of the debris-strewn floor.

Elisabetta put her hand to her mouth to stifle an oath. 'My God!' she whispered. 'How many?'

De Stefano sighed. 'As you can see, our excavations have been hasty and there's undoubtedly jumble and stackage from the cave-in, but there are approximately eighty-five adults and twelve children.'

The bodies were mostly skeletal, but because of the sealed atmosphere some were partially mummified, retaining tan patches of adherent skin, bits of hair and fragments of clothing. Elisabetta made out a few faces with their mouths agape – fixed, it almost seemed, in mid-gasp.

The remains were only incompletely exposed; hundreds of man-hours would be required to extricate them thoroughly and carefully from the rubble. There were so many that she found it hard to focus on one at a time.

Then, out of the tangle of arms, legs, ribs, skulls and spines one singular feature emerged, crashing into Elisabetta's consciousness like a huge wave pounding against a rock. Her eyes darted from one to another until she felt her vision blur and her knees go liquid.

Holy father, give me strength.

It was undeniable.

Every body, every man, woman and child stretched out before her possessed a bony tail.

FIVE

Janko Mulej habitually cracked his knuckles when he became impatient. The gesture wasn't lost on Krek.

'What's the matter?' Krek demanded.

Mulej was in his forties, a decade younger than his host, ugly as the back of a bus, as Krek liked to say, even to Mulej's face. He was almost twice Krek's size, a giant of a man who would have had to go around in tracksuits were it not for his excellent tailor in Ljubljana. 'Perhaps we should pack it in for the night.'

The great room at Castle Krek never got warm even in the height of summer and on this spring night Krek had deemed a fire to be in order. He liked his flames to leap high and throughout the evening he liberally piled on fresh logs to keep the massive fireplace roaring hotly.

The medieval manor had been in his family for four hundred years though it was nominally out of Krek hands during the unpleasant decades of Communist rule. Nestled in several hundred hectares of Slovenian woodlands, a few kilometers from Lake Bled, its original squared-off keep dated from the thirteenth century. The deep moat was stocked with carp and from outward appearances the ragged stonework of the castle suggested a certain shabbiness and disrepair.

That impression was obliterated upon entry. Krek's father had been a reclusive man who had rarely left the grounds. Throughout his life he lavished greater attention on his basement-to-parapet renovation of the castle than on his son. Ivo Krek had concentrated on the guts of the house, the masonry, the plumbing, furnace, wiring. His son shared his father's devotion to the castle but turned his keen eye toward furnishings and trappings of modernity. The reception rooms with their Romanesque arches were lavishly appointed with period antiques but Krek blended in contemporary overstuffed pieces to make the rooms inhabitable. Flat-panel televisions coexisted with medieval walnut carvings. A sixteenth-century cabinet with painted hunting scenes contained a €400,000 Danish audio system. The state-of-the-art chef's kitchen could have sprung from the pages of a decorating magazine.

He chose to receive Mulej and others in the great room. Its magnificent scale dwarfed men, even one of Mulej's size, and Krek liked his people to feel small in his presence.

Krek glanced at the grandfather clock. It was ten o'clock. 'I've been up since four and you're the one who's tired?' he asked Mulej, his voice rising. 'Don't you know what's at stake here? Don't you realize how little time we have?'

Mulej shifted his considerable weight on the armless leather sofa. He was seated uncomfortably close to the fire and was sweating profusely but he would never move from the spot because this was where Krek had placed him. The table between them was piled high with corporate folios, financial reports and a selection of newspapers.

'Of course I do, K,' Mulej said, wiping his damp forehead with his soaked handkerchief. 'I'm sorry. We'll go on as long as you like.'

Krek threw a log down hard onto the pile, making the fire spark wildly. An ember landed on his trousers. He swore and when he flicked it off he continued swearing at Mulej. The man's apology was having little effect. 'The Conclave is in less than a week, there's going to be a new Pope and now we've got this problem at St Callixtus! We have an enormous amount of work to do! You'll sleep when I tell you to sleep, you'll eat when I tell you to eat! Do you understand?'

To the outside world Mulej was Krek's Cerberus, the menacing beast guarding the gates of hell, the managing director of his conglomerate. But when his boss raged at him the hellhound became a small, frightened mutt.

Krek looked upwards as if he could see through the ceilings to the constellations of the night sky. 'Why the hell did Bruno Ottinger have to die? I miss the old goat. I trusted him.'

'You can trust me too,' Mulej said meekly.

'Yes, I suppose I can trust you,' Krek said, calming

down. 'But you're rather stupid. Ottinger was a genius, almost my equal.'

Mulej quickly picked up the copy of the daily newspaper, *Delo*, and dropped it back on the stack, as if anxious to change the subject. 'So what do you want me to do about this?'

The editorial-and-opinions page sported a good-sized photo of Krek, a flattering if somewhat brooding treatment, emerging dramatically from blackness with the headline: DAMJAN KREK – WHY WON'T HE RUN FOR PRESIDENT? A political commentator they knew well, a gadfly of the right, was stirring the pot again.

'We should ignore it,' Krek sighed. 'Why won't this guy leave me alone?'

Mulej answered his question with another. 'How many billionaires are there in Slovenia?'

'The disadvantage of being a large fish in a small lake,' Krek said. 'We do best when we work in the shadows. Politicians!' He spat the word out.

'We've had our share,' Mulej said.

Krek's voice was full of contempt. 'Moths to the flame.'

The phone on the internal line from the gatehouse rang. Krek answered it. 'I'd forgotten,' he said. 'Send her up.'

'Do you want me to stay?' Mulej asked.

'I'll be no more than an hour,' Krek said. 'Yes, stay! Don't you dare leave. When I get back I want to see a proposal of the trades we're going to set up between now and next week.'

'I know what to do, K,' Mulej said wearily.

'And I want you to make sure the statement is checked by one of our Arabic speakers. It has to appear authentic.'

'It's being done.'

'And draw up a press release expressing the company's outrage on behalf of myself and, of course, our Catholic employees. Got it?'

'Got it.'

'And, most importantly, I want a plan for dealing with the catacombs. I can't believe this happened at the worst possible moment. I want our people in Italy to know this is my highest priority. I want the best information, the best plan and the best execution.' He had been gradually creeping closer to Mulej and now he stood over him. He stabbed a finger into his shoulder. 'Got it?'

The big man nodded obediently. 'Yes, K.'

The doorbell chimed and Krek responded personally.

One of his security men was escorting a young woman. Krek welcomed her into the hall with a smile. 'What's your name?'

'My name is Aleida, Mister Krek.' She had a Dutch accent.

'My friends call me K,' he said. 'I was told you were lovely. I'm not disappointed.'

'It's an honor to meet you. Surely one of the great events of my life.' Aleida was a brunette with a film-star face. Her cheeks were flushed with the excitement of the moment.

'Come with me,' Krek said. 'My time is limited.'

'Of course, Mister Krek – K – a man like you has many responsibilities, I'm sure.'

He led her up an ornately carved staircase past a succession of bygone Kreks frozen in portraiture. 'You have no idea.'

Both sides of the hallway were lined with stag antlers, a dangerous gauntlet to run if one stumbled through in a drunken stupor. The residential areas of the castle were also uncontaminated by any traces of femininity. Krek's wife had died of a swiftly moving neurological condition years earlier and what frills of hers he had tolerated were purged when she was gone. His estate was feral, populated with wild boar and roe deer. It was a hunting castle. A man's house.

Krek's bedroom was large but austere. A planked floor with a few small rugs. A huge spiral-carved oak post in the center of the room supporting enormous beams. A medieval chest against a wall. A tapestry. A large bed with a half-canopy covered in striped damask.

Krek sat at the foot of the bed and removed his necktie.

'I was told you're altered,' he said.

Aleida lowered her eyes and whispered something by way of apology.

'I don't ordinarily accept altered women but I was advised I should make an exception.'

'My parents sent me to a boarding school where the girls showered together,' she said softly. 'I didn't want to lose it but they sent me for the operation.'

'It's a common story. I wish these things didn't happen but I accept that they do. Show me.'

Obediently, Aleida began to remove her clothes. First her coat, then her high-heeled shoes, her blouse, her tight skirt. There was no furniture nearby. She let the items drop to the floor.

Krek told her to stop to allow him to feast his eyes on the way she looked in her lingerie. He didn't want her to turn around, not for the moment. 'Keep going,' he finally said.

Aleida unclipped her black stockings from their garters and peeled them off, then deftly shed her bra and slowly pulled down her black thong. She was shaved and smooth.

'Very nice,' Krek said, leaning back on one arm. 'Now turn around.'

She did. There it was: a pale thin midline scar over her sacral spine running about six centimeters.

'Come closer.'

He inspected the scar and traced it with his finger. 'Who did it?'

'Dr Zweens,' she said. 'In Utrecht.'

'I know him. He does good work. So, Aleida, you're quite beautiful. I see no problems here.'

He turned her by the hips to face him. She looked down at him gratefully.

Krek stood, undid his belt and let his trousers fall to the floor. She finished the job and pulled down his shorts.

He guided her hands around his waist. Aleida did

the rest, moving them slowly and sensually to his lower back where she grabbed hold of the thick shaft at the base of his spine. She ran her fingers down its length. It was as meaty as his cock and every bit as hard.

'Pull it,' Krek moaned. 'Pull it hard.'

SIX

Elisabetta's small office was on the third floor of the Pontifical Institute of Sacred Archeology on the Via Napoleone, a bustling Roman street on a gentle hill. Outside, everything was moving at speed – cars, motorbikes and pedestrians – and the cacophony of engines and people made the city seem vibrant. Inside, the pace was languid. The staff shuffled through the halls at a crawl. The catacombs and monuments had been there for centuries, they reckoned, so what was the rush?

Elisabetta didn't share this sense of torpor. Over at Piazza Mastai her classes were being taught without her! Sister Marilena had taken them over so the children were being well-served – that wasn't the biggest problem. This assignment was a schism, a rip through the fabric of her soul, for all the sinister fascination it held for her now. The patterns of her day had a purpose, all to serve God. For the first time in a dozen years she'd been tipped from her gently rocking lifeboat and cast into an unfamiliar sea.

The books and papers on her desk were from a

different time, a different Elisabetta. She recognized her own handwriting, remembered the marginalia she'd made but they seemed alien to her. She resented them, resented Professor De Stefano and resented the staff at the Institute. To her mind, they were players in a conspiracy to pluck her away from the things she loved. Even the clergy at the Institute seemed like inhabitants of a parallel universe with missions different from her own. The nuns were more like clock-watching secretaries, the priests smelled of cigarettes and talked about TV shows in the lunch room. She had to finish this job of hers, whatever it was, and return to precious normalcy.

Elisabetta was thumbing through her old copy of Manilius's *Astronomica* when she felt a sudden need to shut everything out and pray silently.

She closed her eyes and clutched the cross hanging from her neck, hard enough to hurt her hand which already ached frequently from her old palm laceration. 'Dear Lord, I lost all thoughts of myself and that of my old life when I abandoned myself to your divine spirit. I yielded my heart to the power of your love. That heart which was almost pierced by an assassin's knife, that heart now belongs to you. I offer up my actions, my trials, my sufferings that my entire being may be employed in loving, honoring and glorifying you. It is my irrevocable will to belong entirely to you, to live and die as one of your devoted servants. Please let nothing disturb my deep peace. Heal my heart from impurity. Amen.'

Before Elisabetta could reopen her eyes, disturbing images began to invade her thoughts like unwelcome visitors. Pictures of partially mummified bodies with bony tails wafted through her mind.

Then she was seized by a flash, a painful memory she'd all but blocked from consciousness: the half-naked backside of the man who'd stabbed her, that *thing* protruding from his spine, ringed by small black tattoos looking for all the world like a swarm of angry insects.

That thing. It *was* a tail, wasn't it?

Suddenly woozy, she exhaled, unaware that she'd been holding her breath.

It was as if she'd always known.

Elisabetta felt small and vulnerable, a sparrow in a hurricane. God was inside her; He was all around her. But for the first time in a very long while she craved the warm sanctuary of a physical embrace.

'Are you coming?'

Elisabetta heard Marco's impatient baritone through the bathroom door. 'Yes!' she shouted back.

'You said "yes" ten minutes ago. We're going to be late.'

'This time I mean it.'

She put the finishing touches on her eye make-up and stood as far back as she could in an attempt to turn her reflection in the mirror over the sink into something more full-length. She liked her new dress. It was red and summery and it made her look especially shapely. She only needed to pick out a necklace, something nice and long, to show off her cleavage.

She opened the door and watched the impatience melt from Marco's face. 'That was worth waiting for,' he said. 'Look at you!'

She asked if he liked the dress and he responded by running his big hands over the silky fabric and up her stockings.

Elisabetta laughed and pulled away. 'I thought you said we were going to be late.'

'It's only my cousin's wedding. I don't even like him.'

'Well, I'm not going to let you mess up my dress and make-up. Not to mention your new suit – which looks really good, by the way.'

Marco checked himself out in the hallway mirror. 'You think so?'

'Yes, I think so. You're going to make the girls go crazy.'

'They can't have me,' he said, lightly. 'I'm spoken for.'

'For that, I'll kiss you, but later. I'll be right back. I need to get a necklace.'

At that moment he stopped looking like a hulking man and took on the demeanor of a small, excited boy. He reached into his inside jacket pocket and removed a slim velvet box. 'Maybe this will work.'

'Marco, what have you done?'

She opened it and loved it immediately. It was a heart-shaped pendant on a gold chain, half the design done in pavé diamonds, half in rubies.

'You like it?'

'Oh my God! I love it!'

She ran back into the bathroom to put it on and came out glowing.

'It looks beautiful,' he said. 'Like you.'

'Half is me, half is you,' Elisabetta said. 'Which am I, the diamonds or the rubies?'

'Whichever you like.'

She took a couple of steps forward and turned her face upwards to his. He encircled her in his strong arms and tenderly squeezed her ribs. She closed her eyes, put her arms around his waist, and her ear against his heart, feeling as happy and secure as she'd ever been.

'Am I disturbing you?'

Startled, Elisabetta opened her eyes. Professor De Stefano was at her door. 'No, please come in.'

The old man looked apologetic. 'I just wanted to make sure you had everything you needed.'

'Yes, it's all here,' she said, composing herself. 'My box of papers arrived this morning from my father's flat. The computer seems to work.'

'Do you need someone to help you with it?'

'We have computers at the school, Professor. I'm quite proficient.'

'Good, good. I'll have my secretary give you access to my files of photographs from the site.'

'That would be useful,' Elisabetta said.

De Stefano lingered. 'Do you have a plan?' he asked

abruptly. 'I know it's only your first full day and I wouldn't press you, but I've already had calls this morning from the Vatican. They're anxious for a report.'

She tapped on her copy of *Astronomica*. 'I'm thinking about the symbols. I want to try to understand their meaning, the significance they may have had to these . . . beings. And I need to understand the phenomenon better – the tails.'

De Stefano nodded vigorously. 'Yes, this is critical. We need to solve this mystery quickly. Who were these people? How did they come to be in this place? How did they die? By fire? Were they murdered? If so, who was responsible? Was it mass suicide? If so, why did they do it? What do their tails and their symbology tell us about who they were? Were they Romans? Were they pagans? Is there even the remotest possibility that they could have been Christians? It's going to be impossible to prevent the public from finding out about this forever. These things always leak. I only hope that we have some credible explanations to offer if it comes out before the Conclave starts or while it's in session. I'll leave you to it. But let me know as soon as you've made progress.' His voice had a pleading tone.

She opened the small volume to a bookmark. Marcus Manilius was a Roman astrologer whose life straddled the reigns of Augustus and Tiberius, a figure who would have been lost to the sands of time were it not for his epic poem *Astronomica*, intended to teach the art of the zodiac to his contemporaries.

Nor did man's reason set bound or limit to its activities until it scaled the skies, grasped the innermost secrets of the world by its understanding of their causes, and beheld all that anywhere exists. It perceived why clouds were shaken and shattered by so loud a crash; why winter's snowflakes were softer than summer's hail; why volcanoes blazed with fire and the solid earth quaked; why rain poured down and what cause set the winds in motion. After reason had referred these several happenings to their true causes, it ventured beyond the atmosphere to seek knowledge of the neighboring vastness of heaven and comprehend the sky as a whole; it determined the shapes and names of the signs, and discovered what cycles they experienced according to fixed law, and that all things moved to the will and disposition of heaven, as the constellations by their varied array assign different destinies.

This much Elisabetta recalled: the ancient Romans had been astrology mad, passionately convinced that the heavens ruled their fate. Some Emperors, those who were cocksure like Tiberius, encouraged the practice. Others, like Augustus, convinced that the populace was actively trying to predict his demise, banned astrological consultation outright.

But despite the pervasiveness of the zodiac in everyday Roman life she knew that astrological symbols were rarely found on the frescoes of homes or tombs. The symbology splashed across this columbarium was unique and given its context, disturbing.

Elisabetta compared her old notes on the original, now disintegrated wall with her new jottings. The pattern of symbols was identical, the twelve astrological signs simply but beautifully rendered in a large circle in their traditional longitudinal order from Aries to Pisces, followed by seven planetary signs in a peculiar order: the moon, Mercury, Venus, the sun, Mars, Jupiter, Saturn. And in each circle Pisces was always upright, like a standing man.

And what of the mummified and skeletal remains? She'd need to study De Stefano's photos carefully but, more importantly, she needed to get back into the catacombs with a trowel and brush and spend some time with the remains. She started to write a reminder to ask the professor about arranging another visit but she became distracted by a sticky note with an exclamation mark on it that she'd left protruding from a page of *Astronomica* years ago. She opened the book to the mark.

A superior power often intermingles the bodies of wild beasts with the limbs of human beings: that is no natural birth . . . the stars create these unprecedented forms, heaven introduces their features.

Monstrous births.

Elisabetta shuddered, trying to recall why she had flagged the passage.

Her computer chimed the arrival of her first email. She wheeled her chair around and clicked to the inbox, expecting the photos from De Stefano. But it was a message from Micaela – the subject line simply read CIAO.

Here's a bunch of articles for you. Hope they're what you're looking for. It's driving me crazy that you won't tell me what's going on. Mic.

Elisabetta sent the documents to the shared printer in the copier/file room and hurried to pick them up before anyone could see them.

She was relieved to be alone, away from prying eyes as the articles dropped into the printing tray. She stapled each one and waited for the next. Then she realized that she wasn't alone. A young priest had emerged from the rows of filing cabinets and was looking at her.

She turned and stared too long.

He was very tall, certainly two meters, with an oblong face and fine blond hair that made him resemble the screaming man in Munch's painting. He was wearing black plastic glasses with lenses so thick that they magnified and distorted his eyes. But it was his long torso and absurdly long arms that struck Elisabetta most. The arms were too much even for a body as stretched-out as his, and his thin, bony wrists protruded from the too-short sleeves of his black clergy shirt.

She was embarrassed at her involuntary gawking and was about to say something when he scooted out the door and disappeared without a word.

At her desk Elisabetta slipped the journal articles into her bag. Night reading. She would spend the rest of the afternoon poring over De Stefano's computer file of excavation photos.

Gian Paolo Trapani had taken hundreds of shots. The excavation work was rudimentary and the skeletons were only partially separated from one another and the surrounding matrix of rubble. She studied each photo carefully. Her first impressions were that these people were well-off. They had gold and silver bracelets and jeweled pendants on their persons. There were clumps of silver coins here and there suggesting long-ago-decomposed purses. The bodies were pressed together rather uniformly, indicating, Elisabetta supposed, crowding in a small space. But one feature jumped out after she had seen enough shots. The skeletons of children and even infants seemed to be randomly scattered among the adults. She couldn't find one example of an infant sheltered in the arms of one of the adults. Where was the evidence the maternal instinct?

Then a photo of one skeleton stopped her in her tracks.

It was a male, she thought, judging from its overall length and the bulkiness of its skull. As to mummification, it was among the better-preserved, with a good portion of tight brown skin sticking to the facial bones. She knew that post-mortem changes made these kinds of judgment difficult, if not absurd, but there was a frozen look of tortured rage on that rudimentary face.

The skeleton was dripping with gold. Heavy gold bracelets on the wrist bones. A beaten-gold pendant lying among the ribs. Elisabetta searched for a close-up of the pendant but there was none. She magnified the area with a photo-tool but it was no use. If there were markings she couldn't make them out. She made a mental note to seek it out the next time she went to St Callixtus.

But it was the final photo of this skeleton that really seized her imagination. There was something in one of his bony hands: a broken silver chain with a silver medallion. A shiver of expectation ran through Elisabetta. She zoomed in. The resulting image was blurry but she was almost certain what it was: the chi-rho cross, one of the earliest Christian symbols, made by combining the first two letters of the Greek word for Christ.

What was this symbol of the early Church doing in the decidedly un-Christian context of a Roman columbarium decorated with pagan astrological symbols? Elisabetta clicked the folder of photos closed and rubbed her dry eyes.

Yet another mystery.

Elisabetta arrived at Piazza Mastai too late for evening chapel and was obliged to pray on her own while the other sisters took their evening meal together. Because the chapel was at the opposite end of the hall from the kitchen it was peaceful and quiet. When she was done, she crossed herself and rose. Sister Marilena was seated in the last row.

'I didn't hear you,' Elisabetta told her.

'Good,' the old nun said. 'Mama put aside a plate for you. She doesn't like it when someone skips a meal.'

Mama was Sister Marilena's 92-year-old mother. Marilena had years ago sought and received dispensation from the Mother General of their order to allow her mother to live with them rather than going into an old-age home. They had plenty of space. The third and fourth floors of the convent were home to only eight sisters – four Italian, four Maltese – and ten novices, all African. It was hard going these days, recruiting young novices into the fold, particularly from Italy and the rest of Europe, so the women rattled around the facility and had the luxury of their own rooms.

'Making an extra prayer?' Elisabetta asked.

It was their private joke. Marilena was always sneaking into the chapel for extra prayers. The order was under-funded. They needed more books and computers. With the dearth of novices entering the order they had to rely on lay contract teachers who were expensive. Most parents could ill afford a hike in fees. So Marilena was always praying for more resources.

'I believe God heard me this time,' Marilena said, her stock answer.

Elisabetta smiled and asked, 'How did Michele do on her geometry test?'

'Not well. Does that surprise you?'

'No. She'll need extra help.'

'Don't worry,' Marilena said, 'I have vivid memories of Pythagoras and Euclid. How did *you* get on?'

'I don't like it. I hardly had a moment to pray.'

'You hardly have a moment during school.'

'It's different. Here, I'm with you. Their office is alien to me and so are the people.'

'You'll get used to it.'

'I hope not,' Elisabetta said. 'I want to finish the assignment and come back.'

Marilena nodded. 'You'll do what the Church asks of you and I'm quite sure that God will bless you for your service. Now come and eat before we both get in trouble with mama.'

Later, in her room, Elisabetta sat at her study desk in nightgown and slippers, trying to finish the articles that Micaela had sent her. It was hard going. The subject matter was technical and frankly distasteful – a compendium of medical literature on human tails. Most of the reports were in English and these she tackled first. There were a smattering in French, German, Russian and Japanese which she left for later.

She put down her fourteenth paper of the day on

atavistic human tails, a term with which she'd previously been unfamiliar. Atavism: the reappearance of a lost characteristic specific to a remote evolutionary ancestor. Like other atavisms, the scientific literature addressed human tails as one example of our common heritage with non-human mammals.

Elisabetta wasn't going to let herself be drawn into a debate on evolutionary biology. She was trained as a scientist and preferred to let Church doctrine coexist peacefully with truisms about evolution, at least in her own mind. No one in the Church had ever had occasion to question her about her beliefs on the matter and she'd try to keep it so.

Human tails, she learned, were rare – very rare, with only about a hundred well-documented cases in the past century. Elisabetta forced herself to study the photos, especially those of babies. They stirred something inside her, something deeply disturbing and base: a stomach-churning revulsion. And there was more: an element of fear. An ancient Darwinian fear of prey in the presence of a predator. She took a deep breath and pressed on.

Human tails ranged from short nubbins to longer snake-like appendages. They possessed all the structures of mammalian tails with extra bones – up to half a dozen coccygeal vertebrae – covered by sinew and muscle and pink skin. They could move with the full voluntary control of striated muscle.

Most parents opted for surgical removal lest the

child grow up stigmatized and for that reason tails in adults were even more unusual.

Elisabetta's eyelids grew heavy. She'd gotten through all the English-language papers and she was finding them repetitive. A German paper was at the top of the pile. It was from the *Deutsche Medizinische Wochenschrift*, a short piece from 2007. Her knowledge of German wasn't good but she thought the title referred to a case study of an adult human tail. The text was dense and impenetrable.

She'd tackle it in the morning, she decided.

It was time to clear her head and restore her balance with a short period of prayer before sleep overtook her.

As she rose from her chair Elisabetta had a sudden impulse to turn one more page. She tried to fight it but her hand moved too fast.

At the sight of the photo, she lost control of her legs and fell back onto the seat hard enough to make her gasp in pain.

Dear God.

A naked old corpse lay prone on an autopsy table, photographed from waist to knees.

Arising above wrinkled male buttocks was a tail, twenty centimeters from its base to its tip by the measuring rule laid beside it. It was thick at its base, its whole length cylindrical and untapered with an abruptly stubby tip like the cut edge of a sausage.

But there was more.

Elisabetta tried to swallow but her mouth was too

dry. She squinted hard at the photo and adjusted her reading light but it wasn't enough.

Breathing hard, she ran from her room, grabbing at her dressing gown and donning it as she flew down the hall. Sister Silvia, a dear lady with a weak bladder on her way to the lavatory, was speechless as Elisabetta rushed past and careened down the stairs to the classrooms.

She switched on the lights and found what she needed in the science room. Then she ran back up the stairs, clutching a magnifying glass.

She sat back down at her desk. The base of the dead man's spine – that was what had seized her attention like a hard slap to the face.

There they were, visible under the magnifying glass, ringing the tail in concentric semicircles: a flock of small black tattoos. Elisabetta was seized with a para-lyzing fear, as if this naked old corpse might rise from the page and strike at her with a knife aimed for her heart.

SEVEN

The Institute of Pathology at the University Hospital of Ulm in southern Germany was set in woodlands at the outskirts of the expansive campus. A journey by air with a car and driver from Munich airport had been arranged at the insistence of Professor De Stefano over Elisabetta's protestations that the train would do fine.

'Look,' he'd said. 'I'm sticking my neck out by letting you bring your sister into this so indulge me. I want to make sure you're there and back the same day. Speed . . .'

To his non-amusement Elisabetta completed his mantra, '. . . is essential.'

She and Micaela had sat beside each other on the flight from Rome talking in hushed voices about tails and tattoos, star signs and ancient Roman burial practices.

Micaela chomped through her bag of mixed nuts and took Elisabetta's when they were offered, thoroughly enjoying her role as an insider. But Elisabetta already nervous about including her family in this business, began to worry about her sister's commitment to secrecy when she said, 'We should get Papa involved. He's a genius.'

'Yes, I know he's as clever as they come and I guess his analytical powers would be very useful,' Elisabetta replied, 'but we simply cannot tell him. We can't speak of this to anyone else! It was difficult enough to get them to let me bring you inside the tent. I said I needed a medical doctor and De Stefano agreed only because you're my sister.'

The two women who emerged from the Mercedes car at the entrance to the Institute could not have looked more different – Micaela in a tightly fitting print dress with a sharp leather jacket and high heels and Elisabetta in her black habit and sensible shoes.

While Elisabetta hung back, Micaela told the man at the reception area that she had an appointment. After he had placed a call upstairs he looked up again and asked the nun if he could be of assistance.

'We're together,' Elisabetta replied.

He looked them over and shook his head, seemingly uncertain about this apparent collision of two worlds.

Earlier, Micaela had driven Elisabetta to hysterics about the pomposity of German academic titles. So when Herr Professor Dr Med. Peter-Michael Gunther emerged from the elevator Micaela fired off a wicked wink. He looked every inch the Herr Professor. Tall and imperious, and with a smug goatee, his full title was embroidered above the pocket of his lab coat at the expense of a considerable amount of red thread.

'Ladies,' Gunther said in crisp English, seemingly struggling for a proper way to address them, 'it's a pleasure to make your acquaintance. Please follow me.'

Micaela chatted his ear off all the way upstairs. She'd been the one to make initial contact and he seemed far more comfortable with her anyway.

'I'm surprised you were interested in my little paper,' Gunther said, showing them into his starkly modern office that overlooked the Institute's reflecting pool.

'Was no one else interested?' Elisabetta asked, speaking for the first time.

He poured coffee from a cafetière. 'You know, I thought it would generate some wider expressions of interest and comment but that was not the case. Just a few notes from colleagues, a joke or two. Actually, the greatest interest came from the police.'

Elisabetta put her cup down. 'Why the police? Was his death suspicious?'

'Not at all. The cause of death was clearly a coronary thrombosis. The man was in his eighties, found unresponsive on the street and taken to the casualty ward where he was pronounced dead. All very routine until someone removed his trousers. The case took a further unusual turn two days after his autopsy when someone broke into the hospital morgue and removed his body. The same night, my hospital office was burglarized and some of my files were taken, including the notes and photographs of our gentleman. Even my digital camera was stolen, complete with the relevant memory card. The police were quite useless, in my opinion. There was never any solution.'

Elisabetta's heart sank at the news. Had their journey been a waste of time? All she could ask was, 'What did his loved ones do?'

'There were none. The man had no living relatives that we could find. He was a long-retired university professor who lived in a rented flat near the city center. It seems that he was quite alone. The police concluded that someone in the hospital might have talked about his unusual anatomy and some oddball group stole his remains for ritualistic purposes or as a sick joke. Who knows?'

'How did you write the paper if everything was stolen?' Micaela asked.

'Ah, so!' Gunther said slyly. 'Because the case was unique, I printed a duplicate set of photos and a copy of the autopsy report and brought them back to this office the evening of his post-mortem. I wanted to study them at my leisure. It was fortunate that I had two offices.'

'So you have photos?' Micaela asked.

'Yes, several.'

'More than the ones you published?' Elisabetta asked.

'Yes, of course. Now perhaps it's your turn to tell me why a nun and a gastroenterologist are so interested in my case.'

The sisters looked at each other. They'd rehearsed

their reply. 'It's the tattoos,' Elisabetta said. 'I'm doing research on a project concerning early Roman symbology. I have reason to believe this man's tattoos bear a relationship to them but the published photos are too indistinct for me to make them out.'

'What kind of symbols?' Gunther asked, clearly fascinated.

'Astrological,' Elisabetta replied.

'Then you are going to be disappointed,' he said, picking a folder off his orderly desk. He laid out a series of color photographs, one by one, like a dealer at a casino, snapping their edges. They were all of the man's wizened back. The first few were wide-angles and included the two that had been published in the paper. The tail was long, extending below the corpse's buttocks. Its shriveled skin exposed the extra vertebrae underneath.

In other shots the field tightened and the magnification increased as the photographer worked his way up to the conical tip stretched over a tiny coccygeal bone. The tail swelled in diameter at its midsection; fine white hairs covered the skin. Had they been black in the man's youth, Elisabetta wondered?

Then Gunther laid out the critical shots, those from the base of the spine.

It might have been impolite to grab but Elisabetta couldn't help herself. She snatched one of the close-ups and devoured it with her stare.

The tattoos were numbers.

Three concentric semicircles of numbers surrounded the base of the tail.

63 128 99 128 51 132 162 56 70
32 56 52 103 132 128 56 99
99 39 63 38 120 39 70

Micaela, not to be outdone, had gotten her hands on a similar photo. 'What does it mean?' she asked.

'We had absolutely no idea,' Gunther said. 'We still don't.'

They both looked to Elisabetta.

She shook her head hopelessly. 'I have no idea, either.' She put the photo down. 'May we have a copy?'

'Yes, certainly.'

'Do you know anything else about the man?'

'We have his name and his last address, that's all.'

'May we know these?' Elisabetta asked gently.

Gunther shrugged. 'Ordinarily, patient confidentiality would prohibit this, but when the affair went to the police it became a matter of public record.' He produced a data sheet from the folder. 'One day, ladies, you must repay me by telling me the results of your inquiries. I have a feeling you've got something up your sleeves.'

Micaela smiled and said, 'My sister's sleeves are bigger than mine.'

The address on Fischergasse was a short distance from Ulm Münster and if the two women hadn't been rushing to make their return flight, Elisabetta would have tried to pay a flying visit. The cathedral had begun its existence as a relatively modest Catholic building but thanks to the region's conversion to Protestantism and a grand nineteenth-century spire added by its Church Elders, it was now the tallest cathedral in the world.

Their driver parked outside a row of pretty half-timbered houses in the Old Town, close enough to the Danube for the wind to carry a faintly riverine smell. Number 29 was an ample four-story house with a bakery on the ground floor.

When they arrived, Micaela was on her mobile, engaged in an overheated conversation with her boyfriend Arturo, so Elisabetta got out alone.

'If you don't get anywhere, at least bring me back some cakes,' Micaela called after her.

The pleasant street called out to Elisabetta. How marvelous it would be to find a bench and spend some time alone. Except for a few brief moments in the convent chapel at dawn she'd spent an entire day without prayer. She felt unhealthy and unfulfilled and she wondered darkly if her faith was being tested. And if it was, would she pass the test and emerge clean?

A spring-loaded bell chimed her entry into the bakery. The rotund woman at the till seemed surprised to see a nun in her shop and ignored another customer in a rush to serve Elisabetta.

'How can I help you today, Sister?' she asked in German.

'Ah, do you speak Italian or English?' Elisabetta asked in English.

'English, a little. Would you like some bread? Some pastries, Sister?'

'Just some assistance. A man used to live at this address. I wonder if you knew him?'

'Who?'

'Bruno Ottinger.'

It was as if Elisabetta had conjured a ghost. The shopkeeper braced herself against the counter and almost rested her hand on a fresh pie. 'The professor! My God! Funnily enough, Hans and I were talking about him just last night. We were his landlords.'

'I see you're busy. I was just stopping by on the way to the airport and wanted a word with someone who knew him.'

'Let me get rid of her,' the shopkeeper said, pointing her chin at the elderly customer who Elisabetta hoped spoke no English. 'She always buys the same thing so it won't take a minute.'

When the customer was gone, the baker's wife, who introduced herself as Frau Lang, hung a back-in-10-minutes sign in the shop window and locked the door. She touched Elisabetta's wrist and said guiltily, 'Hans is Protestant but I'm Catholic. I should do more with my religion but you get out of the habit, what with our crazy hours and all the family commitments.'

'There are many ways to live a good life,' Elisabetta said, trying to be helpful. 'I wonder if I might get my sister from the car.'

'Is she a nun too?' Frau Lang asked in bewilderment.

'No, she's a doctor.'

'Well, tell her to come inside. Does she like cakes?'

'In fact, she likes them a great deal.'

Krek sat behind his large desk with his mobile phone pressed against one ear. Double-glazed windows cut the street noises of Ljubljana's Prešeren Square to a minimum but he could see that Čopova Street was thick with lunchtime traffic.

'Yes, I know that communication is a perennial issue.'

He listened to the response and said, 'I don't trust the internet. We'll use the old ways. The day before the Conclave our people will see it and they'll know it was us.'

He rang off brusquely and looked up. Mulej was there, filling the door frame with his bulk and wearing a constipated expression.

'What is it?' Krek asked

'I just took a call. There's a new problem, probably not a major one but one that we should monitor closely.'

'Spit it out, damn it!'

'Do you remember that girl, the one from years ago who was snooping around St Callixtus?'

Krek frowned more severely, his look becoming ugly. 'Elisabetta Celestino. Aldo Vani botched the job. She survived. She became a nun, of all things. She became harmless. We let her go. Yes, Mulej, it seems that I remember her.'

'Someone at the Vatican pressed her into service. She left her convent and has begun working at the St Callixtus collapse. I can't confirm it but she may have gone to Ulm today.'

'Ulm?' Krek roared. 'What the hell is she doing in Ulm?'

Mulej looked out the tinted windows rather than face his boss's fearsome stare. 'I don't know, but I'll find out.'

'Get Aldo on the phone right now.' Krek's voice was strained, his throat constricted by venom. 'This time he's going to do the job correctly. I want this woman, this nun, stopped bang in her tracks, Mulej. Tell Aldo to bring her here so I can deal with her personally. If that proves inconvenient, then have him eliminate her. Do you understand?'

The Tribunal Palace was only a few paces from the Basilica, yet it was just one of the anonymous buildings dotting the Vatican complex which tourists barely noticed. A bland administrative building, it housed, among other departments, the Gendarmerie Office.

The Inspector-General of the Gendarmerie Corps, Luca Loreti, was a competent leader, generally liked and respected by his men though the youngest recruits sometimes rolled their eyes at his twisted locutions. The officers who'd been around for a while, like Zazo, always came back to the fact that Loreti consistently stood up to his Swiss Guard counterpart, Oberst Hans Sonnenberg, and defended his men to the hilt against that prick. Not that the officers were completely reverential. Loreti, a lusty eater, had been steadily expanding in girth over time and there was a book running every year on the closest date for his annual uniform refitting.

Most of the Corps's 130 gendarmes were now assembled in the auditorium for Loreti's briefing. The officers sat in the front, the junior ranks behind, all very orderly and hierarchical. Loreti possessed tremendous kinetic energy for a man his size and he strode rapidly back and forth on the stage, making the audience move their heads as if they were at a tennis match.

'First, let me compliment you on the job you did at the Pope's funeral. Our cardinals, our bishops, our Vatican officials, over two hundred world leaders and their security details – all of them came to Vatican City, paid their respects and left in good health,' Loreti boomed into his hand-held microphone. 'But we cannot rest on our laurels, can we? We have five days until the Conclave begins. Many of the Cardinal Electors have already checked into the Domus Sanctae Marthae. As of today, the guest house will be a sterile zone. As of today, the Sistine Chapel will be a sterile zone. As of today, the Basilica and the Museums will be closed to the public. Our tasks will be precisely defined by protocols. I have been working with Oberst Sonnenberg to ensure that we will not be tripping over the Swiss Guards, they will not be tripping over us and there will be no gaps in our security blanket. We will control the guest house, they will control the Sistine Chapel. We will utilize our dogs and our experts to sweep the guest house for explosives and listening devices. The Guards will do the same with their experts inside the Sistine Chapel. I want you to play nice with the Guards but if there's any trouble, let your superiors know immediately and they will let me know. All disputes will necessarily be answered at my level.'

Zazo knew the drill. This would be his second Conclave. At the first one he'd been a wide-eyed corporal, dazzled by pomp, grandeur and the heavy sense of occasion. Now he was immune to that. He had squads of men to command and his accountability went far beyond guarding a doorway.

He nudged Lorenzo Rosa in the ribs. Lorenzo, also a major, had entered the Corps the same year as Zazo and the two of them were now good friends. Initially, Zazo had resisted the urge to befriend Lorenzo because the man bore enough of a physical resemblance to Marco – tall and athletic, crisp facial lines, black hair – that on some level Zazo felt that to make a friend of him would be a betrayal. But Zazo was so naturally gregarious and eager for comradeship that he broke through the psychological block the day both men went through a poison-gas drill together and wound up puking alongside each other in a ditch.

'This isn't going to be as smooth as he says,' Zazo whispered. 'We'll be at war with the Guards by Friday.'

Lorenzo leaned over to whisper into Zazo's ear. 'The Swiss can kiss my Italian ass.'

That was why Zazo liked the guy.

*

Martin Lang, the Ulm baker, was roused furiously from the sofa by his wife and sent to the bedroom to change his shirt. Over Elisabetta's protestations, Frau Lang quickly picked up after him, then left the two women in the sitting room while she put the kettle on and began rattling porcelain and silverware.

Hans Lang came back tucking in a fresh shirt and haplessly combing wisps of hair over a balding pate with his hand. He looked every inch a man who'd been up at the ovens since the middle of the night. 'I'm so sorry,' he said in halting English. 'I wasn't expecting. I'm always the last to know of such things.'

Elisabetta and Micaela apologized for the intrusion and sat stiffly by, waiting for Frau Lang to reappear. Elisabetta tried some small talk about how nice his shop was but the baker's English was not up to the task.

When Frau Lang brought in a tray with tea and cakes, Micaela hungrily tucked into the pastries while Elisabetta nibbled demurely. 'What can you tell us about Herr Ottinger?' she asked.

Frau Lang did the talking. Her husband sat blearily on the sofa looking like he wanted his privacy back. 'He was a proper old gentleman,' she said. 'He lived on our third floor for fifteen years. He kept to himself. I wouldn't say we knew him well. He'd often buy a meat pie for his dinner, maybe something sweet on a Saturday. He paid his rent on time. He didn't have many visitors. I don't know what else I can tell you.'

'You said he was a professor. Do you know anything about his work?' Elisabetta asked.

'He was retired from the university. I have no idea what kind of professor he was but there were so many books in his flat when he died.' Frau Lang spoke in German to her husband. 'Hans says they were mostly science and engineering books so maybe that was his field.'

'And there were no relatives?'

'None. The authorities checked, of course. We had to go through a formal process before we were entitled to sell his belongings to satisfy the unpaid portion of the rental agreement. We didn't do so well out of the process. The man had no significant possessions. More cake?'

Micaela nodded happily and accepted another slice before asking, 'Did you ever notice anything odd about him? Physically?'

Frau Lang shook her head. 'No. Whatever do you mean? He was just an ordinary-looking older gentleman.'

'So, there's nothing left in the flat?' Elisabetta asked, leaving her sister hanging.

'No. Of course we've had new people, a nice couple living there since 2008.'

Elisabetta shook her head slightly. She'd call the university, see if she could track down any former colleagues. There was nothing left to be done here.

The baker said something gruffly in German.

'Hans reminded me,' his wife said. 'We kept a small box of personal belongings, things like his passport, the items in his bedside table in case a relative ever appeared.'

The sisters looked up hopefully. 'Can we see it?' Elisabetta asked quickly.

Frau Lang spoke to her husband in German again and Elisabetta made out curse words as he pushed himself off the sofa and headed out the door.

'He'll get it. It's in the basement,' Frau Lang said, frowning after him and pouring more tea.

In five minutes the baker came back with a cardboard box the size of a briefcase. It was clean and dry, and had obviously been stored with some care. He handed it to Elisabetta, mumbled something to his wife and appeared to be excusing himself with a small bow.

Frau Lang looked embarrassed. 'Hans is going to take his nap now. He wishes you a good trip home.'

Elisabetta and Micaela started to rise but the baker shooed them down with a wave of his hands and disappeared into another room.

The box was light; its contents shifted in Elisabetta's hands when she transferred it to her lap. She pulled apart the tucked-in corners and looked in. A stale mustiness escaped, an old-man smell.

Reading glasses. Fountain pens. A passport. A bronzed medal on a ribbon from, as far as she could tell, a German engineering society. Checkbooks and bank statements from 2006 and 2007. Pill bottles which Micaela inspected and whose contents she declared to be for high blood pressure. A box of dentures. A fading

Kodachrome of a young man, Ottinger himself perhaps, in hiking gear on a steep green slope. At the very bottom was an unsealed Manila envelope with a handwritten note on the outside, written finely in black ink.

Elisabetta lifted out the envelope, prompting Frau Lang to remark that it contained a book, the only one they hadn't sold because of the personal note. Elisabetta, who had a passable grasp of written German, read the note to herself slowly, translating as best she could.

> To my teacher, my mentor, my friend. I found this in the hands of a dealer and I enticed him to part with it. You, more than anyone, will appreciate it. It is the B Text, of course. As you always taught – B holds the key. 11 September is surely a sign, don't you think? I hope you will be with us when M's day finally comes.
> K. October 2001.

Beneath the date was a small hand-drawn symbol.

This sight of it made Elisabetta's head swim.

There was something strangely familiar about it, real and unreal at the same time, as if she'd seen it before in a long-forgotten dream.

She tried to shrug off the feeling as she opened the envelope. Inside was a slim bound book. Its cover was plain, worn leather, ever so slightly warped. The pages were a bit foxed. It was an old book in fairly good condition.

When she opened the cover her head cleared as effectively as if she'd taken a strong whiff of smelling salts.

Elisabetta didn't think she'd ever seen the engraving before, but part of it was as recognizable as her own reflection in the mirror.

It was a 1620 edition of Marlowe's *The Tragical History of the Life and Death of Doctor Faustus*, and there on the frontispiece was the old conjuror wearing his academic robes, standing inside his magic circle with his staff and his book, summoning the devil through the floor. The devil was a winged creature with horns, a pointy beard and a long curled tail.

None of that made Elisabetta's heart race or her skin crawl. None of it made her feel like she was suffocating under her tight veil and gown.

The source of her alarm lay around and within the rim of the magic circle.

Constellation signs.

Aries, Taurus, Gemini, Cancer.

Star signs.

The moon, Mercury, Venus, the sun, Mars, Jupiter and Saturn, presented in the same peculiar order as on the fresco at St Callixtus.

And peeking out to the right of Faustus's robes was Pisces, tilted upright, looking for all the world like a man with a tail.

EIGHT

Rome, AD 37

Dusk was turning to night as two weary boys trudged up the road toward the city centre. An insipid quarter-moon hung limply in the black sky, dimly lighting the way. In silence they kept close to the stinking central gutter to avoid worse piles of refuse that littered their way.

'Where will we sleep?' the youngest asked fearfully as they passed a gloomy alley.

'I've no idea,' snapped his older brother. Sensing the seven-year-old's abject misery he relented. 'The father of my friend, Lucius, says he sleeps in the cattle market whenever he stays in Rome. We'll find a place there.'

Clasping his brother's hand, the younger child shivered. His loose tunic barely warded off the chill.

'Are we nearly there? At the cattle market?' he enquired hopefully.

Quintus groaned, having heard a variant of the same question at least a hundred times that day.

'Yes, Sextus, soon we'll have somewhere warm to rest, after we've had a bite to eat.'

They were travelling to their uncle's brick manufactory in the north of Rome, on the Pincian Hill, and they were hungry and exhausted following a dawn departure from their village. At least they'd made it through the walls, into the city. The two huge Praetorians with scorpion emblems affixed to their breastplates at the Porta Capena had given them a world of trouble and tried to shake them down for a bribe. But they had no coins, nothing at all and they had to prove it by stripping themselves bare and enduring the taunts of the fearsome soldiers.

Quintus, the older by three years, had wondered if his father had looked like these men. Only the vaguest of memories lingered. He was a toddler when the centurion left for active service in Germania. Their mother had to fend for herself with only the help of two older girls to tend their smallholding and look after Quintus and his baby brother.

Only a fortnight ago, their mother had gotten notice of her husband's death in battle against the Cheruscii. On further learning that the bastard had frittered away his accumulated pay on wine and whores all she could do was shed futile tears.

Faced with crippling debts, she quickly sold her land for a pittance to a rich patrician. She and her daughters would have to survive by hiring themselves out as labourers and cloth weavers, but she could ill afford to feed two useless mouths. Rather than sell them into slavery she made the somewhat more humane decision to send the boys to their uncle to earn their keep there.

Judging by the smells, they were getting close to the cattle market in an industrial sector where tenements clung to islands of land in a sea of twisting and claustrophobic alleyways.

At street level, the retaining walls of the tenements were built of stone and reasonably robust. Higher stories listed at precarious angles and looked a good bit flimsier and indeed they passed a block which had suffered a collapse. The dwellings doubled as shops by day, selling bare necessities and cheap, rough wine. The boys dragged themselves along the fetid street towards the ghostly white glow of the stone-flagged marketplace, keeping to the centre, avoiding the glowering shadows.

The open windows at street level leered at them like black sockets in a cadaver's skull. Sextus squeaked in fright as he tripped over a pile of offal festering in front of a butcher shop and set a loathsome carpet of rats in motion. With the last of his fading strength, Quintus managed to jerk him upright before the little boy fell into the mess.

An empty cattle byre beckoned. An emaciated dog emerged from it, interested in seizing the rotting meat before the rats reclaimed their prize. The mongrel succeeded and scuttled off down an alleyway dragging a coil of intestines.

Inside the animal pen, Quintus looked around and declared, 'We'll sleep here.' They busied themselves raking up stray hanks of unfouled straw and dry grass with their hands, laying out a bed of sorts against the plank walls at the far corner of the unroofed shed.

'We won't have far to travel tomorrow, will we, Quintus?' asked the younger boy hopefully.

Quintus wasn't at all sure but he said with feigned confidence, 'If we start early, we'll be at Uncle's before noon.'

He untied the knotted corners of the travelling blanket he'd been carrying over his shoulder and removed the last of their meagre provisions. Handing Sextus half the bread and an apple, the two boys collapsed on the straw bed and ate.

Balbilus heard a dull pounding overhead, an iron rod smashing against stone, a signal that he was wanted.

The underground chamber was well lit by sooty lamps. It was a large space – fifty men could assemble there comfortably, a hundred in a pinch. Live men. There was space for thousands of dead ones if most were cremated and tucked inside urns in the tuff walls. It was newly finished. The columbarium was awaiting its first inhabitant.

Tiberius Claudius Balbilus put down his paintbrush. He disliked interruptions but he was used to them. Many sought him out.

He was in his thirties, a powerful-looking man with the olive skin of his half-Egyptian, half-Greek heritage, a large nose and a well-tended beard which was trimmed to a sharp point and made his face look like some sort of weapon or chisel tool. He had let his tunic go loose for comfort but before he climbed the stairs he cinched his belt and donned a cloak.

Balbilus entered the mausoleum by pushing open a concealed trapdoor. The walls were lined with the tombs and shrines of the wealthy. A fresh corpse, no more than a few weeks old, linen-wrapped and stuffed into a loculum, made the place reek of death. The mausoleum had been in his family for a few generations. It was a good, steady source of income, but because of his recent secret excavation it now had another purpose.

When his time came, he would rest there for eternity, not above ground with these so-called citizens but underground, among his own kind. His followers would rest there too. For the sake of space most would be cremated. But he and his sons and his son's sons could be laid out – all their flesh, all their bones – in all their glory.

There was a solitary figure waiting for him, his face concealed by a hooded cloak. He bowed slightly to Balbilus and said, 'The others are outside.'

Balbilus, together with this man, Vibius, emerged from a rear door into the cold December night. They were within a grove only a few paces off the Appian Way. The mausoleum was a rectangular building with a barrel-vaulted roof made of the finest bricks. Balbilus's lavish villa lay on the other side of the grove.

The quarter-moon reappeared from behind a shroud of purple clouds. Five cloaked figures moved away from the darkness of the fruit trees. Balbilus lined them up like a military unit in front of the mausoleum wall.

'I've studied the charts, and the stars favor action,'

Balbilus said, addressing the men. 'Tonight we light a fire. Although it will be small at first it will spawn another one, and another and another until, one day, there will be a great conflagration that will consume the city. And when that happens we will gain wealth and power beyond our dreams. It is in the stars and I know it to be true. Tonight we will set the Romans against this new Christian cult. I can see in the stars that they will become powerful one day. Their message is seductive, like bread and circuses for the soul. The masses will, I fear, take to it like sheep. If we allow them to become too powerful they will be a formidable enemy. Vibius has my instructions. Tonight you will spill blood because . . .' he took a breath for effect then spat out the rest '. . . *this is what we do.*'

And the men answered in unison, '*And this is who we are.*'

Balbilus left them and went back underground where his paintbrushes awaited him.

The six men moved out in silence. Making use of the concealment provided by the tombs and foliage bordering the Appian Way they headed north toward Rome.

After a while they came upon a dim radius of flickering light cast by pitch torches on either side of a broad postern gate. They flitted from shadow to shadow, getting closer.

The two Praetorians peered dispiritedly into the feeble pool of light and stamped their feet to keep warm.

Vibius made his move. He weaved onto the main road, garbling the words of a drinking song. The sentries became alert and stared as he emerged from the darkness, swaying gently. He stopped to take a swig from a bulging wine-bag.

Resuming his unsteady approach, he came to a stumbling halt, just beyond arm's length from the stockier of the two sentinels.

'Eh, lads, let me pass, will you?' he slurred.

The soldier seemed to relax but he still kept his hand on the pommel of his short-sword.

'It's curfew hour, you drunken fool – all passage is forbidden.'

Vibius staggered a bit further forward, offering the wine sack. 'Drink, my lords, as much as you want. I will pay you for entry. All's I want is to get home.'

With his left hand he waved the bag in the guard's face and when the soldier raised his arm to swat it away Vibius suddenly thrust his right hand upwards, gripping the long dagger he'd concealed beneath his robe. The blade pierced the underside of the guard's chin and with a grisly crunch its point exited through the top of his head.

The second Praetorian didn't have time to draw his weapon. Another cloaked man had crept through the shadows, clamped an arm around the guard's chest and reached for his jaw with his free hand. With a violent motion the cloaked man jerked hard and there was a loud crack as the Praetorian's vertebrae gave way.

Both corpses twitched on the cold ground, then went

limp. The rest of the cloaked men converged on them and joined in a savage choreography.

When they were done with their sharp work, body parts floated in pools of blood like pieces of meat in a stew. Vibius reached inside his cloak and pulled out a silver medallion on a broken chain. It was the chi-rho monogram, the symbol of Christ. He dropped it into the blood and waved the men forward through the Porta Capena into the city of Rome.

The slums at the base of the Esquiline Hill were never quiet. Even late at night there was always enough shouting, drunken brawling and noise from crying babies to disturb the peace. Against this din, the clip-clop of donkey hooves and the clatter of cart wheels on cobblestones went unnoticed.

The cart driver hauled on the reins outside a seedy apartment block on a narrow side street where much of the plaster had fallen from the façade. Had they not been bribed into silence, the city engineers would have condemned the structure years ago.

The driver hopped down between the cart and the building and whispered, 'We're here.'

The straw heaped in the cart moved and an arm appeared, then a bearded head. A tall man climbed down and brushed the straw from his cloak. He looked haggard, much older than his thirty-eight years, his long hair liberally flecked with grey.

'Up these stairs. Knock thrice at the door,' the driver said and with that he was off.

The stairway was pitch black and the man had to find his way by probing with the tips of his sandals. At the top landing he reached out until he felt the rough wood of a door. He banged it gently with his fist.

He heard voices from inside and the sound of a scraping latch. When the door opened he was surprised at how many people were crammed inside the small candlelit room.

The man who opened the door stared at him and called over his shoulder. 'It's all right. It's him.' Then he took the visitor's cool hand and kissed it. 'Peter. We're overjoyed you've come.'

Inside, Peter the Apostle was showered with goodwill as men and women sought to kiss him, give him water, make him comfortable on a cushion.

His visits to Rome were infrequent. It was the home of the enemy, too dangerous for casual travel. He never knew what mood the Romans might be in and whether he had a price on his head. It was only four years since Jesus's murder but the Christians, as they were beginning to be called, a name Peter much preferred to 'the Jewish cult', were growing in numbers and were becoming an annoyance to Rome.

Peter took a bowl of soup from his host, a tanner named Cornelius, and thanked him.

'How was your journey from Antioch?' the tanner asked.

'Long, but I enjoyed many kindnesses along the way.'

A young boy, no more than twelve, drew near. 'You

must miss your family,' the tanner said, looking at his son.

'I do.'

'Is it so, that you were there when Jesus rose from the dead?' the boy asked.

Peter nodded. 'The women, they were the ones who found His tomb empty. I was called and I can bear witness, lad, that He did rise. He died for us and then God called Him to His side.'

'How long will you stay among us?' Cornelius asked, shooing the boy away.

'A fortnight. Perhaps less. Just time enough to meet with the Elders and get the measure of this new Emperor, Caligula.'

Cornelius puckered his mouth. If he'd been on the streets, he surely would have spat. 'He's bound to be better than Tiberius.'

'I hope you're right. But in Antioch, travellers have told me the persecutions persist, that our brothers and sisters are still being tortured and killed.'

Cornelius smiled fatalistically. 'A few years ago we were rounded up for being Jews. Now we're rounded up for being Christians. Unless we kiss the Emperor's ass and pray to Jupiter, we'll continue to be rounded up.'

'What pretext are the authorities employing?' Peter asked, munching a piece of bread.

'There've been some killings. Citizens have been found cut to pieces with our symbols and monograms discovered nearby.'

Peter sighed and put down his bowl. All eyes in the

room were on him. 'We all know that such atrocities can have nothing to do with the followers of Our Lord. Ours is a religion of love and peace – only one sacrifice has been made for it, that of the Christos Himself, and His cruel death has atoned for our sins for all eternity. No, this slaughter must be the work of some evil force at large in this world of conflict and torment. Let us say some words in prayer now. Tomorrow we can begin to discuss what must be done.'

In the cattle stall the two brothers lay close to each other under their blanket on the straw.

The younger boy began to cry, softly at first, then louder.

Quintus opened his eyes. 'Shut up! What's wrong with you? I was asleep!'

'I'm scared,' sobbed Sextus.

'Quiet! Someone might hear you.' The boy's sobs continued unabated and Quintus took a different approach. 'Of what?'

'I'm afraid witches will get us.'

'Don't be silly. Everyone knows witches only live in the countryside. They won't come into town. The soldiers would hunt them down and kill them.'

'What about the Lemures?'

Quintus became defensive, as if he wished his brother hadn't reminded him of their existence.

Lemures, the ones with tails, the kinless and hungry ghosts which skulked around houses and feasted on humans.

'You're a little idiot,' Quintus said. 'Lemures don't hang around cattle pens. Settle down and sleep. We have a long journey tomorrow.'

'You promised we had a short journey,' moaned the child.

'Short, long, don't think about it, just go to sleep!'

Sextus was in the midst of a nightmare. He was desperately trying to run through a swamp to escape a demon. He frantically struggled from the wraith's grasp and floundered in the muck. As sticky warm mud splashed his face, he felt the demon grabbing at his legs, pulling him under. Swamp water covered his face. He gasped for air but a coppery liquid coursed down his throat.

Mercifully, he awoke.

Then the true nightmare began.

He turned his head. A man was straddling his brother's chest plunging a dagger into him. A crimson jet spurted from a great rent in his neck. It was spraying hot blood over Quintus's face and was dribbling into his own mouth.

'Quintus!'

There was enough moonlight to see the attacker's cloak and tunic bunched and riding up his waist. Something was coming out of his back, dancing and flicking in the air.

A great weight compressed him and stifled further cries. A man was on his chest too. A man with dead eyes. When he saw the knife slashing towards his neck he clenched his eyes shut, praying he was still asleep.

The dismemberment and butchery was done quickly. 'Put their heads under the straw but don't hide them too well,' Vibius commanded. 'Wrap everything else in burlap. Make eight parcels and be sure that each contains a hand or a foot.'

The assassins moved down an alleyway toward one of the shops adjoining the cattle market, toting the gruesome products of their work. They stopped at an open windowsill which during the day became a waist-high counter. It was a butcher shop, the only one in the alley marked with the Christian dove.

Vibius stepped onto the cupped hands of a compatriot and was boosted up and over the counter. He dropped soundlessly to the rough-hewn floor and crept toward the rear of the room, stopping in his tracks when he heard loud, guttural rasps.

He inched forward slowly until he was able to peer past the curtain at the back of the shop. The butcher was snoring loudly, an empty jug of wine tipped over beside his bed. Vibius eased his grip on his sword.

Assured that the wine-sodden man was well asleep, he retraced his steps to the window.

He unlatched the door of the meat safe set into the stone wall under the counter, reached inside and began passing cool wrapped packages out the window to waiting hands.

He replaced them with parcels of warm, fresher meat. When was done he vaulted through the window and found the shadows again.

It was dawn when Balbilus finished his fresco but underground he was untouched by the winter sunshine. The oily vapors from the lamps burned his lungs but it was a small price to pay for the satisfying night of work. Vibius had reported back with the news that blood had indeed been well spilled. The Christians would be accused of the massacre of Rome's finest, a couple of Praetorians. And even more heinously, they would now also be accused of killing Roman children and selling their flesh. In addition, the fresco was to his liking.

Could the new day be more auspicious?

Again, the thud of iron on stone.

At the top of the stairs Vibius opened the hatch and whispered something down to him.

'Agrippina? Here?' Balbilus asked incredulously. 'How is that possible?'

Vibius shrugged. 'She's in a wagon. She wants to be carried down to the tomb.'

'It's unbelievable! What a woman! Make sure her wagon is hidden from the road.'

Julia Agrippina. Great-granddaughter of Augustus. Incestuous sister of Caligula. Wife of the Emperor Claudius. The most powerful woman in Rome.

And one of us.

Agrippina was borne on a stretcher by her

attendants and taken carefully down the stairs and placed gently on the floor. Balbilus knew her people. They could be trusted.

Agrippina was swaddled in blankets, her head resting on a silk pillow. She was pale and haggard and wincing in pain, but even in her fragile state her beauty shone through.

'Balbilus,' she said. 'I had to come.'

'Domina,' he replied, falling to his knees to reach for her hand. 'You should have summoned me. I would have come to you.'

'No, I wanted this to happen here.' She turned her head to the wall. 'Your fresco – it's done!'

'I hope it's to your liking.'

'All the zodiacal signs. Beautifully drawn, and by your own hand, I see,' she said, looking at his paint-stained fingers. 'But tell me: this sequence of planets – what does it mean?'

'It's a small personal tribute, Domina. Moon, Mercury, Venus, Sun, Mars, Jupiter, Saturn. This was the alignment of the planets on the day I was born thirty-three years ago. I now question my decision. I should have chosen *your* alignment. I can have new plaster laid.'

'Nonsense, my good seer. This is your tomb.'

'*Our* tomb, Domina.'

'I insist that you keep the fresco as it is.'

There was a faint cry from under her blanket.

'Domina!' Balbilus said. 'It's happened!'

'Yes. Only two hours ago,' Agrippina said weakly.

'After all these years, and all these fucking men, finally: my firstborn.'

One of Agrippina's maids pulled back her blanket to reveal a tiny pink baby. Agrippina pulled the infant's blanket aside and said proudly, 'See. It's a boy. His name is Lucius Domitus Ahenobarbus.'

'This is wonderful,' Balbilus crowed. 'Truly wonderful. 'May I see?'

She turned the baby over. There was a perfect pink tail, wriggling energetically.

'Your bloodlines are strong,' Balbilus said with admiration. 'I assume the Emperor doesn't know?'

'That bumbling, pathetic old man doesn't even know *I* have one! Our unions are absurd affairs.' Agrippina said. 'This is between you and me. You honor me with the title Domina, but you, Balbilus, my great astrologer, you are *my* Dominus.'

Balbilus bowed his head.

'I want to know about this boy,' she said. 'Tell me what will befall him.'

Balbilus had been reading the charts carefully. He knew each day of the week by heart, almost each hour. He rose to his feet and delivered the prophecy with great solemnity.

'The boy's rising sign, Sagittarius, is in tune with Leo where his moon is placed. As the moon represents you, Domina, you and the boy will enjoy harmonious relations.'

'Ah, good,' Agrippina purred.

'The planet that rules this boy and which is his

ascendant is highly propitious. It is Saturn, the evil one.'

She smiled.

'And his moon is situated in the Eighth House, the House of Death. This indicates high position, large income, honors. Jupiter is in the Eleventh House, the House of Friends. From this will come the greatest good fortune and great fame, enormous power.' He lowered his voice, 'There is only one caveat.'

'Tell me,' Agrippina said.

'He is square with Mars. This will serve to diminish his good fortune. How, I cannot say.'

She sighed. 'It is a good reading. To say otherwise would be untrue. Nothing is perfect in our world. But tell me, Balbilus, will my son be Emperor?'

Balbilus closed his eyes. He felt his own tail tingle. 'He *will* be Emperor,' he said. 'He will take the name Nero. And he will be perfectly evil. But you must know this: you yourself, his own mother, may be among the many he will kill.'

Agrippina hardly flinched as she said, 'So be it.'

NINE

Elisabetta held the slim volume in her hands, felt its smooth binding, smelled the mustiness of the yellowing and crinkling vellum pages. It was only sixty-two pages long, yet she had the sense that there was more to it than its value as an antiquarian book.

She'd only asked to borrow it but Frau Lang had pressed her to have it.

'What if it's worth something?' Elisabetta had asked.

Frau Lang had lowered her voice, cocking her head at the wall separating them from her husband. 'I doubt you could buy a loaf with it but if there's money to be made let the Church have it. My eternal soul could use the help.'

The envelope with its neatly written enigmatic message lay on Elisabetta's desk at the Pontifical Commission for Sacred Archeology.

As you always taught – B holds the key.

What was B? The key to what?

11 September is surely a sign . . .

A sign? What was Ottinger up to and who was the writer, K?

And the curious symbol, vaguely astrological, vaguely anthropromorphic. What did it represent? And why was it so familiar?

Elisabetta drew it on her whiteboard with a black marker and glanced at it frequently.

She heard female voices coming down the corridor and hoped that some of the Institute's nuns weren't coming to ask her to join them for coffee. She wanted to shut her door but that, she thought, would have been rude. So she kept her chair turned away in order not to invite eye contact. The voices faded. She opened her desktop computer's browser and searched: *Marlowe – Faustus – B*.

Voluminous results filled her screen. She began to scroll through a load of articles and failed to notice that an hour had flown by or that Professor De Stefano was trying to get her attention by tapping at her door in a fierce staccato.

She'd borrowed Micaela's mobile phone the day before to brief him from the airport but this morning he was anxious for more.

'So?' he demanded a bit testily. 'What does it all mean?'

'I think I know what B is,' she said.

De Stefano closed the office door and sat on the other chair.

She already had pages of notes. 'Two versions exist of *Doctor Faustus*, an A text and a B text. The play was performed in London in the 1590s but the first published version, the so-called A text, didn't appear until 1604, eleven years after Marlowe died. In 1616 a second version of the play was published, the B text.' She scanned her notes. 'It omitted thirty-six lines of the A text but added 676 new lines.'

'Why two versions?' De Stefano asked.

'No one seems to know. Some scholars say that Marlowe wrote the A text and others revised it into the B text after his death. Some say he wrote both A and B. Some say both are differing products of actors' memories of performances years after the fact.'

'And what does this mean for us? For our situation?'

Elisabetta raised her hands in frustration. 'I don't know. We have a collection of facts which may be related to one another, although how is unclear. We have a first-century columbarium containing nearly a hundred skeletons – men, women and children, all with tails. There is evidence of a fire, perhaps coincident with the death of these people. The walls are decorated with a circular motif of astrological symbols depicted in a specific order. The upright Pisces symbol certainly can be seen as having a double meaning. We have the post-mortem photographs of an old man, Bruno Ottinger, with a tail and numbers tattooed on his back. What these numbers mean is unknown. We have a play by Christopher Marlowe in this man's possession. It was given to him by another person, a K. On the note it's written that 'B is the key,' and that September 11 was a sign. The book from 1620 is the so-called B text. The frontispiece of the book shows Faustus summoning the devil while standing inside a circle of astrological symbols which are laid out in the exact same order as in the circle on the columbarium fresco. These are the facts.'

Except, Elisabetta thought, there was one more she'd keep to herself: the fleeting image of her attacker's hideous spine on the awful night when Marco was killed.

De Stefano rubbed his hands nervously together as if cleansing them. 'So we're not in a position to weave them together into a cohesive hypothesis?'

She shrugged. 'From my knowledge of the period, astrology was highly important to the Romans. Aristocrats and common citizens alike placed a great deal of value in the predictive value of star charts. Maybe for this particular cult or sect, the stars and planets were of pre-eminent importance. Its members' physical abnormalities clearly made them different from most of their contemporaries. We know that they clung together in death. It's not too much of a stretch to imagine that in life they were associated in some cultural or ritualistic way. Perhaps they were intensely guided by astrological interpretations. Or maybe they were a sect of actual astrologers. This is all pure conjecture.'

'And you think this cult or sect might persist to this day?' De Stefano asked incredulously. 'Is that what this Ottinger is telling us?'

'I wouldn't begin to go that far,' Elisabetta said. 'That would take us beyond the boundaries of proper speculation. For a start, we need to understand the message on the envelope and to decipher the meaning of the tattoos.'

De Stefano had been growing more haggard and sallow-looking by the day and she was becoming worried about his health. He seemed to labor at the simple act of pushing himself up from the chair's armrests. 'Well, the good news is that the media hasn't gotten wind of the columbarium yet. The bad news is that the Conclave begins in four days and as it gets closer my superiors are certain to get more and more anxious about the risk of a leak. So please keep working and please keep me informed.'

Elisabetta turned to her computer screen, then caught herself. She decided she ought to devote a few minutes to prayer. As she was about to close her eyes she glanced at the title of a search result at the top of the next search page and to her shame, she found herself clicking on the link and postponing her devotions.

The title read: *The Marlowe Society calls for papers to commemorate the 450th anniversary of the birth of Christopher Marlowe.*

There was a thumbnail photo of a mild-looking man with sandy hair, the Chairman of The Marlowe Society. His name was Evan Harris and he was a Professor of English Literature at the University of Cambridge in England. The posting on the Society's web page was an international solicitation for academic papers to be published in book form in 2014 on the milestone anniversary of Marlowe's birth.

Clicking through Harris's biography, Elisabetta learned he was a Marlowe scholar who, among his other interests, had written on the differences between the A and B texts of *Faustus.*

It took little effort to click on his contact button and type a brief email.

Professor Harris:

In my work as a researcher based in Rome, I recently received the gift of a 1620 copy of *Doctor Faustus*. I attach a scan of the title page for your inspection. I have a number of questions about the topic of A versus B texts and wondered if you might be able to help me. As the matter is somewhat pressing, I enclose my telephone number in Rome.

She hesitated before signing her name as Elisabetta Celestino. She couldn't recall the last time she'd used her last name on anything but a government form. Sister Elisabetta seemed, in general, to suffice these days but it wouldn't, she thought, for a Cambridge don.

Elisabetta took the Marlowe book to the copier room, gently pressed the book against the printer glass and scanned the title page to her email address.

On her way back to her office she saw the tall young priest again. He was standing at her door and from the position of his head she was sure that he was staring straight at the symbol on her whiteboard.

When she got halfway down the hall he shot her a sidelong glance and scurried away like a startled deer.

Unsettled, Elisabetta returned to her desk, attached the Marlowe file to the Harris email and sent it off. She felt the need for a strong cup of coffee.

There were two nuns in the canteen who were drinking

coffee. She knew them by name but hadn't gotten much beyond that. She cleared her throat. 'Excuse me, Sisters, I wonder if you could tell me the name of the very tall young priest in the department?'

One nun answered, 'He's Father Pascal. Pascal Tremblay. We don't know him. He arrived the same day as you. We don't know what he's doing here.'

The other nun added, 'But then again, we don't know what *you*'re doing here, either.'

'I'm here on a special project,' Elisabetta answered, sticking to Professor De Stefano's instructions about secrecy.

The first nun huffed, 'That's what *he* said, too.'

The phone was ringing when she returned to her office.

It was an English voice. 'Hello, I was trying to reach Elisabetta Celestino.'

'This is Elisabetta,' she answered suspiciously. This was the first time her office phone had rung.

'Oh, hi there, it's Evan Harris, replying to the email you just sent.'

She'd been out of academia for a long time but she was incredulous that in the interim people had become so responsive to requests for assistance. 'Professor Harris! I'm quite surprised you came back to me so soon!'

'Well, ordinarily I'm a bit more tardy with my inbox but this copy of *Faustus* you've obtained – do you have any idea what you've got?'

'I think so, roughly, but I'm hoping you can further enlighten me.'

'I certainly hope you've got it in a safe place because there are only three known copies of the 1620 edition, all of them in major libraries. May I ask where you got it?'

She answered, 'Ulm.'

'Ulm, you say! Curious place for a book like this to land but we can, perhaps, go into its provenance at a later date. You say you have questions about the A and B texts?'

'I do.'

'And, if I may ask, are you with a university?'

Elisabetta hesitated because the answer would inevitably lead to more questions. But she was hard-wired to be as truthful as she was allowed to be. 'Actually, I work for the Vatican.'

'Really? Why is the Vatican interested in Christopher Marlowe?'

'Well, let's just say that the Faustus story relates to some work I'm doing on the attitudes of the sixteenth-century Church.'

'I see,' Harris said, drawing his words out. 'Well, as you can gauge by my lightning response, this B text of yours interests me a great deal. Perhaps I could come to Rome, say the day after tomorrow to see it in person, and while you have me as a captive audience I can tell you more than you probably care to know about the differences between *Faustus* A and B.'

Elisabetta thought that would be wonderfully helpful and gave him the Institute's address on Via Napoleone. But when she hung up she wondered if she ought to have added, 'By the way, Professor, I should tell you that I'm a nun.'

The Piazza Mastai was deserted and the convent was quiet. Elisabetta was happy to be in the silence of her spartan room. An hour earlier she'd pulled her curtains closed and removed her layers of clerical garb before gladly putting on her nightdress, which by comparison was weightless.

The feeling had crept up on her, the sense that her robes were becoming heavier and more stifling. When she'd first donned the habit after taking her vows, there'd been something magically light about the garb, as if the meters and meters of black cotton were but filmy gauze. But the past few days in the secular world of buses and airports and city streets and young women in their easy spring dresses had taken a subtle toll. Self-aware, Elisabetta launched into a fervent prayer for forgiveness.

Afterward, she was ready for bed. Although her praying had helped to soothe her spirit, she felt no closer to an explanation of the skeletons of St Callixtus. Tomorrow she would immerse herself in *Faustus* and the B text and become as knowledgeable as she could before Professor Harris arrived. But first she had to navigate a turbulent night. The old nightmares of her attack had resurfaced and had become mixed with newer terrors. She dreaded now the jumbled nocturnal world of labyrinths filled with macabre human remains and foul demons with monstrously naked tails.

With one last prayer for her safe passage through the night, Elisabetta slid between the cool sheets and switched off her light.

When Elisabetta's light went out, Aldo Vani tossed a butt into the fountain and lit another cigarette. He'd been discreetly loitering on the Piazza Mastai for an hour or more, watching the windows on the dormitory level. He had a compact monocular scope hidden in his palm and when he was sure there were no passersby he'd swept the lighted windows repeatedly. In the two seconds it had taken for Elisabetta to pull her curtains, he'd spotted her. Third floor, fourth window from the west side of the building. He needed her window and the others on the top floors to go black before he could move.

It took nothing more than a diamond-tipped glass cutter and a small suction cup to quietly remove a pane from a ground-floor classroom window at the back of the school. Vani would have bet his life that the premises weren't alarmed and he grunted in satisfaction when he unlatched the window and slipped through silently. Using a penlight he negotiated the rows of small desks. The hall was dark except for the red glow of exit signs at either end. His rubber soles were noiseless on the staircase at the western side of the convent.

Sister Silvia's eyes opened at the familiar realization that her bladder was twitchy. From long experience she knew she had under two minutes before she'd suffer an accident. She embarked on the first of several night-time visits to the communal toilet.

It was a journey that began with bracing her arthritic knees for the weight of her heavy hips. Then she had to push her swollen feet into slippers and pull her bathrobe from the peg. With under a minute to spare she turned her doorknob.

The door from the stairwell to the third floor squeaked on its dry hinges so Vani had to push it open ever so slowly. The hallway was too bright for his liking. There were night lights at each end and one in the middle. He unscrewed the bulb of the closest one and paused to count the doors. The fourth door on the Piazza side of the building corresponded, he was certain, to the fourth window. It would be better if it was unlocked but it hardly mattered. There were few locks that could slow him down for more than several seconds, especially in an old building. And worse case, with a shoulder to the frame, despite the noise, he'd have his blade through her carotid in no time and would be down the stairs before anyone raised an alarm.

This time he wouldn't fail. He'd promised K. He'd linger just long enough to watch the blood stop spurting from her neck as her arterial pressure dropped to zero.

Sister Silvia washed her hands and shuffled slowly back into the hall. Her room was two down from Elisabetta's. She began to blink. The hall seemed darker than before.

She stopped blinking.

There was a man standing at Elisabetta's door.

For an infirm old woman who sang her hymns in a soft, thin voice, she let out a monumentally piercing scream.

Vani took his hand off the doorknob and coolly assessed his options. It would take ten seconds to rush the screaming nun and silence her. It would take ten seconds to breech the door and finish the job he'd come to do. It would take three seconds to abort his mission and disappear down the stairs.

He made his decision and turned the knob on Elisabetta's door. It was locked.

Other doors began to fly open.

Nuns and novices poured into the hallway, calling to each other as Sister Silvia kept pumping out the decibels.

Elisabetta woke with a start and fumbled for her light.

More doors opened. Vani's options shrank. He knew there was only one thing worse than failing, and that was being captured.

When Elisabetta unlocked her door and swung it open she saw a man dressed in black disappearing down the stairs.

TEN

Cambridge, England, 1584

It was Palm Sunday.

It had been four long years.

Every minute of every hour of every day had led to this moment. His final public disputation.

In many ways the scholar's life had been as arduous as a laborer's or a tradesman's. Six days a week, awake at five in the morning for chapel. Then breakfast and lectures on logic and philosophy. Midday meal at eleven a.m., no more than a bit of meat, bread and broth, then classes on Greek and rhetoric. For the entire groaning afternoon, the study of debate and dialectical disputation, an intellectual tennis match to train young minds. Supper was little better than dinner, then study until nine o'clock when the day was done for everyone but him. While his roommates slept, he would sit at the farthest corner of the room and write his precious verses for another hour or two. Sundays were hardly easier.

Alone, he paced the dusty floorboards outside the lecture hall in his plain black gown. Through the closed doors he could hear the audience shuffling to take its place in the gallery. A few would be supporters but most were a sneering lot who would take more pleasure in seeing him fail.

Success would mean the granting of his BA degree and automatic admittance into the MA curriculum. From there, London would be his oyster. Failure would mean an ignominious return to Canterbury and a life of obscurity.

He balled up his fists, stoking his morale.

I am meant for greatness. I am meant to trample their small minds under my boots and crush their skulls like egg shells.

Norgate, the Master of Benet College, tall and gaunt, opened the doors and announced, 'Christopher Marlowe, we are ready for you.'

Four years earlier Marlowe had made his way from Canterbury to Cambridge, a journey of seventy miles and three days of begged rides on turnip wagons listening to the blather of country folk. Left by a merchant on the outskirts of town he had walked the last mile toting his rucksack. Passersby would have hardly noticed him entering the city through the Trumpington Gate, one more lad streaming into the university for the new December term.

The sixteen-year-old had to ask his way. In an alleyway beside a tavern he saw a man pissing.

'Which way to Benet College?' Marlowe had loudly demanded of the fellow. No 'please, Sir,' no 'might you'. It wasn't his way.

The man had swung his head around, displaying a frown that suggested an inclination to throw the young man into the mud as a reward for his impudence – as soon as he put his member away. But he'd changed his mind after looking the student up and down. Perhaps it was Marlowe's hard, dark eyes or humorless tight lips, the curious gravity of his juvenile beard or the imperious way he carried his slight frame but the man yielded meekly and provided the information the boy had sought.

'Cross over Penny-farthing Lane, go past St Botolph's Church, right turn on Benet Street, into the quadrangle.'

Marlowe had nodded and soon arrived at the place that would be his home for the next six and a half years.

He'd won his position as a Parker Scholar by dint of a laudatory performance at the King's School in Canterbury. That first day in Cambridge he'd been the last of the roommates to arrive at their assigned room at the north-west corner of the quadrangle. His fellow Parker Scholars, Robert Thexton, Thomas Lewgar and Christopher Pashley, all poor as dirt like himself, had been arranging their meager possessions and haggling over the few pieces of furniture allotted them: two beds, two chairs, a table and three stools, some chamber pots and basins. They'd stopped arguing and had taken the measure of the slender, brooding latecomer.

Marlowe hadn't bothered with pleasantries. His stare had darted around like that of a feral animal scoping out a patch of territory. 'I'm Marlowe. Where's my bed?'

Lewgar, a plump boy with a spotted face had pointed at a mattress and said. 'You'll be sleeping with me. I trust you'll keep your breeches on at night, Mister Marlowe.'

Marlowe had thrown his rucksack onto the mattress and managed his first smile in days, a fleeting sardonic one. 'Of that, my man, you can be sure.'

Marlowe stood facing his questioners with his chin thrust out and his arms quietly at his sides. In four years he had grown taller by the better measure of a foot and all traces of boyishness had vanished. His beard and moustache had grown thicker and framed his longish, triangular face in a rakish way. His silky brown hair fell just short of his starched ruff. Whereas most of his contemporaries were beginning to develop the bulbous noses and prognathous jaws that would mark their later years, Marlowe's features had remained delicate, even boyish, and he carried his good looks with an air of haughtiness.

The Master of the college was flanked by three older students taking their MA degrees, all of them with the countenance of sadists aiming to skewer their prey. Once the thesis for the disputation was given, Marlowe would verbally joust with them for four grueling hours and by supper his fate would be known.

Someone in the audience insistently cleared his throat. Marlowe turned. It was his friend, Thomas Lewgar, who would undergo the self-same ordeal the following day. Lewgar winked his encouragement. Marlowe smiled and faced his panel.

'So, Mister Marlowe,' the Master began. 'Here is the final thesis subject of your baccalaureate. We wish you to consider the following and commence your disputation without delay: According to the law of God, good and evil are directly opposed to one another. You may begin.'

Marlowe could hardly suppress his delight. The corners of his mouth curled up, ever so slightly, but enough to unnerve his inquisitors.

The cat's in the bag. The degree is mine.

At the dining hall, the 120 faculty and students of Benet College habitually sat with their own kind. The dirty leaded windows filtered some of the early evening light but as it was spring, the Sizars had no need to light the candles yet.

At the far end of the hall the Master and Fellows sat at High Table on a raised platform. The four Bible Clerks, holding the most prestigious scholarships with the highest stipends, sat directly beneath the Master. The six Nicholas Bacon Scholars came next. Marlowe sat at the adjacent table with the remaining scholars, including his Parker lot. The Pensioners, all rich lads, filled out the tables in the rest of the hall. Unlike the Scholars, they paid their own commons and other expenses. Their interest in the academic life was generally marginal; their lot in life was to drink, play tennis and accumulate just enough education to return to their country seats as Justices of the Peace. Rounding out the student mix were the Sizars, poor lads who were clever enough to attend university but not meritorious enough to receive scholarships. They had to wait on their fellow students for their tuition, bed and board.

Marlowe was high-spirited and ordered up extra bottles of wine for his table. He could ill afford them but his Sizar, a first-year boy, dutifully made the entry in Marlowe's accounts for future reckoning.

'I suppose all of you can have a few more sips, but the lion's share is for Master Marlowe,' Marlowe called out to his table.

'It sounds grand, doesn't it? Master Marlowe!' his friend Lewgar exclaimed. 'By this time tomorrow I pray that I too will have passed my disputation and have received my BA. I shudder to think what will become of Old Tom if I have no degree to carry back to Norfolk.' Lewgar still had spots on his hairless face and remained a beefy lad where most of the others were rail thin. Though Marlowe was notoriously intemperate and prone to pounding his colleagues with his sly, withering sarcasm, Lewgar had remained on his amicable side by dint of perennial self-deprecation.

From across the table, an older scholar, two years Marlowe's senior, a serious fellow taking his MA degree, piped up, 'Rather good show, today, Marlowe. Almost as impressive as my own final disputation.'

Marlowe raised his goblet to the man. Though he had seen him nearly every day for four years, he could honestly say he hardly knew Robert Cecil and, in fact,

Cecil was one of the few men in Cambridge who intimidated him. Yes, of course, his father was Baron Burghley, the Queen's foreign secretary and by rights the most powerful man in a land without a king, but there was more to it than that. Cecil was as strong as a plowman, as smart as any of the Bacon Scholars and as confident in his own skills as Marlowe himself.

But Marlowe was Cecil's better in one area of endeavor and he was boozily grateful when Cecil called for him to demonstrate.

'Go on, Master Marlowe, do us the honor of one of your verses on this, the occasion of your elevation.'

Marlowe rose and steadied himself with a hand on the table. 'Master Cecil, I have just the passage from a small work in progress, my first stage play.'

'Have you been dabbling, then?' Cecil asked.

'As his bedfellow,' Lewgar cried, to howls of laughter, 'I can attest that he dabbles all night long!'

'Quiet, then,' Cecil demanded of the table. 'Let us hear what our man hath wrote and, if it is not to our liking, I will let a birdie fly off to Court to let our Good Lady know that her schools are in disrepair.'

Marlowe raised his arms melodramatically, waiting for his moment, and when all eyes were on him he began.

'What is't, sweet wag, I should deny thy youth,
Whose face reflects such pleasure to mine eyes,
As I, exhaled with thy fire darting beams,
Have oft driven back the horses of the night,
Whenas they would have haled thee from my sight.

Sit on my knee and call for thy content;
Control proud Fate and cut the thread of Time.
Why, are not all the gods at thy command
And heaven and earth the bounds of thy delight?'

He grinned, drained the rest of his wine and sat back down, waving for the Sizar.

The diners waited for Cecil to weigh in. 'Passable, Master Marlowe,' he said. 'Rather passable. My birdie will have to remain in its cage and forsake its journey to London. Who do you have giving this speech and what will you call your play?'

'Thus sayeth Jupiter!' Marlowe said. 'And I am calling the play *Dido, Queen of Carthage*.'

'Well, Marlowe, if, in three years' time, you take your Holy Orders, the world will surely lose an eminent playwright.'

The last to leave the table were Marlowe, Cecil and Lewgar. It was growing dark and Lewgar moaned that he needed to be in bed early.

'I hear the Fellows are not well disposed of your chances, Lewgar,' Cecil said harshly.

'You have heard that?' Lewgar asked fearfully.

'I have indeed.'

'I mustn't fail. My life will be over.'

'If you cast yourself into the Cam, Thomas, I will write a poem about you,' Marlowe said.

'I'll be fine, as long as I'm not given a thesis concerning mathematics. You know how appalling I am at mathematics, don't you, Christopher?'

'I shouldn't worry, Thomas. Tomorrow you'll be as drunk as me. In celebration.'

When Lewgar trundled off, Cecil rose and clapped Marlowe on the back. 'Old Norgate will be letting you know over breakfast, but you'll be one of Lewgar's questioners at his disputation. I shall be another.'

Marlowe looked up quizzically. 'Really? How very interesting.'

His Sizar came to clear away the last of the table but Marlowe sent him for more wine and ordered him to light the candles. The lad obliged. Marlowe stared into the flickering flame of the candle and let his drink-heavy head droop towards his chest. The candlestick, a plain tube of pewter, caught his attention. He'd seen it every day for four years but tonight it jogged his memory. It was very much like a candlestick he'd seen some thirteen years earlier.

His father was always angry, always muttering invectives while he worked. Seven-year-old Christopher sat by the fire, eagerly scribbling on a crossed-out, singed page from his father's ledger book which his mother had rescued from the fire.

> *The sun doth shine,*
> *The birds doth sing,*
> *And lo the bluebird*
> *Takes to wing.*

Pleased with himself, he looked up to see a woman at their door complaining about a job that John

143

Marlowe had done. It was the baker's wife, Mary Plessington. The stitching had already come undone on a recent shoe repair.

His father took the shoes mutely and when the woman was gone he cursed her out roundly.

'Filthy hag. She most likely loosened the stitches by ramming her foot up her husband's ass. She's a bloody recusant, anyway. I shouldn't even take her jobs.'

His mother, Katherine, looked up from her sewing. 'Papist scum. Makes me want to spit on my own floor.'

The shoe shop and their front room were one and the same. His father sat at his workbench all through the day, flaying and puncturing cattle skins and complaining. The Marlowes were meant for more, he would say. It was well and good that he had elevated himself to a freeman and had been able to join the Shoemakers' Guild with all the privileges that entailed. But he was still on a lowish rung of the middle class and he couldn't contain his contempt for the aristocracy and anyone else doing better than himself.

'Katherine,' he called out. 'See how young Christopher gets on with his learning. That's the way to beat the bastards. With a proper education he'll become one of them, or that's what they'll think. Then he'll rise above them and take a Marlowe's rightful place on the top of the pile.'

Christopher was the only son and the oldest child now that his older sister had died of a fever. He attended the petty school at Saint George the Martyr run by the parish priest, Father Sweeting. He'd quickly learned to read from the *ABC and Catechism* and from the first days when the printed page made sense to him verses and rhymes had popped into his head, demanding that he write them down. They were a cheerful counterpoint to the other thoughts that bubbled in his brain, dark thoughts that had scared him when he was younger.

'Are we different?' he remembered asking his mother when he was five.

'We are.'

'Did God make us so?'

'It's nothing to do with God.'

'Sometimes I get frightened.'

'Your fears will go away,' his mother assured him. 'When you're a bit older you'll be happy you're different, believe me.'

She'd been right. The fear faded soon enough and was replaced by something altogether marvelous, a feeling of superiority and power. By the age of seven he genuinely liked who he was and what he was becoming.

The baker's son, Martin Plessington, was in his class at petty school. Thomas Plessington was one of the more successful merchants in Canterbury, a wealthy Protestant with five apprentices and two ovens. Martin was a heavy-boned boy on his way to being a giant like his father. Inside the school he was slow-witted but on the streets he was a bully, using his muscles for primacy.

One day, Christopher was among the last to leave school, reluctant, as always, to part with one of Father Sweeting's books. On his way home he took his usual short cut behind the Queen's Head Tavern and the livery stables.

To his surprise, he saw the thick legs of Martin Plessington poking from a window at the house of the stable master. Martin lowered himself to the ground, clutching something. His eyes met Christopher's.

'Bugger off,' Martin hissed.

'What do you have?' Christopher asked boldly.

'None of your bleeding business.'

Christopher came closer and saw it. It was a pewter candlestick adorned with an ornate Catholic cross.

'Have you stolen that?'

'Do you want me to thrash you?' was the angry response.

Christopher didn't back away. 'I assume you mean to sell it. Unless your family are closet Papists who mean to use it in an illegal mass.'

'Who are you calling a Papist!' Martin said, growing red in the face. 'The Marlowes aren't fit to wipe a Plessington ass.'

'Tell you what,' Christopher said evenly. 'If you let me see it, I'll swear I won't tell a soul what you've done.'

'Why do you want to see it?' the boy asked suspiciously.

'It's pretty, that's why.'

Martin thought about it and handed the candlestick over. It had a heavy round base, the weight of a brick or two. Christopher inspected it closely, then looked up and down the alley. 'Did you notice this?' he asked.

'What?' Martin answered, drawing closer.

'This.'

Christopher swung the candlestick with all the might his small frame could muster and slammed its base against Martin's temple. With a satisfying crunch, the sound of a boot breaking through ice, the boy fell to his knees and pitched forward, blood gushing from the wound. He moved for a few seconds and went slack.

Christopher stuffed the bloody candlestick into his shirt and began dragging the lifeless body toward the stable. It was harder work than he'd imagined but he didn't let up until he had Martin well inside. The tethered horses shifted and whinnied and tugged at their ropes.

He dropped Martin beside a pile of hay and paused to catch his breath. Then he fished inside his shirt for the candlestick. He grasped it by its base, staining his fingers red.

With one hand he opened Martin's mouth and with the other he shoved the stick as far down his throat as it would go and watched blood well up and fill the gaping hole.

The next day, Martin's chair at petty school was unoccupied and Father Sweeting commented prophetically that the boy had better be dead than miss a day of studies. Christopher skipped lightly home, passing by the stables again. The stable doors were shut and no one seemed to be about. When he got home his mother and father were seated at the table talking in low tones, his sisters padding about on bare feet.

'Did you hear?' his father said to him. 'Did you hear about Martin Plessington?'

Christopher shook his head.

'Dead,' his father said, starkly. 'His head stoved in and a Catholic candlestick down his gullet. People are saying the Papists done it, killed a Protestant lad. They're saying they'll be trouble in Canterbury for sure. A right civil war. There's talk of a couple of recusant boys already done in by Protestant gangs. What do you say about that?'

Christopher had nothing to say.

His mother piped up, 'You wore your good shirt today. I found your other one balled up between your mattress and the wall.' She reached down between her legs and produced it. 'There's blood on it.'

'Did you have anything to do with this?' his father demanded. 'Tell the truth.'

Christopher smiled, showing the gap of his missing milk teeth. He actually puffed out his chest and said, 'I did it. I killed him. I hope there is a war.'

His father rose slowly and stretched to his full height, towering over the seven-year-old. His lips quivered. 'Good lad,' he finally said. 'I'm right proud of you. There're dead Catholics today because of you and more to come, I reckon. You're a credit. A credit to the Marlowe bloodlines.'

148

ELEVEN

Elisabetta's first instinct was to call her father but what would that accomplish beyond rousing him from his bed and upsetting him no end? Micaela, she knew, was on hospital duty. She called Zazo instead. He arrived half an hour after the Polizia and sat with Elisabetta in the kitchen while she waited to be interviewed by an officer.

She clutched her robe to her chest. 'I'm sorry I disturbed you. You're so busy.'

'Don't be silly,' Zazo said. He was out of uniform, wearing jeans and a sweater. 'Did you call Papa?'

'No.'

'Good. So the guy was at your door?'

'That's what Sister Silvia said.'

'Did you get a look at him?'

'Only his back.'

'It was probably an addict looking for some cash.' Zazo said. 'And too brain-dead to realize he was breaking into a convent. I've been unhappy that there's no alarm system here.'

'There's never the money for that sort of thing, and anyway . . .'

'Yeah, God protects,' he finished derisively. 'I know the man who's in charge here, Inspector Leone. Let me speak to him.'

Elisabetta's upper lip quivered. 'Zazo, I've got a bad feeling about this.'

'I know you're upset. I'll be right back.'

Leone was a gruff, unpopular fellow nearing retirement. Back in Zazo's day there'd been no love lost between them and Zazo could say with confidence that he hadn't thought about the man once since leaving the force.

'I remember you,' Leone said when Zazo approached him in the residence hall. 'What are you doing here?'

'One of the nuns is my sister.'

'You're at the Vatican, right?' Leone said it with button-pushing derision.

'I am.'

'That's a good place for you.'

In his years of working with the Swiss Guards, Zazo had learned the art of restraint. He drew on it and let the remark pass. 'So what do you have?'

'The guy cut a hole in a ground-floor window at the back and let himself in. The Mother Superior is checking through the classrooms and offices on the first two floors but so far there's nothing missing. He was standing in front of one of the residence rooms when one of the nuns on her way back from the toilet saw him and started screaming her head off. He ran away and probably made his way out a rear door.'

'It was my sister's room.'

Leone shrugged. 'It had to be someone's. Who knows what he wanted? Maybe he was a thief, maybe a rapist, maybe a junkie. Whatever he was it's a good thing he never got to her. We'll do our interviews, dust for prints, check the CCTV footage from surrounding buildings. You remember the drill, right, Celestino?'

'I'm still a police officer,' Zazo spat back.

'Sure you are.'

Elisabetta was sipping at her coffee when Zazo returned. Nuns were busying themselves providing hot drinks for the officers. With so many men on the scene, some of the women, out of modesty, had gone back to their rooms and changed into their habits. 'You don't look so good,' he told her with the bluntness of a brother.

'Thank you.'

'What did you mean when you said you had a bad feeling?'

'There was something about that man.'

'I thought you only saw his back.'

'I know. That's why it's only a feeling.' She whispered now. 'I know it sounds crazy but I think it was the same man who attacked me that night.'

Zazo accepted a cup of coffee from one of the sisters. 'You're right,' he said. 'It does sound crazy. I think you're having some kind of post-trauma psychological reaction. That's all.'

'There's more than that to it, Zazo. There's more that I should tell you.'

'Whenever you want to talk,' he said.

Elizabetta looked scared. 'Now.'

She took him back to her room. Zazo sprawled on her unmade bed and she sat on her reading chair and began by delivering a preamble. She knew that she had no authority to tell him these things but she felt compelled to do so. She demanded an oath of secrecy from him as her brother, as a policeman and as a Vatican employee.

Zazo agreed and listened in rapt attention as his sister told him everything about her work as a student, her flashes of memory about her attacker's spine, the skeletons of St Callixtus, the old man in Ulm, his tattoos, the Marlowe play.

There was a knock on her partially open door. One of the nuns told her the police were ready for her.

'You're not going to tell them anything about this, are you?' Zazo asked.

'Of course not.'

He got off the bed and said gravely, 'I don't think it's safe for you to stay here any longer.'

When he was awoken Krek's head was still thick from the good brandy he'd drunk earlier. Alone in his big bed he answered the phone testily, 'Yes?'

It was Mulej. 'I'm sorry to wake you. I have news from Italy.'

'It had better be good.'

'It isn't. Vani had to abort.'

Krek couldn't conceal his rage. 'I've had it with him. I can't tolerate this incompetence. Did he at least get away cleanly?'

'Thankfully, yes.'

'Tell him this, Mulej. Tell him he has one more chance. If he's not successful he will be terminated. Tell him I will do it personally.'

It was drizzling. From Elisabetta's seat on the bus, Rome looked drained of color and joyless. Her fellow commuters were too preoccupied with their newspapers and earphones to notice the pinched look on the nun's pale face.

At her stop she opened her umbrella and walked the short distance to the Institute. Professor De Stefano's assistant was waiting for her in the lobby.

'The Professor wants you at St Callixtus immediately,' he said. 'Theres' a car waiting for you.'

The St Callixtus catacombs had been closed to the public since the cave-in and the visitors' building looked deserted and forlorn in the rain.

Gian Paolo Trapani was pacing in front of the entrance, water dripping from his long hair. He opened the car door for Elisabetta. 'Professor De Stefano is down at the site. Please come quickly.'

'What's the matter?' she asked.

'That's for him to tell you.'

Elisabetta almost had to run to keep up with the

long-legged young man. The catacombs seemed particularly gloomy that morning. Despite the chilliness of the place, she was sweating and out of breath when they reached the boundary of the Liberian Area and the cave-in site.

De Stefano was at the threshold, immobile except for those hands of his, obsessively rubbing at each other. Elisabetta was alarmed by his abject look of anguish.

'You're the only person I know who doesn't have a mobile phone,' he said angrily.

'I'm sorry, Professor,' she answered. 'What's happened?'

'Look! See for yourself what's happened!'

He stepped aside and let her enter.

The sight was almost as shocking as the one she'd seen the first time but her emotional reaction today was more raw. She was assaulted by feelings of devastation and violation.

The chamber had been picked clean.

Where skeletons had been piled on top of one another, now there were only a few bones left in the dirt: a rib here, a humerus there, toe bones and finger bones scattered like popcorn on a cinema floor.

The fresco too was gone, but it had not been removed. It had been pulverized, certainly by hammer blows, for the plaster lay in clumps and fragments, completely annihilated.

De Stefano was mute with rage so Elisabetta looked to Trapani for help.

'Whoever did this used our shaft,' he said, pointing overhead. 'There's no sign of entry or egress through the catacomb. The night guards at the visitor center heard and saw nothing. We quit yesterday at five o'clock. They must have come when it got dark and then worked all night. Who knows what their methods were but I'd say they dug out one or two skeletons at a time and hoisted them up in crates or boxes to a truck. There are fresh tire marks running through the field. And, to top it off, they destroyed our fresco. It's horrible.'

De Stefano found his voice at last. 'It's more than horrible. It's a disaster of shocking proportions.'

'Who could have done this?' Elisabetta asked.

'That's what I want to ask *you*,' De Stefano said, glaring at her.

She wasn't sure that she'd heard him correctly. 'Me? What could I possibly know of this?'

'When Gian Paolo called me early this morning to inform me of what he'd found here I had my assistant check the phone logs of the few people at the Institute who had knowledge of the work here. Two days ago a call was made from your office line.'

Elisabetta searched her memory quickly before he had even finished. Had she actually used her phone to make an outgoing call? She didn't think so.

'The call was to *La Repubblica*. Why were you calling a newspaper, Elisabetta?'

'I didn't make this call, Professor. You know I wouldn't do such a thing.'

'A call is made to a newspaper and two days later we're cleaned out. These are the facts!'

'If this call was made, I insist, on God's name, that it wasn't me who placed it. Please believe me.'

De Stefano ignored her entreaty. 'I have to attend an emergency meeting at the Vatican. I have to tell you, Elisabetta, that it was a mistake to involve you in this. You are dismissed. Go back to your school and your convent. I've spoken with Archbishop Luongo. You can't work for me any longer.'

TWELVE

Elisabetta felt like she was on a boat that had slipped its mooring line and drifted from the protected waters of a harbor into a vast chartless sea. It was the middle of the afternoon and though she was physically in a place she knew well she found herself in an utterly strange mental and spiritual state.

The bedroom had stayed unaltered from the day when Micaela had left for university. Elisabetta's own bed had the same pink ruffled spread and satin pillow-cases, faded by years of sunlight. Her school books were still there, a precocious mix of French philosophers, theologians and serious novels. Micaela's book-case was, in contrast, filled with such light fare – romances, pop magazines, teen advice books – that it seemed it might float away. Over Micaela's bed was a Bon Jovi poster. Over Elisabetta's was a poster of a beautiful stag with giant antlers, cave art from Lascaux.

Elisabetta lay on top of her bed, fully dressed in her habit but with her shoes kicked off. She couldn't go back to the school or the convent because Zazo had forbidden it and had enlisted Elisabetta's father, Micaela and even Sister Marilena in his crusade. Elisabetta was finally convinced by the argument that she might be putting students and nuns in danger if she stayed there.

She couldn't go back to the Pontifical Commission for Sacred Archeology because, for the first time in her life, she'd been suspended from a job. Her skin danced with anger at the very idea that De Stefano thought she might bear some responsibility for the looting.

And she couldn't even pray in peace without becoming distracted and getting dragged into restless thoughts.

Disgusted, Elisabetta pushed herself up off the bed and put her shoes on. Defiantly, she decided that if she couldn't resume her teaching she would continue with her other job, whether or not she remained on De Stefano's staff. She thrust her chin forward truculently. She would continue out of intellectual curiosity. But there was something more urgent, wasn't there? A deep notion was forming that she *needed* to understand what had gone on in the columbarium of St Callixtus.

For her own survival.

'God protect me,' she said out loud, then went to the kitchen to make herself coffee before settling down in the dining room to peruse some reference works.

There was a sound of a key in the door.

She looked up from her books and heard her father calling her name.

'I'm here, Papa, in the dining room.'

Her books and papers were strewn across the dining-room table. She had used her father's desktop computer in the sitting room to send an email from her private account to Professor Harris in Cambridge – not to cancel their meeting but to change the venue.

B holds the key.

She was midway through a modern copy of both texts of *Faustus* that she'd obtained from a bookstore near the Institute, making notes on a pad about the A text. Then she would tackle the B text, using the paperback and Ottinger's original, looking not only for textual differences but for any marginalia that she might have missed previously.

Her father had finished work for the day. Neither of them was used to the other's presence outside of a Sunday lunch.

'How are you?' he asked, lighting his pipe.

'Angry.'

'Good. I like anger better than forgiveness.'

'They're not mutually exclusive,' Elisabetta said.

He grunted. The pipe went out. He reached for his pipe tool, retracted the long spike and methodically aerated the bowl. 'I've got some tinned soup. Want some?'

'Maybe later. I'll make a proper meal tonight. How would that be?'

Carlo didn't answer. Instead his eyes were drawn to the thing he most loved in the world – numbers.

Elisabetta had copied out the numbers from the Ulm tattoo onto an index card.

63 128 99 128 51 132 162 56 70
32 56 52 103 132 128 56 99
99 39 63 38 120 39 70

'What's this?' he asked, picking up the card.

'It's something to do with the project I was working on. It's like a puzzle.'

'I thought they told you to stop.'

'They did.'

'But you haven't.'

'No.'

'Good girl!' Carlo said approvingly. 'A grid of twenty-four numbers, nine by eight by seven,' he went on. 'A numerical pattern isn't leaping to mind. Can you give me some context?'

'I'm not allowed to, Papa.'

'You've told Micaela things. She told me you had.'

'She shouldn't have said anything,' Elisabetta said.

'She only told me that she was permitted to have some information. What it was, she didn't say.'

'Good. Because, like me, she signed a confidentiality document with the Vatican.'

'And last night you told Zazo some things. Did he sign a document too?'

Elisabetta looked up guiltily. 'I shouldn't have told him but I was scared. I suppose I did what they accused me of doing. Divulging Vatican secrets.'

'Nonsense. Zazo is your brother and a Vatican policeman. It's almost like talking to a doctor or a lawyer or even a priest. Don't worry about it.'

'Zazo is hardly a priest.'

'Well, talking to your father is closer. There's a sacred bond between a father and a daughter, don't you think?'

'In a way, yes,' she agreed.

'I know I wasn't a substitute for your mother but I did my best. It wasn't easy having a university job and raising the three of you.'

'I know, Papa. We all know that.'

'Tell me something. When you were young, were there things you wouldn't tell me that you would've told your mother?'

'I'm sure there were.'

'Like what?'

'Girl things, woman things, but never anything too important. You were always there for me and you were always strong. We felt your strength.'

'Well, after the pounding they've been giving me at the University I'm not feeling so strong but I appreciate your saying that.' Carlo frowned. 'You know I didn't want you to become a nun, don't you?'

'Of course. You weren't shy about telling me.'

'It seemed like you were retreating. A retreat from your life. You'd had a big trauma but I wanted you to be like the American cowboys who get back on their saddles and ride out to fight another day. But instead you ran to the Church and hid. Are you mad at me for saying it?'

'I'm not mad, papa, but you're wrong. In my mind it wasn't a retreat. It was a bold step toward a better life.'

'Look at the way you're treated.'

'I'm treated fine. I'm treated like the other Sisters.'

'What about today?'

'You don't think this kind of thing can happen in academia? Look at how they're treating you – like a pair of worn-out shoes.'

Carlo looked hurt and Elisabetta regretted the remark the moment it left her lips.

'I'm sorry, Papa, I shouldn't have said that.'

'I'm sure you're right. Injustices are everywhere. But if you must know, my biggest regret is not seeing you with children. You would have been a fantastic mother.'

She sighed. 'If I tell you about these numbers, if I tell you everything, do you promise to speak to no one about it.'

'What about Micaela and Zazo?'

Elisabetta laughed. 'You're negotiating with me. Okay, Micaela and Zazo, but only if I'm there too.'

'All right,' Carlo said. 'Let's try to solve your puzzle.'

Elisabetta had to admit that she took a good bit of pleasure in the intimacy of that evening, a father and daughter alone with one another for the first time in many years. She made his favorite dish, ravioli stuffed with goat's cheese, and while she cooked, he smoked, read Marlowe and filled several lined pages with notes and mathematical ideas. As they dined, they happily discussed the pact that Faustus had made with the Devil. They drank wine – Elisabetta half a glass, Carlo the rest of the bottle.

She thought he'd drunk more than his limit but he insisted on bringing out a bottle of grappa and having two glasses while she cleared the table. For years she'd only seen him for Sunday lunches and she really had no idea whether he'd become a heavy drinker. When his speech slurred, Elisabetta moved him to the sitting room and when he dozed in his chair she woke him gently, saw him off to his bedroom and started on the dishes with a new set of worries on her mind.

The Gendarmerie operations center was a well-appointed modern room of video monitors providing real-time feeds of strategic locations around Vatican City. Zazo was huddled in one corner with the two other men of his rank, Lorenzo and a fellow a few years their senior named Capozzoli.

Zazo pointed at the monitor that showed the entrance to the Domus Sanctae Marthae. 'What's the current census? Do you know, Cappy?'

Capozzoli checked his small notebook. 'As of six tonight there were twenty-six Cardinals checked in.'

Lorenzo's men were in charge of airport pickup and delivery. 'I've got seven more coming in tonight.'

Zazo nodded. 'Tomorrow's T-minus-two for the Conclave start. It's going to be a ball-buster.'

'We've got fifty-eight red-hats arriving tomorrow,' Lorenzo said.

'Christ . . .' Capozzoli said.

'Christ is right,' Zazo agreed. 'I've had a couple of minor skirmishes with the Guards. Either of you had any problems?'

'They've been up my butt all day,' Lorenzo said, 'but nothing I can't handle.'

'We swept the Domus for bugs and bombs this afternoon and we'll keep doing it daily until our final sweep the night before the Conclave,' Zazo said. 'Are the Guards on the same schedule for the Sistine Chapel, Cappy?'

'That's what I understand,' he answered. 'They've been cagey about it.'

Zazo swiped the air in disgust. 'We already invited them to observe our last sweep of the Domus. I'll be damned if I'm not going to participate in their last sweep of the Chapel.'

'Don't hold your breath,' Lorenzo said.

Micaela picked at her tray of food. The cafeteria wasn't bad for a hospital but her boyfriend was blunting her normally exuberant appetite.

'Why won't you come with me?' she asked Arturo.

Everything about Arturo was oversized: his hands, his nose, his girth and even, as Micaela liked to tease him, his 'baby-maker'. There was a lot that she liked about him, including the way he could pick her up like a doll, but there were more than a few things she would have changed if she'd had half the chance.

'I had a tough day. Three emergencies, a long clinic. I'm wrecked.'

'All I want you to do is stop off with me to see Elisabetta at my father's place. I'm worried about her. We won't stay for more than a few minutes.'

'I know how these things go,' he moaned. 'A few minutes turns into an hour.'

Micaela pursed her lips angrily and her fierce look made Arturo flinch. 'You don't like my sister, do you?'

'I like her fine.'

'No, you don't. Why? What's she ever done to you.'

Arturo moved some peas around his plate. 'When I was in school, the nuns beat the crap out of me. I guess it's transference.'

'Oh come on!' Micaela said. 'A big strong man like you afraid of what my poor little sister represents to your fragile psyche!'

'You're not being sensitive,' Arturo complained. 'Where's your bedside manner?'

Micaela stood up and grabbed her shoulder bag. 'You're coming with me or you're sleeping by yourself for the next thirty years. There's your bedside manner!'

Elisabetta was immersed in *Faustus* when her father's phone rang. She would have let it go but didn't want him to be awoken. To her surprise, it was for her.

'Elisabetta, it's Professor De Stefano.' His voice sounded thin, squeezed.

'Professor!'

'I called over to the convent. They were reluctant

to give out your contact number but I told your Sister Marilena that it was urgent.'

'What's wrong? You don't sound yourself,' she said.

There was a pause. 'Stress of the day. Not to mention how badly I feel for dismissing you.'

'It was tough being on the receiving end.'

'Will you forgive me?' Elisabetta was struck by his strange pleading tone.

'Of course I will,' she said. 'I'm good at that.'

'I need you to come over to my apartment straight away,' he said suddenly. 'You're back on the job. I have important new information to discuss. I think I know what the message means – B is the key.'

'Tonight?' she asked, looking through the dark windows.

'Yes, tonight,' De Stefano said hastily. There was another pause. 'And bring your copy of the *Faustus* book.' He gave her his address and hung up abruptly.

Micaela rang the apartment's buzzer several times, then used her spare key to let herself in. Inside the apartment the lights were on but no one had been answering her calls. Elisabetta's bedroom was empty, her father's door shut.

She poked her head into her father's room and heard snoring coming from the darkness.

Arturo tapped her on the shoulder and she shut the door behind her quietly.

'There's a note from Elisabetta on the dining-room table,' he said.

It was on a piece of note paper, in Elisabetta's neat handwriting:

I know Zazo told me not to leave the apartment but I had an urgent call to see Prof. De Stefano at his flat at 14 Via Premuda. I'll be fine. Will be back before 11. Elisabetta.

'I'm calling Zazo,' Micaela said, fishing through her bag for her mobile phone.

Zazo flipped his phone shut and looked at his watch. 'Unbelievable,' he muttered.

'What's up?' Lorenzo asked. They were walking together through one of the Vatican staff parking lots.

'Besides my father, my sister Elisabetta's the smartest Celestino but sometimes she's so dumb. I've got to run over to the Via Premuda. It'll take me five minutes to get there. I'll be back in fifteen and we can finish up for the night.'

The taxi driver was held up by some road-repair works that doubled the duration of the ride. Despite carrying a nun as a fare, he insisted on cursing and making lewd gestures out the window most of the way.

He left Elisabetta in front of a smart apartment block clad in pink limestone with freshly painted green window shutters. De Stefano was listed on the first floor. She was quickly buzzed in and walked up one flight to his apartment. She used the small brass knocker and waited.

The door opened too rapidly for politeness.

A man stood there but it wasn't De Stefano.

She recognized his blank face immediately. It was the telephone-booth man, her attacker from long ago, and, she realized in an instant, the man who'd broken into the convent. He had a gun.

Before Elisabetta could do more than let out a horrified gasp he grabbed a handful of her habit and pulled her inside.

Zazo pressed the buzzer for De Stefano's apartment and when he didn't get a reply he pressed all the apartments' buzzers simultaneously until someone buzzed him through.

When he got to the top of the stairs there was the briefest vision down the hall of black cloth disappearing through a door. Then the door slammed hard.

Zazo drew his SIG from his holster, pulled back the slide to chamber a round and tried to steady his shaking hands.

Elisabetta was on her knees, thrown to the ground by the violent jerk of the man's arm. The copy of the *Faustus* book fell from her bag onto the tiles.

She saw through to the sitting room. De Stefano was on the floor, blood oozing from an eye.

She looked up. The man was holding his arm out. He was aiming a pistol at the top of her head.

It was happening too fast – not even enough time to *think* the name of the Lord.

There was a loud crash.

Zazo's boot crashed through the lock plate, splintering wood and throwing the door open.

The explosions were so thunderous that Elizabetta wouldn't be able to hear properly for a week. Zazo fired eight rounds in five seconds. Years of simulator training kicked in automatically: aim for center mass. Keep firing until empty. Expel the spent magazine and slide in the spare.

Elisabetta's pearly-white vest was stained red with the man's arterial blood. Her ears rang so loudly that her own screams seemed far away.

The only thing she was able to focus on was an exceedingly small detail.

A glistening drop of blood clung to the cover of the *Faustus* book, then slowly soaked itself into the porous leather.

THIRTEEN

Surrey, England, 1584

This time it was Thomas Lewgar who was pacing and trying to calm his nerves outside the examination hall. Inside, Christopher Marlowe huddled in a corner of the hall with Master Norgate and the two other questioners for Lewgar's disputation, Robert Cecil and an MA student from another college.

Norgate had a parchment which he waved under the questioners' noses. 'To be perfectly frank, Mister Lewgar is a somewhat marginal candidate. He needs to excel in this disputation to succeed in his baccalaureate. I know his father well. He is a prominent man in Norwich. It would not pain me to see Lewgar do well today which is why I was keen for Master Marlowe to join this committee. As his friend I expect you will do your utmost to be helpful in the line of questioning.'

'Yes, sir,' Marlowe said.

'Now,' Norgate said, referring to his parchment, 'I have three questions we might put to him. The first: In the sight of God sins are then truly venial when they are feared by men to be mortal.'

The committee nodded.

'The second: The love of God does not find, but creates that which is pleasing to it.'

Again nods.

'And the third is less of a theological nature and more of a mathematical and philosophical one. It is: The mathematical order of material things is ingeniously maintained by Pythagoras, but more ingenious is the interaction of ideas maintained by Plato. What say you?'

Something triggered inside him. Marlowe was conscious of the blood coursing through his body; he could almost taste it, metallic in his mouth. 'I would note, Sir, that Thomas has always said to me how much he enjoys the mathematical arts and the contribution of the Greeks to our state of knowledge.'

Cecil looked up in surprise but said nothing.

'Very well,' Norgate said. 'Pythagoras it shall be.'

By three in the afternoon the spectacle was over. Few could remember a more disastrous final disputation. Norgate called the proceedings to a close when it was apparent that Lewgar could do no more than repeat the same inaccurate and insubstantial points over and over. The young man was reduced to wet eyes and chest heaving and by the end only the hardest men in the audience could take pleasure in the spectacle.

When Norgate pronounced from his chair that the candidate had not attained his BA, Lewgar practically ran from the hall.

'Most unfortunate,' Norgate told the committee and was gone himself.

Cecil drew Marlowe aside with a look as much amused as perplexed. 'I thought Lewgar was your friend.'

'He is,' Marlowe said. 'Perhaps my closest at the college.'

'Yet you had him orate on a topic he was least prepared to defend.'

'I suppose I did.'

Cecil leaned in. 'I'm impressed by the cut of your sails, Master Marlowe. The Marlowes are known to us, you know.'

Marlowe thought, Us? 'Is that so?' he said.

'I wonder if you would accompany me to London tomorrow. There's someone I would very much like you to meet.' Then he put his lips an inch from Marlowe's ear and whispered, 'I know what you are.'

He was the most fearsome man that Marlowe had ever seen. He had deep-socketed unforgiving eyes which seemed to be capable of piercing a mind and reading one's soul. His face was finely chiseled and aquiline. The way he could hold his facial muscles perfectly immobile made him seem as though he had been hewn from a block of dusky cold marble. His doublet and cloak were of the finest fabric, befitting a minister of the Queen.

Marlowe was in the man's Great Room at Barn Elms in Surrey, having just arrived by river boat from

London with Robert Cecil. The mansion, built from limestone from the Catholic churches razed by Elizabeth's father, King Henry, was the most splendid house Marlowe had ever seen. From the river, in the last light of the evening, it seemed to go on forever. Inside, the paneling, wainscoting, tapestries and heraldic wall-hangings left him breathless with the desire to possess this kind of life.

'Sir Francis,' Cecil said, 'I present to you Master Christopher Marlowe.'

Francis Walsingham. Principal Secretary to the Queen. Her spymaster and torturer. The man she called her Moor, because of his dark complexion and somber demeanor. The most dangerous man in England.

'Welcome to my house, gentlemen. It's good to escape from Whitehall into the rejuvenating countryside on occasion. Have you seen the Baron Burghley, Robert?'

'I have not. I will seek out father when we return to London.'

'Excellent. Make sure he gives you an audience with the Queen. You must be mindful of your career. Now, I have some good wine for you, a nice Spanish *aligaunte*. It's made by Papists who despise our Queen Elizabeth but one cannot deny its quality.'

Marlowe sipped the chilled wine, admiring its bouquet and wondering why he was sitting in this fine stuffed chair embroidered with a red-and-white Tudor rose. But after some chit-chat about Benet College, Master Norgate and the finals, Walsingham got to the point.

'Young Robert does service for me, Master Marlowe. He helps to root out Papist elements among the ranks of Benet and the other colleges. He also searches for talented men who may also serve the Crown and he has mentioned you several times in his reports over the years.'

Marlowe was stunned. He hardly knew that Cecil had even been aware of him. 'I am honored, my lord,' he said.

'We live in troubled times, Master Marlowe. Since 1547 our state religion has changed three times, from the English Catholicism of Henry, to the radical Protestantism of Edward, to the radical Catholicism of Mary and now to the Protestantism of Elizabeth. The seeds of confusion among the populace have yielded many strange trees. Which is your tree?'

'Our family has always followed the Queen's example.'

'Has it? Has it really?'

Marlowe's excitement turned to misgiving. Had he fallen into a trap? 'We have been loyal subjects.'

Walsingham put his glass down hard on the table. His elaborate ruff forced him to sit ramrod straight. 'I know for a fact,' he said, 'that you are not true Protestants, though you find it convenient to ally yourself with them from time to time. I certainly know you are not Papists; you despise them utterly. Methinks you are something else.'

Marlowe stared at him, not daring to speak.

'I'm told you excelled at the study of astronomy. You understand the stars well, do you not?'

'I have a passable knowledge.'

'Cecil is also an able astrologer. As am I. Neither of us, of course, rise to the level of the Queen's astrologer, John Dee, but we know a thing or two. The stars cannot be ignored.'

'Indeed not,' Cecil agreed.

'So I put to you, Marlowe, that you have a stronger allegiance to the lessons of the heavens than to the lessons of the scriptures.'

Marlowe had an urge to flee.

'Hear me out, Marlowe,' Walsingham said. 'Perhaps there are men who thrive on religious conflict. Perhaps there are men who instigate conflict. Perhaps there are men who may be rather indifferent when Protestants are slain in Paris but purr like stroked cats when Catholics are butchered in York and London. Perhaps there are men who are ancient and determined enemies of the Church of Rome who live in perpetual hope of its destruction. Perhaps you are one of these men.' Walsingham stood, prompting Cecil to spring up and Marlowe to rise more slowly. He was dripping with sweat. Then Walsingham surprised him by putting a hand on his shoulder in a reassuring manner. 'Perhaps,' he continued, 'Cecil and I are also of this mind.'

'I am without words, my lord,' Marlowe sputtered.

'I want you to work for me, Marlowe, even as you continue at Cambridge toward your next degree. I want everything you do to be in aid of our cause and our betterment. The Queen is not one of us but she ardently believes that Cecil and I belong to her. And to the extent that her hatred of the Papists is as acute as ours, then we are well and truly aligned. I want you to become one of my spies, to make mischief abroad in the service of the Queen but more importantly in *our* service. We will expect great things from you.'

Marlowe felt lightheaded. 'I don't know what to say.'

'Say nothing,' Walsingham said sharply. 'Follow me. Deeds speak louder than words.'

Marlowe trailed Cecil and Walsingham down a long hall to an old heavy door, which Walsingham pulled open. There were stone stairs leading to a cellar.

Torches illuminated the damp walls. They walked in silence and came to another door on which Walsingham leaned heavily with his right shoulder. It creaked on its hinges, opening slowly to reveal a large room, about the size of the Great Room above. A dozen people, seven men and five women between the ages of twenty and forty, were drinking wine and lounging on plush furniture in the soft glow of candles. They all stopped what they were doing and stood.

'Ladies and gentlemen,' Walsingham said, 'I present to you Master Christopher Marlowe, the young man I told you of. I wish you to make him comfortable and to demonstrate our full hospitality.'

As if on cue, they all began to astound Marlowe in a way he had not believed possible.

Women and men began stripping off layer after layer of their clothes. The rugs became strewn with doublets, peasecods and breeches, bodices, skirts and farthingales. Soon, there was pink flesh exposed everywhere and

Marlowe trembled and stirred when he saw the full nakedness of twelve comely bodies facing him, the men in full tumescence.

When he turned to his host to register his incredulity he was further astonished to see that Walsingham and Cecil had themselves stripped off.

'Show him,' Walsingham ordered. 'Go ahead and show him.'

In unison, all of them turned away from Marlowe and showed their backs.

Each of them, Walsingham included, had thick pink tails.

'Good heavens,' Marlowe gasped.

Walsingham leered at him. 'Don't be prudish, Marlowe. I urge you to show your natural state.'

Marlowe hesitated for a few moments, then did as he'd been commanded, first removing his shoes, then peeling off his garments until all that was left were his breeches. He let them fall to the floor.

The others broke into applause. They were showing appreciation for perhaps the longest tail in the room. Marlowe's own.

'Choose whomever you like,' Walsingham said. 'You're among your own kind now. You can do what you like. You're a Lemures.'

I'm a Lemures.

Marlowe slowly approached a beautiful fair-haired young man who encouraged him with a gleaming smile.

My life can now begin.

FOURTEEN

The basement tiles of the St Andrea Hospital were a sickly yellow, making it difficult to say if they were clean or dirty. To the outside observer, the presence of a nun standing among policemen outside the morgue might have suggested a scenario of family grief and pastoral attendance.

But Elisabetta was tending her own garden, steeling herself to confront the face of death.

Micaela emerged from the morgue wearing her long white doctor's coat. She pulled Elisabetta off to the side. 'Are you sure you want to do this?' she asked.

'Yes, absolutely,' Elisabetta answered with a pretended confidence. Then, 'I have to.'

Micaela gave her a hug.

Inspector Leone was there, his usual irascible self, looking like he'd slept in his uniform. 'We're coming in too.'

Micaela took on the posture of a fighting cock about to raise its claws. 'The Chief Pathologist said only her. You can speak to him – don't speak to me.'

Elisabetta found it odd how she herself was comfortable with 'old' death but shaky with 'fresh' death, how skeletons and mummified remains were slotted into a cool, academic part of her brain but new corpses were relegated to a more fearful place.

Maybe it was something primeval, feeding on the fear of diseased flesh. Or perhaps, she realized, it was as simple as a childhood memory: trying to reconcile the dead body of her mother in her casket with the vibrant life force she had been.

The man was lying face up on the slab, a small towel covering his private parts – no doubt, Elisabetta thought, in respect for the modesty of a nun. His torso was riddled with angry black holes, the entrance wounds of 9mm slugs. His eyes were open but curiously no more dead-looking than they had appeared during life. His face, fixed in death, was identical to the immobile one she'd seen the night before and again years earlier.

'It's him,' she whispered to her sister. 'I'm sure it's the man who stabbed me.'

Doctor Fiore, the Chief Pathologist, asked whether Elisabetta was ready. She nodded and two thick-armed mortician's assistants turned the body on its face. The exit wounds in his upper and lower back were horrific.

The towel was pulled away to reveal his well-muscled buttocks.

'You see,' Micaela whispered. 'The same.'

Doctor Fiore, visibly shaken by the sight, overheard the remark. 'Same as w – what?'

'Just the same as I told her it would be,' Micaela answered evasively.

It was as if the photo of the old man from Ulm had materialized incarnate.

The stubby tail hanging down to the fold of his buttocks like a dead serpent.

The numbers tattooed in three rings at the base of his spine.

Elisabetta took it in numbly. 'I've seen enough,' she said after a while.

She would have preferred a few minutes alone – perhaps a short respite in the hospital chapel – but it was not to be. There were more people in the basement hall and a heated contretemps had flared up. Zazo had arrived with Lorenzo and immediately got into an argument with Inspector Leone. Zazo started things by insisting that the convent intruder and the man on the slab were likely to be one and the same. Leone responded sarcastically that his investigation clearly demanded a higher level of proof than would satisfy the Vatican Gendarmerie.

The two of them argued and Micaela left to answer an urgent hospital page. Elisabetta was left alone with her thoughts until she felt a presence behind her.

'Are you okay?'

It was Lorenzo, his arms folded across his front, two fingers gripping his major's cap.

'Yes, I'm all right,' she said.

'It was a terrible night for you, I'm sure,' he said, looking down shyly at his feet.

There was something familiar about this. She saw Lorenzo but she felt Marco. The physical similarities weren't so great. Marco was taller, darker, more handsome, at least in her mind's eye. But here was another friend of Zazo's, in uniform, making her feel safe just by his presence. And there was another similarity, she realized. The eyes. Both men had sympathetic eyes.

He glanced at Zazo and shook his head. 'He's fed up to here with the Polizia. They treated him like the criminal last night. Six hours of interrogation and that's only the beginning, apparently. It's complicated when you shoot someone.'

'Have *you* ever . . . ?'

Lorenzo answered quickly. 'Never. I've never fired my gun in anger. Zazo neither – until now – but you know that.'

'It's an awful thing,' Elizabetta said sadly. 'I wish it hadn't been necessary. I wish Professor De Stefano hadn't been killed. I wish evil didn't exist.'

'Your family church,' Lorenzo said. 'It's Santa Maria in Trastevere, isn't it?'

'Do you know it?'

'In passing. Zazo's mentioned it. Maybe when the Conclave is over and the dust has settled, maybe I can come and pray there with you.'

'I'd like that.' Elisabetta caught herself. 'We all need to pray for Christ's forgiveness.'

When the police got their turn in the morgue, Zazo came over to Elisabetta and Lorenzo. 'These idiots have nothing. They've got a name, Aldo Vani, and that's about it. He doesn't have any employment records, no records that he ever paid tax. They searched his apartment and they say they came up empty. His mobile phone didn't have an address book and the log of recent calls was empty. According to them, he's a ghost.'

'I worked in Naples as a young cop,' Lorenzo said. 'This guy is like a Camorra hit man with a life completely off the grid. But what's with the tail? Whoever heard of something like that?'

Zazo looked protectively at Elisabetta. 'We don't know if this is relevant. Maybe yes, maybe no.'

Lorenzo's phone rang. When he stepped aside to answer it Zazo asked her, 'How are you holding up?'

'I'm tired but still grateful to be alive.'

'I told you not to leave Papa's house.'

'The professor called. He was so insistent, the poor man. He must have been threatened by that beast. At least I left a note, thank God.'

Zazo pointed at the morgue doors. 'Jesus, Elisabetta. If you hadn't it would have been you in there. I want you to go back to Papa's and stay there. Don't go out for anything. I'm going to try to get Leone to give you some police protection but I don't think he'll do it. He's more focused on De Stefano and thinks you just stumbled into something. He's not putting the pieces together.'

'I haven't been entirely forthcoming with him,' Elisabetta said.

'Don't. It's not in your best interests to tell him everything. Anyway it would blow the little fuse in his brain. He won't even consider that the bastard in there was the same guy who tried to get you before. Christ, if the Conclave weren't the day after tomorrow, I'd take a leave and protect you full-time myself.'

She touched his cheek. 'You're a wonderful brother.'

Zazo laughed. 'Yes, I am. Listen, maybe it would be better if you went to stay at Papa's farmhouse.'

Elisabetta shook her head. 'I feel safer here. And I can go to my church. But Zazo . . . ?

'What?'

'I'm neglecting my obligations and my devotions. I just want to go back to teaching and get my life back.'

'Soon. I'm sure you'll get it back soon. We'll get to the bottom of this.'

Lorenzo and Micaela finished their calls at about the same time and joined them.

'Inspector Loreti is having a stroke,' Lorenzo says. 'He wants us back at the Vatican right away. The place is crawling with red-hats and the media.'

'Will you take her home?' Zazo asked Micaela.

'Inspector Leone said he wanted to speak with me again,' Elisabetta said.

'Then right after that, okay?'

'I'll take her,' Micaela agreed.

A clatter of footsteps came from the direction of the elevators. Three monsignors were fast-walking towards them, trailed by an archbishop.

'It's Archbishop Luongo,' Elisabetta told them, looking up. 'The head of the Pontifical Commission for Sacred Archeology.'

'Okay, we're out of here,' Zazo said, putting his hand on Lorenzo's shoulder. 'I'll call you at Papa's.'

Elisabetta had an inkling that Lorenzo wanted to hug her goodbye or at least shake her hand but instead he simply smiled and left.

'There you are,' the archbishop called out. 'How are you, my dear?'

'I'm unhurt, Your Excellency.'

Luongo was tall, well over six feet. Elisabetta had seen him at the Institute once without a hat; his head was completely smooth and bald and he also lacked eyebrows and a five-o'clock shadow. *Alopecia totalis*, Micaela had told Elisabetta when she'd inquired about the condition. A completely hairless body. He was an ambitious man – everybody at the Institute said so – and the snippets of gossip that she picked up from the lunch room revolved around whether his malady would interfere with his patent desire to be elevated to cardinal.

He towered over Elisabetta. 'Such a tragedy about Professor De Stefano. He was a marvelous man. I personally recruited him for the job, you know.'

She nodded.

'Who would do such a thing? What are the police saying?'

'They're still investigating.'

The archbishop looked at Micaela over the top of his glasses.

'This is Doctor Celestino, my sister,' Elisabetta said.

'Ah, how wonderful to be involved in the healing arts.'

Micaela managed a tight smile and to Elisabetta's relief kept a lid on any snide retort.

'I wonder if I might have a word with you personally,' Luongo said to Elisabetta.

'If it's about the catacombs and the man who did this last night then you can speak in front of my sister. She's signed a Commission confidentiality agreement. She knows everything about St Callixtus, Ulm and now this.'

'Yes, yes, I recall – we brought you into the fold as a consultant, Doctor, did we not? Thank you for aiding the Commission and the Church. In that case, I'll talk freely. Elisabetta, my message is short and hopefully it will be clear. We have to balance our responsibilities to the secular world and to the Church. I'm sure you will do your duty to be helpful to the police to assist them in finding out why this man . . .' Luongo whispered the next few words '. . . who I understand has a tail – why this man committed these terrible acts. But at the same time, I'm sure you will be sensitive to the situation we are in. The Conclave is upon us. The entire world is focused on the somber grandeur of what we as a Church will be doing to choose our next Pope. We cannot pollute the proceedings by permitting any lurid talk of St Callixtus and men with tails. For this reason we have the complete cooperation of the secular authorities in imposing a news embargo on last night's unfortunate events. And, I must emphasize, despite the odd coincidence of the anatomical abnormality of the man who attacked you and Professor De

Stefano, there is no clear link between the two situations.'

Micaela was becoming red-faced and Elisabetta grew worried that she was going to give the Archbishop a piece of her mind. She tried to preempt her by saying, 'I understand, Your Excellency.'

It wasn't enough. Micaela seemed to struggle to keep her voice at a hospital-appropriate level. 'Coincidence? No clear link? You must be joking! You find these skeletons in the catacombs, then all of them disappear, then someone breaks into my sister's convent, then the professor is murdered and Elisabetta, only by the grace of God, not to mention my brother, is saved. And you want her to stay quiet?'

Elisabetta didn't know Luongo well. She'd only seen him a few times. But now a terrifying change came over his face, a blowback of rage that rendered even Micaela mute. 'Let me make myself completely understood,' he fumed in a hot, whispered discharge like steam escaping from a boiling kettle. 'You are both under the most strict rules of confidentiality. Our secrecy agreements are drafted by the finest law firm in Rome and I can assure you ladies that if these agreements are breached, you will find our lawyers more fearsome than any men with tails.'

In time the hallway outside the morgue thinned out as police and clergy left the scene. The Chief Pathologist departed too and a single mortuary assistant tended to paperwork beside Aldo Vani's draped corpse.

There was a knock at the morgue door and the assistant begrudgingly answered it.

He saw a gangly priest towering over him.

'Yes, what is it?' the assistant asked gruffly.

'My name is Father Tremblay. I am here to inspect the body.' He thrust forward a letter. 'I have been given the highest permission.'

The Domus Sanctae Marthae hugged the lines of a gentle slope of Vatican City adjacent to the Basilica. It was a plain five-story building, modest in its ambitions, a symbol of reserve and austerity. It was no more than a dormitory providing basic accommodation for visiting clergy. Its usual occupancy rate was low but it was notably different from every other hotel in the world: it was designed for Conclaves and on the rare occasions when it was full it meant that there was a sad vacancy of the Apostolic See.

The first floor of the dormitory had a private chapel with a steeply peaked latticed ceiling and a small pipe organ donated by the Knights of Columbus. About two-thirds of the cardinals had arrived in Rome and they assembled in the chapel for a private Mass led by Cardinal Diaz, one of the countless duties during the mourning period for the Dean of the College of Cardinals.

The old boxer towered over the lectern, making it look as though it was meant for a child. The acoustics were perfect and his voice carried to the back without any need for a microphone.

'Dear Brothers, the Basilica of St Peter's, a witness to many meaningful and important moments in the ministry of our dearly departed Father, looks out today on those gathered in prayer who in a special way have had the responsibility and the privilege to be close to him as his direct collaborators, sharing in the pastoral care of the Universal Church.

'In these days of mourning and sadness, the Word of God enlightens our faith and strengthens our hope, assuring us that he has entered into the Heavenly Jerusalem where, as we hear in the Book of Revelation, "God shall wipe away every tear, death shall be no more, neither shall there be mourning nor crying nor pain anymore."

When Mass was over, Diaz strode from the Domus in the company of Cardinals Aspromonte and Giaccone. 'Come back to my office,' Diaz told the other two. 'I've had private conversations with some of our fellow influence-makers. I'd like to share them with you.'

'Electioneering?' Aspromonte asked, making Giaccone snicker.

'Don't laugh, Luigi,' Diaz said. 'You're the one everyone is talking about.'

Aspromonte looked deflated. His large bald head bobbed forward as if its weight had become too much for his neck. For his part, Giaccone closed his eyes and shook his head, setting his jowls into motion. 'We must put a stop to this. I don't want the job.'

The three cardinals passed through several rings of Vatican Gendarmerie charged with sealing off the guest house. Zazo and Lorenzo, on their way to inspect their men, bowed to the triumvirate and continued on to confer with a pair of corporals at the entrance of the Domus.

'What time are the sniffer dogs coming back through?' Zazo asked the men.

'Six o'clock,' one of them answered.

'Give me a report when it's done.'

The corporals looked as though they wanted to ask about the previous night's shooting. Everyone was desperately curious and rumors were running rampant among the Corps. But to raise the subject would have amounted to insubordination and Zazo wasn't about to volunteer any information.

When Zazo and Lorenzo turned to leave they found themselves face to face with one of their rank counterparts among the Swiss Guards, Major Gerhardt Glauser, a small pissant of a man who had an unsupportable air of superiority. Whenever they talked about him Zazo rose on tiptoe as testimony to his belief that Glauser must have cheated to make the Guard's minimum height requirement.

'What's this I hear about an incident last night?' Glauser asked nasally.

'There was a little problem. Zazo took care of it,' Lorenzo said.

'I heard it was more than a little problem. I heard that you killed a man.'

Zazo made a button-the-lips sign. 'Active investigation, Glauser,' he said. 'Need to know.'

'If it involved the Guards, my superiors would surely place the officer on leave pending an inquiry.'

'Well, it *doesn't* involve the Guards, does it?' Zazo said, walking around him.

He and Lorenzo made their way briskly to the Operations Center at the Tribunal Palace and settled into their shared office to review schedules before their afternoon briefing with Inspector-General Loreti. After a while Lorenzo ambled over to Zazo's desk. 'I'm getting a coffee. Want one?'

Zazo nodded and Lorenzo stole a look at his computer screen.

'What are you doing on the Interpol site?' Lorenzo asked.

'Don't be nosy.'

'Come on,' Lorenzo insisted.

'I got the bastard's fingerprint card from the morgue. Leone's such a genius that he probably hasn't run the prints through Interpol. Also, you know the weird markings around his tail? I have to tell you in confidence that Elisabetta knows about an identical tattoo from a man who died a few years ago in Germany. I want Interpol to do a check of old phone records to see whether this fellow in Germany and our guy, Vani, ever exchanged calls.'

'Christ,' Lorenzo said. 'If Inspector Loreti finds out you're doing your own investigation of a Polizia case in the middle of a Conclave – well, you know what'll happen.'

'So don't tell him,' Zazo said. 'Three sugars.'

Krek pulled the curtains in his office closed to get the

afternoon sun out of his eyes. He sat back down and scanned his calendar. There were three more meetings scheduled. Then a dinner at a hotel in the city center with a Swede anxious to unload his construction company. Krek wanted to loosen his tie. He wanted a drink. He wanted a woman. All three would have to wait. He called his secretary. 'Get me Mulej.'

The big man lumbered in, fingering his collar. 'Have you decided what you want to do?'

'Aldo failed us miserably. The nun's still alive and the police have his body. This is as bad as it gets.'

'We should use Hackel. He's already in Rome.'

'Hackel has a more important job. I don't want him losing focus. No, send some men from here. Send them now. Finish this thing.'

FIFTEEN

Rome, AD 64

It was May, the loveliest month, when the meadow grasses were tender and spring flowers were in full color. As the daylight waned and the breezes blew, the crowd of revelers swelled and jostled at the edge of the lake. It would be a long, exotic night, one that would be talked about for generations, a night of spectacle and danger.

It was Tigellinus's doing. Gaius Ofonius Tigellinus was rich, flamboyant and powerful beyond measure. Officially he was Prefect of the Imperial Bodyguard but in practice, he was the Emperor's chief fixer and procurer and tonight he had organized the party of the century. They were surrounded by woodland at the Campus Martius, the splendid villa built decades earlier by Agrippa, Augustus's son-in-law. The centerpiece of the property was the great artificial lake, the Stagnum Aggripae, fed by an elaborate aqueduct, the Aqua Virgo, and drained by a long canal into the Tiber.

Along all the banks of the 200-meter lake guests entertained themselves with wild abandon. There were taverns and brothels and dining halls that had been constructed just for the day. Exotic birds and wild beasts brought from far-flung corners of the empire were everywhere, some roaming freely, others, like tigers and cheetahs, tethered by chains with enough slack to let them snare drunkards with their teeth and claws. Whenever this happened, a swollen roar of amusement would draw hundreds more spectators to watch the hapless man or woman getting torn apart.

The coming darkness and flowing wine set in motion pure licentiousness. One brothel was populated with only noblewomen. In another, professional prostitutes cavorted openly and nakedly and spilled onto the grass. Promiscuous women of all sorts were available – noble and slave, matrons and virgins – and all were obliged to satisfy any request. Slaves had sex with their mistresses in front of their husbands, gladiators took daughters under the gaze of their fathers. All was allowed, nothing was forbidden. As night fell, the surrounding groves and buildings shone with lights and echoed with shouts and moans. There was pushing and shoving, brawls and stabbings. And the night was still young.

At the main pavilion a few dozen of the most important guests reclined on benches and couches. There were Senators, courtiers, diplomats, the richest merchants. Tigellinus sat in the front, the lake lapping only a meter from his sandals. For the night he had shed his heavy uniform as commander of the Imperial Guards for a toga but he'd been tempted to go even further, as some of the high-born guests had done, and wear only a belted tunic. Tigellinus was tall and stern with a heavy brow that made him look like a brawler. At his left, taciturn as always, sat the swarthy astrologer Balbilus. He was in his seventh decade of life but still looked powerful and fit, imperious and unapproachable. To his left sat another of the Emperor's gray-haired toadies, the freedman Acinetus. He had been handpicked by the Emperor's mother, Agrippina, to be one of her son Nero's tutors during his nonage and later he carried out the Emperor's ill-fated plan to drown her by sinking her royal boat. Finally Nero had to dispatch rather more overt assassins to finish the job. When confronted by sword-wielding men in her chambers, Agrippina cried for them to 'Smite my womb' – for bringing a son into the world who was detestable even by her own despicable standards.

Behind Nero, bored and drunk, the Emperor's bejeweled wife Poppaea slouched low, holding her goblet out for one of her handmaidens to refill. Even though she had tired bloodshot eyes and a blotchy rash which her Greek doctor had been unable to remedy, she still had the fetching looks that had first placed her in favor.

Tigellinus leaned over and asked Balbilus, 'Why so glum?'

'You know why. For the second time we have achieved what we always wanted: one of us as Emperor. And this is what he gives us. Listen to the Senators grumbling! I fear a revolt, perhaps violence against him. And us. They killed Caligula. It can happen again. We may not get a third chance.'

Tigellinus snorted. 'There was a comet two weeks ago when Nero was in Beneventum, was there not?'

'Yes. A clear sign of danger.'

'And you advised him to expunge the threat by purging certain elements in the aristocracy.'

'And you, good Prefect, chose well in your slaughter.'

'And that is precisely why you shouldn't worry.' Tigellinus whispered the rest. 'He will fulfill all our desires. He knows his destiny. Yes, perhaps he's gone a little mad – this kind of power has that effect – but he's not so mad as to have lost his way. Let him be merry and indulge himself in his own way.' He winked. 'This is what he does. This is who he is.'

Peter the Apostle was hobbled by bad knees and a constant ache which sent lightning bolts of pain down the back of one leg. The journey ahead was going to be arduous, as it would have been even for a younger man, but he'd risen early, washed himself in a trough behind the small stone house in Golgotha and watched the rising sun brighten the hills.

The house had been owned by a brother of Phillip, one of Jesus's twelve, and upon the man's death it had passed to his wife Rachel. She had been the second to awake that morning and when she saw Peter was no longer in his bed she sought him out.

'Must you go to Rome?' she asked.

He was seated on the stony orange ground. 'I must.'

'You're precious to us,' she said. 'We don't want to lose you. Matthew is gone, and Stephen, and James, and Matthias, and Andrew, and Mark, all martyred like him.'

The rising sun caught Peter's eyes and made him squint. 'When I was a young man, Jesus said something which has stayed with me during my long life. He said, "When you are old you will stretch out your hands and another will dress you and take you where you do not want to go." I do not want to leave you and my beloved brothers and sisters, Rachel, but I fear it is my destiny.'

She did not try to argue with him. 'Well, come on then, at least let's get some hot food into you before you climb onto that mule.'

Fresh breezes swirled through the central courtyard and gardens of Nero's villa at the Campus Martius. Out of sight the vast party heaved and groaned its way toward dawn. Nero sat on a padded marble bench, absently throwing tidbits of food from a crystal bowl to the lampreys in his fish pond while Balbilus and Tigellinus paced and debated.

'May I enter?' Acinetus called out from between a pair of peristyle columns.

'Be quick,' Nero demanded.

Acinetus tugged two handfuls of cloth, each from the shoulder of a young girl's toga. 'Do they please Your Excellency?'

Nero looked the flushed, sobbing girls up and down. 'Who are they?'

'The twin daughters of Senator Vellus.'

Nero smiled. 'Good. I hate that bastard.'

'I knew you'd be pleased,' Acinetus said.

'How old are they?'

'Twelve or thirteen I should think.'

'Take them to my rooms and wait there.' He called Acinetus over and whispered, 'When I'm done with them be sure to make good use of their tender flesh. My fish, dear Acinetus, are famished.' He turned back to the other men. 'You were saying?'

'I was telling Balbilus what he already knows – that the mood in the city is pleasantly ugly,' Tigellinus said. 'The Roman mob has come to hate the Christians even more than they do the Jews.'

'Of course they do,' Balbilus agreed. 'The Christians are an arrogant, loathsome lot who don't even pretend to pay homage to you. At least the Jews go through a pantomime.'

Tigellinus added, 'And the Christians grow in numbers by the month. They breed like mice.'

'I utterly despise them,' Nero said, yawning. 'Their piousness is nauseating. The way they pretend that their weakness is a strength – "Turn the other cheek," they say, "so they may strike you again." To which I say, when they turn a cheek don't waste time by striking them again: run them through with a sword and be done with it.'

'Sound advice,' Tigellinus said.

'Listen to me,' Nero said. 'The Christian cult grows stronger by the day. They challenge my authority. Their leaders, like this scabby dog who calls himself Peter the Apostle, slip in and out of my city without so much as a lashing. If we allow them to escape our wrath we'll live to regret it, mark my words. Pontius Pilate had the right idea when he crucified that hideous little man Jesus of Nazareth. Pilate knew this cult was going to cause us trouble and interfere with our interests.'

'Pilate cut off the cult's head and twelve more heads grew in its place – Jesus's filthy apostles,' Tigellinus said.

'We need to be smarter than Pilate and eradicate all of them!' Balbilus stated. 'Our Emperor tells me that he has conjured a way to use the power of the Roman mob to kill them off once and for all and make ourselves ever richer in the process. My job, as Imperial astrologer, will be to tell him the best date. And you, Tigellinus, your job will be to implement it.'

Nero rose and started to make his way out of the courtyard. 'What this city of ours needs,' he said, looking back over his shoulder, 'is a very large, very hot fire.'

SIXTEEN

On her way back home from the police station, Elisabetta had the taxi drop her off at the Basilica Santa Maria in Trastevere. Her session with Inspector Leone had been difficult and she was exhausted by the mental challenge of giving him enough to be truthful without violating her Church confidentiality.

The basilica was quiet and peaceful with only a few tourists wandering through, snapping pictures and seeking out the church's treasured relics – the head of Saint Apollonia and a portion of the Holy Sponge. Elisabetta bowed at the altar, crossed herself and took her usual position directly under the painting on the wooden ceiling, *The Assumption of the Blessed Virgin* by Domenichino. The only others in the pews were a handful of older local women who always seemed to be there.

Elisabetta lost herself completely in prayer. The dry coolness and low light which had preserved the church's antiquities so well for centuries had a similar effect preserving her sanity. When she had said the last of her amens, she looked around and was surprised to see that there were many more people in the pews. She felt calmer and refreshed. She checked her watch. An hour had slipped by. Back at the school the girls would be finding their desks for geometry.

She rose and tried to keep herself in a state of prayerfulness but it was impossible to control the thoughts moving through her mind.

Vani's hideous back.

The skeletons.

De Stefano's bloody head.

Marco's body laid out in his dress uniform.

And as Elisabetta felt the tears coming the comforting image of Lorenzo's open, friendly face drifted in. Instead of crying she smiled, but when she realized what her mind was doing she shook her head hard, as if doing so would dislodge his image.

Better to look for her mockingbird mosaic high up in the apse, she thought, and that was what she did.

Elisabetta walked back to her father's apartment, stopping only at the greengrocer and the butcher. It was Carlo's day off and she intended to make him a nice supper.

As soon as she let herself in, she heard him calling from the sitting room and fast-walking toward the hall. 'Where have you been?' he said irritably. 'We've been waiting for you.'

He looked uncomfortable.

'"We"?' she asked. 'Who's "we"? What's the matter?'

'Christ, Elisabetta, you didn't tell me you were having visitors. They came all the way from England!'

She closed her eyes in embarrassment. 'My God! I totally forgot! With everything that's happened . . .'

Carlo gave her a quick, reassuring hug. 'It's okay: you're here, you're safe. You had a rough night. I gave them a glass of wine, told them every story I know about Cambridge. Everything's fine. Give me the bags. Go see your guests.'

Evan Harris looked precisely like his photograph. He was slight, bland in appearance, lean but not athletic. His sandy hair, combed to one side over a rounded forehead, made him appear younger than he probably was but Elisabetta thought he must be approaching fifty. He hadn't come alone. A woman was with him, expensively dressed, proper in posture, perfectly coiffed and smelling of good perfume. Her unlined Botox-pricked face and her figurine smile made it hard for Elisabetta to judge her age.

Harris and the woman both stood, blinking their confusion in harmony.

'I'm so sorry I'm late,' Elisabetta said. 'I'm Elisabetta Celestino. I think my father didn't tell you I'm a nun. For that matter, I'm afraid I neglected to mention it too.'

'I'm so pleased to meet you,' Harris said graciously. 'And I must apologize for the fact that I neglected to tell you I was bringing a colleague. May I introduce Stephanie Meyer, a very distinguished member of Cambridge University's governing body, the Regent House. She is also a generous donor to the University.'

'I'm delighted to make your acquaintance,' Meyer said with the careful elocution of the British upper class. 'Your father is absolutely charming. I told him I would suggest to the Chairman of our Mathematics Department that he be invited to give a talk on his Goldberg Conjecture.'

'Gold*bach*,' Elisabetta said, gently correcting her. 'I hope he didn't force a lecture on you.' Suddenly she remembered that he'd been working on her tattoo puzzle. The last time she'd checked, his jottings had been all over the sitting room. There was a messy stack of lined yellow papers covered by some journals on the sideboard. Fortunately, he'd tidied up to some extent.

'Not at all,' Meyer said. 'I hope he cracks it. And I hope his department will treat him with the respect he so clearly deserves.'

'Is there anything he didn't tell you?' Elisabetta said, shaking her head.

'Only, apparently, that you were a nun,' Harris said, smiling.

'So please, sit,' Elisabetta said. 'What can I bring you?'

'Only the book,' Harris said. 'We're very keen to see it.'

It was in her old bedroom, on her small student desk. She took it out of its envelope, brought it back and put it in Harris's outstretched hands. She watched the anticipation on his face, like that of a child receiving his first Christmas present. His hands were trembling.

'One should use gloves,' he mumbled absently. He rested it on his pinstriped trousers and slowly opened the mottled leather cover of the quarto to reveal the front plate. 'Ah, look at this,' he said, almost to himself. 'Look at *this*.'

'Is it authentic?' Meyer asked him.

'There's not a shred of doubt,' Harris said. 'B text, 1620.' He carefully turned several pages. 'The cover's a little shabby but the book is in remarkably good condition. No water damage. No mold. No tears that I can see. It's a remarkable copy of a remarkable book.'

He passed it to Meyer who searched her purse for a pair of reading glasses and perused it for herself.

'And you said you obtained it in Germany,' Harris said. 'In Ulm.'

Elisabetta nodded.

'Can you divulge any details?' he asked. 'Provenance is always of interest in these kinds of circumstances.'

'It was given to me by a baker,' Elisabetta said.

'A baker, you say!' Harris exclaimed. 'What was a baker doing with an extraordinary treasure like this?'

'She was the landlord of a tenant who passed away without next of kin. It belonged to him. He'd been a professor at the University at Ulm.'

Meyer looked as though she was attempting to arch a brow but the Botox was defeating her. 'And do you know where he obtained it?'

'The only information I have is that he received it as a gift,' Elisabetta said.

Just then her father came back in, apologizing for

the intrusion. He was looking for an article he'd copied from a math journal but as he sorted through the stack of material on the sideboard he couldn't help inserting himself into the proceedings.

'What do you think of her book?' he asked Harris.

'I think it's genuine, Professor Celestino. It's a very fine copy.'

'Is it worth anything?'

'Papa!' Elisabetta exclaimed, scarlet-faced.

'I believe it's quite valuable,' Harris said. 'It's rare. Very rare, indeed. That's why we're here.'

'I'm interested in finding out more about it,' Elisabetta said.

'May I ask where your interest lies?' Meyer asked. She was still holding the book on her lap and didn't seem inclined to hand it back.

Elisabetta shifted in her chair and smoothed her habit, a show of nerves she'd developed when forced to tell half-truths. 'As I told Professor Harris, the work I'm doing concerns attitudes of the sixteenth-century Church. Religious themes run large through Faustus.'

'Indeed they do,' Harris said. 'And you indicated that your work pertains particularly to differences between the A and the B texts.'

Elisabetta nodded.

'Well, let me give you some background which might be useful and I can steer you to a host of scholarly work on the subject for further inquiry. I've spent my career on Marlowe. You might say I'm a bit obsessed with him.'

'More than a bit,' Meyer added, pressing her lips into a fleeting flat smile.

'I concentrated on English literature as an undergraduate at Corpus Christi College, which was called Benet College in Marlowe's day, the same college that he attended. And I spent two years living in the same rooms as him. I went on to get my D.Phil. in Marlowe studies and have been teaching at Cambridge since then. I suppose every Marlowe scholar has his personal favorite play and, as it happens, mine is *Faustus*. It's extraordinary in its scope and complexity and the power and beauty of its language. You can have your Shakespeare. I'll take Marlowe.'

Uninvited, Elisabetta's father slipped into one of the chairs and seemed to be listening with interest. She shot him a perplexed look, which was her silent way of asking what he was doing, and he answered with a stubborn pout, his way of saying it was his house and he could do in it what he pleased.

Harris continued: 'Marlowe received his Master's degree in 1587 under somewhat mysterious circumstances, concerning absences from College and his alleged covert activities on the Continent on behalf of Queen Elizabeth's spymaster Francis Walsingham. He most probably left Cambridge for London to take up a career as a playwright. While we don't know the precise order in which he wrote his plays, it's well documented that the first one to be staged in London was *Dido, Queen of Carthage*, an interesting but somewhat sophomoric work.

'The best information we have on *Faustus* is that Marlowe wrote it in 1592. The first documented performance was in 1594, a production by the Admiral's Men troupe with Faustus played by Edward Alleyn, the greatest actor of his day. Marlowe was killed in May of 1593. Did he ever see *Faustus* performed? I would hope so. Perhaps there were earlier performances.'

'And this performance in 1594, was it the A text?' Elisabetta asked.

'Well, that's an excellent question but the short answer is that we don't know. You see, the first known publication of the A-text quarto was in 1604, well after his death. There was a second publication in 1609 and a third in 1611. All told there are only five known original copies of A text in existence, one at the Bodelian Library in Oxford, two at the Huntington Library in California, one in the Hamburg State Library and one at the National Trust's Petworth House in West Sussex. They're all essentially the same, so one might be tempted to say that they represent the earliest stage versions, but that would be a supposition.

'The first B text wasn't published until 1616. That quarto is similar to yours in that it's the first to use the now famous woodcut on the title page that shows Faustus raising the Devil while he, Faustus, stays inside his magic circle. That copy is in the British Museum. The next edition to surface is a 1619 one, essentially the same as the one from 1616. There is a single known copy in the hands of an American collector in Baltimore. Then we come to yours, the 1620 edition. Here, curiously, there's a misprint on the title page – printers were notorious for misprints back then – the word "History" is printed as "Hiftoy". There's a single copy in the British Library. We know that three copies have appeared in the saleroom in the past forty years. All of them have been lost to follow-up. Until now, I'd say. Yours is undoubtedly one of them.'

Elisabetta's father had been scratching at his stubble. He never shaved on his days off. 'So the B text is a third longer than the A text. What else is different?'

Harris looked surprised. 'I'm impressed you know that!' he said. 'I thought your field was mathematics.'

'My father has eclectic interests,' Elisabetta said quickly, begging him with her eyes to stay quiet.

'Well, to be precise,' Harris said. 'The B text omits thirty-six lines of the A text but adds 676 new lines.'

'Who made the changes?' Elisabetta asked. 'Marlowe?'

'That we don't know. Perhaps he wrote a second version. Perhaps an unknown collaborator or hired hand made changes to suit the Elizabethan audience after Marlowe's death. As a playwright of his era, Marlowe would have had nothing to do with the publication of his plays and only a very limited control over the content of the performances. Scenes could have been added or deleted by another writer, by actors – by anyone, really. Unless future hand-written manuscripts turn up we may never know.'

'What would you say are the truly significant differences between the A text and the B?' Elisabetta asked, conjuring the envelope note in her mind: *B holds the key.*

Harris took a deep breath. 'Gosh, where to start? Dissertations have been written on the subject. I myself have made some contributions to the field. I will be happy to send you a detailed bibliography so that you can delve as deeply as you like. In a broad sense, let me say, however, that the similarities far outweigh the differences. In both, our Doctor Faustus summons the demon Mephistopheles from the underworld and strikes a pact to have twenty-four years on Earth with Mephistopheles as his personal servant. In exchange he gives his soul over to Lucifer as payment and damns himself to an eternity in Hell. At the end of these twenty-four rather excellent and sinful years, though filled with fear and remorse, there's nothing Faustus can do to alter his fate. He's torn limb from limb and his soul is carried off to Hell.

'As to the differences, textual differences occur in all of the five acts but the preponderance of additions lie in Act III. In the B text, Act III is far longer and becomes a rather concentrated anti-Catholic, anti-Papist tract – which in and of itself isn't terribly surprising in the Protestant hotbed that England had become under Elizabeth. Faustus and Mephistopheles travel to Rome and observe the Pope, his cardinals, bishops and friars acting like scandalously greedy buffoons. It must have been a real crowd-pleaser in its day.'

'What's your opinion about the reason for this addition?' Elisabetta asked.

'On that we can only speculate. In the A text,

Faustus's visit to Rome was there but was quite abbreviated. Perhaps whenever it was performed and the Pope appeared on stage, the audience jeered and stamped and carried on so much that Marlowe or someone else embellished Act III as part of the B rewrite to milk the sentiment thoroughly.'

Elisabetta jotted some notes on a pad. 'May I ask about astrology in the play?'

Harris nodded enthusiastically. 'Of course. Another subject dear to my heart. Well, astrology was extremely important in Marlowe's day. The Queen had her own court astrologer, John Dee. In *Faustus*, Marlowe would have certainly been influenced by the classic ecclesiastical account of witchcraft, the *Malleus Maleficarum*, which posits – and I'm almost embarrassed to say that I'm able to quote from memory – "demons are readier to appear when summoned by magicians under the influence of the stars, in order to deceive men, thus making them suppose that the stars have divine power or actual divinity." And we see the direct result of these ideas in Act 1, Scene 3 of *Faustus* when Faustus begins to conjure from inside his magic circle:

'Now that the gloomy shadow of the Earth,
Longing to view Orion's drizzly look,
Leaps from th'Antarctic world unto the sky
And dims the welkin with her pitchy
breath, Faustus, begin thine incantations.'"

Harris paused and smiled in a self-deprecatory way. 'I could go on and on.'

Elisabetta looked up from her note-taking. 'I'm curious about the astrological symbols depicted in the magic circle. Do they have a particular significance?'

Harris furrowed his brow at the question. 'Stephanie, may I see the book?'

It was still on her lap. Meyer passed it carefully to him. He opened it to the title page. 'Well, it's the standard zodiac, I suppose. Constellations, planets. To be honest, I've never thought about it in a rigorous way.' He looked up, blinking. 'Maybe I should.'

Perhaps sensing an opening, Meyer broke her long silence. 'I'm sure you've been wondering why I came to Rome with Professor Harris,' she said.

'I don't know about my daughter, but *I've* been wondering why you're here,' Carlo said undiplomatically. Elisabetta cringed and waited expectantly for the answer.

'Let me be open with you,' Meyer said. 'I'm here on behalf of the University. We want this book. We want it badly. It represents a tremendous gap in our library collection. Christopher Marlowe was a Cambridge man, one of our most illustrious and colorful graduates. Yet we do not possess a single copy of one of the early quartos of this, his most famous play. Oxford has one and we do not! This must be remedied. As a friend of the University and a supporter of the humanities I have pledged my personal resources to facilitate the acquisition of this book. Is it for sale, my dear?'

'How much?' Carlo chirped.

'Papa! Please!' Elisabetta begged, staring him down. She turned to face Meyer. 'I don't know what to tell you. I'm so honored that the two of you came all the way to see me. Frankly, it's not something I've thought about.'

'But the book is clearly yours,' Meyer said, pressing on. 'I mean, it's yours and the decision to sell it rests with you, does it not?'

'I have no personal possessions,' Elisabetta said. 'I was given the book as a gift to the Church. I suppose if someone were to buy it, the funds would go to my Order.'

Meyer smiled politely. 'Well, then. Now that we've seen it and Professor Harris is initially happy with its authenticity and condition, perhaps when we return home we can send you an offer in writing. Would you then entertain a formal offer?'

Elisabetta flushed. 'You've been so kind to come and speak with me. Of course. Send me a letter. I'll speak to my Mother Superior. She'll know how to respond.'

When the visitors were gone, Elisabetta slumped wearily on the sofa, surrendering to her fatigue. She removed her tight veil, ran a hand through her short hair and massaged her throbbing scalp. Her father shuffled back with a fresh cup of coffee and a look of paternal concern on his face.

'You need to sleep. No one goes through a night like you had without a need for rest. Have your coffee. Then go to your room.'

Elisabetta took the cup. 'You sound like you did when I was a child. "Go to your room, Elisabetta, and don't come out until you're ready to say you're sorry."'

'Someone had to give you some discipline,' Carlo said. 'Your mother was a very soft person.'

At that moment she could almost see her mother through her misty eyes, young and beautiful, passing from the hall to the kitchen. 'I still miss her so much,' she said.

Her father sniffed defiantly – his way of saying he wasn't going to let himself succumb to emotion. 'Of course you do. We all do. If she hadn't died maybe you wouldn't have done what you did.'

Elisabetta stiffened. 'What did I do?'

'Became a nun.' She could tell that once it was said that he regretted it but it was clear he meant it.

'Maybe you're right,' she said evenly. 'Maybe if Marco hadn't been killed, maybe if mama had been alive, maybe, maybe, maybe. But things happen in a life, God has ways of testing us. My answer to his tests was to find Him. I don't regret it for a minute.'

Carlo shook his head. 'You were a beautiful vibrant girl. You still are. And you've hidden yourself away behind your nunnery and your habit. I've never been happy about this. You should have been a wife and a mother and a scholar. That would have made your mother happy.'

Elisabetta fought the urge to be angry. He was stressed by the events of the past few days and she forgave him.

'Why have you spent all these years going after Goldbach?' she asked.

He huffed a laugh. She knew he was smart enough to see where she was going. 'Because it's my passion.'

'And it's your quest,' she added. 'Well, my passion, my quest, is to be with God, to feel Him deeply within my soul. To honor Him with my work with the children. That's my passion. That's what makes me happy.'

The door buzzer went off. It was like the bell that signals the end of a boxing round. They both seemed relieved.

'Have they come back?' her father said, scanning the room to see if their visitors had left anything behind.

He answered the intercom and came back to the living room to tell Elisabetta that her Mother Superior, Sister Marilena, was here to see her.

Elisabetta rose and hastily put her veil back on. She greeted Marilena at the door.

'My dear,' Marilena said with concern, grabbing her hands. 'I've been so worried about you. Word came to us of your ordeal last night.'

'I'm all right,' Elisabetta said. 'God was with me.'

'Yes, yes, I've been giving thanks all day.'

Elisabetta took Marilena to the sitting room. The kettle was whistling again in the kitchen where Elisabetta had sent her father.

'Such a lovely place,' Marilena said, glancing around the room.

'It's where I grew up,' Elisabetta said.

'So warm, so cultured. Everyone at the school has been worried about you.'

'I hope it's not a big distraction,' Elisabetta said.

'We're strong enough in our mission and our faith not to lose sight of what we must accomplish with the children and with God.' Then Marilena laughed. 'Of course it's a distraction. You know how we talk! Even my mother can speak of nothing else.'

'Tell mama I miss her,' Elisabetta said, realizing with a start that she'd just said something similar.

Suddenly Marilena turned serious. She had the same expression on her face that she wore when preparing to give parents a bad report on their children. 'Mother-General Maria called me today from Malta,' she said somberly.

Elisabetta checked her breath.

'I don't know where the decision was taken, I don't know why it was taken and I certainly wasn't consulted. You're being transferred, Elisabetta. The Order wants you to leave Rome and report to our school in Lumbubashi in the Republic of Congo. They want you there in one week.'

SEVENTEEN

London, 1586

The young man cast nervous glances around a walled garden dominated by a mulberry tree which had grown too large for its small patch of greenery.

'Who did you say owns this house?' Anthony Babington asked.

'A widow woman,' Marlowe answered. 'Her name is Eleanor Bull. She's known to Poley. She's one of us.'

They were in Deptford, on the south bank of the Thames. It was early summer and the preceding weeks had been overly hot and humid. Fetid organic river vapors hung unpleasantly in the air, causing the delicate Babington to sniff at a scented handkerchief for relief. He was twenty-four, fair and beautiful, even with his face scrunched from squinting into the afternoon sun. Marlowe overfilled Babington's mug with beer and the froth ran onto the oak table.

'I must say, Kit, that I don't know how you find the time to do everything you do – engaging in your Master's at Cambridge, writing your ditties and pursuing, how shall I put it, other activities.'

Marlowe frowned in displeasure. 'I don't deny that there scarcely seem to be enough hours in the day. But as to your first point, I have an arrangement with my Master at Benet to be away from college for certain periods as long as I maintain my academic obligations. On the third point, my conscience demands that I pursue these "other activities" and on the second point, I do not write ditties. I write plays."

Babington showed his sincere mortification. 'I've offended you. I did not mean to do so. I am overwhelmed, sir, at your industry and accomplishments.'

'You shall come to my opening night,' Marlowe said magnanimously. 'Come, let us turn our attention to weightier matters. Let us talk of restoring the true Catholic faith to England. Let us talk of dear Queen Mary. Let us talk of that dry hag Elizabeth and what is to be done with her. We have vast sunshine, we have beer, we have our own pleasant company.'

They had met through Robert Poley, one of Walsingham's men, not a run-of-the-mill toady but a choice cut of meat. Ruthless and cunning, he had matriculated at Cambridge in 1568 as a Sizar but had not received his degree because as an alleged Catholic he'd been unable to swear the necessary oath of allegiance to the Queen's religion. Yet apparently he wasn't so principled as to deflect the entreaties of Walsingham's recruiters and he quickly became one of the Secretary's most useful operatives, an informant who easily wheedled himself into Papist plots in England and on the

Continent and for the right compensation even permitted himself to be imprisoned time after time. Her Majesty's jails, he insisted, were the best places to meet Catholic plotters.

During Lent of that year, Poley arranged a supper meeting of young Catholic gentlemen at the Plough Inn, near Temple Bar on the western edge of the City of London. Anthony Babington, an acquaintance of Poley, was invited along with two strangers whom Poley had vouched for, Bernard Maude and Christopher Marlowe. Naive and hapless, Babington was the only one at the table that evening not in Walsingham's employ.

Over ale, wine and whispers, Babington was made aware of certain plans. Mary, Queen of the Scots, had been imprisoned at Elizabeth's pleasure for eighteen years for fomenting revolt against Elizabeth's Protestant reign and for offering herself up as the rightful Queen of England and restorer of the Pope's primacy. Following the collapse of the Throckmorton plot against the crown, Mary found herself in her strictest confinement yet, at Chartley Hall in Staffordshire, isolated from the outside world by Puritan minders who reported her every twitch to Walsingham.

Here was Poley's news. Catholic agents in France, Holland and Spain were passing along their assurances that the Catholic League and the great Christian princes of Europe would commit a force of 60,000 men to invade the north of England, free Mary and assert her rule. Thanks to the genius inventions of Kit Marlowe, a brilliant young recusant recently allied to their cause, a method of communicating with Mary had been devised. Marlowe had imagined a way to smuggle letters to Chartley Hall, hidden and sealed waterproof within kegs of beer, and he had also devised a clever cipher to encrypt them in the unlikely event that they were discovered.

Letters from plotters had already been sent in this manner and Mary had given written replies of general encouragement. However, she had been cautious. None of the plotters were personally known to her. They needed someone whom she knew and trusted.

Enter Babington. In 1579 he had been a page to the Earl of Shrewsbury who was then Mary's keeper. She'd been fond of the boy and five years later he'd been entrusted to deliver several packets of letters directly to the hand of the Scottish Queen. Though he'd dropped out of the dangerous game to take up a gentleman's life in London, his views were well known among her sympathizers.

So the question put to Babington that night was this: will you join with us? Will you help the good Lady?

His response delighted the spies. How could this treason succeed, he whispered, if Elizabeth remained alive? She was popular among her misguided subjects. Wouldn't she be able to rally her armies and effectively counter the invaders? Wouldn't the plot go better if she were brought to, as he put it, a tragical end?

The others assured him that one of their number, a John Savage, was planning to take care of just that and in a giddy response Babington sealed his fate by clinking his mug around the table. Marlowe, who was fresh game and unknown to the likes of Walsingham, would be his go-between. The two young men smiled at each other like fine co-conspirators and there followed another clinking of drinking vessels.

There were sounds from inside the house. Babington started to rise in alarm but it was only Mrs Bull returning from her shopping. She stuck her head out the window and asked if she should bring out a tray of food.

They supped and drank until the shadow of the mulberry tree grew long and dark. Marlowe had news to report which he told Babington had been passed directly to Poley from the French Ambassador to England, Guillaume de l'Aubespine. Invasion plans were taking shape. French, Spanish and Italian armies were committed to the holy task. There were strong indications that English Catholics would also rise to arms at the first sight of foreign troops carrying the Papal colors. What was required was the final assent of Queen Mary, to be obtained by Babington.

Marlowe withdrew the implements of his trade from the portable writing case at his feet. He shaved a quill with his best knife, opened the lid of his ink pot and amused Babington no end by blotting the beer from the table with his rump before placing the case upon the dry spot and laying a few sheets of parchment on its leather pad. 'Would you care to dictate?' Marlowe asked. 'I am a most excellent scribe.'

'You, Kit, are the author. We have well discussed what must be transmitted. Perhaps you can compose.'

Marlowe agreed, saying he would refrain from flowery prose in favor of plain language. As he scratched the parchment he read aloud:

First, assuring of invasion. Sufficient strength in the invader. Ports to arrive at appointed, with a strong party at every place to join with them and warrant their landing. The deliverance of Your Majesty. The dispatch of the usurping Competitor. For the effectuating of all which it may please Your Excellency to rely upon my service.

Now forasmuch as delay is extreme dangerous, it may please Your Most Excellent Majesty by your wisdom to direct us, and by Your Princely Authority to enable such as may advance the affair; foreseeing that, where is not any of the nobility at liberty assured to Your Majesty in this desperate service and seeing it is very necessary that some there be to become heads to lead the multitude, ever disposed by nature in this land to follow nobility, considering withal it doth not only make the commons and gentry to follow without contradiction or contention but also doth add great courage to the leaders.

Myself with ten gentlemen and an hundred of our followers will undertake the delivery of Your Royal Person from the hands of your enemies.

For the dispatch of the usurper, from the

obedience of whom we are by the excommunication of her made free, there be six noble gentlemen, all my private friends, who for the zeal they bear to the Catholic cause and Your Majesty's service will undertake that tragical execution.

'Are you well satisfied with this concoction?' Marlowe asked when he was done.

Babington's throat seemed raspy with anxiety. 'It seems to properly convey our knowledge of the affair and our requests for the Queen's blessings.'

'Then I will place it into a cipher forthwith. While I undertake the task you might ask the Widow Bull to bring us more beer. I will drink only for thirst. The process of substituting letters for numbers and words for symbols is ever taxing and my head must remain as clear as Narcissus's reflecting pool.'

Babington shuffled off with the foreboding of a man heading to the gallows. When he returned with a full jug Marlowe said, 'I will make as much haste as I am able. Poley will need to get this letter to the brewer in Chiswick tonight for I believe tomorrow is the day the next keg goes to Mary. Then we need only await the reply of the dear lady.'

Babington drank two tankards in quick succession. He had no such desire to keep a clear head.

The Palace of Whitehall was a city unto itself. It surpassed the Vatican and Versailles in sheer size and pomp and it was no small task to navigate among

1,500 rooms. To find one's destination required prior knowledge or the good graces of a friendly gentleman or lady to take you by the hand and lead you through the labyrinth of offices and private residences.

By now Marlowe well knew his way around the palace and eagerly presented himself at Walsingham's privy chamber, his pulse racing, his face triumphant. Walsingham's private secretary greeted him cordially and announced his arrival.

Walsingham was in conference with Robert Poley, severe as always with a sun-beaten face and his greasy black hair pulled into a knot. In this state one would take him for a brigand or a soldier, not a gentleman who had matriculated from Cambridge.

The first words Marlowe spoke to them were 'I have it!'

Walsingham looked down his narrow nose. 'Let me see.'

Marlowe opened his writing case and proudly slid the parchments across the desk. Walsingham plucked them up like a hawk swooping on a vole. While he pored over them, Marlowe stood, pinching white hairs from one of Mrs Bull's cats off his doublet.

'This is good, very good,' Walsingham said. 'I'll have the cipher sent to the brewer immediately. Mary possesses the new code?'

'She has it,' Poley said. 'It was in her last keg. She will safely believe that no others could have deciphered it.'

'May she answer soon and reply forcefully,'

Walsingham cried. 'Once we've intercepted her letter we'll have her fucking Catholic head, by the stars!'

'I'd like to be there when it happens,' Marlowe said, imagining the bloody denouement.

'I'll see to it that you are. And you'll be there to see Babington with his insides out, howling to his God. And the other plotters too. Then the serious game will begin. The Pope's lot will want their revenge for Mary's downfall. You know what that will mean?'

'A war, I should think,' Marlowe said.

'Not one war, many. Europe ablaze, and in due course the world. And ourselves as the only clear winners. Taking pleasure in the growing piles of Catholic corpses. Seizing land and commerce from all parties. Swelling our coffers.'

Marlowe nodded, still standing.

'Sit,' Walsingham said. 'Have some wine. You've done well. You always do well. Whatever task we've given him, be it in Rheims or London, Paris or Cambridge, he's handled it with dispatch, wouldn't you say, Poley?'

Poley stiffly raised his glass. 'Yes, he's quite the marvel.'

'Thank you, my lord,' Marlowe said. 'I seek only your pleasure and the furtherance of our cause. But to continue to do so I will need a letter from the Privy Council to the Master's of the University excusing my absences. They aim to deny me my Masters for they believe that I go to France to mingle with and encourage the Papists.'

'That's because you are a convincing actor,' Walsingham said. 'Poley, give him the letter we've prepared.'

Marlowe read it in gratitude. It was perfect. Short and authoritative, leaving no doubt that Marlowe had been serving abroad in the service of Her Majesty. 'That will do nicely.'

Walsingham took back the document and began to heat some wax to affix the Privy Council seal. While he was fussing with the wax and candle he said, 'Let me ask you something, Marlowe. I am most curious to know why you seek to engage in the frivolous business of writing plays. I hear the Admiral's Men will perform one of your works before long. How does this most effectively further our cause? I can set a brilliant mind such as yours to a hundred tasks that will credit the Lemures. How can this be a higher priority?'

Marlowe poured himself a goblet of the Secretary's wine and tasted it. It was excellent, far better than his own usual swill. 'Have you ever been to the theater, my lord?'

Walsingham nodded disdainfully. 'I do so only because the Queen is keen on such things and oft requires her Privy Council to attend her. What about you, Poley? Are you a theater man?'

Poley snorted. 'I'd rather spend my evenings with a whore.'

'Yes, I've heard of the trail of destruction you leave when you go a-whoring.'

'I can't very well leave them alive once they've seen my arse.'

'Hardly,' Walsingham chuckled.

Marlowe leaned forward, ignoring Poley. 'So, my lord, you've seen then the effects that plays have on the audience. How they stir emotions like a cooking ladle stirs stew. How they evoke all manner of passions – mirth, rage, ardor, fear – and make those in attendance think as one. I will use my plays, my lord, to stir discord, to start fires in men's hearts, to set Protestants against our great enemy, the Catholics. With my plays I can make mischief on a grand scale. And I am good at it. No, *more* than good.'

Walsingham walked slowly around his desk and sat beside Marlowe. He took some wine and began to laugh. 'I cannot disagree with your ideas, Marlowe, or the confident state of your mind. It is not our usual way but there was one of us, a very great one, a long time ago, who fancied himself an artist. Do you know of whom I speak?'

'Was it Nero?'

'Yes, indeed. He was, it is said, one of the great performers of his age. But you know what happened to him? He went mad. All his gains came to dust. You won't go mad, will you, Marlowe?'

'I would hope to remain sane.'

'That's good. If you were not to do so, I might have dark words to impart to Mister Poley.'

Summer passed and then the autumn. The new year came and, with it, frost on the fields and ice on the ponds. And in February, with the winter winds howling across Northamptonshire, Marlowe arrived by coach at Fotheringay Castle.

The stabbing air couldn't chill his hot excitement. These had been heady months. From the day he'd drafted Babington's letter in Mrs Bull's green garden to this moment when the massive doors of Fotheringay were cast open for him, he'd felt as though he was living his destiny. His bloodlines and his intellect had always given him a sense of mightiness but the actual wielding of real power was truly intoxicating.

After Walsingham intercepted Mary's reply to Babington he quickly rolled up the plotters. Marlowe was there at St Giles in the Fields on the late-September day when Babington's confused stare found him in the crowd moments before the unfortunate young man was hoisted by the neck onto the scaffold and then strapped to a table, very much alive. His executioner used a none-too-sharp knife to slice open Babington's flat belly. The brute in his bloody butcher's smock slowly roasted Babington's entrails and his severed penis as his screams finally faded to silence and his eyes went mercifully dull. Some of the crowd that day were sickened by the ordeal. But not Marlowe.

The trial of Mary followed and though it was conducted with all the proper formalities that great matters of state required, the outcome was never in doubt. The hour of her execution inside the Great Hall of Fotheringay had come, the same chamber where her trial had been held.

Marlowe, for obvious reasons a keen student of theater, marveled at this particular stage. A black-draped platform, five feet high, twelve feet wide, had been erected beside a log fire which blazed in the huge fireplace. Mary stood between two soldiers, her ladies weeping behind her. The hooded executioner stood, hands clasped across his white apron, his ax standing against the scaffold rail.

As Mary prayed in Latin and wept, Marlowe pushed his way through the crowd to be near the stage. When the time came for her to disrobe, she managed to say, 'Never before have I had such grooms to make me ready nor ever have I put off my clothes for such a company.'

The audience gasped at her petticoats: blood-red satin, the colors of her Church, the colors of martyrdom.

Marlowe held his breath as the executioner raised his ax high over his head and brought it down with all his might.

Nonetheless, the blow was clumsy. It missed its mark, hit the knot of Mary's blindfold and glanced off, cutting deeply into the back of her skull. The Scottish Queen made a small squeaking noise but stayed upon the block, still. The second blow found a better mark and the blood gushed as it should, but even that blow failed to completely sever head from body. The executioner was forced into a crouch, whereupon he used his ax like a knife to cut through the last bits of gristle.

He grasped her head by its pinned cap, rose and held it high. But as he shouted his practiced line – 'God save the Queen!' – her head fell from his grip and he was left holding the cap and an auburn wig.

It had been known only to herself and her ladies but Mary had gone almost completely bald. Her bloody head rolled off the scaffold and landed at Marlowe's feet.

He watched her mouth open and close as if she were trying to kiss his boot, and with each deathly movement he felt his tail twitching with life.

I am a Lemures, and I have helped kill the Catholic Queen.

EIGHTEEN

Michelangelo's Sistine Chapel was not created for hordes of tourists craning their necks and strobing the chamber with their digital flashes.

It was created for this.

Sealed and empty, it was grandly silent and expectant, evenly and naturally lit from the high windows which lined the chapel from their position just below the painted ceiling.

Rows of brown-velvet-topped tables were carefully laid out on either side of the chapel, facing each other, each table with a simple white card bearing a cardinal's name.

There was a sound of an ancient key in an ancient lock and a heavy door groaned open. Then a sound of sniffing and claws scratching on the mosaic floor.

The Alsatian dog strained at its leash, its ears erect and eager, its tail wagging with purpose. Its handler from the security contractor Gruppo BRM let it do its job. It went straight for the nearest table, sniffed at the floor-length velvet drape and poked its large black and brown head underneath.

The dog resurfaced, its tail in the same state of readiness. It strained for the next table down the line.

Hackel motioned to his man, Glauser, who seemed overjoyed that he'd been given a plain-clothes assignment for the Conclave, a black suit cut with enough room to conceal a modified Heckler & Koch submachine gun. 'Bring in the electronics team to start sweeping behind the dog.'

Glauser nodded and went to fetch the bug sweepers.

When they were done with the chapel, the security detail proceeded en masse to the small adjoining rooms including the Room of Tears – where the new Pope would briefly contemplate his fate alone – the Vestments Room and on down to the basement rooms where they completed the sweep.

In the courtyard behind the chapel, Hackel watched the Gruppo BRM people packing up their gear and loading the dog into a van. Glauser approached him and said, 'From this point on, I'll double the guard and maintain the highest level of sterility.'

Hackel pointed a finger at him and growled, 'You make sure of that.'

Elisabetta had the apartment to herself. She'd returned there after mass at Santa Maria in Trastevere and the day stretched out oddly in front of her. She wasn't at all used to unstructured time but she wasn't going to turn on the television, was she?

First she spent an hour on her father's computer

researching Lumbubashi and the Republic of Congo. Such a poor country, she thought. So many needs. But despite the poverty, the children on the Order's website seemed so cheerful and fresh-faced. That, at least, buoyed her spirits.

She sighed and rose. The light streaming through the windows accentuated the dust on the furniture. Unlike her father's cleaning lady, she could move his books and papers with impunity and dust and polish under surfaces that hadn't been tended for years.

Elisabetta went to her bedroom, slipped off her shoes and then her robes. The drawers of her old dresser were swollen with humidity and it took several determined tugs to open them. She hadn't looked at her clothes in years and the sight of her old jeans and sweaters brought back a torrent of memories. She reached for a faded pair of Levis she'd bought on a school trip to New York and her fingertips brushed something underneath them.

It was a velvet box.

She sat back on her bed, her chest shuddering, trying to suppress tears. The box was on her bare knees. She opened the lid. The sunlight caught Marco's pendant and bounced wildly off its faceted surface. It was as pretty and sparkly as the day she'd first put it on.

It was a hot night. Elisabetta's window was wide open but the air was hardly moving.

Marco put his forefinger onto the heart-shaped pendant, pressing it lightly against the top of her breast.

Her skin was glistening and she was breathing heavily. They were bathed in candlelight.

'Do you still like it?' he asked.

'Of course I do. Don't you notice I never take it off?'

'I have noticed. Even when you make love.'

'With the other boys, I take it off,' she said, poking him in the ribs.

He pouted. 'Ah, very nice.'

Elisabetta kissed his cheek, then ran her tongue playfully over Marco's stubble. He tasted salty. 'Don't worry. You're the only one.'

He sat up beside her in the bed, pulled his knees against his chest and suddenly said. 'We're going to get married, aren't we?'

She sat up too and looked at him quizzically. 'That's not a proposal, is it?'

Marco shrugged. 'It's just a question. I mean, I think I know the answer, I just want to make sure you know it too.'

He was like a man-child that night. So big and potent, but at the same time so vulnerable and insecure. 'Who else would I marry?' Elisabetta placed her palm on his naked back and moved it slowly down over his spine until she got to the hollow at the small of his back. It was smooth and strong and, for a reason she didn't understand, was her favorite spot on his body.

Elisabetta put the velvet box back into the drawer, as carefully as if she were handling a saint's relic. She pulled on the old Levis – which still fit – and then a musty sweatshirt.

As she cleaned the apartment, she tried not to think about Marco. She had always been good at blotting out thoughts of him but today the only thing with any chance of accomplishing that was Africa.

The news from Sister Marilena had shaken her deeply. She'd spent the night in denial, suppressing a sense of indignation, even anger. Who was playing with her life, pulling strings as if she were a marionette? Why was she being ripped from her convent and her students, indeed from the very membrane of her life?

But as she'd prayed at Mass that morning her attitude had begun to shift and her mood had lightened. How arrogant and self-important of her to question her fate! Not only was she in God's hands but it dawned on her that the Congo was His gift. It was a chance, Elisabetta realized, to shed the heavy load she'd been forced to carry. She could leave behind the skeletons and the men with tails and their dark little tattoos and get back to her true calling, the service of God and the education of His children. The convent school in Lumbubashi was far away and pure and good and she would be restored there. Of course she would miss her family and her community of Sisters but her sacrifice was nothing compared to the sacrifice that Christ had made. Christ's love would sustain her in a foreign land and the happy faces of the little children called to her from the pages of Lumbubashi's website.

The sitting room, kitchen, dining room, hall and guest lavatory were gleaming and smelled of fresh cleaning products. She'd do the bedrooms next, starting with her own and doing her father's last. Elisabetta pushed the vacuum cleaner into her bedroom, plugged it in and began to run it over the carpet when the *Faustus* book and Bruno Ottinger's envelope caught her eye. She turned off the machine and sat at her desk, rereading the inscription from this mysterious K to Ottinger.

She sighed at her weakness. She couldn't let go.

I'm not leaving for six days, she thought. What would it matter if I spent some of my time before I got on the plane doing more than cleaning?

Armed with a cup of coffee and a phone number from the University of Ulm web page, Elisabetta sat in her father's kitchen cradling a telephone under her chin. She talked her way past an imperious secretary and was soon on the line with the Dean of the Faculty of Engineering Sciences, Daniel Friedrich.

Dean Friedrich listened quietly to Elisabetta's request for information about Bruno Ottinger but as soon as she spoke she knew he couldn't be helpful. He was relatively new at the University and although he had a vague knowledge that Ottinger had been in the department years earlier, he had no personal knowledge of the man. He also sounded as if he had more important things to attend to.

'Are there any older faculty members who might remember him?' she asked.

'Maybe Hermann Straub,' the Dean said irritably. 'He's been here forever.'

'Might I speak with him?'

'Tell you what,' Friedrich snapped. 'Call back and leave your number with my secretary. She'll see if Straub wants to contact you. That's the best I can do.'

Elisabetta had already pulled Straub's office number from the website and she rang it the instant the line went dead. An older-sounding man answered formally in German but switched to serviceable English when she asked if he spoke English or Italian.

Straub was instantly charming and, she imagined from his syrupy tone, something of an aging ladies' man. She didn't risk putting him off by mentioning she was a nun.

'Yes,' he answered with surprise. 'I knew Ottinger quite well. We were colleagues for many years. He died some years ago, you know.'

'Yes, I know. Perhaps you can help me, then. I came into possession of one of his treasured possessions – an old book – through a mutual acquaintance. It made me curious. I wanted to try to find out something about him.'

'Well, I have to say that Ottinger wasn't the easiest man in the world. I got along with him fairly well, but I was in the minority. He was quite hard, quite tough. Most students didn't like him and his relations with other faculty members were strained. Some of my colleagues refused to speak with him for years. But he was a very brilliant man and an excellent mechanical engineer and I appreciated his work. And *he* appreciated *my* work, so that was the basis, I think, for an acceptable departmental relationship.'

'What did you know of his life outside the University?'

'Very little, really. He was a private man and I respected that. To my knowledge he lived alone and had no family. He acted like an old bachelor. His collars were frayed, his sweaters had holes – that sort of thing.'

'You knew nothing about his non-academic interests?'

'I only know that his politics were a little on the extreme side. We didn't have big political conversations or anything like that, but he often made small comments that showed which direction he tilted.'

'And that was?'

'To the right. To the *far* right, I'd say. Our University is quite liberal and he was always muttering about socialist this and communist that. I think he also had some biases against immigrants. The students we had from Turkey and such places, well, they knew Ottinger's reputation and they stayed away from his courses.'

'Did he belong to any political party?' Elisabetta asked.

'That, I wouldn't know.'

'Did he ever mention an interest in literature?'

'I don't recall.'

'Did he ever talk of Christopher Marlowe or the *Faustus* play?'

'To me? I'm certain he didn't.'

'Did he ever bring up someone he called "K"?'

'Again, not that I recall. These are very odd questions, young lady.'

Elisabetta laughed. 'Yes, I suppose they are. But I'm saving the oddest for last. Are you aware of any anatomical abnormalities that he might have had?'

'I don't know what you could possibly mean.'

She took a breath. Why hide it? 'Bruno Ottinger had a tail. Was that something you knew?'

There was a longish pause. 'A tail, you say! How marvelous! Of all the characters I've known in my life, Ottinger, that old devil, would certainly be the one man to have a tail!'

Once Elisabetta had pulled back the heavy curtains and let the light pour in she discovered that her father's bedroom wasn't the disaster she had expected. True, his bed was unmade and books and clothes were strewn everywhere but there wasn't much dust and the en suite bathroom was acceptable. The cleaner, it appeared, had periodic access to his inner sanctum.

She stripped the bed, gathered the towels and dirty clothes and began to assemble a load of laundry.

She left the second bed untouched. The bedspread was perfectly draped, the decorative pillows in precise rows of descending size. It seemed as though it was protected by some force field – the only surface unencumbered by her father's things.

Her mother's bed.

Returning to the bedroom, hands on hips, Elisabetta

surveyed the untidiness. She reckoned there'd be hell to pay for organizing his books and papers but she was determined to take a stab at it. Besides, she could do it with more care than anyone else: Goldbach monographs in one place, Goldbach notebooks and scraps of paper in another. Lecture notes here. Detective novels there.

One bookcase was neat as a pin, the one next to her mother's bed. Flavia Celestino's books, most of them on medieval history, remained in the same exact order as on the day she died. Elisabetta reached for one, *Elizabeth and Pius V – The Excommunication of a Queen*, and sat on the bed. The dust jacket was bright and clean, a pristine copy of a 26-year-old book. She opened it to the inside back flap and gazed at the author's photo.

It was like looking into a mirror.

Elisabetta had forgotten how much she looked like her mother; the photo had been taken when Flavia was about her own age. The same high forehead, the same cheekbones, the same lips. Even though she'd been a young girl when the book came out, she remembered the soirée her parents threw and how proud and radiant her mother had been over its publication. Her academic career at the History Department at La Sapienza was launched. Who could have known she'd be dead within a year?

Elisabetta had never read the book. She had avoided doing so in the same way that one avoids dwelling on the memory of a painful love affair. But at that moment she resolved to take a copy to Africa. She'd start reading on the flight. It would be a long-neglected conversation. Absently, she thumbed through the pages and dipped into a paragraph or two. There was a light turn of phrase evident in the style. Flavia, it seemed, was a good writer and that pleased her.

An envelope dropped onto her lap – a bookmark, she supposed. She turned it over and was surprised to see the Vatican seal. The envelope was unaddressed, unused, never sealed. There was a card inside. With a curious anticipation she pulled it out and instantly froze.

There it was!

She *had* seen it before. She remembered.

The bedroom door loomed large and scary.

'Go in,' her father said. 'It's okay. She wants to see you.'

Elisabetta's feet seemed to be stuck.

'Go on!'

The doorknob was at a child's eye level. She turned it and was assaulted with the unfamiliar smells of a sickroom. She crept toward her mother's bed.

A thin voice called to her. 'Elisabetta, come.'

Her mother was propped up on big pillows, covered by bedclothes. Her face was hollow, her skin dull. Every so often she seemed to be fighting off a wince so as not to scare her daughter with facial contortions.

'Are you sick, momma?'

'Yes, sweetheart. Momma's sick.'

'Why?'

'I don't know why. The doctors don't know either. I'm trying my hardest to get better.'

'Should I pray for you?'

'Yes, why not? Praying is always good. When in doubt, pray. Are you eating all your food?'

Elisabetta nodded.

'Your brother and sister too?'

'Yes.'

'And Papa?'

'He's just picking.'

'Oh, dear. That won't do. Elisabetta, you're only young but you're the oldest. I want you to promise me something. I want you always to take care of Micaela and little Zazo. And if you're able, try to take some care of Papa too. He gets distracted by his work and sometimes needs to be reminded of things.'

'Yes, Mama.'

'And don't forget to take care of yourself too. You're going to have your own life to lead. I want you to try always to be the happy little girl I love so much.'

Her mother had a spasm, strong enough that it couldn't be denied. She clutched involuntarily at her stomach and when she did a small pile of papers slid off her belly. A card slipped off the bed onto the floor. Elisabetta picked it up and looked at it.

'What's that?' Elisabetta asked.

Her mother snatched it from her fingers and tucked it in back among her papers. 'It's nothing. It's just a picture. Come closer. I want to kiss you.'

Elisabetta felt dry lips against her forehead.

'You're a good girl, sweetheart. You've got the best heart I know. But remember: not everyone in the world is good. You must never let your guard down against evil.'

Elisabetta held the card in her hand and sobbed. At that moment her mother's death felt as raw and fresh as the day it had happened. She desperately wanted to reach back and speak to her one more time, ask for an explanation, ask for help.

There was a sharp rapping coming from the front door, the sound of a single insistent knuckle against heavy wood. She tucked the card back in the book, dried her face with her palms and began to wonder how someone had got past the entrance without being buzzed through. Was it a neighbor?

She put her tearful eye against the peephole and pulled back with a start.

The pale, elongated face of Father Pascal Tremblay filled the fisheye lens and Elisabetta's first confused instinct was to run and hide underneath her mother's bed.

NINETEEN

Rome, AD 64

It was mid-July and many of the noble families of Rome had retreated from the scorching heat to the breezier climes of their villas on the western coast or their estates high in the piney hills. A million of the less fortunate were left behind. The shimmering air above the metropolis reeked of smoke from tens of thousands of cooking fires and a thin layer of black ash settled on roofs and cobbles like a sinister summer snow.

Everything was parched: men's throats, the sandy soil, the fissured timbers and rafters of the ancient tenements. Water, always important to Rome, was never more vital than during the rainless drought of that hot summer.

A thousand freedmen and slaves worked perpetually in the city's water gangs, keeping the aqueducts, reservoirs and kilometers of pipes in order. A hundred public buildings, five hundred public basins and bathhouses and dozens of ornamental fountains received running water around the clock but for weeks the loudest sound that the system produced had been grumbling.

Water wasn't flowing as it should; it was trickling. The basins were dangerously low, the bathhouses were raising their prices, the brewers were charging more for beer. The vigiles, the night-owls of the city, knew the hazard. Organized into seven cohorts of a thousand men each, they slept by day and by night they patrolled the impossibly narrow dark lanes of the vast capital, prowling for incipient house fires. Their only effective weapons were bronze and leather buckets which they passed from hand to hand in human chains from the nearest basin or, if close enough, the Tiber. But this season the water levels were too meager to do much good and the vigiles knew why. It was more than drought.

The puncturers were relentless and the water commissioner, a close relative of Prefect Tigellinus, was getting rich.

Before decamping for Antium a fortnight earlier, Nero had told Tigellinus, 'Have your brother-in-law bleed it dry,' and virtually overnight corrupt water bosses had their gangs of puncturers tap into the system with illegal pipes. Torrents of tax-free water rushed to Lemures privateers and the vigiles could do little more than bite their nails to the quick as they watched Rome turn to kindling. It had been twenty-eight years since the last major fire.

July was a festival month and the chariot-race season was in full swing. Nothing distracted the masses from the misery of the heat and humidity like a day of sport at the Circus Maximus. Up to 200,000 Romans crammed into the stands to root for one of their teams, the Blues, Reds, Greens or Whites, each controlled by a corporation. Quadrias – four-horse chariots – raced around the long narrow U-shaped track and if the drivers and animals survived the hairpin turns the prizes were great. Below the stands were several bustling floors of wine bars, hot-food shops, bakeries and plenty of prostitution dens.

The day was propitious in other ways, too. Balbilus had told Nero that it would be so after poring over his astrological charts. Sirius, the Dog Star, rose in the heavens that night, signaling the hottest days of the summer. But furthermore its path took it through the House of Death. That had sealed it. The time of destiny had come.

There was a full moon that night but because it was cloudy it shone little light on the thousands who were queuing at the Circus Maximus gates for a dawn admission to the grounds.

Deep in the bowels of the Circus's grandstands, Vibius, Balbilus's creature of the night, and another man crept through a dark passageway into a cheerfully lit shop. There a leather-aproned baker was sliding loaves into a roaring oven.

'We're not open,' the baker barked.

Vibius walked calmly toward him and ran a sword through his gut upwards to his heart. The baker fell hard and when his wife ran from the second room where the dough was curing the other man killed her likewise with one hard thrust.

A man screamed. Out of the corner of his eye Vibius saw the baker's son bursting from the curing room with rage in his heart and an iron bar in his hand. With a dull thud of crushed bone Vibius's colleague crumpled. Vibius wheeled and pounced on the strapping lad, sliced his neck hard and clean and watched him fall onto his mother's lap.

Cursing, Vibius stepped around the bodies and used the baker's pallet to scoop embers from deep inside the brick-lined oven. With a flick of his wrists he dumped a red-hot heap into a corner. Instantly the floorboards began to smoke and hiss and in mere moments a line of flame crept up the wall to the rafters.

Vibius returned to the dark corridor and hustled down the stairs, his job imperfectly done. Soon he was mingling with the crowd, waiting for the show to well and truly start.

One floor above the baker there was a lamp-oil shop, laden with heavy amphorae. The clay vessels burst in the heat and fed the fire so spectacularly that the northeastern corner of the Circus Maximus exploded in a fireball. With a collective gasp, the crowd pointed at the blaze and began to stampede. The flames leapt skyward and almost immediately the fire bells of the nearby vigilis station of the district known as Regio IX began to jangle.

A cohort of vigiles mobilized but their bucket brigades quickly exhausted the meager local water supply and all they could do was shout evacuation orders into the night. The circus was ringed with rickety tenements, some with illegally built upper stories so shoddily constructed that they practically leaned onto each other across narrow cobblestone lanes. The blaze ran quickly through the blocks of tenements, leaving behind collapsed buildings and charred bodies. Whipped by a strong seasonal wind the fire spread south into Regio XII and then to Regio XIII before jumping the Servian Walls which had once marked the southern boundary of Rome before urban sprawl had stretched the city limits.

The streets filled with frightened, powerless people as the inferno hurtled down some blocks and danced across roofs. One narrow winding street after another was consumed by flames, often with masses of men, women and children trapped by fallen masonry or walls of fire. And although there would be tales of men helping others to escape and beating back pockets of flames, there would also be reports of shadowy figures moving through the city, throwing burning brands into hitherto untouched buildings.

By morning light a pall of heavy smoke hung over many of the southern regions of Rome and the fire was advancing up the Aventine Hill toward wealthy homes and temples. Then the winds shifted ominously and started to drive the fire in the north to the southern slopes of the Palatine and Caelian Hills. The city was doomed.

From the highest balcony of his villa on the Via Appia, Balbilus looked north to the billowing clouds of smoke. Vibius joined him, sooty from his exertions, and was offered a goblet of wine to slake his thirst.

'It's too close for comfort,' Balbilus growled.

'The wind is turning southerly,' Vibius said.

'I can predict the movement of the heavens, but not the wind,' the swarthy astrologer said. 'I would rather not lose my house.'

'I think mine has already gone,' Vibius said without a trace of emotion.

'Your family can come here. All the Lemures families who are in peril can come. Put the word out.'

A Praetorian cavalry contingent arrived at Antium as the sun was setting. The city had a new port which Nero had built but the Praetorians trusted their horses more than boats. Nero had turned Antium into a protected enclave settled by Praetorian veterans and retired centurions. He had rebuilt the seaside palace of Augustus to his liking and included a raised columned complex that extended for two thousand meters along the seafront. For his amusement he had built numerous gardens, temples, pools and most importantly, a theater where he could practice his art.

When the cavalry arrived to inform him about the fire in Rome Tigellinus received the report impassively but refused to let the messenger, who was carrying a personal dispatch from the Prefect of Rome, see the Emperor. Nero was in the wings preparing to take the stage for an evening competition. Dressed in an unbelted, Greek-style tunic he mingled with his competitors, all local lads who knew with certainty that Nero would be the judges' favorite. When it was his turn he took to the stage of the half-moon theater and peered out at an audience of toadies – retired soldiers, senators in his entourage, local Antium magistrates and a cohort of his special troops, the German bodyguard. Though Antium was a good distance from Rome, there was a faint smell of ash in the air and the news of the fire was beginning to take hold. The audience whispered and fidgeted and if not for the royal performance they would have sought out the messengers for more information.

Nero lifted his lyre and began to sweetly sing a song, The Sack of Ilium, about the destruction of Troy by the Greeks during the Trojan War. He would win the competition, of course, but no one seemed pleased to be entertained about a great city being laid waste by fire.

In the slums of the Esquiline Hill stray embers settled onto roofs and balconies and were stamped out by vigilant citizens and slaves before they caught hold. Peter the Apostle was there on one of his pastoral missions as Bishop of Rome. He was a weary but persistent traveller, enduring the months-long mule-train journeys to Jerusalem and Rome from his home in Antioch in Greece where he also served as bishop. Rome had been a tough assignment. His disciples were converting as many slaves and freedmen as they could but the citizens were hostile to the Christian cult, as they called it. But Peter had a small flock and, like lambs, they needed the guidance of a shepherd's staff from time to time.

Cornelius the tanner had become a priest of the new church and his house was one of their common prayer and meeting points. Peter stood by one of the tenement's windows in a room packed with devotees. A glowing ember floated by and Peter watched it for a moment before turning back to the papyrus in his hand. He had recently written an epistle to his faithful followers and he wanted them to hear it come from his own lips. 'So, dear brothers and sisters, work hard to prove that you really are among those whom God has called and chosen. Do these things, and you will never fall away. Then God will give you a grand entrance into the eternal Kingdom of our Lord and Savior Jesus Christ. Therefore, I will always remind you about these things – even though you already know them and are standing firm in the truth that you have been taught. And it is only right that I should keep on reminding you as long as I live. For our Lord Jesus Christ has shown me that I must soon leave this earthly life, so I will work hard to make sure you always remember these things after I am gone. For we were not making up clever stories when we told you about the powerful coming of our Lord Jesus Christ. We saw His majestic splendor with our own eyes when He received honor and glory from God the Father. The voice from the majestic glory of God said to Him, 'This is my dearly loved Son, who brings me great joy.' We ourselves heard that voice from heaven when we were with Him on the holy mountain. Because of that experience, we have even greater confidence in the message proclaimed by the prophets. You must pay close attention to what they wrote, for their words are like a lamp shining in a dark place – until the Day dawns, and Christ the Morning Star shines in your hearts.'

When Peter was done, Cornelius drew him aside to a corner by the cooking stove. 'Fine words,' he said.

'They are from my heart,' Peter answered.

'You spoke of leaving your earthly life.'

Peter seemed resolute. Another ember blew past the window. 'It will happen soon. Rome is being consumed by the fires of hell and I fear Nero will be looking to place the blame.'

'They'll look to us, but some say it's the Lemures.'

'Superstitions, surely,' Peter said.

Cornelius whispered, 'I know a man who swears he saw a charred body in the rubble of the Circus Maximus. It had a tail.'

Peter arched an eyebrow. 'If true, then evil may indeed be among us.'

'You should leave Rome,' Cornelius insisted. 'Let's have you returned to Antioch.'

'No,' Peter said, 'I will stay. It was meant to be. Christ suffered for me and now it is my turn to suffer for Him. You know, Cornelius, what they don't understand is that killing us only makes us more powerful. Come, friend, let's try to help our brethren. And if there's evil about, let us confront it.'

*

Tigellinus held the messenger at bay until the morning. He knew Nero was in a revelatory mood and wouldn't have appreciated the interruption of matters of empire. Besides, Nero had known about the fire before it happened, hadn't he? Still, the Prefect of Rome's message had to be delivered and when the Emperor was gently awakened by his private secretary, Epaphroditus, an attentive Greek Lemures, he was informed that a contingent of Praetorians had arrived from Rome bearing important news.

After an hour of bathing and perfuming, Nero received the soldiers in his grand reception room, attended by Tigellinus, Epaphroditus, and his devoted assassin, Acinetus. The letter he was handed was stark. The Circus Maximus was destroyed. The southern regions of the city were ablaze. The fire was uncontrollable.

'And what am I to do?' Nero asked rhetorically. 'Am I to carry a bucket? Surely this is a matter for Prefect Sabinus to deal with. That's his job! My job is to sing tonight in competition. There is said to be a Thracian with an excellent voice who will be my rival. I cannot disappoint my audience.'

'Shall I deliver a written reply to Prefect Sabinus?' the Praetorian commander asked.

'Tigellinus can pen something if he likes,' Nero said. 'By the way, is there any danger to the Esquiline Hill?'

The soldier replied he didn't believe so and Nero dismissed the cohort with an imperial wave.

Nero called for some watered wine. 'It seems you've done a good job of it, Tigellinus.'

'Rome took many a day to build but it can be destroyed in a very few,' Tigellinus said with a smile.

'Remember,' Nero said irritably, 'I'm as interested in destruction as you, but I just completed the Domus Transitoria and I fancy living there until the Domus Aurea is built on reclaimed land.'

The Domus Transitoria was a long, colonnaded palace that ran from the Palatine all the way to the Gardens of Maecenas, occupying much of the Esquiline Hill in Regio III. But building the Domus Aurea was his ultimate goal, a palace so grand and audacious it would eclipse all buildings in Rome. He had personally approved the plans and drawings. It would sit on 200 acres of burnt-out land at the foot of the Palatine Hill. The entrance hall would be high enough to accommodate a 40-meter statue of himself, a true Colossus of Rome. This entrance hall, three stories high, which Nero dubbed the Millaria, would run for two kilometers along the Forum valley through the fire-ravaged Carinae and Suburba districts. There would be an enormous pool, a veritable sea in the middle of Rome which he would use for lavish pageants.

'I am confident that the land you need for the Domus Aurea is already consumed,' Tigellinus said. 'If the winds are favorable, the Domus Transitoria should be safe. I too am worried about my shops at the Basilica Aemilia.'

Nero was not inclined to offer sympathy. He had made Tigellinus the second-most powerful man in Rome and immensely wealthy.

'If you lose your precious Basilica you'll build a larger one with smaller shops and charge higher rents. You know how it works. We'll use Lemures marble quarries, cement and timber works for our new constructions. We'll give prime land to our allies. We'll get our personal levy on every transaction. We'll make a fortune on the back of all the suffering and death. How fine is that? By the way, are we spreading the word that the Christian Cult is behind this?'

'It's being done.'

Nero rose and stretched. 'It's a good day, Tigellinus. Leave me now. I'm going to rest my throat for the evening's competition.'

The fire raged on. Flames climbed the Palatine, Caelian and Aventine Hills and fierce winds drove them north toward the Esquiline Hill and the heart of Rome.

Later in the day a Praetorian messenger arrived with news which firmly caught the Emperor's attention. The Domus Transitoria was threatened. With that, Nero angrily sent back orders that everything had to be done to protect his properties and ordered preparations for his departure to Rome by sea the following morning.

Nero arrived in one of a flotilla of small boats that sailed up the Tiber under a filthy brown sky. As his boat drew closer to the city he marveled at the great clouds of smoke and the fierce balls of fire which rose majestically into the air. The usual dock areas in Regio XIII had been razed so the flotilla had to find a landing downstream beside the Campus Martius.

Accompanied by Tigellinus, Nero was taken by litter to meet with Sabinus, the Prefect of Rome, who gave him a sober summary: the city was at the mercy of the fire. It was beyond the control of man. They passed through the Esquiline Gate, then entered the smoldering Gardens of Maecenas which days earlier had been the loveliest spot in Rome. Nero climbed to the top of the hill and ascended the squat Tower of Maecenas for the ultimate view of his burning city. Across the valley the Palatine Hill and all the old imperial palaces of Augustus, Germanicus, Tiberius and Caligula were burning. The Forum Romanum was gone, the House of the Vestals, the Temple of Vesta, the Regia, the ancient home of the kings of Rome – all consumed. With a heavy sigh, Nero watched the flames licking at the Domus Transitoria. A firebreak constructed by Praetorian cohorts and imperial slaves had failed.

'I'm sorry your palace is burning,' Tigellinus said glumly.

Nero shrugged. 'It will all be for the good. Meanwhile, let's stay here and watch the fire. It possesses a certain beauty, does it not?'

On the fifth day of the fire Nero toured the city, acting like a proper emperor: directing the firebreaks, ordering temporary shelter for the refugees on the Campus Martius and calling for grain stores to be delivered from Ostia. Yet despite his public overtures, there were widespread rumors that he and his henchmen were behind the conflagration and there was growing resentment that he had taken so long to return to Rome.

When informed of the rumors, Nero's creative response was 'Fight fire with fire.' Soon every Praetorian and vigiles commander was ordered to pass the word to the citizens of Rome that they had evidence that Christian arsonists were to blame – their retribution for the Roman crucifixion of Christ. Before long, vigilantes were patrolling the city, hauling known Christians from any unburned dwellings and shops and killing them on the spot.

By the next morning the winds had died down and the fires had stopped spreading. But one piece of news sent Nero into fits of rage. While he had completely lost his Domus Transitoria and would have to make ready a temporary palace, he learned that Tigellinus's pride and joy, the Basilica Aemilia, had survived the inferno without so much as a scorch mark on its marble façade. Tigellinus was even said to be boasting of his good fortune.

Nero's underling had fared better than his emperor! So he sent word over to Balbilus's estate that some rough justice was in order. That evening a fire broke out in a fancy silk and linen shop on the lowest floor of Tigellinus's building.

It soon engulfed the entire complex – and so began the second phase of the great fire. It would spread up the Capitoline Mount and ravage the sacred temples that had escaped earlier destruction. The Temple of Jupiter the Stayer would be lost, the Temples of Luna and Hercules, the Theatre of Taurus. On the down-slope of the Capitoline Hill the fire would breach the Servian Walls and demolish large public buildings on the southern edge of the Campus Martius where hoards of refugees were huddling. Had it not been for an expanse of stone colonnades and a sudden drop in the wind, the fire would have burned through the refugee camp and killed thousands more. When it finally ended two days later only four of Rome's fourteen districts would have escaped destruction.

When word spread that the Basilica Aemilia was burning, the priest Cornelius was summoned because several members of his congregation had stores within the building and Christians were duty-bound to help their brethren. Peter the Apostle was by Cornelius's side when the messenger arrived and the two of them rushed to the scene with a contingent of Christian men.

Vibius had not been pleased by the order to torch the Basilica Aemilia in broad daylight but Balbilus had been unwilling to disobey a direct command from the Emperor. As Vibius emerged from a rear window just before a plume of fire burst into the rear alley, a shop-keeper saw him and gave chase but lost him in the winding side streets.

When Cornelius, Peter and their lot arrived, the complex was fully ablaze and there was little for them to do but join the swelling crowd and comfort distraught shop-owners.

Peter placed his arm around the shoulder of a sobbing wine merchant and whispered that Christ would look after the man and his family. The merchant suddenly stiffened and pointed. 'That's the man I saw who started the fire.'

Vibius had returned to watch his handy work from a vantage point six-deep in the crowd. At the sight of the merchant pointing at him he hurried to the rear of the throng.

In his youth in Bethesda Peter had been a fisherman; he and his brother Andrew had gotten into plenty of hard scrapes to protect their fishing grounds. Jesus had preached non-violence but Peter never shied away from an injustice. 'Let's give chase!' he shouted and the group of Christians moved as one.

The younger men kept close with the fleeing Vibius but the older ones stretched out, struggling to keep their nearest comrade within view. Peter and Cornelius took up the rear, trotting southwards as best they could through the crowded smoke-filled lanes.

When Peter and Cornelius reached the Porta Appia, Peter was obliged to stop and rest. 'We've lost sight of them,' Peter said ruefully. 'I'm sorry to be burdensome.'

'I hope I'm half as fleet when I'm your age,' Cornelius said.

Soon one of their group was running back toward them. 'We've got him trapped,' the man said breathlessly. 'He's nearby in a villa.'

Balbilus's villa had become a haven.

Nearly a hundred Lemures were gathered in Balbilus's

reception rooms, their own homes threatened or burned. Most of them were wealthy, the women and children spoiled, and the lack of their usual comforts had made for a surly competitiveness for basic necessities. Balbilus had good personal stores of grain and wine but he would need to ask Nero to send special provisions within a short while.

He was in his bedchamber on the top floor of the villa bitterly muttering at the ruckus that had erupted below when his servant Antonius knocked urgently at his door.

'What is it?' Balbilus asked the man irritably. 'What are my visitors complaining about now? Aren't they grateful they've a roof over their heads?'

'There's a mob,' Antonius said breathlessly. 'They've entered the gates.'

'What mob?'

The servant pointed out the window.

Balbilus slipped on his sandals and went onto the balcony. A crowd was in his garden, wielding torches, and when they saw the tall olive-skinned patrician peering down at them they began shouting.

'What is it you people want?' Balbilus called down.

One shouted back, 'We want the man who started the fire at the Basilica Aemilia! We know he's here!'

'I assure you, there's no one here who started any fires,' Balbilus bellowed back.

Another man yelled, 'Give him to us or we'll burn you out.'

'I am the Emperor's astrologer! Leave here at once or you'll have to answer to the Praetorians!'

Balbilus turned away.

'Go away, scum,' Antonius shouted down at them before closing the window.

'Who are they?' Balbilus asked him.

'I don't know, master.'

'Find out.'

Balbilus hurried down the stairs and found Vibius drinking wine in the crowded courtyard.

'You were followed,' Balbilus growled at him.

'So I hear,' he answered coolly. 'I told you we should have waited until nightfall.'

'Maybe so. Now what do we do?'

Vibius finished his drink, tossed the goblet into the reflecting pool and unsheathed his sword.

'What good will that do against a mob?' Balbilus asked.

'While they're chasing after me, take everyone down to the columbarium. It's your only hope. They may burn the villa but they'll leave as soon as their stomachs start growling. Get word to Nero. Go to Antium. You'll think of something. I'll kill as many of them as I can.'

There were more shouts from the garden and a torch flew through one of the reception room windows. A young Lemures quickly plucked it from the floor and doused it in the pool.

In the garden Peter and Cornelius had arrived. 'Cease your violence!' Peter shouted at the torch-thrower. 'Know you whether there are innocents inside?'

Vibius waved his sword and ran out a side door. Roaring and swearing fiercely at the assembled throng he fled toward the Via Appia. The younger Christian men were upon him like dogs on a hare.

A strong young Christian caught up with Vibius and tackled him from behind. The two men grappled fiercely on the ground for a few seconds. At first contact, Vibius had dropped his sword but he managed to get his hands around the young fellow's neck and pressed his thumbs hard against his windpipe. Gasping, the man pushed Vibius away with a foot to the chest. As they separated, a chain around the man's neck broke off in Vibius's hand.

Vibius cast it away and grabbed the nearby sword. Rising to one knee, he sliced the Christian's belly open in a deft move, spilling coils of guts. On his feet again, Vibius fled toward the Appian Way, the men in hot pursuit.

'Quickly!' Balbilus yelled at the Lemures. 'To the columbarium! Follow me!'

They streamed from the villa through his fruit grove and entered the rectangular mausoleum with its barrel-vaulted roof. Antonius held the trapdoor open until his master and all his guests had descended the narrow stairs. Then he pushed a small altar over the trapdoor to conceal it and ran toward the grove, hurdling over the man with spilled guts. Something he saw on the ground caused him to stop: a silver medallion attached to a broken silver chain. He picked it up, swore an oath and ran back to the columbarium.

Satisfied that the coast was still clear, Antonius slid the altar aside and banged on the trapdoor.

'Master, it is Antonius! I know who they are! Open quickly!'

Balbilus did so and looked up the gloomy shaft. Antonius dropped the medallion into his hands, closed the trapdoor and once again concealed it with the altar. In the grove he stopped under a tree, sat down and without a second's hesitation defiantly slit his own throat.

By the light of a smoky oil lamp Balbilus examined the pendant.

The chi-rho monogram.

It was the Christians!

Damn them to the heavens! May Nero slay every Christian man, woman and child. May they be cursed for eternity!

A hundred Lemures crammed into the columbarium, fighting for every centimeter of floor space.

Balbilus stood under his fresco of astrological signs and demanded quiet. A small child cried. He threatened to kill her if someone didn't shut her up.

'Hear me,' he hissed. 'We need only to survive the night. In the morning we'll find sanctuary elsewhere. We're stronger than they are. We're better than they are.'

Above ground one of the Christians had seen Antonius running away from the mausoleum. He found him still twitching and warm, blood pouring from his neck. Soon the Christian man was running to find Cornelius and Peter. 'Come!' the man insisted. 'You must see this!'

When they stood over Antonius's corpse, the man pulled down the slave's breeches.

'Dear Lord!' Cornelius cried.

Peter steadied himself with an outstretched arm against the trunk of a tree.

Antonius had a tail.

When the young Christian men returned to the villa, their fists and sandals stained with Vibius's blood, they found Peter by the tree. One of them had a knife in one hand – and something else in the other. He showed it to the Apostle. It was a bloodstained pink length of tail.

'There is no denying it,' Peter said, shaken. 'They are not ghosts. They are real. What must we do when we find true evil – evil such as can only be the work of the Devil himself – in our midst?' he asked.

'We must purge it,' Cornelius said.

'There is no other answer,' Peter whispered. Then he raised his voice. 'In the name of Almighty Christ you may set the torch and send these devils back to Hell.'

Balbilus looked to the dark ceiling and heard the muffled shouts of the Christian marauders and the sound of their stamping feet.

The Lemures squatted in front of him, packed tight like salted fish in a barrel: the men stoic, the women angry, the children fidgety. Above their heads, the loculi in the walls were full of ash-filled urns and the skeletal remains of their recent ancestors. The pungent smell of rot filled their nostrils.

Suddenly the muffled shouting above their heads stopped and all grew quiet.

Balbilus strained and listened.

He heard the voice of Peter but couldn't make out the words.

Balbilus heard a faint whooshing sound and felt his ears pop as a roaring fire took hold above and sucked some of the air out of the chamber.

He felt his skin tingle as the temperature in the vault crept higher by the minute.

After a long while he heard a thunderous rumble when the vaulted roof crashed down onto the mausoleum floor.

More time passed and he saw the oil lamps sputter out one by one in the depleted air. When the last one died they were in complete darkness.

And in that darkness he heard the gasps and wheezes of a hundred men, women and children.

He was the strongest and the last to go. Sinking to his knees in the blackness and angrily clutching the chi-rho pendant so hard that it made his hand bleed, his final emotion was a shuddering rage so great and hot that it seemed to incinerate his brain.

It would be weeks before the soil of Rome was cool underfoot but Nero swiftly set about bringing some cheer to his beleaguered citizens.

His soldiers rounded up every Christian who had survived the fire and had been foolish enough not to flee. There were few public spaces left to celebrate their mortification properly so Nero invited Rome's refugees to the gardens of his only untouched estate, across the Tiber.

There, at his personal racetrack, as hungry citizens feasted on fresh bread, Nero made a grand entrance dressed as a charioteer astride a golden quadria. To a blare of trumpets Peter the Apostle was dragged onto the track. He'd been arrested along with the priest Cornelius and several followers at a Christian house near the Pincian Hill. When the soldiers arrived Peter had smiled at them as if he were welcoming old friends.

Pater was hauled onto a high wooden platform at the center of the racetrack for all to see and Tigellinus loudly proclaimed him to be the ringleader of the plot to destroy Rome. When he finished his speech he sat beside Nero in the royal stands and they watched together as the Praetorians began their work with hammer and spikes.

'We have it on good authority that this man Peter and his mob were the ones who trapped Balbilus and the others,' he told Nero.

'My hate for them was already great,' Nero said through clenched teeth. 'Now it is a thousand times greater. They killed my great astrologer and have taken from us the cream of the Lemures. Members of their Church will forever be our foremost enemies. Kill them. Crush them. Damn them to eternity.'

'What shall we do with Balbilus?' Tigellinus asked.

'He is at rest in his own columbarium. Let him lie there in peace with the others.'

Peter was laid out on a wooden cross not so different from the one that Pontius Pilate had used to crucify Jesus. Iron spikes were driven through his palms and ankles but whereas Jesus had been suspended in the usual manner, Nero bestowed upon Peter the further indignity of being nailed upside down.

The gentle old man died slowly and painfully in the afternoon heat, proclaiming to the end – too softly for anyone to hear – his love for God, his love for his savior and friend Jesus Christ, and his absolute belief that good had vanquished at least some of the evil in the world.

For the crowd's immeasurable pleasure, as Peter's life was ebbing away, two hundred Christian men and women were dragged into the stadium, stripped naked, flogged and tied to stakes. Ravenous dogs, mad at the scent of blood, were brought in to finish them off.

And that night and for nights on end Nero's gardens were the scene of a ghastly display: Christians whom Nero had dipped in animal fat and turned into human torches to illuminate the husk of a city that had once been the great Rome.

TWENTY

Elisabetta stood in the hallway, trying to decide what to do. If she remained quiet perhaps the young priest would leave of his own accord.

'Sister Elisabetta,' Tremblay called through the door, his Italian laced with a strong French intonation. 'Please, I know you're there. I must talk to you.'

She answered hurriedly, trying to think fast. 'My brother's in the Vatican Gendarmerie. He told me not to speak to anyone. He'll be here any second.'

'I know who your brother is. Please, you don't have to be afraid of me. We're on the same side.'

'And what side is that?' she called out.

'The side of good.'

Against all her instincts Elisabetta let him in. Though she braced herself against some kind of physical attack he followed her quietly into the sitting room and took a chair. Tremblay was less imposing seated, his long praying-mantis legs crossed, his spindly arms folded on his lap. He had a slim leather file which he wedged between himself and the arm of the chair.

'I'm glad you weren't hurt,' he said.

'You heard about last night?' she asked, still standing.

He nodded.

She couldn't ignore the rules of hospitality. 'Would you like some tea or coffee?'

'No, thank you. I'd just like to talk.'

'Then please start with who you are.'

'Father Pascal Tremblay.'

'I know your name.'

'I work for the Vatican.'

'So I gather,' she said frostily.

'I'm sorry for my reticence. You see, the facts don't trip off my tongue easily. I've been trained to be discreet. No, more than discreet – secretive.'

'Trained by whom?'

'My superiors. Actually, my superior. I have only one.'

'And who is that?'

'I answer to Cardinal Diaz, Dean of the College of Cardinals. I whisper in his ear, he whispers in the Pope's ear.'

'What about?'

'Evil,' he said simply. 'I *will* have tea if you're still offering.'

Elisabetta left him, trying to compose herself while waiting for the kettle to boil. Though she briefly lost track of time the noise of the hissing spout brought her back. When she returned with two cups she saw that Tremblay hadn't moved an inch nor unfolded his limbs. She handed him his tea and stared too long at his exaggeratedly bony fingers.

'I have a condition,' he said suddenly.

'I apologize,' she said.

'It's all right. It's called Marfan Syndrome. It's a disorder of the connective tissue. It's why I look the way I do.'

'It's none of my business,' Elisabetta said, sitting.

'It's better for you to understand me.'

'Why?'

'It just is.'

When she crossed her own legs she realized she was wearing jeans. 'I'm sorry I'm not dressed properly. I was cleaning. You were speaking of being a whisperer. Is that on your business card?'

'I don't have a card,' Tremblay said after taking a sip. 'I don't have a title. I'm simply a Special Assistant to the Cardinal. My predecessors have been Special Assistants, no more, no less.'

'Your predecessors?'

'There's been an uninterrupted chain for centuries.'

'Whispering to Cardinals and Popes about evil.'

'Yes.'

Tremblay volunteered a brief personal history: how he'd been tagged at his seminary in Paris as more likely to succeed as an administrator than as a parish priest. Though he assumed they considered his appearance might be offputting to parishioners, he was told it was his aptitude and his degree in accountancy which had attracted the attention of the diocese. After taking his oaths he was assigned to the Archbishop of Paris's ecclesiastical office and rose quickly through the administrative ranks until he began having regular contacts with the Vatican on diocesan issues. On one visit to Rome, seven years earlier, he'd been summoned to an audience with an Italian bishop he didn't know in an unfamiliar wing of the Apostolic Palace. There was one other man present in the bishop's office, an elderly Italian Monsignor with a pronounced tremor in his hands.

You are being selected to come to Rome, Father Tremblay was told. You are to take over the duties of the Monsignor who is retiring.

And what are these duties?

Vigilance, he was told.

Against what? Against whom?

Lemures.

'What are Lemures?' Elisabetta asked.

'You saw one in the morgue,' Tremblay said.

Elisabetta shivered. He seemed to notice but didn't try to soothe her.

'And you saw their skeletons at St Callixtus.'

'I don't understand.'

'I think you do,' he said. 'Professor De Stefano told me how smart you are. He said you'd wondered if some kind of a sect might have persisted to the present.'

'You worked for him?'

'No, I told you who I worked for. I was assigned to the Pontifical Commission for Sacred Archeology after the skeletons were found. I was instructed to keep tabs on what you were turning up. What Professor

De Stefano told you was true enough – there was, there is, a lot of concern within the Vatican about St Callixtus, particularly because of the Conclave and the confusing and damaging publicity if the story leaked out. The few officials who are aware of the Lemures were particularly worried. But De Stefano knew not much more than you did. Enough to make him nervous, maybe. He didn't need to know more.'

'And now I do?'

'I need your help.'

'I don't see what I can do. I was dismissed.'

'Yes, I heard.'

'And I'm being sent to Africa.'

Tremblay appeared surprised at that. 'When?'

'A week from now.'

'I can try to get that reversed.'

'No, don't! I want to go.'

'Then we haven't much time. Lemures,' he said again, putting his cup down.

Lemures. The ghosts of the ancient Romans, the shades of the dead. Malevolent, restless, unwanted souls. Invaders of the home, they were said to come at night to do fearsome things.

Tremblay said there had been a public festival every May during which the Romans performed rites to exorcise these horrible entities from their homes. At midnight in every Roman household the head of the family, the paterfamilias, would throw black beans over his shoulder and say nine times: 'These I cast. With these I redeem me and mine.' The Lemures were

270

supposed to become distracted as they gathered up the beans. Suddenly the worshipper would spin around, throw clean spring water in their direction, then clang bronze plates together, demanding that the demons depart. And for a year they would, with luck, be obliged to do so.

The origin of the name Lemures was obscure. But the modern association was clear enough. Lemurs, the African primates with nocturnal habits, haunting stares, ghostly calls and long, thick tails. The Roman ghosts had been the inspiration for the name given to the animals by the eighteenth-century taxonomist Carl Linnaeus.

Tremblay uncrossed his legs and leaned forward. 'At St Callixtus we have a first-century group of men, women and children who possessed tails and died together, perhaps violently by fire. The early Romans feared them, thought they were ghosts. But, Elisabetta, they were *real*. They were there in ancient Rome. They were there throughout history. They're still here. Your man from Ulm was one of them. Aldo Vani was one of them. They stole the skeletons from St Callixtus, for what purpose I don't know. They killed Professor De Stefano. They tried to kill you. They are among us.'

'How do you know all this?'

'It's my job. The Vatican – or rather, a very small number of people within the Vatican – has known of the Lemures for centuries. The Church has quietly done what they can to counteract them, to defeat their evil at every possible turn. There have been successes but also many failures. They are difficult adversaries. I'm a tracker – more detective, unfortunately, than priest. I look for their signs, I follow their trails which are sometimes as vaporous as rumors. I travel, I read, I monitor the internet, intelligence reports, and even, like you, the medical journals.'

Elisabetta looked shocked.

'I confess I looked at your email box.'

'You went to my desk?'

'I'm sorry. In this day and age you should log off an email account when you leave the office.'

'Did you also call the newspaper from my desk phone?'

'No! Someone did, but it wasn't me.'

'I imagined it was.'

'Why?'

'You made me nervous.'

Tremblay laughed. 'I have that effect on people.'

'Who are they? What do they want?'

'That's like asking why is there evil in the world? I'm not the best theologian, Sister. My skills lie more towards organization and administration. I'm content to simply acknowledge that evil exists in many forms and the role of a compassionate God is to give us the strength to fight it and learn from it. The Lemures are quite amoral. They revel in attaining power, wealth, domination. Those seem to be their gods. And we, the Church, are their great enemy. Why this is so, I don't know – but it is most assuredly a fact. It reaches back for centuries, perhaps millennia to the Church's very beginnings. I like to think that we represent the good in the world and they represent evil. That we represent light and they represent darkness. Naturally opposing forces.'

'One of the corpses at St Callixtus had a chi-rho pendant in his hand,' Elisabetta said.

Tremblay arched an eyebrow, making his face appear even more elongated. 'Really? The Church was young at that time. Very young. So the battle *is* quite old, then. They enjoy killing us, harming our interests, setting others against us. Throughout the ages, at every anti-Catholic turn of history, it now seems that we may suspect unseen Lemures hands.'

'And what of their tails?'

'Ah, the tails. They are a phenotype.'

'I'm sorry?'

'A scientific term. The long-held view of the Vatican is that the tails are a physical embodiment of evil. From the decidedly modern field of genetics we know the genotype is said to control the phenotype.'

'Are you saying they have evil genes?'

'What I'm saying is that they are extreme psychopaths, an almost alien subset of humans, completely lacking the ability to feel guilt or remorse. They have shallow emotions. They engage in antisocial behaviour, often involving violence. They understand the difference between right and wrong – they just don't act like they do. There's an evolving field in neuroscience linking specific genetic abnormalities of brain neurotransmitters like serotonin and dopamine with antisocial or psychopathic states. But the most visible phenotype of the Lemures' genetic constitution is unquestionably their tails. The anomalous tail has always been associated with evil. You don't need to look any further than representations of the Devil since early times.'

'If what you're telling me is true, how could they have stayed hidden for so long?'

'Because they are exceedingly careful and probably because there aren't so many of them. They associate with their own kind. They couple and marry with their own kind. If they have to go into the army or some situation where others will see them, then we believe they're sent to one of their own surgeons to have their tails amputated. They get sick, they go to one of their own doctors. They die, they go to one of their own funeral homes. Dropping dead on the street before their own kind can get to the body, as happened to Bruno Ottinger – that is a very rare occurrence. And getting shot like Aldo Vani by your brother – that's even rarer.'

'What about the tattoos?'

'These have never been understood. I've personally scoured the Vatican to see if any of my predecessors had any credible theories, but there's nothing. I was hoping you might have come up with something.'

'No, I don't have an answer.'

'But you have clues. This message you found on the envelope in Germany – it's a living document. We've never seen this kind of intimate communication among them.'

'You know about it.'

'Professor De Stefano showed me a copy of the note. And I couldn't help but notice the Monad you drew on your whiteboard.'

'Monad?'

'You hadn't identified it?'

Elisabetta felt her chest fluttering. 'No, what is it?'

Tremblay pulled out his leather file, unzipped it and took out a page. 'Look at this.'

It sent a chill over Elisabetta's breastbone. 'The symbol,' she said quietly.

Tremblay nodded. 'It's from the frontispiece of a book published in London in 1564 by John Dee. He was an alchemist, an astronomer, a mathematician, a philosopher and the court astrologer to Queen Elizabeth I. We believe he was also a Lemures. The book, the *Monas Hieroglyphica*, the *Hieroglyphic Monad*, was an exhaustive text purporting to explain this glyph, this symbol of his own making which he claimed represented a mystical unity of all creation, a singular entity from which all material things on Earth derive. The glyph is constructed from four distinct symbols: the astrological signs for the moon, the sun, the cross, and the zodiac symbol for Aries, the ram, one of the fire signs. The text is hugely convoluted and technical but the gist, according to Dee, was that the sun and the moon of the Monad desire that the elements be separated by the application of fire.'

Seemingly in response to Elisabetta's look of confusion Tremblay added quickly, 'Don't worry about understanding it. I'm not sure any contemporary scholar really has a handle on the text. Apparently there was a secret oral tradition that properly explained the Monad but it's been lost to time. The important thing for us is that the Monad was adopted by the Lemures as one of their symbols, a quick and easy way for them to identify themselves, a shorthand, if you will, for recognition.'

'What makes you so sure? And what makes you think Dee was one of them?'

'There's a 450-year trail of breadcrumbs scattered throughout the Vatican. My predecessors have done most of the work. I've added a few documents here and there to the mix but we know that by the late sixteenth century secret correspondence between known Lemures began to adopt the Monad by way of signature. It clearly had some profound significance for them and we presume that John Dee was one of them. But no direct evidence has ever been found.'

Elisabetta looked at the frontispiece again. 'The Monad. It looks as though it has a tail, doesn't it?'

'Yes, it does.'

'I need to show *you* something.'

She left Tremblay behind with a quizzical expression on his long face and went to her father's room. She returned with her mother's book and handed Tremblay the Vatican envelope. When he pulled out the card he puckered his lips as if he'd sucked hard on a lemon.

'It was my mother's,' Elisabetta said. 'She died when I was eight. I thought I'd seen the symbol before and I had. At her deathbed.'

'A Vatican envelope,' Tremblay said. 'What was her connection?'

'None that I know of. She was an historian at La Sapienza.'

'This book? It's hers? Flavia Celestino?'

'Her first and only one. She died young.'

'Do you know if she ever did any work, any research at the Vatican?'

'I was a child. Perhaps I can ask my father.'

'Let me see the book.'

Tremblay turned to the acknowledgment section and scanned it. 'Here. She thanks the Vatican for giving her access to certain documents.'

Elisabetta sighed at her ignorance of her mother's life.

Tremblay stood suddenly and checked his watch. The band was too loose, as if nothing could properly fit a wrist so thin. 'What are you doing tomorrow morning?'

'I've no plans.'

'Good. You're coming with me to the Vatican Secret Archives. We need to find out why your mother had the Monad.'

TWENTY-ONE

Even though it was a full day before the Conclave and only six in the morning, St Peter's Square was buzzing with eager pilgrims and an assemblage of international journalists setting up their first shots of the day.

Zazo made a detour from his usual route from the Gendarmerie parking lot to the Tribunal Palace so he could pass through the square and check his men who had been on the night shift. Except for a drunken tourist who'd wandered through at two AM making a ruckus, all was reportedly peaceful.

At 6:30 there was a joint meeting of officers of the Gendarmerie and Swiss Guards. For the sake of harmony the venue of these meetings had alternated between the Tribunal Palace and the Garrison of the Guards. At the podium were Inspector General Loreti and his counterpart, Oberst Franz Sonnenberg. Standing behind them, at ease, were their vice-commandants, Sergio Russo for the Gendarmerie and Mathias Hackel for the Guards.

Zazo and Lorenzo sat together. A row behind them,

Major Glauser of the Guards deliberately bumped the back of Zazo's chair with his boot. 'It's time for the big game, Celestino. Are you guys going to be ready?' he said with his usual condescending tone.

Zazo glowered back and said nothing. 'I'm ready to kick his ass,' he whispered to Lorenzo.

'Did you get a look at his suit?' Lorenzo asked.

'It was probably half-price because of his half-size,' Zazo said.

Loreti tapped the microphone. 'Okay, gentlemen, let's begin. I welcome Oberst Sonnenberg and his men to our home for the final group briefing before the Conclave begins. You are all aware of our modus operandi: we leave nothing to chance. Nothing. Everything is planned to the minute and there will be no deviations. This morning we will review the order of events for tomorrow, Day One. After Day One, the final length of the Conclave is clearly out of our hands, but each day will have the same schedule until there is a new Pope. Then the post-Conclave program of events will begin and that too is planned to the minute, without any possible deviations. The security of the Cardinals, the new Pope, the Holy See, the employees and the world's visitors to the Vatican depend on our strict observance of the joint security plan. Everything must run as precisely as Oberst Sonnenberg's wristwatch.'

Amidst small guffaws at Loreti's quip, Mathias Hackel took the microphone. He was a head taller than the others and as broad as the podium. From his stern look and his tight lips it was clear that he had no intention of warming up the audience with a joke.

He pressed the remote control and called up the first PowerPoint slide. 'Here is the program for Day One,' he began. 'We will go over it now in detail. I will expect every officer to ensure that each of his men will have their precise assignments perfectly understood. The Swiss Guards will do their jobs. The Gendarmerie Corps will do their jobs. There will be faultless command and control. The entire world will be watching and we must be perfect.'

Zazo turned to his printed presentation and worked hard to concentrate. He knew the details by heart and Hackel's monotone only made him aware how early he'd woken that morning.

8:45 AM. Buses arrive to transport Cardinal Electors from the Domus Sanctae Marthae to the Basilica for the *Pro Eligendo Romano Pontifice*, the Mass for the Election of the Roman Pontiff.
9:15 AM. Beginning of Mass.
10:15 AM. Conclusion of Mass.
10:30 AM. Buses back to Guest House.
12:00 PM. Private lunch for Cardinals at Guest House.
3:00 PM. Buses arrive to transport Cardinal Electors from Guest House to the Hall of Blessings in the Basilica.
3:30 PM. Procession from Hall of Blessings to Sistine Chapel.

4:00 PM. Doors of Sistine Chapel locked. Conclave begins.

7:00 PM. First ballot slips burned in chimney of Sistine Chapel.

7:15 PM. Buses from Sistine Chapel to Guest House.

With Hackel's bloodless briefing done, Zazo and Lorenzo went for a quick coffee and headed to their office. They had only a few minutes before mustering their platoons but Zazo glanced at his inbox and clicked hopefully on an email from Interpol.

He was stunned that they had responded so quickly but when he began to read the message he understood.

Aldo Vani's fingerprints had lit up Interpol's computers like a Christmas tree.

Under the name Hugo Moreti – wanted in Switzerland for assault.

Under the name Luis Crea – wanted in Spain for rape.

Under the name Hans Beckmann – wanted in Germany for an explosives charge and murder.

Vani was quite the international criminal.

In the fax, Interpol asked for Vani's Italian police file and death certificate to enable them to close the pending cases, and by attachment they were providing, with compliments, the requested German telephone records of Bruno Ottinger from 2005–6. The only item that gave Zazo pause was a query at the end of the message as to why the Vatican Gendarmerie Corps was involved in the case.

Before grabbing his cap and running off to meet with his men, Zazo sent the phone records to his printer, doubtful whether he'd have time to do more than run them off and take them with him before the Conclave was over. He stuffed the printed sheets into his leather jacket.

There was a steady stream of Cardinals coming and going from the Domus to various appointments around Vatican City. Ordinarily they'd have been allowed to roam freely, accompanied only by aides, but security was tight and each one required at least one Gendarme to shadow him. Zazo was at the Domus after lunch, adjusting to an ever-shifting appointment schedule, when his mobile rang. It was Inspector Loreti's office. He needed to report immediately.

'I'm up to my eyeballs,' he told Loreti's assistant. 'This had better be important.'

Loreti saw him straight away; he didn't look happy. He asked Zazo to sit. He did, his hat in his lap.

'I got a call from Interpol,' Loreti said flatly.

'Look, Inspector . . .'

Loreti shut him up angrily. 'I didn't ask you to speak. Apparently you've been making inquiries on behalf of the Vatican about the man you shot. They wanted to know what business this was of our Corps. It's a good question. Tell me, Major, what business is this of the Gendarmerie Corps? Now you may speak.'

'My sister was almost killed,' Zazo exclaimed. 'She was a Vatican employee at the time, assigned to the

Pontifical Commission of Sacred Archeology. And besides, the Polizia don't have a clue. They're bungling the case.'

Loreti took a deep breath, puffed out his cheeks and let the air out slowly. Zazo looked like he pretty much knew what was going to come out of his mouth. 'I've heard some ridiculous excuses for inappropriate behavior in my day, but coming from one of my top officers this is one for the record books. Here are some facts: number one, the crime took place outside Vatican City and is therefore not in our jurisdiction. Number two, the Polizia did not request our assistance. Number three, you were a principal at the crime scene. You shot and killed the assailant. One does not investigate one's own involvement in a crime. And number four, in case you didn't know it, the Conclave begins tomorrow. This kind of distraction from your duties in unacceptable.'

Zazo nodded like a chastened schoolboy. 'I'm sorry, Inspector. This involves my sister. Perhaps you would have done the same thing if your sister was attacked this way. But I should at least have talked to you and gotten your permission.'

'I would have said no!'

'That would have been the end of it, I suppose. I accept your criticisms and I'll accept, of course, whatever sanctions you choose to impose.'

'Well, that's good. You're not going to like it, your comrades are not going to like it and I don't like it, but I have no choice. You'll be taken before a tribunal to answer for your actions and until then you're relieved of duty, effective immediately.'

'But Inspector! The Conclave! My men!'

'I'm going to give Lorenzo temporary command of your men. He's going to have to work double and thank you for it. I can't risk having a seriously distracted officer such as yourself responsible for the lives of the Cardinal Electors and the next Pope. You are dismissed, Major.'

Lorenzo found him sitting disconsolately at his desk, staring out the window.

'Christ, Zazo,' he said.

'I'm sorry. I screwed up.'

'I would have done the same thing if it were my sister. What are you going to do now?'

Zazo shrugged miserably. 'Go home? Go to a bar? Watch you do my job on television? Hell, Lorenzo, I don't know.'

Lorenzo patted him on the shoulder and walked him out.

Near the parking lot Zazo ran into Glauser who was looking particularly smug. 'Hey, Zazo, I heard what happened,' he called out. 'Next time I see you, if they ever let you back, you'll have to salute because we won't be the same rank.'

'Hey, Glauser,' Zazo replied. 'Go fuck yourself.'

A tall priest with ghostly skin accompanied by a pretty young nun entered the Tower through the Porta di Santa Anna. They were challenged instantly by two Swiss Guards.

285

Father Tremblay showed his identification card and when the Guards questioned Elisabetta he said, 'The Sister is with me.' The guards asked again and this time Tremblay said louder, 'I said, the Sister is with me!'

The guards let them pass.

'It's the Conclave,' Tremblay whispered to her. 'Everyone's on edge.'

They passed through an enormous pair of brass doors adorned with a bas-relief of Old Testament scenes.

They were in the Tower of the Winds.

'Welcome to the Secret Archives,' Tremblay said, leading Elisabetta up a narrow winding staircase.

She followed on his heels but had to pull up abruptly when he stopped partway up the staircase, breathing heavily and wheezing audibly.

'I'm sorry,' he said. 'It's my condition. I'm not very fit.' He kept talking, apparently giving himself a chance to catch his breath. 'The tower was built by Ottaviano Mascherino between 1578 and 1580 as an observatory. If we had more time I'd give you a tour. Higher up, the Hall of the Meridian is covered in frescoes depicting the four winds. There's a tiny hole high in one of the walls. At midday the sun shines through the hole and falls along a white marble meridian line set into the floor. On either side of the line are various astrological and astronomical symbols once used to try to calculate the effect of the wind upon the stars.'

'I'd very much like to see that one day,' Elisabetta said.

Tremblay was composing himself and breathing more easily now. 'In the seventeenth century, under the orders of Pope Paul V, the Secret Archives were separated from the Vatican Library and remained absolutely closed to outsiders until 1881, when Pope Leo XIII opened them to researchers. The Archive, you see, is the central repository for all of the acts promulgated by the Holy See: state papers, correspondence, papal account books, and many other documents that the church has accumulated over the centuries. Researchers have to apply for access with specific document requests. They can do a search in the Index Room and documents are brought to them by the staff. Officially, no one is allowed to simply browse.'

From the way he said that Elisabetta added, 'But *you* can, right?'

He started climbing again. 'Yes. I am allowed.' He stopped on the landing and opened a door. 'Come. The Index Room and the librarians are next to the Old Study Room.'

The Old Study Room had canary-yellow walls and a high vaulted ceiling. Life-size statues of saints were set into niches in the walls. Large windows overlooked the Vatican Gardens. There were row after row of white laminate desks with gooseneck reading lights and power plugs for computers. All the desks were empty.

'It's closed,' Tremblay said. 'Because of the Conclave.'

287

The Index Room, also devoid of people, was lined with card catalogs and computer terminals. Tremblay knocked on a door with the nameplate of the Head Librarian and a woman in her fifties wearing heavy make-up responded.

She greeted him warmly. 'Father Tremblay! How nice to see you.'

'Signorina Mattera,' he replied. 'I'm sorry to trouble you without notice. I'd like to introduce a colleague to you, Sister Elisabetta.'

The woman politely nodded to her. 'How can I help you, Father?'

'We need to find any material you might have on a woman named Flavia Celestino. She was an academic researcher who was given access to the Archive in the 1980s.'

'Well, I might be able to find her in the logs, but the information on researchers is usually very sparse.'

'Would there be a record of the documents she requested?' Tremblay asked.

'Possibly, but usually not.'

'Well, anything you can find would be helpful,' the priest said.

Tremblay and Elisabetta waited in the Old Study Room at a table with a view of the garden which was showing the first exuberance of spring greenery. The new Pope would have a lovely place for respite.

'May I ask you a question?' Tremblay said.

'Of course.'

'Why did you become a nun?'

Elisabetta smiled but countered with 'Why did you become a priest?'

'Me first, eh?' he laughed. 'Okay. For me it was easy. I was an altar boy. I was comfortable in the Church. In college I was awkward. I never fit in so well. Well, maybe I would have been fine in an office doing accountancy, but I was never going to have a social life. I mean, my condition, the way I look. Women were scared of me so celibacy wasn't the biggest sacrifice, I suppose.'

She pursed her lips. 'I'm wondering, Father, if you've asked other nuns why they'd entered the clergy?'

'No, never.'

'Why me?'

He hesitated then blurted it out. 'Because you're so beautiful. When a beautiful woman becomes a nun, I imagine the sacrifices are greater and the commitment to God is proportionately greater too.'

Elisabetta felt her cheeks flush. 'It's a complicated question. Was I running from something? Was I running toward something? My faith is deep and I think that's the important thing for me.'

'It's a good answer.'

The clipping of heels against the stone-tiled floor signaled the return of the librarian. She had an index card in her hand. 'It's most unusual, but it seems this researcher has her own file. I can't imagine why but here's the accession number. Do you want me to have it brought to you?'

Tremblay took the card and inspected it. 'No, I'll

find it myself.' He said to Elisabetta, 'We're going to the basement.'

Descending was easier for him and Tremblay was able to make it down several flights of stairs without stopping. The subterranean archives, excavated some thirty years earlier, was vast, stretching under the full length of the Vatican Museum. Unlike the Tower of the Winds with its breathtaking frescoes and dark wooden cabinets containing older, more precious material, the basement had the look of an industrial site. There were some eighty kilometers of file cases – metal, beige, utilitarian – laid out on concrete floors beneath a low concrete ceiling. The priest told her that insiders called it the Gallery of Metallic Shelves.

Tremblay looked at the card's file number and said, 'It's a good thing nuns wear sensible shoes.'

They walked for several minutes through the seemingly endless grid of shelving. Elisabetta felt a strange association. It was like being in some kind of latter-day catacombs. In the past bones were revered. Now it was paper.

'Many of these files,' Tremblay said, 'are more "secret" than the documents in the Tower of the Winds. Officially, there's the hundred-year rule that keeps most of the Vatican's correspondence and documents closed for one hundred years, to protect them from being released to the public during the lifetime of those concerned. From a practical standpoint, everything later than 1939 is strictly off-limits.'

'But not for you,' Elisabetta said.

'I have no restrictions.' He checked the numbering on the cases. 'I think we're close.'

They finally came to a halt in the middle of a row. Tremblay used his finger to pick out the numbers on each pale yellow file box.

'This one,' he said. 'Sometimes it's helpful to be tall.' He reached high above his head and wriggled a box free. 'It's a long way back to the Reading Room. Do you mind if we just look at it here?'

The box was almost empty; it contained only a dozen or so loose papers. Tremblay removed them, put the box at his feet and held the papers so that both of them could see.

The first page was a typed letter on University of Rome letterhead dated 12 June 1982.

Elisabetta's mother's signature was bold and confident, written with an italic-nibbed fountain pen. It brought tears to Elisabetta's eyes but she sniffed hard once and stifled her sobs.

'It's her letter asking for permission to use the Archives,' Elisabetta said, reading it quickly. 'It's on the subject of her book, Pope Pius's excommunication of Queen Elizabeth.'

Tremblay put the letter at the back of the stack.

There were other, similar letters, requesting readmittance to do further searches. One of the letters summarized the documents she had already reviewed: *Regnans in Excelsis*, the Papal Bull of 1570 excommunicating Elizabeth, Queen of England for heresy; a letter from Matthew Parker, Archbishop of

Canterbury to Pope Pius V (1571); a letter from Edmund Grindal, Archbishop of Canterbury to Pope Gregory XIII (1580); a Papal Bull of 1580, Pope Gregory XIII's Clarification of the *Regnans in Excelsis*; a letter from the Papal Nuncio in France to Pope Clement VIII informing him of the death of Elizabeth (1603).

Tremblay looked to see if Elisabetta had finished, then turned to the next page.

It was Flavia's cover letter dated late 1984, referencing the gift of her book on the excommunication of Elizabeth to the Vatican Library.

Then another letter, this one dated 22 April 1985 to the Chief Archivist asking to return to do research for her second book. Flavia wrote: 'In the course of doing work on my Queen Elizabeth book, I happened upon an interesting correspondence between the English mathematician and astronomer John Dee, and Ottaviano Mascherino, the astronomer who built the Tower of the Winds. I would like to search the Archives for further letters between the two astronomers to elaborate on my hypothesis that, while the religious schism between Rome and England was absolute, there was nevertheless vigorous and persistent scientific and cultural intercourse among the luminaries of the day.'

'Did you know of this?' Tremblay asked.

'No. Nothing.'

The next page caused Elisabetta to inhale sharply.

It was a memo to the file from the Chief Archivist,

dated 17 May 1985, withdrawing Flavia Celestino's Archive privileges. It asserted that she had obtained unauthorized access to File Box 197741-3821 and that her notes had been confiscated.

'This seems suspicious,' Tremblay said. 'She could only have received files specifically requested. As I said, there's no browsing allowed.'

A lined piece of notebook paper was stapled to the memo. It was in Flavia's distinctive italic.

'Her notes!' Elisabetta said.

The notations were sparse:

> *Letter from Dee to Mascherino, 1577:*
> *Brotherhood*
> *Common Cause*
> *'When I am observing the full eclipse of the moon on 27 September from London, I take heart in knowing you will be gazing on the same sight from Rome, dear brother.'*
> *Lemures*

'My God!' Tremblay exclaimed. 'She found direct evidence. I've never seen this letter she refers to. Come with me. The file box that's referenced – ones with these numbers are up on the Diplomatic Floor with the older documents.'

'Wait,' Elisabetta said. 'We're not finished.'

There were two more sheets in Flavia's file.

The first was a memo to the file from a physician, Dr Giuseppe Falcone, addressed to no one but marked 'Hand-delivered, 6 June 1985.'

On the request of the Vatican I examined the patient, Flavia Celestino, who is under the care of Dr Motta at the Gemelli Hospital. She is in serious condition with diarrhea, vomiting, anemia, liver and kidney dysfunction and periods of disorientation. My differential diagnosis includes hemolytic uremic syndrome, viral encephalomyelopathy, amyloidosis, and intoxication with heavy metals or arsenic. The latter would have to be my leading suspicion. I have spoken with Dr Motta. He informs me the arsenic and toxicology tests are negative and while surprised I have to accept what he says. I believe he has considered all relevant possibilities but at this stage there seems to be little to be done for her.

'She was poisoned,' Elisabetta whispered. Now she made no attempt to staunch her tears and Tremblay looked on impotently.

The last page was a copy of the death certificate, dated 10 June 1985, listing Flavia's cause of death as kidney and liver failure and noting that a post-mortem was not requested by the coroner.

'I'm sorry,' Tremblay said, touching her hand. 'But we have to find the Dee letter.'

He placed the file box back in its place and with

long strides backtracked rapidly toward the Tower. Elisabetta followed, her body and mind so numb that she could hardly feel her feet against the floor.

Going up the stairs, Tremblay cursed his weak constitution but forced himself to keep going until they'd reached the second floor of the Tower. At the landing Elisabetta was worried that he might pass out from air-hunger.

'It's this way,' he gasped.

Here in the Archive of the Secretariat of State, they passed through room after room of seventeenth-century walnut cabinets. Tremblay had written the file number on a scrap of paper and he referred to it as he searched the rooms. He finally found it, high up. Facing the tall library ladder he said, 'I'm so puffed out I don't trust myself.'

Elisabetta climbed the ladder and pulled open the door he was pointing at. He called out the file number to her. She found the box.

After climbing down she laid the file on top of one of the low cabinets in the center of the room and let Tremblay open the box.

It was full of parchments tied in a ribbon, all from the sixteenth century.

With a practiced eye he scanned the Latin, French, English and German scripts, looking for the one he wanted. Two-thirds of the way through the pile he stopped dead at a modern sheet of paper with a hand-written note in ballpoint ink.

1577 Letter from John Dee to Ottaviano Mascherino, removed to a personal collection. Signed, R.A. 17 May 1985

'Who is R.A?' Elisabetta asked.

Tremblay shook his head sadly. 'I have no idea, but by God I'm going to find out. Let's go. There's nothing more for us to do here. I have work to do. I'll contact you as soon as I have something. Please, say nothing of this to anyone.'

The phone rang in the librarian's office.

'This is Signorina Mattera in the Secret Archives. Yes, Your Excellency. Thank you for getting back to me. I wanted to inform you that Father Tremblay requested access to a red-flagged file today. It was regarding a woman who did research here in the 1980s, a Flavia Celestino. Yes, Your Excellency, per protocol, he was granted access and now, per protocol, I have duly informed you.'

TWENTY-TWO

Elisabetta unlocked the front door of her father's apartment and blinked in confusion. Zazo was in the kitchen.

'Where were you?' he said with exasperation. 'Haven't I told you to stay put?'

'I had an appointment.' She didn't want to lie but she said, 'At the school.'

Zazo started to lecture her, 'Elisabetta . . .'

'What are *you* doing here?' she countered. 'How come you're not in uniform?'

As he told her what had happened Elisabetta's tears flowed again. 'This is all my fault.'

'How is it your fault?'

'I don't know,' she said, wiping her eyes. 'It just is.'

Zazo laughed. 'You used to be so intelligent. What happened? Stop crying and make me some coffee.'

Later, while she washed their cups and saucers, Elisabetta asked Zazo if he wanted to go to church with her.

'No more churches for me for a while,' he said. 'But I'll walk you there.'

It was one of those wind-whipped afternoons where dense cumulus clouds blocked the sun intermittently, turning the light from yellow to gray and back to yellow again. Zazo couldn't decide whether to keep his sunglasses on or not. He gave up finally and stuffed them into the inside pocket of his jacket where they got entangled with the phone records.

'These were my undoing,' he said, waving the papers at his sister.

'Have you looked at them?'

'No. Maybe later tonight or tomorrow. Whenever I sober up.'

'Please don't drink,' Elisabetta said.

'Are you a nun or a Puritan?' her brother joked. 'Of course I'm going to drink. A good long toast to the end of my career and to the new Pope, whoever he may be.'

They stopped at a corner, waiting for the crossing light to turn green. 'I'm sure they'll just give you a slap on the wrist. Zazo, I'm so cross with you. You couldn't leave it alone, could you?'

'No, I couldn't.'

'Me neither,' Elisabetta confessed as she started across the street at the green signal.

Zazo caught up with her. 'What did you do?'

'I called the University at Ulm and found an old colleague of Bruno Ottinger's. It turns out that Ottinger was a mean old fellow, a right-winger.'

'That's it?'

'Nothing else too remarkable. He didn't have

many friends. The initial K didn't mean anything to the colleague. Nor did Christopher Marlowe.'

'Is Papa still working on the numbers?'

Elisabetta nodded.

'Here's hoping he'll have more luck than with Goldbach,' Zazo said dismissively.

'Don't be mean.'

Suddenly he said, 'I'm really going to miss you.'

She gave him a tight-lipped smile, holding on to her composure. 'I'm going to miss you too. And Papa. And Micaela. And my school.'

'Then don't go.'

'It's not my choice.'

'Whose choice was it? It wasn't God's, you know.'

'I don't know whose decision it was but of course it was God's choice.'

'Someone wants you out of the way. It's obvious, Elisabetta. First someone makes a call from your office to the newspapers, a call that gets you fired. Then you're transferred a day after someone tries to kill you. This is not the hand of God. It's the hand of man.'

The dome of the church came into sight.

'Maybe we'll find out the truth of this affair one day, maybe we won't. What's important for me is that I resume my life. If that's in Africa, so be it.'

'You know,' Zazo said slyly, 'the people you just mentioned won't be the only ones who will miss you.'

'Who else?'

'Lorenzo.'

She stopped and stared at him.

'He hasn't said anything, of course,' Zazo said, 'but I can tell.'

'But I'm a nun!'

'Maybe so, but sometimes women leave the clergy. I can't say that he's thinking this, but I can see there's something in his eyes. He's my best friend.' Zazo dropped his voice. 'Next to Marco.'

'Oh, Zazo.'

'Let me tell you something else,' her brother said, touching her black sleeve. An old woman with a shopping bag stopped to take in the scene of a nun and a young man having an intimate discussion on the street. Elisabetta smiled politely at her and she and Zazo began walking again. 'I know why you became a nun.'

'Do you? Why?'

'Because Marco was perfect for you. There wasn't ever going to be anyone who was as good.'

She gestured at the sky, 'And because of that I married Christ instead? Is that what you're going to say? Don't you think that's awfully simplistic?'

'I'm not a complicated guy,' he said.

'You're my brother, Zazo, but you're also an idiot.'

They were at the Piazza S. Maria in Trastevere. He shrugged and pointed toward the church. 'I'll wait for you in the café.'

'You don't have to.'

'If I can't protect the new Pope I'll protect you instead.'

A Mercedes Vito panel van slowly poked its nose into the Piazza from the street they'd been walking along. It was a pedestrian zone. Before Zazo could motion to the driver that he'd made a mistake the van went into reverse and disappeared. In a short while a man with a reddish beard emerged from the van in a side street, walked back, and sat on the edge of the Piazza's fountain to smoke a cigarette. He was halfway between the church and the café and seemed to be taking pains to keep both Elisabetta and Zazo in sight.

'What are you doing here?' Zazo's father asked as he dropped his briefcase in the sitting room.

'Runs in the family,' Zazo mumbled. He repeated the entire story while Carlo poured himself one aperitif – and then another.

'First Elisabetta gets in trouble, now you. What's next? Something with Micaela? Bad news always happens in threes.'

'Is that superstition or numerology, Papa?' Elisabetta asked.

'Neither: it's a fact. What are we doing for dinner?'

'I'm going to make something.'

'Make it simple,' Carlo said. 'I've got to go out tonight.'

'A date?' Zazo asked.

'Funny. Ha, ha. A retirement party for Bernadini. He's younger than me. The writing's on the wall.' Carlo opened his briefcase and swore.

'What's wrong?' Elisabetta asked.

'I was going to spend an hour working on your puzzle but I left the goddamned book in my office. Let me have the old one.'

'No!' she protested. 'You heard that it's valuable. You'll spill your drink on it. I've got a paperback in my room. You can even write in that copy if you like.'

Elisabetta cooked a bowl of pasta with pecorino and chopped a garden salad while Zazo drank a couple of his father's beers.

'Micaela's coming over after supper,' she told him.

'I'll take off when she gets here.'

'You don't have to wait if there's someplace you'd rather be,' she said.

'It's okay, I'm hungry.'

'Well, get Papa then. Tell him it's ready.'

Zazo rapped on his father's bedroom door. When there was no reply he knocked louder and called out.

There was a testy, 'What?'

'Supper's ready.'

Through the door came, 'Wait a minute. I'm busy.'

Zazo returned to the kitchen, put a fork into the pasta and twirled a taste. 'He said to wait a minute. He's busy.'

They waited ten minutes and Elisabetta tried again. Carlo sent her away, promising he'd be ready in another minute.

Ten minutes later they heard his door swing open. He stepped slowly into the kitchen, scowling, with the *Faustus* paperback and a notebook in one hand.

'Are you okay, Papa?' Elisabetta asked.

Suddenly Carlo's scowl turned into a giant smile, like that of a kid playing a trick. 'I've cracked it! I've solved your puzzle!'

TWENTY-THREE

London, 1589

Marlowe practically sucked in the rough and tumble of London as he strolled through the crowded, jostling streets of Shoreditch. He smiled at every blackguard, whore, blackamoor, cheating monger and filthy urchin he brushed past. *I was born to live in such a place,* he thought.

Today was a day of high expectation and even the stench of the open drains couldn't diminish his pleasure: in a short while he would see the first performance of his new play, *The Tragical History of the Life and Death of Doctor Faustus.*

Marlowe had donned his best suit of clothes, the same that he had worn four years earlier when, pockets laden with Walsingham's payments, he had posed for a commissioned portrait. In an unheard-of act of hubris, which had thoroughly seized the imagination of his fellows, he had presented the portrait to the Master of Benet on the occasion of his leaving the college in 1587. Somewhat flummoxed by the gift, Master Norgate had had no choice but to hang it in his wood-paneled gallery next to a bevy of vastly more notable academics and alumni.

In the painting, he had assumed a cocky pose with his arms folded, his lips pouty and rebellious, his hair flowing and his moustache wispy. His doublet was close-fitting, black with a red velvet lining, trimmed with gold buttons down the front and up the sleeves. His linen shirt was open-necked with a floppy cobwebbed collar, far more rakish than the usual starched and ruffled collars that graced the worthies on Norgate's wall. The garments, which had seen their share of use in England and the Continent, were a bit worn now, but they still looked splendid and fit perfectly. Still, if the play were a success he'd already laid a plan to visit Walsingham's tailor for a new ensemble.

London, this dense metropolis of 100,000 souls, was now Marlowe's oyster. In a short time he'd repeatedly pried open its unyielding shell, plucking out one treasure after another; he had little doubt that *Faustus* would give him his most lustrous pearl yet.

Marlowe had taken to London like a witch to a cauldron. By night he frequented the riotous Nag's Head in Cheapside, the dark brothels of Norton Folgate where he could try to hide the truth of his anatomy under his drawn-up breeches, and the feverish salons of Whitehall where – among Cecil, Walsingham and his kind – he had no need to hide. And by day, when his head had cleared from the previous night's excesses, he sat in his rooms and put quill to parchment until his hand ached.

He found his theatrical home among the Admiral's Men, a troupe of players under the patronage of Charles Howard, Elizabeth's Lord Admiral. The Admiral had lured the leading actor in England, Edward Alleyn, to his company and when Alleyn, an imposing man with a baritone voice like a fine brass horn, first read *Tamburlaine the Great* it was the beginning of an intense artistic partnership. Alleyn could scarcely believe that a masterpiece like *Tamburlaine* was penned by a 22-year-old. Nor could the audiences, and the play about a simple shepherd who rose to be the murderously blaspheming ruler of Persia became the talk of London and a commercial sensation.

The Theatre was London's first purpose-built playhouse and Marlowe still felt a shiver of excitement every time he entered. It was a great timbered polygon, built partly by Burbage's own hand, he a master carpenter by trade. There were three galleries surrounding a cobblestoned yard fronting a raised stage. For a penny a few hundred could stand on the stones pressed hard against one another. For another penny, a few hundred more could ascend the galleries and for yet another penny they could rent a stool. A half a dozen Lord's Rooms were fashioned into the galleries, private cozies for the wealthy.

Outside the Theatre Marlowe had to fight his way, unrecognized, through an unruly smelly crush of patrons, prostitutes, procurers and pickpockets. He arrived at the turnstile whisking at his doublet with the back of his hand in case something nasty had stuck to it.

'Kit! Over here!' Thomas Kyd was waving at him from the other side.

'Tom!'

The gatekeepers let him pass and Tom closed the distance with a few loping steps. He was much taller, as fair as Marlowe was dark. 'I thought you'd be late for your own opening.'

Marlowe beamed. 'They hardly need me any longer. The words, after all, have long been writ.'

Kyd clapped him on the shoulders. 'Such is our lot in life, my friend. But without our small contribution, the actors would have naught to do but fart and stammer.'

Marlowe had met Kyd shortly after leaving Cambridge. Kyd was a fixture of the Mermaid, one of the young lions of the theatre. His *The Spanish Tragedy* had been one of the most successful productions in recent memory. He was six years older than Marlowe, like him of rather humble origins, and was further disadvantaged by having never attended university. He had triumphed solely on the basis of his creative talent and a winning personality. Marlowe took to him instantly and vice versa but the younger man resisted for the longest time his entreaties to become his paramour.

Finally, after one particularly ale-filled night, they

found themselves in the same bed. Marlowe pulled away from Kyd's ardent kisses and said hoarsely, 'I have a certain feature.'

'Really? How intriguing. Is it very large, very small or very crooked?' Kyd asked, propping himself on one elbow.

'Do you swear never to tell anyone?'

'I do so swear,' Kyd replied melodramatically.

Marlowe got off the bed, stood, turned his back and lowered his breeches.

Kyd screamed in delight. 'I always knew you were a devil! How marvelous! May I touch it?'

'You may,' Marlowe said. 'It can take rough treatment.'

Kyd stroked the tail in fascination. 'Does this peculiarity run within the bloodlines of your family?'

'No,' Marlowe lied. 'I am the only one. Perhaps the only one in the world.'

'This will be our special secret, then,' Kyd said. 'Come back into my bed as quick as you can.'

The two men pushed their way through the crush to the stage. In the wings Edward Alleyn, England's leading actor, in the full academic robes and hat of Doctor Faustus, was warming up his vocal chords with a harmonic exercise.

'Kit!' he exclaimed. 'And Tom! How's the house looking?'

'Oversold, judging by the crowds,' Kyd said. 'You're looking the part.'

'I look it well enough but will I remember it? I've done three new plays in the past week.'

'Do not, good sir, forget my lines,' Marlowe scolded. 'Remember, the other plays were mere meat pies. This one is a top cut of beefsteak.'

'I shall do my very best, of that you may be assured.'

James Burbage sidled over and escorted Marlowe and Kyd up a narrow staircase to one of the Lord's Rooms where they surveyed the crowd.

'Look at them all!' Burbage exclaimed. 'I hear there's a mob at the gates, all clamoring for tickets. I'll have to dispatch armed horsemen to keep order! Word of mouth is a powerful ally, is it not?'

'Well, the play has it all!' Kyd said. 'Kit's notions – summoning Mephistophilis with magic, selling one's soul to the Devil in exchange for the secrets of the universe – these are heady themes.'

There was a flask of wine on the table. Burbage poured out three glasses. 'Here's to heady themes and frothy success, gentlemen.'

The stage manager called for quiet and announced the players to the audience. At the mention of Edward Alleyn there were rousing cheers. The Chorus marched onto the stage and the play began.

When the Chorus set the scene and exited, Alleyn, as Doctor Faustus, entered and at the mere sight of the great man the house erupted in cheers. He managed to stay in character as the robed Faustus while pausing smugly to let the audience exercise their lungs. Soon he was standing in an elaborately drawn magic circle of astrological signs, done precisely to Marlowe's specifications. His voice boomed:

> *Now that the gloomy shadow of the Earth,*
> *Longing to view Orion's drizzling look,*
> *Leaps from th' antarctic world unto the sky,*
> *And dims the welkin with her pitchy breath,*
> *Faustus, begin thine incantations,*
> *And try if devils will obey thy hest,*
> *Seeing thou hast pray'd and sacrific'd to them.*
> *Within this circle is Jehovah's name,*
> *Forward and backward anagrammatiz'd,*
> *Th' abbreviated names of holy saints,*
> *Figures of every adjunct to the heavens,*
> *And characters of signs and erring stars,*
> *By which the spirits are enforc'd to rise:*
> *Then fear not, Faustus, but be resolute,*
> *And try the uttermost magic can perform.*

The audience gasped collectively as Mephistophilis appeared in a flash of phosphorus, green-suited, complete with horns and wings.

Kyd whispered into Marlowe's ear. 'Marvelous!'

And Marlowe smiled back at him, well satisfied.

The stagecraft intensified as Faustus, having made a pact with Lucifer to trade his soul for twenty-four years on Earth with Mephistophilis as his personal messenger, embarked on his journey of worldly exploration.

Alleyn's soaring elocution, combined with fireworks

and flames, enthralled the audience. When it was time for Lucifer to claim his bounty a terrible dragon of a creature rose out of the smoke, breathing fire. Overhead, shaggy-haired devils swung across the stage on wires with sparklers in their mouths. Drummers made thunder and stagehands made lightning.

And near the end, before being carried off to Hell, Faustus was granted his final wish – to see with his own eyes the fair Helen of Troy. Alleyn, his voice soaring, moved the house to tears.

Was this the face that launch'd a thousand ships,
And burnt the topless towers of Ilium!
Sweet Helen, make me immortal with a kiss.

By the time the applause had faded and the audience had largely dispersed, evening had come and with it a cooling mist. In an alleyway behind the Theatre, Kyd and Marlowe shared a moment.

'Why must you go?' Kyd pouted. 'Come with me to the Mermaid. You're triumphant, Kit. Celebrate among friends.'

'I've men I must see,' Marlowe said. 'I'll be there later. Wait for me, will you?'

'I will, if you'll come closer.' Kyd kissed him, slid a hand down the back of his breeches and sensually stroked his tail.

In the shadows a lone man watched them for a while, then crept off silently into the haze.

*

At the Palace of Whitehall, within his privy chamber, Francis Walsingham poured Marlowe and Robert Cecil glasses of good French brandy. Robert Poley was there too, sitting by the fire, nursing a tankard, gloomy and taciturn.

There was a knock on the door and Walsingham's private secretary announced, 'He is here.'

Marlowe wasn't expecting another party. With curiosity he watched as a small man, no taller than an adolescent boy, entered. He wore an academician's black robe that scraped the floor. His face was wizened with age and he possessed the most remarkable beard that Marlowe had ever seen, white as a snow goose, bushy enough to hide a bird's nest and as long as his head. The man was clutching a polished, inlaid box the size of a Bible.

Walsingham went to him, obsequiously kissed his bony hand and asked, 'Is that it?'

The man handed him the box and said, 'It is.'

Walsingham placed it carefully on his desk, pointed toward Marlowe and said, 'This is the man I wanted you to meet. Christopher Marlowe, I give you Doctor John Dee.'

The bearded man seemed to glide to him. 'The young playwright and poet. I am most pleased to know you, sir.'

Marlowe felt the excitement of the occasion wash over him. The great Lemures astrologer! The Queen's astrologer! 'No, sir,' he said, bowing deeply. 'It is I who am humbled and immeasurably favored to meet you.'

Walsingham filled a glass for Dee while Poley remained mutely by the fire, uninvited into the circle.

'So, your new play opened this afternoon, I hear,' Dee said.

'Indeed it did,' Marlowe said.

'And how was it received?' Walsingham asked.

'The audience seemed to take to it,' Marlowe said modestly.

'Perhaps we should assume disguises and see it for ourselves,' Cecil said to his host.

'I do not frequent plays unless the Queen insists,' Walsingham said. 'Perhaps, Master Marlowe, you'd be so good as to inform Doctor Dee how this new production serves our larger purposes.'

Marlowe nodded. 'Certainly: nothing is more important than our mission and my small play is merely meant to sow sweet seeds of confusion and hatred.'

'How so?' Dee asked.

'Well, for one, it is about good and evil and I am happy to report that evil, in the form of Lucifer, soundly trounces good. Damnation well and truly trumps salvation, which will, no doubt, foment a sense of dismay and bewilderment among the masses.'

'Good,' Dee said. 'Very good.'

'And I have aimed to cloud their minds with respect to the central precept of Protestant doctrine – absolute predestination. I need not remind you that, according to Calvin, God alone elects which men will be saved and which will be damned. Man has no control of his ultimate faith. The Papists, of course, see this as complete heresy and if any of their numbers see the play they will be sorely troubled. Protestants in the audience will see the hideous fate of my hero Faustus, who rejects God but later is utterly unable to repent, as a worthy tribute to Calvinism. But some, I suspect, will secretly despair at its sharp message and wallow in their certain torment over the fact that repentance is pointless and their fates are sealed. If that is the case, they will think, then why not continue to sin?'

'Why indeed not?' Cecil piped up.

'While we despise the Catholics with all our might, I am happy enough to poke sticks at Protestants too. Faustus says this in a speech,' Marlowe said, 'The reward of sin is death. That's hard. If we say that we have no sin, we deceive ourselves, and there's no truth in us. Why, then, belike we must sin, and so consequently die. Aye, we must die an everlasting death. What doctrine call you this? Che sera, sera. What will be, shall be.'

Walsingham said approvingly, 'I can see how this will torture their fragile minds.'

'And, as an homage to our traditions,' Marlowe said, 'Faustus summons the Devil from within a magic circle containing the star signs of the great Balbilus.'

Dee pounded the arm of his chair. 'This! This pleases me greatly! Balbilus is my hero. Lost as he is to the memory of ordinary men, he is locked forever in *our* hearts.' Dee let Walsingham refill his glass and said, 'Have you told Marlowe what we are asking of him?'

'I was waiting for you to put it to him,' Cecil answered.

'I will,' Dee said. 'Marlowe, have you ever heard of the Irish saint Malachy?'

'I have not,' Marlowe replied.

'More's the pity,' Dee said. 'He was the twelfth-century bishop of Armagh – well-traveled on the Continent, a confidant of Bernard of Clairvaux and Pope Innocent II. And he was a secret Lemures, a great one, an astrologer who ably carried the torch of his art. While visiting Pope Innocent in Rome, he witnessed, it is said, a particularly propitious eclipse of the moon and from his observation an important prophecy concerning the papacy emerged. He foresaw a finite number of future popes, numbering 112 – no more, no less. And he further foresaw an identifying feature of each of the popes. So, for the last pope, Sixtus V, Malachy foresaw and did write of him, 'the axle in the midst of a sign'. Sixtus had a coat of arms which bore an axle in the middle of a lion. For the present pope, Urbanus VII, Malachy wrote, 'from the dew of the sky'. Urbanus was Archbishop of Rossano in Calabria, where sap called 'the dew of heaven' is gathered from trees. You see?'

Marlowe nodded in fascination. 'And when the number 112 is reached?' he asked.

'The prophecy is apocalyptic,' Dee said evenly. 'The Church will be no more, and I venture to say that a new order will ensue. Out of the chaos the Lemures will triumph.'

Marlowe narrowed his eyes. 'What will happen?'

'Alas, we shall not be there to see for ourselves. Have you read my *Monas Hieroglyphica*?'

'I have labored at it. At college. It is a most challenging text,' Marlowe admitted.

'Well, our friend Walsingham, the code-master, will well appreciate it when I tell you that the work has one meaning, challenging as it may seem for the ordinary reader, but another altogether hidden message for our brethren. Do you recall my illustration of the Monad?'

'I do, sir.'

'My own prophecy is that the world will end at a time when both the moon and sun are in the House of Aries. Aries is a fire sign. The world will surely be consumed by fire. The Monad carries this meaning. Would that it might become our symbol!'

'It can,' Cecil said, raising his glass. 'It shall.'

'I cannot say whether my vision of the apocalypse will coincide with the prophecy of Malachy. No one can. But the possibility cannot be denied.'

'Why is it that I have never seen Malachy's prophecy?' Marlowe asked.

'This is the reason I am here,' Dee said. 'You will have a vital part to play in setting the next stage of our plan in motion. I cannot stress too strongly the importance of our collaboration in the achievement of the ultimate destiny of the Lemures. Malachy's text has been passed from astrologer to astrologer and has stayed among us as a sacred document. We believe the time has come to make it more widely known.'

'Indeed,' Cecil muttered.

'These are difficult times,' Dee said. 'In England we

are well served by the Protestant zeal of the Queen. Here we have done well and we are safely established. But on the Continent things are not so favorable. The Pope is inflamed by the death of Queen Mary. He and his closest Cardinals are convinced there was a Lemures hand in the affair.'

Walsingham laughed. 'They are despicable but they are not stupid.'

'Quite so,' Dee said. 'They have captured a number of our agents in Italy, Spain and France and have tortured them most grievously. I am told that they have kept their tails as trophies to gloat over. We have become dispirited and this will not stand. Our brethren need inspiration and encouragement to maintain their fighting spirit. According to the prophecy, there are only thirty-eight popes left. While this may span some considerable time – indeed, centuries – it would be well if Malachy became a rallying flag for all Lemures to carry in their hearts. I have always said that he who foresees the future will control the future. The Lemures can and should prosper greatly in the period to come and I fervently believe that when the last grain of sand trickles through the hourglass of history and the last pope has come and gone, the world and all its riches will be within our hands.'

'And there is more,' Cecil said. 'Tell him of our plot concerning the next Pope.'

Dee nodded enthusiastically. 'We would like to realize something we have never achieved before: a Lemures pope. Imagine our power if we commanded the Papacy and, through out own influence at the English court, simultaneously controlled the Protestant Queen? With the help of Malachy we would like to assist our man, Cardinal Girolamo Simoncelli, to attain the prize. Malachy identifies the next pope as '*ex antiquitate urbis*' – from the antiquity of the city. Simoncelli fits the role admirably as he is presently Cardinal of Orvieto, which, in Italian, means "old city".'

'Tell me what I can do,' Marlowe said, feeding off the fiery excitement in the old man's eyes.

'Walsingham, give him the box.'

Marlowe took the box in his hands and unlatched it. Inside was a rolled parchment secured with ribbons.

'It is a copy of the prophecy in Malachy's own hand,' Dee said. 'Keep it close to your person. Take it to Rome. We have a trusted friend there, an astronomer named Mascherino. Walsingham will provide you with good reason to be in Italy but when you are there you will, with Mascherino's assistance, deposit the manuscript within the Pope's Library and shortly thereafter Mascherino will, *mirabile dictu*, find it and make it known. Once it is read and appreciated, the Cardinals will see Malachy's undeniable accuracy over the centuries and this will serve to make the case why they must elect Simoncelli as the next pope.'

'May I?' Marlowe said, holding up the parchment.

'Of course,' Dee nodded.

Marlowe untied the ribbons and unrolled the parchment carefully. He read in silence and for a while the only sound in the chamber came from Poley taking a poker to the logs. When Marlowe was done he let the manuscript roll itself up and re-affixed the ribbons. A smile creased his face.

'Why the wicked grin, Kit?' Cecil asked.

'An idea has crossed my mind, a trifle, really,' Marlowe said, closing and relatching the box. 'I'm already hard at work on revisions to my Faustus play which are extensive enough to have it considered a new version. It had occurred to me that I could do more to ridicule the Pope's Church and I am in the process of adding more meat to my third act which is set within the papal palace in Rome. I would like your permission, good gentlemen, to encrypt a message to future generations of Lemures, a message of pride and aspiration concerning the Malachy prophecy derived, perhaps, from the differences between my two versions.'

Walsingham looked to Dee, then nodded. 'As you know, I have always had a fondness for codes.'

'I think it's an excellent notion,' Cecil said. 'By all means, Kit. I look forward to your masterpiece of encryption.'

Dee rose and straightened his robe. 'Come, Master Marlowe, walk me to the street and let us gaze at the night sky together.'

Left behind, the other three men kept at their drinking.

'I believe Doctor Dee liked him,' Cecil said.

'He is likeable enough,' Walsingham said. 'I don't

318

understand his compulsion for the theatre but his particular talents are certainly useful.'

'Nero too had a compulsion for performance,' Cecil observed.

That made Walsingham snigger. 'He's hardly a Nero! Poley, what do you think about all this? You've been as silent as a slug all evening.'

Poley turned away from the fire. 'I was at the Theatre tonight.'

'Why, pray tell? Have you become a devotee?'

'Hardly. I've had my suspicions about Marlowe. I observe him from time to time.'

'And what,' Walsingham asked, 'did you observe?'

'I witnessed Marlowe and Thomas Kyd in an amorous embrace. Kyd had his hand upon Marlowe's posterior parts.'

'Kyd is not one of us!' Walsingham said sharply.

'Indeed not,' Cecil said.

Walsingham gripped the arms of his chair in frustration. 'Marlowe is brilliant, but he is intemperate and does not share our cautious ways. Accompany him to Rome. Make sure he accomplishes his assigned task. When he returns, we'll let him write his plays and do our bidding. But, Poley, I want you to keep an eye on him, a very careful eye, and, as always, keep me closely informed.'

TWENTY-FOUR

Elisabetta's father made Zazo and Elisabetta clear the supper table so that they could gather round the *Faustus* book.

'Look!' Carlo said. 'There's a difference between your copy and the one I've been working from.'

Elisabetta glanced at hers. 'They're both B texts. What's the difference?'

'Yours is numbered. See the numbers on the right margins? Every five lines, see? The beginning of each act resets the line numbers back to one. It's a common notation system for plays so actors can find their lines easily and teachers can send their students to a passage. Only my copy didn't have numbers.'

Elisabetta grew excited. 'Yes! I see.'

'I've been getting nowhere looking at this as a number-progression or a substitution code. So then it hit me: what if these tattoos refer to line numbers! Lines which differ between the A text and the B text. "B is the key." That's what the letter said.'

'But there are so many differences between the two versions,' Elisabetta said. 'Where to begin?'

'Exactly. I realized this could be a very difficult task, one better suited to computational power than trial and error and I began to think how I could write a program to accomplish it. But then I remembered something your Professor Harris said. Remember? The biggest differences were in Act III which was much longer in the B text and was turned into an anti-Catholic rant. On a hunch – and don't roll your eyes, Zazo, mathematicians sometimes have hunches, just like policemen – I went straight to Act III and started playing with the line numbers. If each of the twenty-four numbers in the tattoo array corresponded to a line number then we might have the only solution that wouldn't require a computer to sort out.'

'Okay,' Elisabetta said. 'What was the first number?'

Carlo put his reading glasses on, then took them off. '63.'

She found the line. '*May be admired through the furthest land.* Now what?'

'Well, again, the simplest solution was going to be taking the first letter of the first word. Believe me, I was prepared to have to dig deeper but I think it's that straightforward.'

'So it's M,' she said. 'What's the next number?'

'128.'

'*And curse the people that submit to him.* A.'

Zazo almost shouted. 'Please! I'm starved! Can you please just cut to the chase.'

321

Carlo put his glasses on again. 'The message is: **MALACHY IS KING HAIL LEMURES.**'

Elisabetta caught her breath when she heard the word *Lemures*. She forced her mind to skip to Malachy and barely managed to squeak out, 'Malachy was an Irish saint, I think. There's something else about him too. I can't remember . . .'

'Me neither,' Carlo said. 'And what the hell are Lemures? Anyway, I'm just the mathematician and my work is done.' He sniffed happily, finally aware of the kitchen aromas, and said, 'Smells good. Let's eat.'

Elisabetta thanked God for the internet.

Without it she would have had to wait until the morning, then find a library and spend a day or more in the stacks.

After supper, alone in the apartment and waiting for Micaela to come over, she surfed her way frantically toward an understanding of the coded message.

From the myriad web pages devoted to Malachy she saw that the saint had become a newsworthy subject, particularly since the recent death of the Pope.

Elisabetta shook her head at her earlier lack of awareness of Malachy's topicality. *I'm not cloistered,* she thought, *but it seems that I'm out of it.*

The facts were simple enough: Saint Malachy, whose Irish name was Máel Máedóc Ua Morgair, had lived from 1094 until 1148. He was Archbishop of Armagh. He was canonized by Pope Clement III in 1199 and became the first Irish saint. And he was the purported author of *The Prophecy of the Popes*, a premonitory vision of the identities of the last 112 popes.

Much of what was known of his life came from *The Life of St Malachy*, a biography written by his French contemporary, St Bernard of Clairvaux, the great twelfth-century theologian whom Malachy visited on his journeys from Ireland to Rome. Indeed, on his last such visit to Clairvaux Malachy fell ill and literally died in St Bernard's arms.

Malachy's prophecy was unknown, or at least unpublished, during his lifetime. It was the Benedictine historian Arnold de Wyon who first published it in 1595 in his book *Lignum Vitae*, naming St Malachy as its author. According to de Wyon's account, in 1139 Malachy was summoned to Rome by Pope Innocent II for an audience. While there he experienced a vision of future popes which he recorded as a sequence of cryptic phrases. His manuscript stayed unknown until it was mysteriously discovered within the Roman Archive in 1590.

Malachy's prophecies were short and abstruse. Beginning with Celestine II who was elected in the year 1130, he foresaw an unbroken chain of 112 popes lasting until the end of the papacy – or, as some believed, until the end of the world.

Each pope was assigned a mystical title, pithy and evocative: *From a castle of the Tiber. Dragon pressed down. Out of the leonine rose. Angel of the grove. Religion destroyed. From a solar eclipse.* Over the centuries, those who tried to interpret and explain these symbolical prophecies always succeeded in finding *something* about each pope embedded in Malachy's titles, perhaps related to their country of origin, their name, their coat of arms, their birthplace, their talents.

Elisabetta skipped through the list with rapt fascination. The prophecy concerning Urban VIII was *Lilium et Rosa*, the Lily and the Rose. He was a native of Florence and a fleur-de-lis figured on the arms of Florence; he had three bees emblazoned on his escutcheon, and bees, of course, gather honey from the lilies and roses.

Marcellus II was *Frumentum Flacidum*, trifling grain. He was trifling, perhaps, because he was pope for only a very short time, and his coat of arms featured a stag and ears of wheat.

Innocent XII was *Raftrum in Porta*, rake in the door. His given name, Rastrello, meant lake in Italian.

Benedict XV was *Religio Depopulata*, religions laid waste. During his reign, World War I killed twenty million people in Europe, the 1918 flu pandemic killed one hundred million, and the October Revolution in Russia cast aside Christianity in favor of atheism.

In 1958, following the death of Pius XII, Cardinal Spellman from Boston had a little fun with Malachy's prediction that the next Pope would be *Pastor et Nauta*, shepherd and sailor. During the Conclave that would elect John XXIII, Spellman rented a boat, filled it with sheep and sailed up and down the Tiber. As it happened, Angelo Roncalli, the Cardinal named as the new Pope, had been patriarch of Venice, a maritime city famous for its waterways.

Pope John Paul II was *De Labore Solis*, which literally means 'the labor of the sun', though *labor solis* was also a common Latin expression for solar eclipse. Karol Jozef Wojtyla was born on 18 May 1920, the day of a partial solar eclipse over the Indian Ocean, and was buried on 8 April 2005, a day which saw a solar eclipse over the southwestern Pacific and South America.

And Malachy's prophetic chain led all the way to the 267th and penultimate pope who was now freshly interred within three nested coffins in a crypt beneath the Basilica of St Pietro.

The 268th pope, to be chosen at the Conclave which would begin tomorrow, would be the last. Malachy called him Petrus Romanus and gave him the longest title:

In persecutione extrema S.R.E. sedebit Petrus Romanus, qui pascet oves in multis tribulationibus: quibus transactis civitas septicollis diruetur, et Iudex tremendus iudicabit populum suum. Finis.

During the final persecution of the Holy Roman Church, the seat will be occupied by Peter the Roman, who will feed his sheep in many tribulations; and when these things are finished, the seven-hilled city will be destroyed, and the formidable Judge will judge his people. The End.

To Elisabetta, the vague nature of these prophecies reminded her of the quatrains of Nostradamus, notions concocted by a charlatan so that people might find one or two snippets from a pope's life to connect the man to his title. In fact, diverse scholars claimed Malachy's Prophecy was no more than an elaborate sixteenth-century hoax intended – unsuccessfully – to help Cardinal Girolamo Simoncelli reach the papacy.

Yet here, embedded within Marlowe's *Faustus*, was the coded message: **MALACHY IS KING HAIL LEMURES** – a message important enough for these Lemures to tattoo over their sacrums.

Elisabetta's training in anthropology kicked in. The documented use of tattoos reached all the way to the Neolithic period, and probably even further than that. Tattoos were evidence of rites of passage, marks of status and rank, cultural affiliation, symbols of religious and spiritual devotion. The symbolism and importance of tattoos varied from culture to culture, but she was certain of one thing: these sacral tattoos were important to the Lemures.

So it stood to reason that Malachy was important to them too, perhaps forming the basis of some kind of belief system. And Marlowe must have either known of them or been one himself!

HAIL LEMURES. Elisabetta fingered her crucifix.

She wanted to reach out to Father Tremblay but realized she didn't have a contact number for him.

There was a sound at the front door, someone fumbling at the lock.

She approached cautiously. The door swung open and Micaela burst in. 'Sorry I'm late. I had a patient to see.'

They kissed and Elisabetta put the kettle on.

'Where's Papa?'

'A retirement dinner for someone in his department.'

Micaela frowned. 'I'm sure he was thrilled about that. Arturo's coming later – do you mind?'

'Of course not.'

Micaela stripped off her jacket. She was looking stylishly professional in a blue skirt and silk top and seemed compelled to comment on the sartorial gulf between herself and her sister. 'For heaven's sake, Elisabetta, why are you wearing your habit around the house? Aren't you off duty?'

Elisabetta held up her left hand, showing off her gold wedding band. 'Still married, remember?'

'So how's Christ been treating you in His role as a husband?' Micaela asked dryly.

Elisabetta remembered her recent daydream about Marco. 'Better, I think, than I've been treating Him in my role as a wife.' She changed the subject abruptly. 'Did you hear about Zazo?'

Micaela knew; he'd called her. She went into a rant, heaping invectives upon the Vatican, stupid bosses and assholes in general. Elisabetta halted her diatribe. 'If you calm down, I'll tell you something.'

'What?'

'Papa solved the tattoo code.'

'Tell me!'

They were interrupted by the sound of the buzzer. Micaela said it was probably Arturo and scrambled to answer it but she came back shaking her head. 'It wasn't him. It's a Father Tremblay. He said you're expecting him. Is it okay?'

'Yes, but . . .'

'But what?'

'Please don't comment on the way he looks, all right?'

Elisabetta greeted Father Tremblay at the door and showed him into the kitchen where, upon seeing Micaela, he immediately apologized for intruding. Elisabetta assured him that it wasn't a problem and hastened to add that she wanted to speak with him anyway. She introduced him. Micaela looked him up and down and promptly asked, ignoring Elisabetta's request, 'You have Marfan's, don't you?'

'Don't be so rude!' Elisabetta scolded.

'I'm not rude, I'm a doctor.'

'It's okay,' Tremblay said, his ears glowing with visible embarrassment. 'Yes, I do – you're a good diagnostician.'

'I knew it,' Micaela said, satisfied.

At the kitchen table it was left to Elisabetta to explain to Micaela Father Tremblay's involvement in the affair and to inform the priest what her sister knew about it.

'So it seems we all have some knowledge, albeit incomplete,' Tremblay said. 'But I have some important new information.'

'So do I,' Elisabetta said.

'Should I flip a coin to see who goes first?' Micaela asked.

'No, please, Sister Elisabetta,' Tremblay said politely. 'Tell me what you've found.'

'My father's a clever man, a mathematician. He broke the code. We know what the tattoos mean. I was about to tell my sister. The answer came from differences between the A and B texts of Marlowe's *Faustus*. The tattoos say: "Malachy is King. Hail Lemures."'

Tremblay's face fell. 'My God . . .'

'What are Lemures?' Micaela asked.

While Tremblay sipped nervously at his tea, Elisabetta reminded him that Micaela was subject to a Vatican confidentiality agreement and asked if she, Elisabetta, could speak freely. He nodded uncomfortably and Elisabetta passed on what he had told her about Lemures and what they had learned at the Secret Archives.

When she was done, Micaela asked, 'You expect me to believe this? And you're telling me that our mother was involved with these people. That they might have poisoned her?'

'I'm afraid everything Sister Elisabetta says is the absolute truth,' Tremblay murmured. 'They are difficult foes. It would be better if they didn't exist but they do.'

'And Malachy?' Micaela asked, shaking her head. 'Who's he?'

Tremblay said, 'I can answer that.'

To Elisabetta's surprise, the priest was fluent in his knowledge of the prophecy and presented a brisk summary. When he finished, he curled his long index finger through the handle of the cup and raised it to drain the last of his tea, then added, 'I can tell you, Elisabetta, we had no idea that the Lemures were involved with the Malachy business. No one in the Vatican took it seriously. That was a mistake and now we've arrived at the moment of Malachy's last pope. And maybe our world's last *hope*.'

Micaela displayed her characteristic blend of scepticism and exasperation. 'Am I the only one who feels like they're in a carnival hall of mirrors? It's too much! None of this makes any sense to me.'

'You saw Aldo Vani in the flesh,' Elisabetta said. 'You saw the photos of Bruno Ottinger. These men were Lemures. The Prophecy of Malachy was important enough for them to tattoo it onto their spines! I'm scared, Micaela. Your carnival analogy – this isn't a hall of mirrors, it's the terror ride. I think these men mean to do the Church great harm.'

Tremblay reached for the leather portfolio he'd deposited at his feet. He unzipped it and took out a sheaf of copier pages. 'Your sister is right, Micaela. Sister Elisabetta, when you left this morning I went back to my office and began working to find out who this "R.A." was who signed the Dee letter out of the Secret Archives in 1985. It involved a lot of work, looking through old Vatican personnel files. I think I have the likely man: a certain Riccardo Agnelli. He was the private secretary to a bishop, a man who is now a cardinal.'

'Who? Which cardinal?' Elisabetta asked.

'In a minute. But this is something much more important. By the time I had my answer, I saw my email inbox was full of messages. I subscribe to a service that scans newspapers and magazines for certain key words and symbols, like the Monad.'

'What's the Monad?' Micaela asked.

Elisabetta leaned forward and shushed her. 'Wait!'

Tremblay was laying pages down, one at a time. 'Here's a classified ad in today's *New York Times*.' Elisabetta saw a small image of the Monad with no accompanying text. 'Here's an ad in *Pravda*. Here's *Le Monde*. The *International Herald Tribune*. *Corriere della Sera*. *Der Spiegel*. *Jornal do Brasil*. *The Times* of London. *Sydney Morning Herald*. There are more. They're all the same. Just the Monad. I called a reporter I know at *Le Monde*. I asked him if he could find out who placed the ad. He got back to me. They received a letter with no return address with cash for the ad and instructions to run the image today.'

'It's a message,' Elisabetta whispered, barely audibly.

'Yes.' Tremblay nodded.

'A message? A message about what? What are you two talking about?' Micaela exclaimed.

Elisabetta rose suddenly and felt faint. She steadied herself with a hand on her chair. 'I know what's going to happen!'

'So do I,' Tremblay said, his slender fingers shaking.

'All this urgency to keep the skeletons of Callixtus hidden,' Elisabetta said. 'All the attempts to silence me. It's because of the Conclave. These Lemures. They're communicating among themselves to be ready. They're going to fulfill the Malachy prophecy. They're going to strike tomorrow during the Conclave!'

'Have you gone *mad*?' Micaela said.

Elisabetta ignored her. 'I'm going to call Zazo.'

'Zazo's on suspension. What can he do?' Micaela snapped.

'He'll think of something.'

There was a light rapping from the hall.

'Good,' Micaela said. 'Someone sane's here. That's Arturo.'

Micaela got up and opened the door.

There was a man filling the doorway, a man with a reddish beard holding a pistol. Two more were close behind, all of them neat, ordinary, unsmiling.

TWENTY-FIVE

Micaela yelped but the men pushed their way inside, closed the door and forced her to the ground. Elisabetta sprang up in panic and ran to the hall to witness a bearded man standing over her sister pointing a gun, trying to quiet her with a finger held in front of his lips. Two other clean-shaven men were aiming guns directly at her. Elisabetta froze. The man with a beard spoke in a language she didn't recognize, then immediately switched to English when she didn't respond.

'Tell her to be quiet or I will kill her.'

His tone was coldly matter-of-fact, his eyes dull.

He's one of them, Elisabetta thought.

'Please, Micaela, try to stay calm,' she said. 'We'll be all right. Please, let my sister up.'

'You will be quiet?' the man asked her.

Micaela nodded and Elisabetta helped her to her feet.

There was a small sound from the kitchen.

One of the men ran there and in seconds was

marching out Father Tremblay at gunpoint. The priest was breathing heavily.

'What do you want?' Elisabetta asked.

'Go back, all of you,' the bearded man said, pointing his gun toward the sitting room. 'Is anyone else here?'

'No.'

The bearded man seemed to be instructing one of the others to search the flat while he forced the sisters and Tremblay onto the sitting-room sofa. The man who stayed at his side was toting a large empty duffel bag.

Micaela's lips were trembling. Angry tears streaked her cheeks and made her mascara run.

'Are they?' she whispered to Elisabetta.

'I'm sure of it.'

Elisabetta's eyes were dry. She fingered her crucifix and watched their every move, desperately trying to figure out a way to get Micaela out of this and fearful that her father or Arturo would stumble into their midst.

The other man came back from his search and gave an all-clear sign.

The bearded man took out a mobile phone, punched in a number and began speaking rapidly in a guttural dialect. When he was finished he barked some orders.

The man with the duffel bag put it down on the carpet, unzipped it and took out two more collapsed bags from inside.

'All of you are coming with us,' the bearded man said.

'Where?' Elisabetta demanded.

'If you don't resist, you won't be hurt. That is the important fact.'

The other man unzipped a smaller bag and removed a metal bottle and some wads of gauze.

Micaela sniffed and stiffened. 'Jesus, it's ether! There's no fucking way I'm going to let them etherize me.'

'My God,' Tremblay croaked. 'Please, just take me. Let the women go.'

The bearded man addressed Elisabetta in a casual tone. 'They want you, but they say, "Okay, take them too." If they resist they won't care so much if we leave them here with bullets in them.'

'Listen to me, Micaela,' Elisabetta said gravely. 'Let them do it. Don't put up a fight. God will protect you.' Then she added 'I will protect you.'

It was the hardest thing she'd ever done, watching her sister's wild eyes as a brute pressed a reeking cloth over her mouth and nose, watching Micaela writhe and kick. But something was keeping Elisabetta's mind lucid and working and while the men were focused on their awful work she snatched something off the end table and hid it in a pocket within her habit.

Micaela went limp and the gauze was removed from her face.

Father Tremblay began to pray in rapid-fire French. He sounded very young and looked very scared as the square of gauze was pressed onto his face.

When his body went slack Elisabetta smelled fresh

ether and she too began to pray. As the fabric got closer to her nose the caustic stench made her gag.

She tried not to struggle but her body wouldn't let herself go down without a fight. But the struggle was brief and soon it was over.

Zazo was trying to fulfill his promise to get good and drunk. But he was behind schedule, only a couple of beers into the scheme. He should have been on duty. It was the night before the Conclave and he knew that his men were busting their balls and that Lorenzo was running around like a madman to keep the wheels on his over-burdened cart.

Getting plastered somehow didn't seem right.

The TV was on – some inane quiz show which he wasn't watching. It was just noise.

His mobile rang.

'Where are you?' It was his father. He sounded stressed.

'I'm home. What's the matter?'

'Did Elisabetta or Micaela call you?'

'No, why?'

'Arturo came over before I got home. The apartment door was unlocked. They weren't there.'

Zazo was already standing, putting on his jacket. 'I'll be right there.'

There wasn't enough air. Elisabetta's mouth was uncovered but she was in some dark constricted space that didn't allow her to shift her position. Her knees were drawn up uncomfortably to her chest. Then she realized that her wrists were bound in front of her. She lifted her hands to explore what was constraining her and felt the roughness of nylon mesh. Reaching up she felt her veil in place. It wasn't helping her breathing.

There were vibrations coursing through her back and the sounds of tires on a rain-soaked highway.

She whispered 'Micaela!' and when there was no response she raised her voice and tried again.

Over the road noise she heard a soft and groggy 'Elisabetta!'

'Micaela, are you okay?'

Micaela's voice grew a little stronger. 'What happened to us? Where are we?'

Elisabetta's fear was tempered by her sister's presence. 'I think I'm in a carry-bag.'

'Me too. I can't move.'

'I think we're in a car or a truck.' Then she remembered something. 'Father Tremblay?' she called. 'Father, are you there?'

There was no response.

'I don't know if they took him,' Micaela said. 'Where are we going?'

'I have no idea.'

'Who are they?'

Elisabetta knew the answer but hesitated to say it for fear of completely unnerving her sister – and herself. But she couldn't hold it in. 'The Lemures.'

*

Zazo almost lost it when Inspector Leone said, 'Look, calm down, Celestino. You've been drinking. I can smell it on your breath.'

'I had a couple of beers. What does that have to do with the disappearance of my sisters?'

Leone wouldn't let go. 'The Conclave starts tomorrow and you're having beers? Don't you guys have work to do?'

Zazo took a deep, self-controlling breath. 'I'm on leave.'

Leone smirked. 'Really. Why am I not shocked?'

If Zazo threw a punch he knew he'd be in handcuffs and the Polizia's attention would be on him, not on his sisters. His father seemed to sense the hazard and put his hand on Zazo's shoulder.

Zazo said slowly and carefully, 'Let's talk about my sisters, not me – okay, Inspector?'

'Sure. Let's talk about them. You haul me and my men out here and what do we find?' Leone waved his arm around the sitting room. 'Nothing! There's no sign of forced entry, no sign of burglary, no sign of a struggle or violence. Me, I see a couple of ladies who went out for the night and forgot to lock the door behind them. And it's still early, only 10:15. The night's still young!'

'You're talking about a nun, for Christ's sake!' Zazo screamed. 'She doesn't go out on the town!'

'I hear she's on leave too.'

Carlo took over for his sputtering son. 'Inspector, please. Since the attack on her she's been very cautious.

Except for Mass she's hardly gone out. She and Micaela would never have left here without telling us or leaving a message. And why isn't Micaela answering her phone?'

Leone raised his eyebrows as a signal to the two officers who were with him. 'Look, there's nothing we can do right now. In the morning, if they haven't crept back into their beds, give me a call and we'll treat them as missing persons.'

Soon, father and son were alone.

Zazo rubbed wearily at his eyes with the heels of his hands. 'I'll call Arturo again to make sure they didn't go to Micaela's hospital or her apartment.'

Carlo looked around the room distractedly, then banged out the pellet from his pipe bowl on an ashtray. As he was filling a fresh bowl he asked, 'Then what?'

'Then you're going to call every hospital casualty ward in Rome while I knock on every door in the apartment building to see if any of the neighbors heard or saw anything.'

'And then what?'

Zazo had sounded like he expected they'd come up empty. 'Then we wait. And pray.'

Blessedly, Elisabetta fell asleep for a time. She awoke abruptly to an awareness of a lack of motion. The air inside the bag was so depleted that she thought she would lose consciousness again. There were voices in that foreign language and the sound of a door unlatching. Then she was in motion again, but this time sliding and jerking and bouncing up and down.

'Micaela?'

There was no response.

'Micaela!'

Elisabetta bounced around for a minute, maybe two, suffering breathlessness and agitation, calling her sister's name in vain. Then the bouncing stopped and she was on a hard surface again. There was a long, slow sound of unzipping, one of the most welcome sounds she'd ever heard. She gulped at the cool air and reflexively closed her eyes against the harsh light.

When her pupils had adjusted to the brightness, the first thing she saw was that wretched red beard. There was the click of a knife snapping open. She closed her eyes again when she saw the blade and started to pray, waiting for the agonizing sensation she'd felt once before – steel penetrating her body.

There was a slicing sound, quick and clean, and her hands went free.

The red-bearded man had cut the duct tape which bound her.

Elisabetta opened her eyes and awkwardly pushed herself to her feet. She was standing unsteadily in a collapsed black holdall in the middle of a large windowless cellar. The room was loaded with pine crates, each the size of a bathtub. But she was more interested in the two unzipped duffel bags which lay beside her.

'Let them out!' she demanded.

Another of the kidnappers unzipped the first bag. Micaela was curled in a fetal position, unmoving.

Before anyone could stop her, Elisabetta ran to Micaela's side, kneeled down and touched her cheek. Thank God it was warm.

She looked up at the bearded man. 'Cut her free. Please.'

Elisabetta stroked her sister's hair while the man obliged and sliced the tape. Then she rubbed Micaela's wrists and hands to get the blood flowing. Micaela was breathing slowly, too slowly, but suddenly she opened her mouth and started gasping for air. Her eyes blinked open and squinted. She uttered a weak 'Elisabetta.'

'I'm here, my darling.'

'Are we alive?'

'Thanks to God, we are.' She pivoted to face their captors. 'Let the priest out!'

They unzipped Father Tremblay's bag.

His long body was folded upon itself; he was motionless, his thick eyeglasses dangling from one ear. Elisabetta went to him and felt his face. It was cool as stone. 'Micaela, can you come? He needs help!'

As the men watched impassively, Micaela crawled over to his duffel bag and felt for Tremblay's carotid pulse. She put her ear to his chest.

Crestfallen, she said, 'I'm sorry, Elisabetta. He's gone. The ether. Marfan's patients have bad hearts. He couldn't take it.'

Elisabetta stood and pointed at the bearded man. 'Bastards! You killed him!' she screamed with an anger she hadn't known she was capable of mustering.

The man shrugged and simply told his colleagues to take the body away. 'There are beds there,' he said, pointing at three single beds against one stone wall. They were unmade but sheets, blankets and pillows were laid out. 'And through that green door is a lavatory. We will bring food. There is no way out so there is no reason to try to escape. You should also be quiet because there is no one to hear you. Okay. Goodbye.'

'What are you going to do with us? What do you want?' Micaela demanded.

The bearded man backed away from them, heading toward a sturdy wooden door. 'Me?' he answered. 'I want nothing. My job is done and I go home now to sleep.'

The men left, dragging Father Tremblay's body with them.

There was the scraping sound of a bolt sliding into place. Elisabetta helped Micaela to one of the beds and sat her down. There were bottles of water on a table. Elisabetta twisted one open, sniffed at it and had a sip. 'Here,' she said, handing it to her sister. 'I think it's all right.'

Micaela drank half of it in one go. Only then did Elisabetta let loose and start crying. Micaela cried too and the two of them held each other.

'The poor man,' Elisabetta choked. 'That poor, poor man. He didn't deserve to die like that. No last rites. Nothing. I need to pray for him.'

'You do that,' Micaela said, rubbing her tearful eyes. 'I need to pee.' Shakily, she made for the green door.

Elisabetta said a hasty prayer for the young priest's soul, then decided that God would want her to concentrate on saving Micaela and herself. She rose and began to explore.

The bolted door wouldn't budge. It didn't look as though there was any other way out. The walls were cool, pale limestone and the ceiling was high and vaulted. It was an old cellar, she reckoned, possibly medieval. The crates suggested it was meant for storage, not guests. The metal bed frames looked out of place, brought in for the occasion.

Micaela came back in, shaking her head.

'How were the facilities?' Elisabetta asked.

'The toilet flushed.'

'Any windows?'

'No.' Micaela made her own tug at the door. 'I think we're in big trouble.'

'What time is it?'

Micaela checked her watch. 'Just past seven. In the morning, I suppose, but we could have missed a whole day.'

'I doubt it,' Elisabetta said. 'What language do you think they were speaking?'

'It sounded Slavic.'

'If we were on the road all night we could be in Germany, Austria, Switzerland or Slovenia.'

'Your brain's working better than mine,' Micaela said. 'You probably got less ether.'

'Probably.'

Elisabetta used the bathroom herself. It was the size

of a closet, only a toilet and a sink, no windows. The walls were the same yellow limestone.

When she came out she started making up her bed.

'You're adapting well to your captivity,' Micaela said.

'We should get some rest. Lord knows what's ahead for us.'

Micaela reluctantly began to lay the sheets on her thin mattress and tuck them in. 'Why didn't they kill us?' she asked suddenly.

'I don't know.' Elisabetta was looking around the chamber again. 'Perhaps they need something from me.'

Micaela finished unfolding her blanket and smoothing it into place. She punched at the lumpy pillow. 'The beds are terrible.' She sat back down, kicked off her shoes and rubbed her feet.

'God willing, we won't be here long.' Elisabetta wandered over to a pile of crates stacked high against one of the walls. The boxes were unmarked. She rapped on one; the dull sound told her that it was full.

Because the crates were arranged several boxes deep and weren't flush with one another they formed an uneven staircase to the top.

Elisabetta hiked up her habit and began to climb.

'What are you doing?' Micaela asked. 'You're going to fall!'

'I'll be fine. I want to see if I can open one.'

'Why?'

'Curiosity.'

'I thought you said we should rest.'

'In a minute.'

Elisabetta climbed to the top and stood on one of the crates about twelve feet off the ground.

'Oops!'

The crate shifted a couple of centimeters.

'Come down!' Micaela said.

'No, it's okay – I think. I'll be careful.'

Elisabetta couldn't very well try to open the box she was standing on so she went for the one closer to the wall. She knelt down and inspected the lid. It looked heavy and fitted tightly but it wasn't nailed or screwed down. She pulled at the edge and it gave a little.

What was she going to find? Weapons? Drugs?

She pursed her lips. She didn't think so.

With all her strength she managed to lift the lid a couple of centimeters, just enough to insert her fingertips. She yanked up hard and the lid pulled open enough to let her have a good look inside.

Micaela was on her feet again, hands on her hips. 'So what is it, what do you see?'

The light was dim but Elisabetta could make out the contents.

In a way, she wasn't surprised by what she saw.

The crate was filled with red tuff dirt and human bones.

There were two complete skeletons, maybe three. The one on top had an articulated tail the length of her hand. And the face – she recognized his howling expression. She easily spotted the gold pendant in the ribcage because the light glinted off it. It was heavily incised with star signs, the exact same zodiacal ring from the fresco and from Faustus's magic circle.

Who are you? Elisabetta thought, staring at the raging face.

She transferred all the weight of the lid onto one hand and reached in with the other, ignoring the gold disc and going instead for the smaller silver object among the finger bones. She pulled it out. A pretty little chi-rho medallion.

'What is it?' Micaela called out. 'What have you found?'

'It's them,' Elisabetta called down. 'The skeletons of St Callixtus.'

TWENTY-SIX

Rome, AD 68

At the age of thirty, pudgy and balding, Nero no longer looked anything like his ubiquitous image on statues and coins. The years since the Great Fire had taken their toll.

In the hours of the day when he was sober he had obsessed and labored over every detail in the construction of his Golden House. The Domus Aurea wasn't so much a palace as a statement. A vast tract of burnt-out Rome was now his and he could shape the land at will into his golden image. When it was done, a flabbergasted visitor would see a vista of open countryside filled with woods, pastures, exotic animals and grand buildings surrounding a lake, all set in a valley surrounded by hills.

The main residential complex dazzled the eye because its 360-meter south-facing façade was built so that its gilded surface caught and reflected the sun throughout the day. Its vestibule was tall enough to house a colossal effigy of Nero, the largest statue in Rome. There were dining rooms with fretted ceilings of ivory and with panels that could be opened by slaves to shower his guests with flower petals. There were pipes for sprinkling guests with perfumes. The main banquet hall was circular and set on a revolving platform that slaves slowly rotated throughout the day and night to mimic the earth moving through the heavens. His heated baths were supplied with sea- and sulphur water.

Its construction greatly enriched a bevy of Lemures corporations but drained the coffers of the empire. But Nero felt wholly entitled. When it was sanctified and dedicated he would say that finally he could live like a human being.

As he moved from room to sumptuous room, from one debauchery to another, the empire groaned under his profligate rule. The Roman statesman Gaius Calpurnius Piso had tried to unseat him a year after the fire before Nero got wind of the affair and slaughtered the multitude of plotters and all their blood-kin. The following year there was a Jewish revolt in Judea which required Nero to implore his esteemed general Vespasian to come out of retirement.

Cost overruns at the Domus Aurea and other Roman building projects and the massive expense of keeping order within his far-flung empire led Nero to bleed more taxes out of the provinces.

'Get me more money!' he was always bellowing to Tigellinus who would oblige as best he could, carving out his personal take from every transaction. He'd grown used to Nero's increasing demands. More money, more food, more wine, more spectacles, more orgies, more blood – especially Christian blood.

None of this bothered Tigellinus in the least but he and the leading Lemures families were growing worried about losing the control they had enjoyed since the days of Caligula. How they wished that Balbilus were still among the living to read the star charts and tell them what was due.

A new and serious threat had emerged in the form of Gaius Julius Vindex, the over-taxed governor of Gallia Lugdunensis, and Gaul was in open rebellion. True, Nero's legions had defeated Vindex at the bloody battle of Vesontonio but, far from continuing to fight for Nero, the victorious Praetorians promptly proposed their own commander Verginius as the new emperor. He refused to participate in treason but support was growing across the empire for Galba to seize power from the fat, crazed lyre-player in the Golden House.

Yet whatever adversity befell him during these troubled times Nero could always find escape in a jug of wine and solace in the arms of Sporus.

In the summer of 65, Nero, who was immune to the notions of regret and remorse, committed the one act he would have taken back if he could. In a drunken rage brought on by something he couldn't even remember the next day, he stomped his wife Poppaea Sabina and her unborn child to death. When he awoke the next morning, bilious and hungover and saw her broken carcass on the marble floor and her blood on his hands and feet he wailed like a child.

He'd killed his own mother, he'd raped a Vestal Virgin, he'd committed countless unspeakable acts but none of them had ever stuck with him like the murder of Poppaea. After she was gone it occurred to him that he missed her terribly. An emptiness gnawed at him and he attempted to fill it as quickly as he could. Every time he heard of a woman who looked like Poppaea he had her brought to him and if the likeness was appealing enough he kept her as his concubine. But none met his expectations like a boy, a freedman named Sporus, who bore an uncanny resemblance. Nero took to him immediately and rewarded the lad with castration to seal the deal.

When his wounds healed Nero had him wigged, gowned and made-up like Poppaea and married him in a formal ceremony where Tigellinus held his nose and gave the 'bride' away. He took him to his bed every night and told him he'd slit his throat if he ever whispered about his tail. And while tongues wagged all over the city, Nero perpetually pestered his Greek surgeons about some way of turning the eunuch into a proper woman so he could kiss his face while they fornicated.

In June the gardens of the Domus Aurea were at their most fragrant but the only ones who seemed to notice were the slaves who tended the flower beds and fruit trees. Nero and his court were otherwise occupied with news of the traitor Galba who was gaining steam as the summer heat began to bear down.

Nero had briefly rejoiced at the defeat of Vindex weeks earlier, not for least because he'd heard the Gallic governor had called him a bad lyre-player, but Galba had taken up the mantle of rebellion and was rolling his legions towards Italy. It reassured the court not a bit when Nero had announced his mad plan for defeating the insurrection: he would travel to the advancing legions armed with wagons laden with theatrical props and water organs accompanied by concubines who would be given masculine haircuts and dressed as Amazonian warriors. When he met Galba he would, at first, do nothing but weep. And thus, reducing the rebels to penitence, he would stage a grand performance for them with songs of victory he was composing.

After dark one day, a messenger arrived at the Domus Aurea with a message for Tigellinus. He read it and shook his head. The time had come for him to leave. He'd been expecting the news and his slaves had already cleaned out his villa and loaded the carts and wagons. General Turpilianius, the last of the loyalists commanding the advance force against Galba, had defected. Tigellinus had no desire to die for Nero and despite the riches that had accrued to him over the years he still had a bitter taste in his mouth over Nero's torching of his precious Basilica Aemilia. No, he would decamp to his estate in Sinuessa and keep a low profile there among other Lemures families. They would find a way forward. They always did.

'What is it?' Nero drunkenly asked Tigellinus when he entered the dining hall.

'A dispatch from the field.'

Nero put his arm around Sporus and knocked over a precious glass goblet in the process. 'Well, tell me what it says then! I'm busy, can't you see?'

'Turpilianius has gone over to Galba.'

Nero stood wobbly on his feet. His secretary, Epaphroditus, ran to his side to steady him.

'What shall we do?' Nero demanded.

Tigellinus thought for a moment and before stamping off he delivered a line from the *Aeneid*, a biting, sarcastic send-off. 'Is it such a wretched thing to die?'

Nero sputtered as his courtiers fled and the dining hall emptied. He managed to compose himself enough to rasp a few orders to those who remained. He wanted a fleet prepared at Ostia to take him to Alexandria. In the meanwhile he'd leave his Golden House that very night. It was too large to defend every entrance and he was feeling vulnerable there. The walled Servilian Gardens across the Tiber were more secure. Nero threw gold at any of his Praetorian and German cohorts who would flee with him but most of them deserted on the spot.

'Where's Sporus?' he ranted to Epaphroditus. 'Bring him to me!'

Epaphroditus found him in the kitchens, speaking to a man at a rear door by the herb garden. The man disappeared into the night.

'Who was that?' Epaphroditus asked.

'Just a friend,' Sporus pouted.

'You have but one man to attend to, wretch,' Epaphroditus said, 'and he commands you.'

As Nero and his small entourage made their way across the Tiber, the majority of the Senate marched to the Praetorian barracks, declared Nero an enemy of the state, and gave their allegiance to Galba. Nero's German Cohorts were ordered to stand down.

It was after midnight when Nero and Sporus finally bedded down for the night in Nero's chamber at the Servilian Gardens.

Nero suddenly sat bolt upright.

'Can't you sleep?' Sporus asked wearily.

'Something's wrong,' Nero announced, leaping up and calling for Epaphroditus. The man confirmed Nero's fears. The imperial bodyguard had melted away.

Nero bolted hysterically from the villa to the riverbank and when it appeared that he might fling himself into the dark waters one of his few remaining friends, the freedman Phaon, suggested they flee to his own villa a few kilometers to the north. Some horses were found and Epaphroditus dressed Nero in an old cloak and a farmer's hat since their route led directly past a Praetorian barracks. His last entourage was small indeed: Phaon, Epaphroditus and Sporus.

It was a harrowing final journey for an emperor. He held a handkerchief over his face to conceal his identity as they journeyed along the well-traveled road. As they passed a farmer and his mule, Nero's horse lurched, forcing him to use both hands to steady the beast. When he lowered his handkerchief the farmer, who had once been a soldier, recognized him and cried, 'Hail, Caesar! How could they declare you an enemy of the state?'

Nero said nothing and rode on.

They reached Phaon's villa where Nero collapsed on a couch. 'What do they do to an enemy of the state?' he asked.

'The punishment is the ancient one,' Phaon said miserably, rummaging for a flask of wine.

'And what is that?' Nero cried.

'It is a degrading fate, Caesar,' Epaphroditus informed him. 'The executioners strip their victim naked, hold his head down with a wooden fork and then flog him to death with rods.'

Nero began to whimper.

Horses were coming.

Nero panicked, grabbed a dagger and put it to his throat but then let it drop from his limp hand and clatter to the floor.

'Will no one help me?' he pleaded.

Epaphroditus retrieved the dagger and held it to Nero's throat again, its tip just indenting the soft pink flesh.

'Make sure my body is burned,' Nero whimpered. 'I want no one to see what I am.'

'Yes, Caesar,' Epaphroditus answered.

Nero looked at the fresco on Phaon's ceiling. It depicted a seated woman playing a lyre. 'What a great artist dies with me,' he whispered.

'I can't do it,' Epaphroditus said, his hand wavering.

Sporus was hovering behind him. The boy, who had been held down and castrated and then buggered for years, took hold of the dagger handle.

'I can,' he said, thrusting the blade through one side of Nero's neck and clean out the other.

And as Epaphroditus knelt numbly beside his master's body, Sporus turned and left the chamber alone, fingering the medallion in his pocket which had been given to him by the man in the herb garden.

It was a chi-rho symbol, a fine one, rendered in gold.

'I am a Christian now,' Sporus said out loud. 'And I have rid Rome of this monster.'

London, 1593

It was an unseasonably warm May and the Mermaid tavern was sweltering. The tavern smelled of stale and fresh ale, old and new piss and a sickly miasma of sweat.

Marlowe was bone weary and mightily peeved that he wasn't getting drunk as quickly as he would have liked. Seated at a long crowded table, he raged at the landlord about watered ale but the burly server ignored him and let him seethe.

'I shall take my business elsewhere,' he bellowed to no one in particular. 'The ale is better in Holland.'

He knew Dutch beer well.

He'd spent much of the past year in the stinking port city of Flushing doing the double and triple dealings at which he had become so adept. Walsingham was dead, nigh on three years now, and Marlowe had a new master, Robert Cecil, who had continued to play on his father, Lord Burghley, for connections with the Queen. Cecil had successfully wheedled himself into Walsingham's position as Secretary of State and chief spymaster. Robert Poley, Cecil's loyal toad who willingly shuttled in and out of dank prisons to maintain his cover as a Catholic sympathizer, was put in charge of all Her Majesty's agents in the Low Countries.

Marlowe often found his covert duties petty but they paid well – better than the theatre – and afforded him time to write plays to further the agenda that he admired: chaos, confusion and calamity. Burghley was infirm and not long for this world. The elderly John Dee had become dotty and the Queen had put him out to pasture as Warden of Christ's College in Manchester. Robert Cecil was primed to become the most powerful Lemures in England and Marlowe was his man. He would ride his coat-tails to new heights of fame, wealth and power. He felt altogether deserving; he'd paid his dues.

He'd lived in a stinking room in the port city of Flushing, drunk Dutch beer in the inns and taverns, gathered intelligence masquerading as a Catholic supporter, counterfeited coins by day with a ring of conspirators and found the time to write for a few hours most nights.

And following his triumph with *Faustus*, each of his new plays had been well received. *The Jew of*

Malta was next, then the historical drama *Edward II*, then *Hero and Leander* and finally *The Massacre at Paris*, which Pembroke's Men had performed months earlier.

Never content and always striving, Marlowe found much to irritate him. He lived like a pauper compared with someone like Cecil. They were of the same stock, same education, similar intellect, but Cecil had a Burghley for a father and Marlowe's father was a shoemaker. And on the literary side, he now had a formidable rival. A young actor and writer from Stratford-upon-Avon had burst upon the London scene with a play called *Henry VI*, which had debuted a year earlier with astounding financial success. William Shakespeare also lived in Shoreditch. They saw each other frequently at the Rose Theatre and local taverns where they circled one another warily like two bucks ready to charge at one another and bang antlers.

The only true pleasure in Marlowe's life was Thomas Kyd, his great love, whom he'd persuaded to share a room in Norton Folgate.

He shouted for another flask of ale, insisting that it should come from a new barrel, and went to empty his bladder in the ditch behind the tavern.

There, in the shadows as was his wont, was Robert Poley.

'Poley!' Marlowe yelled at his black outline. 'Is that you? Do you ever come into the light? You're like the shades of Hades, lurking, lurking, always lurking.'

'I'll show myself well enough if you buy me a drink,' Poley said.

'Good. Come and be my dark company, then.'

Poley had come straight from Robert Cecil's privy chamber.

They had been Walsingham's rooms but Cecil had them decorated with better paintings and tapestries, finer silver and plate. He had improved his own bearing, too, adopting a slow, regal stride, commissioning the finest clothes and fussing obsessively over his pointed beard and thick swept-back hair.

'What do you have to report, Poley?' Cecil had asked.

'I've done as you instructed and have been closely watching Marlowe.'

'And how fares our talented friend?'

'His indiscretions mount.'

'How so?'

'He's sharing a bed with Thomas Kyd now. Openly.'

'Is he, now?'

'There have been rumors about Thomas Kyd which have been passed to me by our people in Rome.'

'What rumors?'

'It's said that he is in the employ of the Church. The Pope has tasked his men to find Lemures and root us out.'

'And you're saying that Kyd is their spy?'

'I am.'

Cecil had sighed. 'Marlowe could have easily found pleasure among his own kind.'

'He's bent on destroying himself,' Poley had said.

'Then we must help him,' Cecil had said. 'But it must be done carefully. The Queen likes his plays. Still, I hear this new man, Shakespeare, while not one of us, is the better writer of plays. The Queen will soon enough be distracted by another bard.'

Marlowe poured strong liquor from a flask into Poley's mug. They were at a small private table. 'What occupies you these days, Poley?'

'There are plans afoot,' the other man said cryptically. 'Foul winds blow from Flanders. Cecil aims to send us there before too long.'

'Will he pay well?' Marlowe grumbled.

'He says he will pay exceedingly well. The matter is serious and if it is handled to perfection, Cecil believes it will strengthen his position with the Queen. Further, this venture could make all of us rich.'

'Tell me more,' Marlowe said, suddenly interested.

'In a fortnight or so the plan will be ripe for discourse. When Cecil passes the word, we'll meet at Widow Bull's house in Deptford.'

'Let me know,' Marlowe said. 'I've conducted a good fill of business there and it has a further advantage. Mrs Bull is a most excellent cook.'

Marlowe knew trouble was brewing when a week later a venomous letter was posted on the wall of a London church that was frequented by Dutch Protestants. It was a diatribe in blank verse aimed at stirring mob violence against these immigrants and their multitudinous vile ways. The missive evoked passages from Marlowe's *Jew of Malta* and *The Massacre at Paris* and was provocatively signed 'Tamburlaine'.

Marlowe hadn't written the letter but the general assumption at Court was that he had.

To Marlowe's horror, Thomas Kyd was arrested by the Royal Commissioners at Cecil's command and under extreme torture at Bridewell Prison attested that he had seen Marlowe composing the letter.

The Queen was informed and the Privy Council, with Burghley and Cecil sitting in attendance, authorized a warrant for Marlowe's arrest.

He was hauled off to Bridewell but was treated gently enough with nary an interrogation. In two days Poley arrived to bail him out.

'Why is this happening, Poley?' Marlowe demanded angrily when they were out on the streets. 'You and Cecil know I had nothing to do with this Dutch letter.'

'Someone is doing you mischief,' Poley said, shaking his head. 'Let's find a tavern.'

'Damn the taverns! What's happened to Kyd?'

'He's being held. You were likely close to him these past days. He says you were the culprit.'

'Under torture?'

'I expect so,' Poley said. 'At least you weren't touched. Cecil made sure of that.'

'To protect me or the knowledge of the existence of my nether parts?' Marlowe whispered.

'Both, I'm sure.'

Marlowe suddenly stopped in his tracks. 'I know who did this, Poley! By the stars, I know!'

Poley took a small step back as if expecting a blow.

'I'm certain it was Will Shakespeare, that jealous worm, that sorry excuse for a playwright.'

Poley smiled because he had written the letter himself and was rather proud of the effort. 'I'm sure you're right about that. Before you're off to Flanders you should kill the wretch.'

The Widow Bull laid on a fine meal in one of her upstairs rooms: a feast of neat's tongue, lamb, capon and stag.

Marlowe was uncharacteristically anorectic. His appetite had been failing since the business of the Dutch letter and furthermore he had to suffer the daily indignity of reporting his whereabouts to the Privy Council while they continued their investigations.

Poley ate heartily, as did the other two men, Nicholas Skeres and Ingram Frizer, two Lemures hooligans and swindlers whom Marlowe knew well enough. Yet just because they were his kind didn't mean he had to like them. He had no problem with killers but little time for uncultured ones.

Marlowe fidgeted and drank his wine. 'What of Flanders?' he asked.

Poley spoke through a mouthful of meat. 'King Phillip of Spain is preparing an invasion force.'

'He already lost one armada to Elizabeth,' Marlowe said. 'He's itching to have another joust with the Lady?'

'Apparently so,' Poley said.

'Well, I'm keen to go,' Marlowe said. 'Can you have Cecil give the word and let me away from these damnable shores?'

'He's preparing the ground,' Poley said.

'And what of you two?' Marlowe said, pointing his dining knife in the direction of Skeres and Frizer. 'Are you also to Flanders?'

The men looked to Poley who nodded at them.

Frizer rose. 'Are you pointing a knife at me?' he demanded huskily.

Marlowe rolled his eyes at him. 'What of it?'

'No one points a knife at me.'

'Apparently you're mistaken,' Marlowe said sarcastically. 'I just did. Perhaps I mistook you for a plump ox testicle, ripe for the skewer.'

Suddenly Frizer had a dagger in his hand.

Marlowe had never backed off from a fight in his life and now all his pent-up frustrations came to a satisfying boil. He was an able brawler and this wiry scoundrel would go down hard. Marlowe's eating knife wasn't very long or very sharp but it would do.

He started to stand.

But suddenly there were arms around his chest and shoulders, pinning him to his chair.

Nicholas Skeres had stolen around behind him and was holding him immobile.

Frizer was coming around the table fast.

Marlowe heard Poley say, 'Do it!'

He saw the dagger streaking toward his eye.

He wouldn't yell and he wouldn't beg.

Like Faustus, about to be dragged to Hell, Marlowe reckoned he'd made his bargain.

The three men stood over Marlowe, waiting for his twitching body to become still. The flow of blood from his eye had receded to a trickle.

'That's that,' Skeres said. 'It's done.'

'Let's divide the money, then,' Frizer demanded.

Poley grunted and took a purse from his belt. It was heavy with gold.

'An equal split?' Skeres asked.

'Aye,' Poley said.

Later, in his chambers, Cecil asked Poley, 'How did he die?'

'He died well. A proper Lemures death. Violent. Quick. Quiet.'

'Well, it's over then. The Queen will soon enough be pleased he's dead. I'm already pleased he's dead. Make sure that no one examines the body beyond the wound to his head. Bury him in an unmarked grave. Make sure that Kyd dies, too. Let Marlowe's legacy be his plays and his codes, not his tail. Hail Lemures, I say. Hail Marlowe.'

TWENTY-SEVEN

Elisabetta awoke to the sound of the door creaking open. She called to her sister and both of them threw back their blankets.

The first person through the door was a mountain of a man in a black suit. The other was smaller, older, handsome and dapper in a tight blue cashmere sweater, dark trousers and tasseled loafers.

'I'm sorry to wake you,' the older man said in heavily accented English. 'I know you had an uncomfortable night but I didn't want you to sleep through the big day.'

Elisabetta stood, smoothed her habit and stepped into her shoes.

'Who are you?' she demanded.

The man ignored her question.

Micaela was standing, adjusting her blouse. 'My sister asked you who you were, asshole. You're going to wish you hadn't messed with us.'

Mulej pulled a large pistol from under his jacket and swore at her.

'Fat men with small dicks like to threaten women,' Micaela snarled.

'Micaela, please,' Elisabetta pleaded. 'Don't make the situation worse.'

The older man laughed. 'Put the gun away, Mulej. There's no need. My name is Krek. Damjan Krek.'

Krek. Could this be K?

'Where are we?' Elisabetta asked.

'Slovenia,' Krek replied. 'You are in my home. Come upstairs with me.'

'What about Micaela?'

'She'll be fine. You and I need to discuss some things. And we need to watch a little television, too.'

'Television?' Elisabetta asked.

'The whole world is watching the Vatican and we must watch as well,' Krek said. 'The Conclave is about to start.'

Zazo hadn't wanted to sleep but his body had shut itself down in agitated exhaustion as the sun rose over the Tiber. When he awoke it was ten o'clock and the apartment was quiet. Mad at himself, he jumped off the sofa and rushed to his sisters' room in the vain hope that they had tiptoed in while he was napping.

As he feared, the room was empty.

He peeked in on his father. Carlo was asleep on top of his bed, fully clothed. Zazo let him be.

He rang Arturo again. The man sounded as rough as he did. 'Anything?' he asked.

There was nothing.

Zazo had spent the long night waking neighbors, calling casualty departments, calling Sister Marilena, driving to Micaela's flat, walking the streets of the neighborhood. Just before he'd decided to wait for daylight he'd left an angry message on Inspector Leone's voicemail telling him that his, Zazo's, sisters hadn't come home and asking how missing someone needed to be for the Polizia to start a missing-person investigation.

Zazo parted the sitting-room curtains and sunlight streamed in. He paced. He swore. He didn't know what to do with himself. He reached for his jacket. He'd get some fresh air, get a coffee.

At the café he picked up his coffee at the bar and went to a window table. When he sat he was aware of something stiff in his inside jacket pocket. He reached in and pulled out the folded papers.

There were twenty pages of phone numbers, a couple of years of Bruno Ottinger's outgoing calls from his home. Zazo slurped his espresso, flicked through the pages and stopped, muttering to himself about wasting his time. He looked out the window, hoping he'd see a nun's black habit floating past.

He looked at the pages again. The great majority showed numbers within Germany, mostly local ones in Ulm. He picked up the phone and rang the most-called number. An operator at the University of Ulm answered; he hung up on her without speaking.

Scattered through the pages was a number with a country code that he didn't recognize – 386. He tried it. A man's voice answered, 'Da? 929295.'

Zazo tried Italian first. 'Hello. Who am I calling please?'

'Kaj?'

He shifted to English and asked again.

The voice responded in English. 'This is private line. Who do you try to reach?'

'I'm a friend of Bruno Ottinger,' Zazo said.

There was silence and a muffled sound as if someone had a hand over the mouthpiece. The voice came back on. 'I can't help you.' The line disconnected.

Zazo wearily rubbed his eyes and made a mental note to look up the 386 code. He began folding the pages.

Something caught his eye and he stopped. He smoothed the pages and stared. A single number was leaping out at him.

It was Italian – a Vatican exchange.

He punched in the number as fast as he could. A woman answered in Italian but with a German accent: 'Pronto.'

Zazo spoke to her in Italian. 'This is Major Celestino of the Vatican Gendarmerie. Who am I speaking with?'

'This is Frieda Shuker.'

'Ah, Corporal Shuker's wife?'

'That's right. Klaus is on duty today, of course. How can I help you, Major?'

'I'm sorry to bother you,' Zazo said. 'Just a simple question. This number is one of the Swiss Guard's residences, correct?'

'Yes, it's our flat.'

'And how long have you been assigned to it?'

'We moved here in 2006.'

'Do you know who lived there before you?'

'I've no idea. Sorry. Shall I have Klaus ring you?'

'Not to worry, it's okay. Thanks for your time.'

Zazo couldn't stay seated. His mind was too unsettled for him to stay inside. He was on his feet and out the café door. He scrolled through the contact list on his phone and speed-dialed Omar Savio at the Vatican City IT department.

Omar, a pizza-and-beer buddy, seemed surprised that he was calling. 'This must be important,' he said.

'Why do you say that?'

'Because the Conclave's about to start. You must be up to your ass in it.'

Omar, it seemed, hadn't heard about his suspension. 'Yeah, it's important. I need you to look something up for me.'

'Shoot.'

'Who lived in Klaus Shuker's flat in the Guard's Residence before him? Shuker moved there in 2006.'

'Give me a second.' Zazo heard Omar's fingers on a keyboard.

'Okay, Flat 18, almost got it . . . It was Matthias Hackel. He had it from 2000 until 2006. He's in the Oberstleutnant Apartment now. He must've moved out when he got promoted.'

'Hackel, eh?' Zazo said, trying to think. He stopped to wait for a street light to change.

'Why's it so noisy?' Omar asked. 'Aren't you at the Vatican?'

'Yeah, I'm nearby. Look, Omar, what I've got to ask you to do is time-sensitive and extremely delicate. I need you to email me Hackel's telephone logs for his residential and cellular numbers going back to 2006.'

His friend sounded incredulous. 'You're joking, right?'

'No, I'm deadly serious.'

'I'd need a written authorization from Hackel's boss to do that. If I didn't have it, the Guards would run me through with their pikes.'

'Omar, I wouldn't ask you if it weren't a matter of life and death. Please believe me. I can't let the Guards know I'm looking into one of their own. I'll never reveal you as a source. Send it to my private email address. You're in IT. You know how to make these things invisible.'

'Free pizza for life?' Omar asked.

'Yeah, for life.'

Waiters hustled around the dining hall of the Domus Sanctae Marthae, serving the dessert course and pouring out coffees. The Cardinal Electors were taking care not to stain their cassocks. These days a good telephoto lens could pick up a splash of gravy from a hundred meters.

The nine Cardinal Bishops sat at the raised dais overlooking tables where the other Cardinals dined with the conclavists, the small number of attendants who were entitled to accompany them into the Sistine Chapel. Cardinal Diaz sat in the central chair, befitting his position as Dean of the College of Cardinals. His old friends, Aspromonte and Giaccone, flanked him.

Diaz pushed a piece of pie around his plate and mumbled to Giaccone, 'The sooner we have a new Holy Father, the sooner we get back to proper food.'

Giaccone wasn't as picky. He took a big forkful but agreed. 'It's not so much the food. For me it's the bed. I want to sleep in my own bed.'

Aspromonte leaned his big bald head in to listen. 'The walls are too thin.' He pointed his fork in the direction of an American cardinal. 'All night I heard Kelley snoring.'

Diaz snorted. 'Well, in an hour we'll be in the Chapel. We'll do our duty and then life will go on.'

Suddenly, Giaccone winced and put his silverware down.

'What's the matter?' Diaz asked him.

Giaccone scrunched his fleshy face and pushed at his round belly. 'Nothing. Maybe some gas.' He winced again.

Aspromonte looked concerned. 'Maybe you should see the doctor. He's right over there.'

'No, honestly, I'm fine.'

Diaz patted him on the shoulder. 'Go and lie down. There's time for a little rest before we're called.'

'I don't want to fall asleep,' Giaccone protested.

'Don't worry about that,' Aspromonte said. 'We won't let you sleep through the Conclave!'

TWENTY-EIGHT

The great room of Castle Krek made Elisabetta feel like a speck of dust. The huge hearth was blazing, the furniture was oversized, the gallery and wood-beamed ceiling were impossibly high.

Krek had made her sit on a sofa. There were doors on three sides of the room, all shut. There was no sign of the fat man. They were alone.

Elisabetta watched him closely, trembling and frozen like a rabbit trying to remain hidden from a prowling wolf.

Krek was impeccably groomed, with barbershop-fresh silvering hair and a perfectly aligned posture. He poured himself coffee and with an afterthought offered her a cup. She declined with a single head shake.

'I've never actually met a nun,' he said suddenly. 'Can you believe that? Particularly with my long interest in the Church. And no ordinary nun. A professional woman, an archeologist. An expert in the catacombs – which have always fascinated me. I'm also fascinated by the choices you've made. You see, I'm always learning. Do you nuns have the opportunity to keep learning too? Or do they stifle this when you join a convent?'

Elisabetta stared mutely back at him, refusing to answer.

Seemingly unperturbed by her snub, Krek checked his watch and said, 'Look at the time!' He picked up a remote control, turned on a large flat-screen TV which hung above a sideboard and put on a pair of wire-rimmed glasses. The wall became alive with a bright helicopter's view over St Peter's Square where tens of thousands of pilgrims were so packed in that they could hardly move.

Krek seemed gleeful.

'Can you believe how many people are there? It's going to be a big, big day for them. Some of them will tell their children and their children's children: "I was there! I was at St Peter's that day."'

Elisabetta finally spoke. 'I know what you are.'

'You know what I am,' he spat back. '*What* am I?'

'Lemures.'

'So, I knew you were clever. This is just a confirmation.'

'You killed Professor De Stefano. You killed Father Tremblay. You're a monster.'

'Labels. Always labels. A monster! Too glib, don't you think? I define myself as a successful businessman who happens to be a member of a very old, very elite club.'

'You must not do this.'

Krek looked at Elisabetta over the top of his wire-framed glasses and smiled. But there was no hint of humor in his expression. It was the smile of a predator closing in on its prey. 'What do you think I'm going to do?'

She trembled inwardly but said nothing more, causing him to stare at her fiercely.

'Please understand this: I'll do whatever I please.'

Three luxury coaches, each with a capacity of forty-two passengers, idled at the Domus Sanctae Marthae, waiting for the Cardinal Electors and the conclavists to file out for the one-minute ride to the courtyard behind the Basilica. True, all the electors were under eighty years of age, their older brethren banned from the task, and all possessed enough mobility to walk the short distance. But security concerns dictated this part of the ritual.

Cardinals Diaz and Aspromonte boarded the first coach and took adjoining seats. 'Did you hear about Giaccone?' Diaz asked.

'No, what?'

'He's still in his room. He can't come.'

'What happened?'

'He called the doctor. It seems that he has the runs. Too much food, I suspect.'

'Will he join us later?'

'The rules permit him to do so but he can also cast ballots from the Domus. I've assigned a monsignor to bring him a ballot if necessary.'

'A disaster,' Aspromonte whispered. 'He's the popular choice. But who knows how easy it will be to get votes *in absentia*. People like to see the face of the new man.'

'Well, God willing, he'll recover quickly.'

On the television there was a bird's-eye view of the coaches crawling away from the guest house and their brief journey to the rear of the Basilica. One by one the Cardinals filed out of the coaches and disappeared inside a door manned by Swiss Guards in full ancient regalia.

'It's a colorful spectacle,' Krek said. 'Full of tradition. That much I respect.'

From their sofas, both he and Elisabetta had a good view of the TV and with every passing second Elisabetta's anxiety ratcheted upward. Out of desperation to do something, anything, she decided to engage him.

'And what part of it *don't* you respect?' she asked, her voice tremulous.

He seemed delighted to have her come alive. 'Well, the belief in God, of course, is a fundamental weakness. A crutch as ancient as man himself. I believe the more you rely on a god to govern your life, the less you govern it yourself. But besides that, the Catholic Church has always been the most smug, most repugnant, most hypocritical of all the religions. A billion people slavishly following some old man tarted up in robes and a hat! We've been fighting it since its earliest days.'

'You say you believe that men should rely on themselves, not on God. What else do you believe in?' Elisabetta asked.

'Me? I very much believe in myself. I believe in the heavens, too. The stars and planets clearly influence human events. That much is factual but I confess I haven't a clue how it works. So that, I suppose, is my suspension of rationality in favor of a belief system.'

'You believe in astrology,' she said, bemused.

'Our kind have respected astrology for many centuries,' Krek sniffed.

'I found astrological symbols at St Callixtus.'

'Yes, I know. If there had been a way to quickly remove the wall intact I would have been very happy to have the fresco in my home. My men said they tried, but it crumbled. They were hardly conservationists and they had a more important task.'

'The skeletons.'

'Yes. Again, a crude job – but speed was necessary.'

'What will you do with them?'

'I intend to give them the respect they deserve. The bones are in a jumble. I need them to be properly assembled, every man, woman and child. Somewhere within that confusion is our greatest astrologer – Balbilus, and I would like his remains to be identified and given pride of place in my family crypt. He was Emperor Nero's personal astrologer, imagine that! Nero was one of us, you know. Tradition tells us that the burial chamber belonged to Balbilus and that he and his followers perished during the Great Fire of

Rome. It can't be verified but Peter the Apostle was said to have been involved in their demise.'

'There were signs of a fire.'

'You see. Science! That's why I need you.'

'To do what?'

'You're going to handle the bones for me. You're an archeologist and a woman who respects the past and the sanctity of the dead. I think you'll do a marvelous job.'

Elisabetta shook her head. 'You think I'd do this voluntarily?'

Krek shrugged. 'I really hadn't thought about that. I simply decided you were going to do it.' Before she could express outrage he added, 'What did you make of the star signs at St Callixtus?'

'I hadn't fully worked them out.'

'You took note of the particular order of the planets, didn't you?'

She nodded.

'That was the alignment at the moment Balbilus was born in 4 AD. Check the charts if you don't believe me. I think it was a personal homage to his greatness. It became a symbol for us – of his power, of *our* power.'

'Marlowe used it in *Faustus*.'

'Yes! Bravo! You noticed the illustration. I told you that you were the one for this job. We've had many powerful astrologers through the ages. Bruno Ottinger was my personal astrologer. I believe you know certain things about Bruno.'

'I have the book that you gave him.'

'I want it back,' Krek said icily. 'Maybe you'll give it to me as a present.' He checked the TV and turned up the volume. 'So, there they are, all of them in the Pauline Chapel. We should watch.'

Hackel stood immobile inside the Pauline Chapel of the Palace of the Vatican. He was in front of the Pauline Door which led to the Sala Regia, a frescoed hall which connected the Palace to the Sistine Chapel. The Cardinal Electors stood in rows facing Cardinal Diaz who was about to address them. There were two videographers who'd been cleared to broadcast the brief ceremony, the last that the public would see of the Cardinals before the Conclave began.

Hackel heard chatter in his earpiece. Minor things: a tourist had been removed from the Square for public drinking. There were pickpockets about. He controlled his breathing, slow and smooth. It would be over soon. Perhaps his role would come out in the investigation, perhaps not. One could never underestimate incompetency. Regardless, *he*'d know what he'd done. And, more importantly, K would, too. If it looked as though the authorities were on to him, he would disappear into the Lemures network. There would be choices. He fancied South America. There were beautiful women there.

The Master of the Papal Liturgical Celebrations, Cardinal Franconi, held a microphone up to Diaz's mouth. He made a short speech in Latin, reminding the

Electors of their responsibilities to the Church for the solemn task they were about to undertake and led them in a brief prayer to give them the strength and wisdom to choose a new Holy Father.

It was Hackel himself who opened the Pauline Door to let the procession begin.

TWENTY-NINE

Zazo watched the Cardinals in rows of two walk slowly through the Sala Regia flanked by an honor detail of Swiss Guards. He swallowed hard. It was other-worldly to be seeing this play out on TV. He should have been there. He caught a fleeting glimpse of Lorenzo in the background and wondered how he was holding up.

Zazo's father was puttering about the apartment in an agitated state, unable to go to the university, unable to pick up his Goldbach notebook. By turns he stared out the windows and at the phone as if he could will his daughters to materialize. Zazo tried to get him to eat but he wouldn't.

Both of them jumped when Zazo's mobile rang. He answered immediately and shook his head quickly to signal that it wasn't Micaela or Elisabetta.

He listened and said, 'Omar, you're the best. I swear to you that you won't get in trouble for this.' Then he clicked off and sat down at his father's computer.

'Who was that?' his father asked.

'One of my friends in IT at the Vatican. He's emailing me a file of phone records.'

'Whose records?'

'This morning I found out that in 2005 Bruno Ottinger placed a call to a private residence in the Vatican. Matthias Hackel, the man who's currently second in command of the Swiss Guards, used to live there. I asked for Hackel's phone logs.'

'What does this have to do with Micaela and Elisabetta?' Carlo asked.

'I don't know. Maybe nothing. But it's curious, isn't it? Why is a man like Ottinger communicating with a Swiss Guard? Anyway, I'd rather follow my nose than sit like a lump. I don't trust the Polizia to be doing anything productive.'

His father agreed and hovered over his shoulder while Zazo opened Omar's email and sent the attachment to the printer.

The printer was still churning out fifty pages. Zazo grabbed a sheaf and groaned, 'This guy made a lot of calls.'

'What are we looking for?' Carlo asked.

'I'm not sure. Patterns. Frequently dialed numbers.' He pulled out the Ottinger logs and unfolded them. 'Maybe any calls to third parties common to the two sets of logs.'

At the sight of dense rows of phone numbers, Carlo perked up. He pulled the pages from his son's hand. 'You go make me some toast and leave the numbers to me.'

*

The somber procession of Cardinals in scarlet and white seemed to fascinate Krek.

They were chanting the hymn *Veni Creator Spiritus.*

Veni, creator Spiritus
mentes tuorum visita,
imple superna gratia,
quae tu creasti pectora.

Come, Holy Ghost, Creator blest,
And in our hearts take up Thy rest;
Come with Thy grace and heavenly aid,
To fill the hearts which Thou hast made.

'Please tell me why you're doing this!' Elisabetta asked Krak desperately.

He looked heavenward in a wry sign of cooperation, then muted the TV's volume so he wouldn't have to compete with it.

'Nine hundred years ago, one of us, a great astrologer and visionary, made a prophecy.'

'Malachy,' she said.

'Yes! Malachy. More cleverness from my nun. For us, this prophecy has been like a beacon and as one of the proud leaders of my people it has been my personal responsibility to use my resources to make sure it is fulfilled.'

'To destroy the Church,' she said sadly.

'Yes, of course. This has always been our strongest desire.'

'Malachy said the world would end. You want that too?'

'Look,' Krek said. 'I enjoy my life. I'm very comfortable as you can see. But this is something that has been anticipated for a very long time. I say, destroy the Church. That much I can help to accomplish. Whether the world ends too because of my actions, well, we'll just have to see.'

Elisabetta shook her head. 'It's despicable.'

Krek stood and liberally stoked his fire as if he wanted a backdrop of leaping flames. If that was his intention, then it achieved its dramatic effect. As he stood in front of the fireplace it appeared to Elisabetta as if he were emerging from an inferno.

'Despicable?' His voice rose, 'How is your Catholic dogma so different? You speak of a Final Judgment Day. The day the world as we know it ends, no? Your version has Christ returning, mine does not. That's the principal difference.'

'In the Last Judgment there will be different fates for the good and evil. That's what the Church teaches,' Elisabetta said, fighting to match his anger with gentleness.

'Believe me,' Krek said, settling back down, 'I have no interest in debating your theology. I welcome the perceived differences. Religious discord has always been a source of bounty for us.'

She felt sick. 'You say you want to destroy the Church. Toward what end? What do you want?'

'Our credo?' he ejaculated contemptuously. 'Our

raison d'être? We're interested in the dark beauty of power, wealth, domination. Fighting the Church has always enriched us. Every conflict brings opportunities. Wars make us rich – and, besides, they're quite enjoyable.'

'You get pleasure from human suffering?'

Krek set his jaw. 'Personally, yes, especially the suffering of sanctimonious religious zealots, but maybe I'm a little extreme in this regard. Most of my brethren are more businesslike in their attitudes.'

'You're psychopaths.'

He laughed. 'Labels again. You know, I'm an educated man. I've read and studied all my life. I understand the meaning of this term. Look, we are what we are just as you are what you are. I like to think we're more evolved, more specialized, more efficient. We're not hindered by emotionality and I believe that's a strength. If you want to use the term "psychopath", then go ahead. How should I label *you*?'

She was wrong-footed by the way he'd turned the tables. It took several moments for her to compose her thoughts. 'I'm a woman of faith. I believe in God. I always believed in Him, from my earliest childhood memories. I believe in goodness and the power of redemption. When people suffer, I suffer. I am a servant of God. I suppose that's my label. It defines me and it makes me happy.'

Krek glanced at the television to make sure he wasn't missing anything, then replied, 'Yes, but becoming a nun is a big step, no? No more parties. No more sex,

I suppose. No more freedom to do whatever the hell you want to do when you want to do it. Why did you do it?'

He knows why, she thought. She wasn't going to give him the sadistic satisfaction of spelling it out for him. She wasn't going to say, *you* did it, you bastard! Your thugs put a knife in my chest. They snuffed out the life of the man I loved. You made me suffer as much as a person can suffer. My only salvation lay in a total commitment to Christ.

Instead, she said, 'I can thank you for it. I suppose I owe you a debt of gratitude.'

Krek found this amusing and clapped like a seal. Then he pointed at the TV. 'Look!' he said like an excited child. 'They're closing the door!'

Hackel and his underling Gerhardt Glauser were among the plain-clothes Swiss Guards trailing the procession, mostly men who had provided close security for the deceased Pope. When the last of the conclavists had passed through the great portal of the Sala Regia into the Sistine Chapel, Cardinal Franconi, the Master of the Papal Liturgical Celebrations, was the one to close the heavy door. Hackel knew there was a ritual to be performed before the door was locked from the inside but as far as he was concerned the game was almost done.

A contingent of Guards in ceremonial costume took their place in front of the closed door. Hackel and Glauser saluted them, then Glauser said, 'Can I talk to you?'

The two men walked away from the prying lenses of the videographers and stood beside Agresti's fresco of Peter of Aragon offering his kingdom to Pope Innocent III. The vaulted ceiling of the Sala Regia amplified sounds so Glauser bent to whisper into Hackel's ear. 'One of them, Giaccone, is sick. He's still in the Domus.'

Hackel looked alarmed. 'Why wasn't I told of this?' he whispered back angrily.

'I'm telling you now,' Glauser replied. 'We've got it covered. I put two men on him. The Gendarmes are there as well. When they send a messenger for his ballot, we'll shadow him too.'

'Does Oberst Sonnenberg know?

'I'm not sure. Not from me, anyway. I follow the chain of command.'

Hackel shot back, 'You stay here.'

'Where are you going?' Glauser asked.

'To the Domus to check personally on Giaccone's security.'

'I apologize for the delay in informing you, Oberstleutnant. I didn't think it was such a big deal.'

Hackel stomped off in a huff. *One stray lamb.* He'd pay a visit to Cardinal Giaccone and take care of him properly.

Carlo Celestino was hunched over the dining-room table, his reading glasses low on his nose. He was circling phone numbers with his pencil and grumbling. 'I wish you hadn't marked up Ottinger's records. It's interfering with the system I'm using.'

'There's nothing I can do about it,' Zazo said wearily. 'Find anything?'

Carlo flipped through Hackel's log and muttered, 'This is the kind of thing a computer could do in a nanosecond. Maybe it's not surprising that most of the out-of-country calls of a Swiss Guard are to Switzerland. Probably family, but that's for you to figure out. Ottinger may have called Hackel's number but Hackel doesn't seem to have called Ottinger. Wait a second, here's a funny one. Hackel made a few calls to a 386 number. Didn't I see that exchange in Ottinger's records?' He checked the Ottinger files. 'I knew it! 929295. Hackel and Ottinger both called this number.'

'Let me see,' Zazo said, reaching for the Ottinger pages. 'Christ, I called it this morning!'

'Who was it?'

'They said it was a private line and hung up.'

'Where is it?'

Zazo was already on the computer, looking up the code. 'It's in Slovenia, the Bled region. It's not far from the Italian border. I'm going to call the Slovenian National Police in Ljubljana and ask them to do a reverse look-up. We've got to find out who lives there.'

THIRTY

Behind closed doors and away from the prying eyes of the media the Cardinal Electors found their assigned places and stood somberly at their tables, hands folded. Three items were laid out before them: The Gospels, a simple plastic pen and a ballot slip.

Cardinal Diaz strode to the podium, surveyed his colleagues and looked upwards to Michelangelo's magnificent ceiling. He focused on his favorite panel, *The First Day of Creation*, where God divides light from darkness, filled his chest and read out an oath in Latin. All those present would observe the procedures set down by the apostolic constitutions. If elected, they would defend the liberty of the Holy See. They would maintain secrecy and disregard any secular interests in voting.

When he was done, each Cardinal, one by one, touched the Gospels and simply stated, 'I do so promise, pledge and swear.'

Diaz took his place at his desk and Cardinal Franconi slowly made his way to the door of the Sala Regia.

He pushed it open and called out in a loud voice, '*Extra omnes!*'

Everyone but the Electors and conclavists were thereby ordered out. Several minor attendants dutifully left. Then Franconi closed the door behind them and slid the heavy bolt into place.

Hackel knocked on the door of Room 202 of the Domus Sanctae Marthae. The long hallway was empty.

Through the door, Giaccone asked who was there.

'Oberstleutnant Hackel of the Swiss Guards.'

In a few moments the door opened. Giaccone was wearing a bathrobe and slippers. He looked pale, his face even more droopy than usual.

'Oberstleutnant, how may I help you? Is everything all right?'

'Your Excellency, I need to speak with you in private on a matter of great urgency. May I come in?'

Giaccone nodded, allowed Hackel to enter and closed the door.

'So, now there is nothing more for us to see,' Krek said, sitting down across from Elisabetta. The television coverage had shifted back to St Peter's Square. 'The Conclave has begun. We must wait. But not for too long, I think.'

There was a crystal whiskey decanter on the table. Krek twisted off the ground-glass top and poured himself a good measure.

Elisabetta watched him enjoy a mouthful. She didn't

know what, other than curiosity, then compelled her to ask, 'Do you have them? The tattoos?'

'Would you like to see?'

'No!'

'Pity. It's been a tradition among us men since the late eighteenth century. Do you know what they stand for?'

'Malachy is King. Hail Lemures,' she said mechanically.

'My goodness! How did you figure that out?'

'A versus B. Your note to Ottinger with the book.'

'I'm genuinely impressed!' Krek knocked back another gulp of amber liquid. 'It would really be great if you worked for me.' He glanced at his watch and then at the television. He was drinking faster, becoming more voluble. 'Marlowe was an important person, associating with the other great English Lemures of his day – Francis Walsingham, Robert Cecil, John Dee. His coded message became a rallying cry for us: Malachy is King! Hail Lemures! It was a prideful thing. The numbers became deeply meaningful. To wear them out of sight where only we would see . . . well, that was very special.'

Krek poured himself another whiskey.

'And today you're trying to turn Malachy into a reality.'

'Since World War Two, just six popes ago, we began to get really focused on the prophecy and during John Paul II's papacy the 9/11 attacks happened. So I and some of my colleagues got to thinking, let's mobilize around this event and make sure that Malachy happens.

And the radical Muslims made it so simple for us, with 9/11 and the rest. Just like that – the Crusades are back! And all we have to do is fan the flames a little. So we were completely ready to spring into action when this pope died – and he was kind enough to give us plenty of warning with his nice slow cancer.'

As he was talking, Elisabetta felt clammy. A nausea started in her gut and a bilious rush rose in her throat. Krek wasn't looking at her anymore. His attention was fixed on the television.

'So the two hundred and sixty-eighth pope will be the last one. An Islamist group will take credit for what happens today. It should set the stage perfectly for the greatest religious war in history. There will be fire – no, it will be more than fire. It will be a conflagration. We'll watch it together, then have a little celebration.'

Zazo thanked the police officer in Ljubljana and put the phone down.

'They gave it to you?' his father asked.

'No problem. I told them it was a Vatican emergency. It's an unlisted number registered to someone named Damjan Krek.'

Carlo shrugged at the name.

Zazo did a search. 'He's a Slovenian billionaire. He owns a company that does construction, heavy equipment manufacturing, mining, that kind of thing.' Zazo stood and thrust his hands deeply into his pockets. 'So what's a Slovenian businessman doing with a German professor with a tail and an officer of the Swiss Guards?'

'K!' Carlo exclaimed. 'Krek could be the K who sent the book to Ottinger. This guy Hackel, I don't know.'

Zazo picked up the phone again. 'You speak German, right?'

His father nodded.

'I'm calling Krek's number. When it rings, say you're Matthias Hackel calling for Krek.'

'And if he picks up?'

'Then I'll take over, in English or Italian. I'll tell him the Gendarmerie's conducting a routine investigation. I'll improvise.'

'What's this got to do with Micaela and Elisabetta?'

Zazo shook his head. 'Maybe nothing, maybe everything.' He put the phone on speaker mode and called Krek's number.

When a man answered, Carlo identified himself as Oberstleutnant Hackel and asked for Krek.

There was a pause on the line and the man replied in German. 'I'm sorry, Herr Hackel. You're calling from a non-authorized line. I will have Mister Krek ring you back immediately on your authorized mobile number.'

The line went dead.

'Damn!' Zazo said, squeezing the back of his neck.

'Now what?' his father asked.

'Something's very wrong here. Krek's at the center of this. I'm going to call the Slovenian police again and see if I can get them to send some men to his house.'

'Looking for what?'

'Micaela and Elisabetta.'

*

When Hackel left the Domus he avoided the crowds by passing behind the Basilica, the Sistine Chapel and the Palaces of Gregory XIII and Sixtus V to get to his flat. The route obliged him to skirt the Swiss Guards barracks. Just past them a voice boomed out, 'Hackel!' He recognized the caller's voice, closed his eyes in frustration, and turned.

It was his superior, Oberst Sonnenberg, rushing out of the barracks with a squad of plain-clothes men.

'Hackel, what are you doing here? You're supposed to be at the Chapel,' Sonnenberg said.

Hackel turned and reversed his direction. 'There was a report of suspicious activity outside the Church of Saint Pellegrino. I left Glauser for a short while to check it out.'

'No, no, you must be mistaken,' Sonnenberg insisted. 'I've heard nothing of the sort. The problem is at the eastern entrance to St Peter's, at the metal detectors. Someone tried to pass through with a gun. The Gendarmes have him but there may be a second man. Come with me.'

Hackel sputtered, searching in vain for an excuse to disobey. He sighed and followed along.

He hadn't gone more than a few paces when he felt his phone vibrating in his pants pocket and pulled it out. It was Krek's number. He had to take the call and fell back a few paces.

'Yes?'

One of Krek's men was on the line. Over the crowd

noises from St Peter's Square he heard, 'Herr Krek is returning your call, Herr Hackel.'

Hackel slowed further to make sure he was out of Sonnenberg's earshot. 'I didn't call him!' Hackel declared.

'I'm sorry? Just now – I took the call myself.'

'Well, obviously it wasn't me. What number was it from?'

'I will send it to you by text, Herr Hackel, and inform Mister Krek of this irregularity.'

'Do it right away. And tell him that I'm a little behind schedule but that all is well.'

Krek was on the phone, making no attempt to hide the conversation from Elisabetta. 'Find out who made the call claiming to be Hackel and let me know immediately.' He put the handset down hard and tossed another log on the fire. The heat was making his forehead glisten. 'It seems we have a little more time,' he said to Elisabetta. There was a huskiness in his voice. 'Have a drink with me.'

'I don't drink,' Elisabetta said.

'I have some very good reds,' Krek said. 'You could pretend it was communion wine.'

'No.'

'Well, I'm having another.'

Elisabetta had never been so aware of her own heartbeat.

She couldn't sit there any longer with this monster, waiting for some catastrophe to erupt.

She had to do something.

While he was pouring another whiskey she bolted toward one of the doors. Krek reacted quickly enough. He grabbed a fistful of her robe and twisted her down to the rug. When she tried to rise he hit her hard with his closed fist, striking her jaw.

Elisabetta's head snapped back. The pain lasted only a second before her consciousness slipped away.

Zazo slammed the phone down.

'No?' his father asked.

'They wouldn't do it,' Zazo said. 'They routed me to the Deputy Head of the Slovenian State Police. He said that Krek was an important man and he wouldn't send people out to his house on a whim. There was nothing I could say.'

'What can we do, then?'

'I'm going myself.'

'To Slovenia? It'll take you all day.'

'Then I'd better get moving. I'm going back to my flat to get my car. Stay by the phone and call me if you hear anything.'

Micaela heard the cellar door creak open. Mulej was coming in. His jacket was off, his tie loosened. 'I thought you'd be lonely,' he said drunkenly.

She got off her cot. She'd already had a good look around for something that could serve as a weapon but there was nothing. No table lamps, no bed or table legs to pull off, no loose pieces of wood, not even a towel rack in the bathroom to wrench from the wall.

She was defenseless.

Mulej pointed at her with a fat finger. 'Stay there,' he ordered, shutting the door behind him.

'What do you want?' Micaela asked.

'What do you think I want?'

He came closer.

'There's no way,' she said defiantly.

Mulej didn't seem concerned by her attitude. 'Then I'll shoot you. Krek doesn't care. You're no use to him. If you want to stay alive, you'll cooperate. If not, then it's not a problem for me.' He patted his waistband. 'What have I done with my gun?' he slurred.

At that, she made a dash for the crates and began to scale them as Elisabetta had done.

Mulej watched in amusement. 'What are you doing up there?'

'Isn't it obvious, you fat pig?' she called down.

'That's hurtful,' he said. 'Come on down. Be more obliging.'

'Screw you.'

'If you don't come down I'll just have to get my gun and *shoot* you down.'

Micaela kept climbing. A wobbly crate shifted under her weight. She scrambled off it onto the highest one, the crate that Elisabetta had opened. She sat on it and glowered down at Mulej.

'Okay,' he said, unsteady on his feet. 'I'll be back and then I'll shoot you.'

'No!' she shouted. 'Don't go!'

'Why?'

'Convince me to come down. Be nicer to me.'

He looked confused. 'Nicer?'

'Sure. Like a proper gentleman, not a fucking rapist!'

Micaela dug her heels against the wobbly crate and pushed off with all her strength. It creaked and slid and reached a tipping point.

Mulej watched in a drunken, soft-focused way, half grinning, hands on hips, suggesting either that he didn't understand what was happening or that he thought he might be able to jump out of the way in the nick of time.

Gravity took hold of the crate. Perhaps its descent happened more quickly than he had anticipated.

His mouth opened to say something just before the crate struck him, pulverizing his face and crushing his big frame under a pile of splintered wood, red dirt and Lemures skeletons.

Micaela climbed down and tried to find an arm or a leg that belonged to Mulej under the debris. She dug around and found a wrist.

'Good,' she said out loud when she couldn't detect a pulse.

Elisabetta regained consciousness quickly but it took several moments to get her bearings.

She was lying on her side in the center of the great room. The fire was crackling and popping fiercely. The big television was still showing the crowds at St Peter's. Her jaw hurt terribly.

Where was Krek?

There was a weight on top of her.

Then she felt herself being turned onto her back.

A hand slipped up under her robes and she smelled the whiskey on her assailant's breath.

'I've always been curious,' Krek said, breathing hard, his cheek touching hers. 'I've always wanted to know what nuns wear under these habits.'

Elisabetta didn't want to give him the satisfaction of weeping or pleading. Instead she squirmed and thrashed like a bucking horse and tried to throw him off.

'Good, good!' he shouted. 'I like this. Fight harder!'

He had her robes up around her waist and as they bunched she felt something sharp against her stomach.

She remembered.

Elisabetta kept fighting Krek off with her left hand while she thrust her right one into the pocket of her tunic. She felt for the object and when she had it in her grasp she eased it open.

Her father's pipe tool. This simple, comforting little implement.

Krek let up for just a couple of seconds to arch his back and undo his belt and that was all the time Elisabetta needed.

She slid the pipe tool from her pocket and punched

it into Krek's chest with all the strength she had in her arm.

He said nothing. She didn't know she'd accomplished anything at all until she let her hand go and saw the tool sticking through his sweater, the aerator spike fully buried. There was no blood.

Krek looked down, rolled off Elisabetta and rose to his feet. He looked amused. 'What is this? What did you do?'

He pulled out the pipe tool and laughed. 'No, thank you! I smoke cigars!'

To Elisabetta's horror, he seemed perfectly fine. As she lay on the rug he casually lowered his trousers, enough to reveal his lower back. 'Have you ever seen one of these?'

He made a half-turn to show her his spine. His tail was thick, twitching like an angry snake. His tattoos were black and crisp, menacing but, to Elisabetta, no longer mysterious.

She started to crawl away.

But as Krek turned back to her something was happening inside his chest.

Blood was leaking from a small wound in his heart into the pericardial sac and when the sac was full it squeezed his heart like an orange in a juicer.

He inhaled sharply and began to wheeze.

Krek clutched at his chest and lifted up his sweater as if that might help give him more air.

He began to teeter, then slowly pitched forward like a felled tree.

He tried to speak but nothing came out.

And just before he crashed down pure rage possessed his face.

Elisabetta had never before seen a look of such hatred.

THIRTY-ONE

It had been a false alarm.

The man apprehended by the Vatican Gendarmes at the metal detector was an off-duty Rome policeman with an unloaded service weapon in his backpack. He'd come to St Peter's Square to join in the Conclave vigil and had forgotten he'd brought his gun. He was chagrined and apologetic. His identity checked out. The man with him was his cousin.

Hackel waited outside the incident van where the men were being held. He shifted his weight from foot to foot and finally said to Oberst Sonnenberg, 'I should be getting back to my post at the Chapel.'

'Yes, go ahead, Oberstleutnant,' Sonnenberg said. 'I'll check in with you soon. I don't think we'll be lucky enough to have white smoke tonight, but you never know.'

Hackel saluted and peeled away. When he was out of Sonnenberg's sight he reversed direction and made for his flat.

*

Micaela briefly considered digging at the rubble to see if the fat corpse had a mobile phone but the task seemed too formidable. She put her ear to the door and listened. The falling crate had made a terribly loud sound. If someone were nearby they would surely have noticed it.

Hearing nothing at the door she opened it a crack, then wide enough to poke her head through. The cellar hall was mostly dark; there was a naked bulb ten meters away. There was no one about. She began to walk toward the light.

Elisabetta stood over Krek's prone, lifeless body. The tail which only moments ago had seemed so terrifyingly menacing now struck her as nothing but an anomalous piece of meat.

She felt her heart thumping wildly and tried to think. She had to sound the alarm. Krek's telephone beckoned. She reached for it, then froze. What if the line was monitored? Would placing a call alert Krek's people that she was running free and put Micaela's life in danger? She had to save her sister first.

The great room had four doors and all of them, she found, were locked from the inside. Krek seemed to have liked his privacy.

Two of the doors along one wall led to different sides of the entrance hall. This was the way she had entered. Elisabetta visualized the route from the basement: up a set of stairs, into a hall off a small study, through a paneled library to the entrance hall and then into the great room. She was about to go into the hall when she heard heavy footsteps approaching. She retreated, closed the door and examined the other two.

The third door led directly to a stairway that went upstairs. The fourth one led to a dim, undecorated hallway – a servant's passageway, perhaps. The coast seemed clear and she took the passageway.

Micaela shucked off her shoes to enable her to tread more silently and kicked them against thc wall. The basement hall stretched a considerable distance without any sign of stairs and she wondered if she should have gone in the other direction. She tried several door latches along the way. Some were locked, others led to dark storage rooms.

Finally a poorly lit flight of stone stairs beckoned. Micaela climbed them gingerly, praying that she didn't meet anyone along the way.

Elisabetta crept into a dining room with a banqueting table long enough to seat thirty comfortably. Through its leaded windows she could see a young man with a slung rifle patrolling the grounds. She ducked and frog-walked below the window line. At the opposite end of the dining room she stopped to put her ear to a set of double doors. Through the wood she heard the noise of a clattering of pots.

*

Micaela's stairs took her to a rabbit warren of pantry rooms stocked with canned and dried goods. She found herself looking hungrily at labels and briefly searching in vain for a can opener to get at a tin of peaches.

She heard a gasp behind her and turned to see a huge woman wearing a chef's apron looking as shocked as she herself must have looked. The woman let out a short shriek and began to flee but Micaela pursued her with the peach tin, laying her low with a single heavy blow to the back of her head. The woman went smashing into a shelf, taking a month's worth of provisions to the floor with her.

Elisabetta heard a sharp cry and loud noises coming from the kitchen area. She crouched behind a large oriental vase in case someone came flying into the dining room but after several minutes all remained quiet. Cautiously, she entered the kitchen. Seeing nothing, she went through to the pantry where she found a hefty female chef lying unconscious, her chest heaving with grunts and snores. To one side was a flight of stairs to the basement. Elisabetta uttered a quick prayer and made a dash for them, wondering what had befallen the woman.

Micaela left the kitchen and found herself in the entrance hall, a vast expanse of marble and oversized ornamental furnishings. She stole across the hall, trying first one door, which was locked, then another. The second door was unlocked. She eased it open a centimeter at a time, trying to avoid any creaking.

Through the gap she took in a great room with an enormous fireplace before she spotted a half-naked body on the floor.

Micaela slinked inside and quietly locked the door behind her. The body lay still, with a cashmere sweater bunched up around its chest and slacks rolled down around its ankles. She approached it slowly and swore at what she saw.

A long, lifeless tail.

Elisabetta scurried down the basement hall, her habit sweeping the concrete floor. Suddenly something made her stop short. Micaela's shoes! She cringed in fear but carried on to the room with the crates where she leapt inside, calling for her sister.

The room was in a shambles with planks from a burst crate, tufo earth and ancient bones scattered everywhere.

The sight under the mess of a hand that still had flesh on it almost made her scream but she gasped with relief when she saw a chunky man's ring on one finger.

Micaela, she thought, *where are you and what have you done?*

Micaela armed herself with a fireplace poker and made doubly sure that all the doors were locked.

She stared at the phone, wishing that she knew the

Slovene number for emergency services. Just then the phone rang and she backed away from it as if it were a coiled viper.

One of the doorknobs squeaked.

She inhaled deeply, unlocked the door, gripped the poker like an ax and raised it high above her head.

The knob turned and the door opened.

At that instant Micaela began her downward swing but at the last second was just able to check it when she glimpsed a nun's black sleeve.

Zazo started to jog. The traffic was bad at this time of day and he thought he'd do better on foot than taking the bus. He started to form a plan. He'd get his car, head north and drive like hell to Slovenia. With luck he'd get to Bled before midnight. He'd demand to speak with Krek. They'd probably call the authorities and have him arrested but what else could he do? He was a policeman and this was his only lead.

His mobile phone chirped.

He plucked it from his pocket as he ran but came to a dead halt at the sight of the number.

929295.

Krek's number!

'Yes?' he answered cautiously, panting from his running.

The whispering voice he heard was distraught and frantic. 'Zazo! It's me!'

His mind disconnected from his body at the sound

of Elisabetta's voice. It seemed to take him an eternity to answer.

'My God! You're in Slovenia! You're with Krek!'

'How did you know?'

'Forget about that. Are you okay?'

'Yes! No! He's dead. I killed him, Zazo!'

'Jesus! Is Micaela okay?'

'Yes, we're together. I'm sorry I've got to whisper but we're hiding. Krek's men are everywhere but they don't know he's dead.'

'Okay, listen. If you're safe where you are, stay put. I'll call the Slovenian State Police.'

'No, Zazo. I'll call them. You've got to go to the Vatican.'

'Why?'

'There's a bomb in the Sistine Chapel, I'm sure of it. You've got to go there! You've got to stop the Conclave!'

Zazo was on Via Garibaldi. Cars and motorbikes were whizzing past. He stared at his phone for a moment to gather his wits and then speed-dialed Lorenzo. He got his voicemail.

He tried Inspector Loreti.

Voicemail there, too.

He was three or four kilometers away from the Vatican – too far to run.

On impulse Zazo stepped into the street, stretched his arms wide and blocked an approaching red Honda 1000. The rider almost lost control and stopped a half-meter before hitting him. The young man ripped off his helmet and began swearing.

Zazo pulled his badge from his back pocket. 'Police! This is an emergency! I'm taking your bike!'

'The hell you are!' the man shouted.

Zazo instinctively reached for his gun but it was back at his flat. Instead he pointed a finger and menaced the Honda's rider: 'Do you want to go to jail for obstructing a police operation?' When the fellow didn't respond, Zazo pushed him hard with both hands. The bike tipped over and the young man fell to the ground. Zazo righted the Honda, mounted it and put it in gear. All the rider could do was scream at him and toss his helmet uselessly at his back.

Hackel locked the door of his flat and opened one of his west-facing windows to let in some fresh air. His building was too low for him to see the Sistine Chapel but the spire atop St Peter's was visible against a hazy late-afternoon sky.

He turned on his television. The crowd in the Square was placid, expectant.

He went into the bedroom and slid open the top drawer of his dresser. Behind the folded stacks of black socks was a black and green box, the size of three packs of playing cards.

Hackel sat on his bed and tested the on-off switch of the Combifire detonator. He knew the batteries were fresh but just in case he was wrong he had spares.

A small bulb glowed green.

He put the detonator down and sighed.

He was troubled by the call that had been made to Krek's residence by someone claiming to be him. The number texted to him was from a Rome exchange. Someone was onto him. Who? How? The notion of riding out the investigation was now absurd. He'd have to disappear immediately.

Hackel went to his closet and retrieved an empty suitcase.

Zazo gunned the Honda like a madman, weaving in and out of traffic, passing through gaps between cars so tight that he scraped their doors with the handlebars. The combination of rush-hour traffic and the extraordinary congestion around Vatican City made for total gridlock.

On the Via Domenico Silveri the traffic came to a complete stop. He looked up at the Dome of the Basilica, turned the handlebars and jumped the motorbike over the curb and onto the sidewalk.

Pedestrians yelled at him and he yelled back, making it clear that he wasn't going to stop. Dodging and zigzagging, he made it to the Via della Stazione Vaticana where the sidewalks too became impassable.

Zazo ditched the Honda and ran.

He fought through the crowds and arrived, chest heaving, at the Petriano Entrance on the south side of St Peter's where three of his own men were guarding a checkpoint.

He came barreling up to them. From the look in

their eyes he could tell that they knew he was on suspension.

A corporal said, 'Major Celestino, I thought—'

Zazo interrupted him. 'It's okay. I've been reinstated. Inspector Loreti called me back in.'

They saluted and let him pass.

It was pointless trying to cut through the Square. He'd never seen it so packed. Instead he ran through the non-public zones by the Domus Sanctae Marthae and the back of the Basilica to a rear entrance of the Palace off the Square of the Furnace.

The smokeless Conclave chimney was overhead.

He made it into the Sala Regia unchallenged. Even the Swiss Guards saluted him curiously.

The hall was bright and ornate, filled with archbishops, bishops, monsignors and lay officials awaiting the conclusion of the first day.

Lorenzo was at the Palace end of the hall with Major Capozzoli. He spotted Zazo, called out in surprise and intercepted him.

'What the hell are you doing here?' he asked.

Zazo looked at him with wild eyes. 'I need your gun.'

'Are you crazy? What's the matter with you?'

'There's a bomb!' An archbishop overheard him and began whispering to one of his colleagues.

Lorenzo eyed him with alarm. 'Be quiet! How do you know?'

'Elisabetta found out! I think Hackel placed it.'

'Why hasn't Loreti or anyone notified me?'

'No one knows yet. For God's sake, Lorenzo! Give me your gun. Cappy, clear the hall. Lorenzo, find Hackel and stop him before it's too late!'

Hackel zipped his suitcase and put it by the front door.

There was a drawer in his study desk that contained an accordion folder of private papers and false passports. He took it out and stuffed it into an outer flap of his case.

He'd be traveling. He wanted to be as anonymous as a man of his size could be. His black suit wouldn't do. He took it off and folded it carefully, peeked at the television, then looked in his closet for something more comfortable. He'd be taking his car as far as a taxi stand, getting a ride to a rental-car facility, then calling Krek. An escape plan would quickly fall into place. He wasn't all that worried.

Glauser saw Zazo and stiffened.

'Celestino! You're suspended. Who let you in here?'

The costumed Swiss Guards at the Sistine Chapel door clutched their ceremonial pikes tightly and looked to Glauser for instructions.

Zazo tried to control his tone lest he should sound deranged. 'Glauser, listen to me carefully. We have to evacuate the Chapel. There's a bomb.'

'You're out of your mind!' The small man began to lift his arm to speak into his cuff microphone but Zazo stopped him by pulling Lorenzo's SIG from his waistband, breeching a round and pointing it at Glauser's head. There was a commotion in the Sala Regia as people murmured and backed away.

'Glauser, keep your hands folded in front of you,' Zazo ordered. 'I'll shoot you if I have to.' He spoke to the Swiss Guards. 'Men, there's a traitor in your midst. Your duty is to protect the Pope. One of the cardinals inside the Sistine Chapel will soon be that man. Help me clear the area.'

Glauser seethed at him. 'The only traitor is you, Celestino. I've always had my suspicions about you. You're going to rot in jail for this.'

Glauser reached inside his suit jacket for his weapon and Zazo reacted. He fired a bullet into Glauser's right knee and when the man fell screaming Zazo reached inside the jacket and ripped out Glauser's Heckler & Koch MP5A3. He clicked the safety off and pointed the weapon at the stunned Guards. He barked at one of them: 'You, put a tourniquet on him or he'll die. And you other men – for God's sake clear the Sala Regia!'

At the other end of the hall Capozzoli was at the Pauline Door, yelling for everyone to get out. Clergy and laity streamed urgently toward him.

Zazo kept the sub-machine gun aimed at the Guards and kicked at the door of the Sistine Chapel with his heel. 'It's an emergency!' he shouted. 'It's Major Celestino of the Gendarmerie! Let me in!'

It seemed to take an eternity but eventually he heard the bolt slide back.

Cardinal Franconi was at the door with an

expression of equal parts apprehension and confusion on his face. The sight of a non-uniformed man holding a sub-machine gun sent him into a state of panic.

Zazo rushed past him into the Chapel. A hundred elderly men wearing red hats stared at him in stunned silence and put down the pens they were using to mark their ballot papers.

Zazo had been inside the Chapel hundreds of times, perhaps thousands, and he hardly noticed its majesty anymore. But he'd never seen it like this, steeped in the gravitas of all the Cardinal Electors fulfilling their ancient duty. The magical ceiling was softly illuminated by afternoon light pouring through the high windows. Zazo stopped in the center of the Chapel. Directly above his head the hand of God reached to the outstretched hand of Adam, bestowing life.

Cardinal Diaz rose from his desk and straightened his spine. He recognized Zazo. 'Major, why have you come to this holy place with a weapon and interrupted our sacred rites?'

Zazo's voice reverberated in the chamber and sounded, to him, other-worldly. 'I'm sorry, Your Excellency. But everyone must leave immediately.'

'We are in the midst of a ballot. We cannot leave.'

'There's no time to explain but I believe there's a bomb inside the Chapel.'

Diaz scanned the faces of his fellow cardinals.

Cardinal Aspromonte rose. 'Why do you believe this? Who has told you?'

'A nun. A nun named Elisabetta.'

Some of the cardinals tittered nervously.

'You've committed this great sacrilege because of the word of a nun?' Diaz roared. 'Leave us! Leave at once!'

Zazo looked at Diaz and placed the tip of the gun under his own chin. He curled his thumb around the trigger. 'I'm sorry. I won't leave. This nun, she's my sister, and I believe in what she says with all my heart. If I can't save you, I'll die trying.'

Hackel sat in his favorite chair. The vantage point gave him a simultaneous view of the television and, through his window, the Dome of St Peter's. That way he'd see the flash twice. He'd hear the explosion twice. He'd feel the percussion ripple through his body once.

The night of the Pope's death, in the basement of the Sistine Chapel, he had placed his utility bag on one of the simple wooden tables, unzipped it and removed a continuous roll of rubberized sheeting which resembled some kind of building material. Primasheet 2000. An RDX-based plastic explosive, two millimeters thick and with a sticky backing. Military-grade and lethal, particularly within a vaulted space.

The width of the Primasheet had been perfect but it had needed to be cut to the right length and then stuck to the underside of the table. Hackel had plucked a component from a plastic bag and firmly pressed a thumbnail-sized RF microchip into the sheet, firmly anchoring it. He had turned the table back on its feet and inspected the job.

Each of the chips was set to discharge at the same frequency. One switch on a remote detonator would do the job. Over the next hour he had repeated the process 108 times, one for each Cardinal Elector in the Papal Conclave.

They had a man inside the security-contractor company. The Alsatian dog he used for the explosive sweeps wouldn't have detected Primasheet if it had been crammed up its rear.

Hackel extended the antenna on the Combifire detonator to its full extent.

This is what we do, he thought. *This is who we are.*

He flipped the on switch and pushed the red detonate button.

The high windows of the Sistine Chapel were the first to go.

They blew out in an orange flash, the old glass fragmenting into millions of shards.

Then the shock wave took the ceiling.

The brightly painted frescoes which had taken Michelangelo four years to paint, vaporized in an instant into a fine, colorful mist.

The vault of the Chapel came down in great chunks, burying everything beneath under tons of ugly grey rubble. A vast cloud of smoke rose over St Peter's Square, blotting out what was left of the sun and turning day into night.

THIRTY-TWO

The blast caught Zazo like a train hurtling through the Sala Regia, pushing him through the Pauline Door well into the Palace. Because he was the last one out he took the hardest hit but some of the cardinals closest to the explosion were toppled like bowling pins.

Concussed and unconscious, he missed the immediate aftermath of ambulances and first responders. Loreti and Sonnenberg immediately activated a disaster plan called Code Citadel which summoned the full resources of the Italian state. The Nucleo Operativo Centrale di Sicurezza, the SWAT Team of the Polizia di Stato, and the Carabinieri swarmed through Vatican City and with the assistance of the Vatican Gendarmerie evacuated the traumatized crowds in St Peter's Square.

Though there were injuries from flying glass and chunks of masonry, most of the casualties came from the subsequent stampede, though, miraculously, at the end of the day there was not a single fatality. Zazo was among those more seriously hurt. A broken rib lacerated his liver and within an hour he was in an operating theater undergoing abdominal surgery. In an adjoining suite, Glauser was getting his knee reconstructed.

The Swiss Guards closed ranks around the cardinals and those who didn't require medical triage and hospitalization were bundled onto coaches and brought back to the Domus Sanctae Marthae, which was cordoned off by a ring of armed men. A Polizia di Stato helicopter hovered overhead.

Lorenzo, soot-streaked and shaken, found Loreti and Sonnenberg outside the Domus.

Loreti asked him, 'You were there. What the hell happened?'

Lorenzo spoke too loudly, a victim of blast-induced hearing loss. 'Five minutes before the explosion Major Celestino entered the Sala Regia.'

'He did this?' Sonnenberg roared. 'One of your men did this, Loreti?'

'No, Oberst Sonnenberg,' Lorenzo said. 'Major Celestino saved them. He found out about the bomb and forced the cardinals out of the Chapel. They would all have died.'

Major Capozzoli came rushing over and joined them.

'Where did he get his information?' Loreti asked. 'Why didn't he inform anyone else?'

'His sister told him.'

'Who in God's name is his sister?' Sonnenberg demanded.

'She's a nun.'

416

Both men stared at him.

'Look, I don't know the details,' Lorenzo said, 'but she was right. Zazo told me that Matthias Hackel was involved.'

'Hackel!' Sonnenberg cried. 'You're insane.'

'Where is Hackel?' Loreti asked.

Sonnenberg tried hailing Hackel on his radio but got no reply.

'The last time I saw him he was here at the Domus,' Capozzoli said. 'It was about forty minutes before the blast.'

'Why was he here?' Loreti asked.

'He said he wanted to check on Cardinal Giaccone.'

'Christ!' Loreti said. 'Let's get up there. Cappy, come with me. Lorenzo, take some men and look for Hackel. Check everywhere. Check his residence.'

Loreti, Capozzoli and Sonnenberg stood outside Room 202.

Loreti knocked.

There was no answer.

'Cardinal Giaccone?' he yelled. 'Open it,' he said to Capozzoli.

Capozzoli had a pass key. The small room was empty, the bed made. Giaccone's robes were neatly laid out on the bedspread.

The bathroom door was closed and they heard a shower running.

'Hello?' Sonnenberg called out.

There was nothing but the sound of water.

Sonnenberg tried again, louder. 'Hello?'

The water stopped and a moment later the doorknob turned. 'Hackel? Is that you?'

Giaccone opened the bathroom door, fat, naked and dripping wet.

At the sight of the three men in his room he tried to shut the door again but Capozzoli stuck his foot against the jamb, then threw the door open.

'You were expecting Oberstleutnant Hackel?' Loreti asked. 'Why? Come out and speak with us. Do you know what has happened?'

Giaccone said nothing.

He rushed forward like a small pink bull, tripping up Sonnenberg who fell unceremoniously on his backside.

Giaccone reached for something on the desk, under his red hat. When he turned they saw it.

He had a dangling pink tail.

They hardly noticed the small silver pistol in his hand.

But he pressed it to his temple, shouted, 'I am Petrus Romanus!' and pulled the trigger.

Lorenzo forced the lock of Hackel's flat and burst inside.

The men swept through. It was empty.

'Search the place,' Lorenzo ordered. 'Put on your gloves. Treat it as a crime scene.'

It was a small flat and meticulously tidy, which made it easy to sort through Hackel's possessions and papers.

Among his household bills was a very non-domestic account that stood out: an invoice to a Geneva-based mining corporation, which would prove to be a shell outfit with a fake import license. It was from a US company, EBA&D, for a roll of flexible RDX explosive, Primasheet 2000.

They had their man.

Now they needed a motive.

Cardinals Diaz, Aspromonte and Franconi huddled together in a corner of the chapel on the ground floor of the Domus. Their cassocks were soiled and their faces were still grimy but they were unhurt.

'Did you see his body?' Franconi asked.

Aspromonte nodded. 'I did. I tell you, Giaccone had a tail.'

Franconi rubbed his hands in agitation. 'Lemures?' he asked nervously. 'One of *us* – a Lemures?'

Aspromonte said, 'Before he shot himself he declared to the officers, "I am Petrus Romanus."'

Diaz sputtered, 'My God! Malachy! Is this prophecy coming to pass?'

'We have many more questions than answers,' Aspromonte said. 'But there is no doubt now that the Church faces a time of unprecedented turmoil and struggle, the outcome of which we cannot be certain.'

'Nothing must be said to the press about Giaccone's "condition" or the circumstances of his death,' Diaz insisted. 'He had a heart attack when he heard the explosion. A heart attack. We must close ranks.'

'The tragedy!' Franconi sobbed. 'Our greatest treasure, Michelangelo's Chapel, gone!'

'No, you're wrong!' Aspromonte scolded. 'Somewhere in the world, perhaps here in Italy, is another Michelangelo. Buildings can be rebuilt. New paintings can be commissioned. But our greatest treasure, the Church, thank God, and its leadership have been saved because of the acts of a simple policeman and a simple nun.'

Diaz nodded. 'We have work to do. I'm told that the Basilica only has damage to its northern exterior façade. The Sala Regia is quite badly damaged but the Palace is intact. We must find a place for the Electors to convene tomorrow. The Conclave must continue. We need a new Holy Father, now more than ever.'

Elisabetta and Micaela held each other and wept as they watched the terrible images on the television.

A reporter for RTV was interviewing a Slovenian family on pilgrimage to St Peter's Square when the bomb went off.

The camera shook and thousands of people fell to the ground as one, screaming at the fireball that rose into the air.

'Oh, God! Zazo!' Elisabetta screamed.

Before Micaela stepped over Krek's body, she kicked his chest just to make sure. She snatched the telephone from the coffee table and rang Zazo's mobile. It went straight to voicemail.

'I'm sure he's okay,' she mumbled. 'He's got to be okay.'

Elisabetta fell to her knees and began to pray.

She prayed for Zazo.

She prayed for the Cardinals.

She prayed for the Church.

She prayed for Micaela.

She prayed for herself.

In the distance they heard sirens. The insistent whooping got louder and louder until it stopped.

There were shouts in Slovenian, a brief but terrifying exchange of gunfire from the entrance hall and finally, after an unpleasantly long time, an urgent banging against the heavy oak door.

'Police! We're coming in!'

THIRTY-THREE

The mood inside the Basilica was as somber as it had been for any funeral Mass ever held under its hallowed dome. A few dozen Vatican insiders huddled in the dust-filled pews praying silently, as shell-shocked as the victims of the physical blast the day before.

Matthias Hackel's black suit, white shirt and polished black shoes had been found on the bank of the Tiber near the Ponte Sant'Angelo. Perhaps he'd drowned himself, perhaps not, but the internal investigation was in its infancy and there were certainly no conclusions about possible accomplices yet. Because of this, Oberst Sonnenberg reluctantly ceded primary security to the Polizia di Stato and the Swiss Guards were remanded to barracks. The Gendarmerie were deployed to seal off Vatican City to all but critical employees and a small pool of international reporters.

Elisabetta, Micaela and their father sat in a rear pew, waiting silently.

At noon, Monsignor Achille, Cardinal Aspromonte's

private secretary, approached them, leaned over and whispered into Elisabetta's ear.

She told Micaela and her father. 'Wait here. They want to speak to me now.'

Elisabetta followed Achille through the aisle under the monument of Pius VIII to the passageway of St Peter's Sacristy and Treasury. They walked over the marble floors to a museum-like room where three plush chairs faced each other. She looked up at the Crux Vaticans, the Vatican Cross, covered in leather, silver and precious stones. It was the Vatican's greatest treasure, said to contain fragments of the True Cross.

Achille asked her to wait. Soon Cardinals Aspromonte and Diaz appeared. When Elisabetta rose to greet them Aspromonte smiled and told her to sit down again. They joined her, their chairs so close that their knees almost touched.

Diaz was rigid and imposing but Aspromonte's full face was kind and avuncular; she warmed to him immediately.

'Elisabetta Celestino,' he said, clasping her thin, cold hand in his warm, generous ones. 'Sister Elisabetta. The Church owes you an incomparable debt of gratitude.'

'I was only serving God, Your Excellency. He has been my guide through this ordeal.'

'Well, you've served Him well. Imagine what the world would look like today if you hadn't succeeded. Tell me, how is your brother?'

'We saw him this morning. They hope to release him from intensive care later today. He's doing well.'

'Good, good. He was so bold, so brave,' Aspromonte said. 'He saved many lives.'

'Yes, he's amazing,' Elisabetta said. 'But it's sad that good men like Professor De Stefano, Father Tremblay and Cardinal Giaccone died. It's sad that the great Sistine Chapel is no more.'

'The Chapel will be rebuilt,' Aspromonte said, releasing her hand. 'De Stefano and Tremblay are greatly mourned. Cardinal Giaccone is a different matter.'

'He was one of them,' Diaz said curtly. 'The head of the Pontifical Commission for Sacred Archeology was one of them!'

'My God,' Elisabetta said. 'That's how they knew. Even years ago when I was a student. He was a Lemures?'

The cardinals were dumbstruck by her response. 'You know of them?' Diaz whispered.

Elisabetta nodded. 'I discovered some facts. I shared them with Father Tremblay and in return he told me certain things in the strictest confidence.'

'Then you understand what we've been up against. Lord knows what harm Giaccone would have done to the Church if he'd been the only Cardinal Elector left,' Diaz said angrily.

'He would have been Pope,' Aspromonte said.

'A disaster,' Diaz said, gritting his teeth and pumping a fist, as if the old boxer in him was itching to leave his corner and go another round.

Aspromonte opened his palms. 'Sister, you must tell us what you think because you have seen them up close. You have spoken with one of their leaders.'

'And God forgive me, and forgive my sister,' Elisabetta said, 'we took lives.'

'Later, you will give your confession and you will be forgiven,' Diaz said impatiently. 'What is your impression of them?'

Elisabetta took a breath. 'They want to destroy the Church. They hate it and everything it stands for. They want to trample all that is good, and if everything is destroyed in the process they'll feel satisfaction at seeing the world in flames. They are pure evil.'

Aspromonte listened to her, doleful, his head shaking, as if keeping time to an unseen metronome. 'We speak of the Devil all the time,' he said, 'but even for me, a man who is quite literal in my beliefs and my interpretation of the Bible, the Devil has always been something of a metaphor. Evil exists, of that there can be no doubt, but for there to be a physical embodiment like this! It is a fearful notion.'

Elisabetta felt she should only listen, not speak anymore, but she couldn't hold back. 'It makes the word of Christ that much more important, doesn't it?'

'Yes!' Aspromonte agreed. 'You are exactly right, Sister. We've always had work to do. Today we have work to do. Tomorrow we have work to do. It will never be done until the day Christ returns. We must be perpetually vigilant.'

Elisabetta felt an overwhelming sadness wash over her. 'Could I ask a question of you?'

'Of course, Sister,' Aspromonte said.

'My mother died when I was a girl. She was an historian. She found a document in the Vatican Secret Archives, a sixteenth-century letter from John Dee, a man who could have been a Lemures. Her research privileges were cancelled and within days she became ill and died. I think she was poisoned.'

'What was her name?' Aspromonte asked.

'Flavia Celestino. She passed away in 1985.'

The Cardinals whispered among themselves. 'We don't know of her,' Diaz said.

'Before we were abducted, Father Tremblay told me that he knew the name of the man who had the John Dee letter removed from the archive. It was Riccardo Agnelli. He was the personal secretary to someone who is now a cardinal.'

'I know Agnelli!' Diaz exclaimed. 'He died some years ago. I'll tell you who he worked for! He worked for Giaccone!'

'Then she *was* murdered,' Elisabetta said, her eyes stinging.

'I'm so sorry, my dear,' Aspromonte said. 'Your life has been traumatized again and again by these fiends.' He reached for her hands and she gave them up freely. 'Why, we must ask, has the Lord tried you so?'

Diaz interrupted impatiently. 'An important question, I'm sure, but we have some practical work to do first. We have concerns about these matters becoming public. Imagine what the reaction would be among the faithful if they knew about the Lemures. And we aren't even sure what we're up against. Where are they lurking? And who knows how many of them even exist? Do you have any idea about these things?'

Elisabetta shook her head and Aspromonte released her hands.

Diaz leaned closer. 'Perhaps these Slovenians and Giaccone were the leaders. Perhaps there aren't so many of them. If Hackel hasn't drowned himself he must be caught. Regardless, he will be identified as the perpetrator of the bombing. He was deranged, bitter, disgruntled after becoming aware that he would never become the head of the Guards. We have worked this out.'

Elisabetta listened incredulously. 'I'm sorry, Your Excellency, maybe it's not for me to say – but do you think it's the right thing to suppress the truth?'

Aspromonte jumped in before Diaz could answer. 'After hearing a preliminary report of your ordeal and reviewing the facts as we know them, the Cardinal Bishops met late into the night discussing the matter. I mustn't speak of these deliberations but perhaps some members, myself included, were more inclined than others toward the view which I believe you possess. But we debated the issues with great solemnity and with prayerful guidance and we speak as one. We think it is better to spare the world such a great anxiety. We think there is more harm to be done than good.' Then he added, 'In the afternoon, we will start the Conclave again in this very room, under this great symbol, the Crux Vaticans. We will have a new Pope. Perhaps the new Holy Father will have a different view. We shall see.'

'In the meantime,' Diaz said, 'we must have your silence. We know that Major Celestino will do his duty. We need your sister and father to do likewise. Can you guarantee their discretion?'

Micaela had never been accused of discretion, Elisabetta thought, but she nodded. 'I will speak to them. I'm sure they will agree. But what about Krek? And the other man Micaela had to kill? Krek was a very wealthy man. The police were there. Surely this will come out!'

'I think not,' Diaz said. 'The Slovenian Ambassador to the Vatican has had a busy night. The Slovenian government has no desire for the facts ever to be known about Damjan Krek. He was quite far to the right, certainly no friend of the country's political leaders. They've already begun circulating the word that Krek and Mulej died in a murder-suicide. It seems that they were having a homosexual affair. Their bodies will be cremated.'

Elisabetta held her tongue. 'And the skeletons of St Callixtus? What will become of them?'

'They're already on their way back to Italy. They'll go into storage. The new Pope will choose the next President of the Pontifical Commission for Sacred Archeology. Decisions will be made in good time.'

Elisabetta had only one more question. 'And what of me?' she asked.

Diaz rubbed his face. 'I have to tell you, Sister, that you could be of great service to us here in the Vatican. I, for one, would like to see you pick up the staff that fell from Father Tremblay's hand and continue his important work. No one is in a better position to fight these Lemures than you.'

Elisabetta's lower lip quivered uncontrollably. 'Please, Your Excellency. I will do whatever the Church demands of me but I beg you, please let me go back to my school.'

Aspromonte smiled. 'Of course you can, my dear, of course you can. Go in Christ.'

After Elisabetta had left them, the two cardinals faced each other, their expressions grim. 'It's a pity,' Diaz said. 'She's young with an agile mind. It seems it's left to old men like you and me to carry on this struggle.'

It was five o'clock in the afternoon.

They had been meeting for just three hours but the Cardinal Electors looked weary and shell-shocked.

They sat in the Sacristy of St Peter's in a chamber that had never been intended for this purpose. Tables and an altar unused since the last Papal Synod had been brought in from the adjacent Paul VI Audience Hall.

A new batch of ballots had been hastily printed,

each beginning with the words: *Eligo in Summum Pontificem* – I elect as Supreme Pontiff.

When they had put their pens down, Cardinal Franconi summoned the Electors one by one, in order of their precedence, to the altar where each man presented the ballot to one of the Cardinal Scrutineers and swore in Latin, 'I call as my witness Christ the Lord who will be my judge, that my vote is given to the one who before God I think should be elected.'

When all the ballots had been cast, one Scrutineer shook the container and another removed a ballot and read the name aloud.

As the balloting progressed there was a growing chorus of whispers but when the senior Scrutineer read the results the whispers were replaced by silence.

Cardinal Diaz rose and stretched himself to his full height.

He strode to the row of tables on his right, stood in front of one man and looked down.

'*Acceptasne electionem de te canonice factam in Summum Pontificem?*' Diaz asked. Do you accept your canonical election as Supreme Pontiff?

Cardinal Aspromonte had been looking down at his clasped hands.

He turned his eyes upwards, met his old friend's gaze and hesitated for a very long time before nodding. '*Accepto, in nomine Domini.*'

'*Quo nomine vis vocari?*' Diaz asked. By what name will you be called?

Aspromonte raised his voice for all to hear. 'Celestine VI.'

The old oven and chimney of the Sistine Chapel were gone so the fireplace in the Papal residence was used in its place. It was an eerie sight. St Peter's Square was still cordoned off and empty except for a smattering of Vatican workers. But there were crowds outside the gates craning their necks and at the sight of plumes of white smoke against a pale evening sky a roar went up that echoed throughout Rome.

Elisabetta kicked off her shoes and lay fully dressed on her old bed, in her old room, in her old school.

It felt unimaginably good to be back with the nuns of the convent. After communal dinner, Sister Marilena had made a little speech about the two joyous events she urged them to dwell on – the election of a new pope and the return of their Elisabetta – rather than the horrific ones of the previous day.

She was scared to close her eyes lest she see Krek's raging face and flipping tail so she prayed with her eyes wide open. And when she felt the courage to test the darkness behind closed lids, she was relieved to see not Krek but the young, sweet face of Marco, just as she remembered him.

There was a light tap on her door.

It was Sister Marilena. 'I'm sorry to interrupt you, Elisabetta, but there's someone to see you, here, in the chapel.'

Monsignor Achille, Aspromonte's secretary, was waiting patiently. He held a snow-white envelope in his hands. 'The Holy Father wanted me to deliver this in person,' he said.

With trembling hands Elisabetta opened the envelope and pulled out a handwritten letter.

Sister Elisabetta,
There were two reasons why I chose the name Celestine VI.
The first is, like Celestine V, who was a famously reluctant Pope, I too was reluctant to accept the Papacy.
The second, dear Elisabetta, was you,
Celestine VI

Elisabetta reached into the pocket of her habit and pulled out the silver chi-rho pendant.

'Please give this to the Holy Father,' she said. 'Tell him it's from the columbarium of St Callixtus. Tell him it was the one small ray of goodness in a place of great darkness and evil.'

THIRTY-FOUR

Two weeks passed and the rhythms of the Vatican began to return to a semblance of normality – with the jarring exception of the cranes, construction vehicles and workmen attending to the orderly demolition and cleanup of the smoldering remains of the Sistine Chapel.

Few artistic treasures were salvageable but a small army of art-restoration experts from the major Italian museums were fussing over the blast damage to the Sala Regia and planning a restorative campaign.

Pope Celestine VI seized on the symbolic importance of rebuilding the Sistine Chapel. He established a special Pontifical Commission to supervise the project and conduct an international contest to select an artist to paint a fresh ceiling fresco that would capture, in a new way, Michelangelo's grandeur and would endure for centuries to come.

And on a sunny Saturday afternoon a small ceremony was taking place in the auditorium of the Scuola Teresa Spinelli on the Piazza Mastai.

In the audience were nuns, teachers, students and parents.

On the stage, Sister Marilena and Sister Elisabetta sat beside Evan Harris and Stephanie Meyer and the Mother General of the Augustinian Sisters, Servants of Jesus and Mary, who had flown in from Malta.

Sister Marilena took the podium and announced, 'Today is a happy one for our dear school and our dear order. Nothing is more important to us than our mission of educating our children for good, productive and faithful lives. Our chronic lack of funds has forced us to make difficult choices in the past but thanks to Sister Elisabetta and our new friends here with us today we see bright days ahead. Please, let us welcome Professor Evan Harris and Miss Stephanie Meyer.'

Both of them rose and stood at the podium. Harris took the microphone. 'I apologize for my lack of Italian but, since this is such an excellent school, I have been assured that English will work just fine. Nothing is more satisfying than a win-win situation. Cambridge University has educated many prominent men and women in its long and storied history but perhaps none more illustrious than the playwright Christopher Marlowe.'

Elisabetta winced at the name.

'Marlowe's most famous play,' he continued, 'was *Dr Faustus* and, as a Marlowe scholar, it has always pained me that Cambridge did not own an original early text of the play. That is now rectified.' He raised the book for all to see. 'This magnificent volume will take pride of place in our university library and will be an inspiration for generations of scholars and students to come. And now may I present Stephanie Meyer, a distinguished member of the University Regent House and the generous donor who has made this purchase possible.'

Meyer smiled and spoke into the microphone in her plummy accent. 'It is with great satisfaction and great pleasure that I present this check for one million euros to the Augustinian Sisters, Servants of Jesus and Mary.'

Elisabetta awoke the next morning feeling light-hearted and contented, her happy Sunday routine rekindled. Zazo was out of hospital and had been informed that he'd been reinstated in the Gendarmerie and could resume his duties when his condition allowed. The entire family would take Mass together and have lunch at her father's.

She showered, put on a robe fresh from a dry-cleaning bag and walked to the Basilica of Santa Maria in Trastevere in sparkling sunshine.

Elisabetta felt reborn.

The detour that her life had taken, this sorry interlude, had sparked a re-examination that felt, in a way, like the one she'd undertaken a dozen years earlier while she convalesced. Back then she had resolved to leave her old life behind and become a person of all-sustaining faith. Now she had decided to re-commit herself to this path.

Her father, for one, had lobbied insistently for a

different decision. Seize the moment, he'd argued. You're still young and vital. You can still be a wife and a mother. Go to church all you want, pray till you're blue in the face, but please leave the clergy and rejoin the secular world.

'Will you give up Goldbach?' Elisabetta asked.

'No, of course not,' Carlo replied. 'It's my passion. It's what makes me tick.' And then he wagged his finger at her. 'It's not the same thing,' he said.

'Isn't it?' she said. 'I don't think it's so different.'

Zazo was taking small, gingerly steps but his color was good. Outside the church Elisabetta kissed him and told him that he'd lost weight, but not to worry, she'd fix that with her meal. Lorenzo was with him, in uniform. She could tell that he wanted to spend the afternoon with the family but he was obliged to report for duty after Mass. Micaela was with Arturo. Her father was the last to arrive. He smelled of pipe tobacco and Elisabetta could see a fresh ink stain on his fingers. He'd been working on Goldbach, for sure.

They entered the church as a group and occupied a central pew in the nave.

As parishioners filed in Micaela leaned over and whispered in Elisabetta's ear, 'Doesn't Lorenzo look splendid?'

'Why are you asking me that?' Elisabetta whispered back.

'He admitted to Zazo that he fancies you. I think he's embarrassed about it because you're a nun.'

'He should be embarrassed,' Elisabetta whispered back with a laugh.

'Well?' Micaela asked wickedly.

'You and Papa need to leave me alone,' Elisabetta scolded as Father Santoro appeared and took his place at the altar.

She couldn't remember ever having enjoyed Mass more, particularly the moment when Father Santoro extended his hands, raised them and intoned the *Gloria* in his lovely clear voice.

Gloria in excelsis Deo
et in terra pax homínibus bonae voluntatis.
Laudamus te,
benedicimus te,
adoramus te,
glorificamus te,
gratias agimus tibi propter magnam gloriam tuam.

Glory to God in the highest,
and on Earth peace to people of good will.
We praise you,
we bless you,
we adore you,
we glorify you,
we give you thanks for your great glory.

When Father Santoro was done, Elisabetta chimed in with a hearty *Amen*.

Zazo was moving slowly, refusing to lean on anyone,

so their group was among the last to leave the church. From the archway Elisabetta squinted into the high sun.

The piazza and its fountain looked particularly pristine and lovely. There were children playing outside the café and lovers holding hands. Father Santoro approached to give the family his Sunday wishes and he put his hand on Zazo's shoulder.

Suddenly Elisabetta saw Zazo's face contort and a single word bellowed from his mouth.

'Gun!'

She turned to see a man pushing through the crowd of parishioners with a pistol pointed directly at her.

Matthias Hackel had the wooden expression of a man who had simply come to complete some unfinished business.

A shot rang out.

Elisabetta waited to feel the bullet piercing her heart.

She was ready. Far from willing, but ready.

Hackel's head erupted in a splash of red. He pitched forward, his big body thudding onto the cobblestones.

Micaela dropped instinctively and pulled Elisabetta down to the ground with her.

Lorenzo was standing over Hackel's body, his gun drawn, ready to fire a second round. It wasn't needed.

He saw Elisabetta and ran to her.

'Are you all right?'

She looked up at him. His head blocked the sun but its light spilled around it, creating a very real halo.

She saw his face clearly enough, but she also saw the face of Marco and the face of Jesus Christ.

All of them had saved her.

'Yes, I'm all right.'

The limo driver pulled into the circular drive of Stephanie Meyer's secluded Georgian mansion.

Evan Harris was beside her in the back seat.

'It's good to be home,' she said.

'Indeed.'

'Won't you come in for a drink?' she suggested. 'I can run you back to your house in a bit.'

Harris agreed.

'Don't forget the book,' Meyer said. Harris's briefcase was by his feet.

'No fear of that.'

Inside, they left their bags in the hall and went into her sitting room.

'It's a terrible blow that it's come to nothing,' Meyer sighed.

'Don't you know Pope Celestine VI's full name?' Harris suddenly asked.

'I believe it's Giorgio Aspromonte,' Meyer said.

'Giorgio *Pietro* Aspromonte,' Harris added quickly.

'Petrus Romanus!' Meyer hissed.

'See?' Harris said. 'Don't be so gloomy. Aren't you going to offer me a drink?'

She poured them both large gins.

'Why not get the book?' she asked.

He removed it from its bubble wrap and put in on

her mantel, opened to the frontispiece. Old Faustus seemed to be looking down at them from his place within the magic circle.

'Tomorrow we'll start making calls,' Harris said. 'K is gone. But there are others.'

'Why not you?'

'Indeed. Why *not* me?'

They clinked glasses.

'This is what we do,' Harris said.

'And this is who we are,' Meyer replied.

Library of the Dead

Glenn Cooper

The most shocking secret in the history of mankind is about to be revealed . . .

A murderer is on the loose on the streets of New York City: nicknamed the Doomsday Killer, he's claimed six victims in just two weeks, and the city is terrified. Even worse, the police are mystified: the victims have nothing in common, defying all profiling, and all that connects them is that each received a sick postcard in the mail before they died – a postcard that announced their date of death. In desperation, the FBI assigns the case to maverick agent Will Piper, once the most accomplished serial killing expert in the bureau's history, now on a dissolute spiral to retirement.

Battling his own demons, Will is soon drawn back into a world he both loves and hates, determined to catch the killer whatever it takes. But his search takes him in a direction he could never have predicted, uncovering a shocking secret that has been closely guarded for centuries. A secret that once lay buried in an underground library beneath an 8th Century monastery, but which has now been unearthed – with deadly consequences. A select few defend the secret of the library with their lives – and as Will closes in on the truth, they are determined to stop him, at any cost . . .

arrow books

Book of Souls

Glenn Cooper

They guarded it with their lives, but now the greatest secret of all mankind must be told...

A shocking truth lies within the pages of an ancient library, locked inside a high-security complex deep beneath the Nevada desert. And the US government will stop at nothing to keep it classified. But now a shadowy group of ex-employees want the world to know – however terrifying the disclosure might prove to be. And when a single volume missing from the original collection mysteriously surfaces at a London auction house, they persuade former FBI agent Will Piper to help them obtain it and unlock the ultimate secret of the library, once and for all.

Travelling to England, Will discovers the text contains a sonnet that holds a series of clues – clues that reveal the book has had a profound effect on the history of mankind. But all the time he is being watched. And as he gets nearer to the final revelation, he and his young family become a direct target for a deadly group of men whose duty it is to guard the library's secret – whatever it takes. However, the truth is too powerful to keep hidden...

arrow books